CLOSE ENCOUNTER

"I'm worried about you."

Evaline's heart flopped in her chest. "I'll be fine, Gabe."

"You sure?" His thumb traced the arc of her brow. Evaline longed to close her eyes and savor his deft, gentle touch, but couldn't allow her feelings for him to show. Instead, she gazed up at him.

Before she could move, she felt Gabriel's mouth closing upon hers, warm and firm and questing, asking for something she wasn't certain she should give. His kiss plunged her back to an altered state of consciousness where time hung suspended and unnoticed. She heard a ragged sigh and realized with a blush that the sound had come from her.

"Evaline," he murmured against her lips.

"Patricia Simpson is one of the premier writers of supernatural romance."
—*Romantic Times*

Books by Patricia Simpson

Whisper of Midnight
The Legacy
Raven in Amber
The Night Orchid
The Lost Goddess
Lord of Forever
Mystic Moon
Just Before Midnight

By Debbie Macomber, Linda Lael Miller, and
Patricia Simpson

Purrfect Love

Published by HarperPaperbacks

Just Before Midnight

⋊ PATRICIA SIMPSON ⋉

HarperPaperbacks
A Division of HarperCollinsPublishers

HarperPaperbacks
A Division of HarperCollinsPublishers
10 East 53rd Street, New York, N.Y. 10022-5299

This is a work of fiction. The characters, incidents, and
dialogues are products of the author's imagination and are not to
be construed as real. Any resemblance to actual events or
persons, living or dead, is entirely coincidental.

ISBN 0-06-108494-8

Cover illustration by Jon Paul

First HarperPaperbacks printing: February 1997

Printed in the United States of America

Visit HarperPaperbacks on the World Wide Web at
http://www.harpercollins.com/paperbacks

❖ 10 9 8 7 6 5 4 3 2 1

To my daughters, Jessica and Camille,
and a very special, pleasant hibiscus.

Just Before Midnight

1

University of Washington Medical Center, Seattle

"*Mr. Durrell?*" Evaline Jaye stuck her head around the half-open door and peeked into the conference room of the hospital. Normally the long narrow room would be filled with nurses or doctors, but this afternoon the rosewood table and ring of chairs was empty except for a man at the far end. He was dressed in a navy blue suit that set off his shoulder-length blond hair, which was styled so perfectly he looked just like his publicity shots. He rose, and Evaline felt a definite shift in the atmosphere, as if someone had just opened a curtain to let in a ray of light.

A glow hovered around him, and when she looked closer, she discerned two barely noticeable curving lines just above his head—like translucent tubes or the horns of a beast. This phenomenon was similar to the ones Evaline had trained herself to see in the old days, and it enveloped

Durrell in a misty shape, moving when he moved in an unmistakable outline of an animal. She recalled the teachings of the elders on the reservation and their interpretation of the meaning of different spirit animals: *a ram's head. Seek spiritual not material pleasures.* Impossible. She couldn't be seeing a vision. She had turned her back on that part of her life.

The moment Evaline doubted her "sight" and stared at the man directly, the vision disappeared. A cool rush of relief washed over her. Perhaps the animal shape had been the result of viewing Durrell's blond hair against the slate gray thunderclouds behind him, and could be attributed to a simple shock to the retina. Rain splattered the window, the sound as hard as gravel striking stone, driving her back to the logical, rational world of modern medicine, where spirit animals didn't belong.

"Miss Jaye," Durrell called out in a rich liquid voice she had heard many times on TV, pushing her completely into the here and now. "Come in."

Quietly, she slipped into the room, having had years of practice easing unnoticed into a crowd. Though she no longer had a reason to seek invisibility, her old habits clung to her. As she approached, Stephen Durrell surveyed her, and she braced herself for the reaction she had endured for eleven years: the stare of disbelief at her face and the nearly instant glance away. Her crooked eye and ruined mouth had been too hideous for some people to bear. But those days were gone, along with the spirit animals which had disappeared from her life after the attack. She was different now. Surgery had changed her forever.

Still she was surprised when strangers didn't turn away in horror and pity. "You asked to see me?" she inquired.

"Yes. Do sit down." He swept the air with his hand, then waited for her to take a seat before he lowered himself to the chair at the head of the table. Then he turned and smiled at her.

The smile sent a golden glow beaming toward her, enveloping her. No wonder he was such a popular evangelist. Was that what people called him? Or was he considered a guru, a New Age teacher? She'd never paid enough attention to his broadcasts to know for sure just what his title and credentials were.

"I don't believe we've met," Stephen remarked, laying one hand over the other. His left hand still bore red blotches from the burns he'd suffered in the tragic fire at the villa, and he seemed to be unconsciously covering the splotches.

"No, we haven't, but I've seen you at the hospital a lot," Evaline replied. "And on TV."

"Really? Are you a follower of The Path?"

"No." Evaline blushed. "I'm not involved in any religion right now."

"It isn't so much a religion as a journey, a way of life, Evaline. A way of thinking. Of becoming."

"I don't know, Mr. Durrell—"

"Here." He reached into the inside pocket of his suit coat and produced two tickets. "Take these passes to my show. We're taping in Seattle now, since I've had to stay near the hospital."

"Yes, I know."

"Come as my guest. Bring a friend. You might be surprised by what you'll learn." He urged her to take the little rectangles of paper. Evaline didn't know what else to do but accept them.

"Thank you."

"If you'd like, I could even have you tagged as an active audience participant. You could be on national television."

"Definitely not for me." She laughed nervously and tucked the tickets in the pocket of her lab coat.

"Why? With that face of yours, you'd boost my ratings, Evaline, you surely would."

She flushed. Until her plastic surgery at the age of twenty-three, she'd been a social pariah, and spent her days as a recluse at a clinic on the Saquinnish Indian Reservation north of Seattle. Now, four years later, she had a new face, a new career, and a new life, but she still hadn't learned to accept a compliment, especially from a man. Did men, she wondered, see only her alluring but surgically created features? Did any of them look beyond the large dark eyes and slender nose to the woman behind the medical miracle? She doubted it.

Besides her father only two men in her entire life had treated her as a normal human being: one was a new-comer to the reservation named Carter Greyson, and the other a man who had rescued her at sea. Her father was now a fugitive from the law, Carter had married a white woman, and her rescuer, after plucking her from the frigid water off the Washington coast, had sailed away before she could thank him and discover his name.

"Think about it, won't you?" Stephen put in when she made no response.

Evaline shrugged off her dark thoughts and nodded, deciding to turn the conversation from her face and his career to the business at hand. "Mr. Durrell, I'm told you are looking for a physical therapist."

"Yes. My step-daughter"—he broke off—"I mean my wife-to-be's daughter, has been in serious condition for many weeks." He leaned back in his chair. "But of course, I don't have to tell you that. You probably know all about her case."

"Everyone knows about Allison," Evaline said, nodding. "And you, too. You're all the hospital staff talks about. The tragedy of it all—"

"Yes." He clasped his hands together tightly. "And the

media have fed off poor dear Allison like a pack of hyenas. She has suffered, I'm afraid—suffered terribly."

Evaline thought of the articles she'd read about the fourteen-year-old Allison, how the girl had started the fire that had killed her own mother and then taken off in a car she didn't know how to drive, crashing on a cliffside road in the sea and almost plunging to her own death hundreds of feet below. The maid and gardener had tried valiantly to save Meredith Delaney, and Stephen had nearly lost his life by dashing into the inferno to save his fiancée. But he'd been too late. Allison's mother perished in the flames.

Reporters all over the world were in a frenzy for weeks, speculating on the reasons for the death of wealthy Meredith Delaney, known by millions as a beautiful jet-setter and the most famous convert to The Path. Evaline could still remember seeing Stephen on television after the fire, breaking down in grief from every camera angle and on every station.

While Stephen appeared on talk shows all over the world, Allison lay comatose in a hospital. While Stephen received more airplay from the fire than he got for his own broadcasts, Allison's reputation disintegrated. Numerous witnesses stepped forward to verify the domestic problems of the Delaney household: how Allison had been nothing but trouble, how Allison had fought with her mother constantly, how Allison drank and partied and made life miserable for everyone around her. Some reporters even went so far as to speculate that Allison might have wanted charismatic Stephen Durrell for herself, and had killed her own mother in a fit of jealousy.

Allison claimed to have no memory of the awful night, and the Greek police had not found enough evidence to charge her, but most people doubted she was telling the truth.

"Perhaps when Allison recovers her memory, she'll be able to explain what really happened," Evaline put in.

"For her sake," Stephen replied, "I hope she *doesn't* remember that night. I wish to God I couldn't." He sighed. "And the situation hasn't gotten any better for her. In fact, it's just gotten worse."

"What do you mean?"

"A complication in Allison's treatment has come up. And I need your help."

"What's the complication?"

"Allison's natural father."

"Why is he a problem?"

"Why?" Stephen pursed his lips, then lowered his dark brows. "Let me just say that this insensitive rube of a man wants to take his fourteen-year-old daughter, whom he hasn't seen since she was two, to a remote bay on the Strait of Juan de Fuca. There, he expects her to recover, both mentally and physically, from a trauma that has left her without a memory or the use of her legs."

"He intends to take her away from the hospital?"

"Exactly." Stephen leaned forward. "I've met him. He's a bullheaded idiot entirely incapable of dealing with Allison's current psychological and medical problems, let alone a teenage girl who has just lost her mother."

"Or might have killed her mother," Evaline put in.

"I prefer not to believe Allison capable of murder. I'm convinced it was an accident." He steepled his fingers in front of his chest. "Whatever happened, Allison shouldn't be taken away by a redneck fisherman."

"He is her father, though. There's something to be said for blood ties."

Stephen rolled his eyes. "Blood is the only thing this character has in common with Allison. You've seen her, haven't you, Evaline?"

"Yes." Evaline recalled the slender blond young woman

whose delicate bone structure and classic beauty couldn't be camouflaged by casts, bandages, or a bad attitude. "Allison is an attractive girl."

"Just like her mother, may she rest in peace." Stephen paused thoughtfully for a moment, in honor of his deceased fiancée's memory, and then pressed on. "Meredith was a lady, in every sense of the word. I miss her, and all I have left of her is her beautiful daughter, whom I wish to protect in all ways. All her life Allison has known nothing but the best money can buy. Meredith and I saw to that. Right now, Allison needs all the support she can get. And yet this Townsend character, the complete opposite to Meredith in every way, thinks he's going to whisk Allison off to a house out in the middle of nowhere and give her a miracle cure."

Evaline frowned slightly. She didn't believe money was the answer to everything, but yanking a teenager out of her everyday routine wasn't a good idea, either. Teenagers were notoriously inflexible about certain aspects of their lives, especially if they were accustomed to designer labels and moneyed independence.

"I can't let it happen, Evaline," Stephen continued. "I know what they say about Allison. But I believe that under all the problems there's a great kid, if I can only have the chance to reach her. I consider myself a father to her, I really do."

Evaline studied Stephen. He didn't look like anyone's dad. He was far too glamorous for such a mundane role. Good dads were frayed around the edges, a bit careworn, like a pair of favorite shoes, dependable and comfortable, not like the shining, perfectly groomed man at her elbow. Besides that, Stephen dropped her name into the conversation much too frequently, the way a salesman used a name to create a false sense of familiarity. She'd never liked that. A niggling sense of distrust of

Stephen dulled the memory of the bright aura she'd seen when she first met him.

"She's lucky to have two men to care about her," Evaline replied at last, remembering her own father who had betrayed her in the end, leaving her without a soul in the world. "But as you know, Allison is suffering from amnesia."

"Yes. Post-traumatic amnesia, they tell me." He tilted his head. "I don't follow you—"

"Perhaps she won't remember her former way of life. Perhaps a remote house won't seem that bad to her."

"Oh, she remembers plenty. Just not the night at the villa. And knowing Allison, this house scenario with her father will be the absolute worst experience for her. I am afraid she'll lose what little progress she's made." Stephen frowned. "But there's nothing I can do to block Townsend. He has every legal right to regain custody of Allison, now that Meredith is no longer with us."

"I don't understand how I fit in to all this," Evaline commented.

Stephen glanced at her. "Allison needs therapy and someone to see to her safety, and I have offered to help pay for Allison's physical therapy, to ensure that she gets the care she needs."

"But she'll be away from the medical center."

"Exactly. The therapist will have to go to her."

"You mean travel back and forth from Seattle?"

"No. Live there."

"At the remote cabin?"

Stephen nodded slowly, allowing the impact of his words to register.

Evaline sank back and clutched the arms of the chair in an effort to subdue a swell of concern. "For how long?"

"Months. The doctors say Allison will need extensive therapy, since she seems unable to move her legs, even though there is no medical reason why she can't."

"We call it a conversion reaction," Evaline explained. "It's a psychological condition, not a physiological one."

"Yes. That's what the doctor said. And it might take the whole summer to regain her strength. Plus follow-up trips afterward. But you could do that on a weekly basis."

"You mean to say that I would have to live in a cabin with two strangers for the whole summer, no days off?"

Stephen nodded.

At her look of protest, he held up a long slender hand. "Before you say anything, Evaline, just let me mention that I am willing to make it worth your while."

"What do you mean?"

"I've heard you want to attend medical school."

Evaline glanced at him in surprise. Had he talked to her fellow co-workers about her? She wondered if he had selected her at random or for a particular reason.

"You do want to go back to school, don't you?" he added.

"Well, yes."

"I could set up a grant that would pay for your expenses—tuition, room, board—"

"You'd pay for my entire medical education?"

"Yes. That's how important Allison is to me, and to her grandparents. They have agreed to contribute to your education as well."

Evaline blew out a puff of air, too surprised to respond. The offer seemed too good to be true. Yet, how could she refuse? She had worked her way through undergraduate school in only three years, done her internship, and had become a physical therapist. But medical school was her dream, her chance to make something of herself, her chance to make a difference in the world.

"Cat got your tongue, Evaline?" Stephen asked, smiling.

"It seems so—so—so generous," she stammered. "I don't know what to say."

"Say you will do it. It would mean a lot to us to know Allison is getting the best care possible."

"I don't know, Mr. Durrell. Why me?"

"You're young, healthy, unattached. I realize you're new at this, but I've heard you're good at what you do." He touched her arm. "Three months is a long time to ask of anyone, but I am confident you can do it."

"It's a long time to be away." Her voice trailed off with indecision.

He sighed and stood up. She watched him slip his burned but still elegantly shaped hands into the pockets of his dark blue trousers. For a moment he paced the room, his head lowered as if trying to decide something. Then he stopped suddenly and leveled his gaze on her.

"All right. Maybe you should be told everything, Evaline."

Her stomach pinched together, anticipating bad news to come. She twisted in her chair to face him. "What do you mean, everything?"

He sighed again and studied her face for a long moment. Then he wiped the sides of his face with his finger and thumb, down past his mouth and over his chin. "There's another reason I need someone to accompany Allison."

The sinking feeling intensified. "What reason is that?"

"Meredith told me once—" He paused, looked down at the floor, and then back into her eyes. "And I don't want this to go any farther than this room—no farther, Evaline, do you understand?"

"Of course." She stared at him, her gaze riveted to his face.

"The media would eat Allison alive if you spread this around. Anyway"—Stephen frowned—"Meredith told me that she'd been abused by her first husband."

"Abused?" Evaline's voice cracked.

"Yes."

"You mean beaten?"

"Yes. And more." Stephen's eyes narrowed. "He raped her. That's how she became pregnant. Marital rape."

"Allison was the result of a rape?"

Stephen nodded gravely.

"My God!"

"Meredith stayed with him because of the child, but when he turned on Allison, she left him."

"Townsend abused his own child?"

"Yes. But there's no proof, Evaline. That's the trouble. The bastard has never been charged with abuse, and so the courts will give him his daughter, no questions asked."

"That's awful!"

Stephen sank to the chair again. "So you see why you must go with Allison? She must be protected, Evaline. Townsend must be watched. And the first proof you get of abuse, you call me, and we'll have him arrested."

"But what if he turns on me?"

"We've arranged to get you a small handgun, the kind you can carry on you at all times. You'll be safe."

Evaline shook her head and stared at the wall, where a print of children playing in the sunshine clashed with the upsetting turn in the conversation. "I don't know, Mr. Durrell."

"I've been told you are an excellent marksman."

Her head shot up. "How do you know all these things about me?"

"Do you think I would choose just anyone for this job? Do you think Allison means nothing to me, nothing to Meredith's parents? We want the best. The best physical therapy and the best personal protection. That combination was difficult to find, Evaline. But we found it in you."

"I could be killed."

"I doubt Townsend is that violent."

"I'm beginning to see why the pay is so good."

"Yes." Stephen shrugged. "But I'm a firm believer in decent compensation, Evaline. The stakes are high. You will need to be constantly vigilant. A medical education isn't too much to offer for the peace of mind you'll provide us in return."

Evaline sighed, and drummed the table with her fingertips. She wanted the medical school grant, but she wasn't willing to risk her life for a degree. On the other hand, how could she let a child be taken into the wilderness by a man capable of rape and abuse—a girl too injured to run away? How could she let a motherless child be subjected to such a danger? Hadn't she been in need of a mother, once, too—someone to love her, someone to keep her from harm? Wouldn't her life have been vastly different had a mother prevented her from walking alone that fateful day when she was twelve years old?

The memory of that day loomed up, and she shut it off immediately, but not before she'd broken out in a cold sweat. Beneath the lab coat, her blouse stuck to her torso. Evaline clutched the arms of the chair, fighting off the panic, fighting off the heartache, but knowing what she had to do.

"Okay," she said, her heart pounding.

"You'll take the job?" Stephen's voice rose in hope.

"Yes."

"Excellent!"

The next morning, just as Evaline reached for the door of Allison's private room, she was stopped by the sound of a familiar voice behind her.

"Evaline!" Patty Johnson exclaimed in a hushed tone. "I can't believe you're taking this on!"

"Well, I am," Evaline replied. Allison was being discharged, and a van loaded with Evaline's suitcases and equipment, and Allison's expensive leather bags, idled outside the hospital, waiting for them. "The pay's too good to refuse."

"Have you seen the father?" Patty jerked her thumb toward the door of the room. "Do you know what he's like?"

"No." Evaline paused. "I haven't met him."

"From what I've seen, they're both bad apples." Patty gave a snort of disgust. "Some things aren't worth it, no matter how much they pay you."

"They can't be that bad."

"Wanna bet?"

At that moment a deep male voice bellowed inside the room. "She is not riding in some goddamn wheelchair!"

Evaline glanced at the door and then back at her friend. Patty raised her eyebrows.

"If you can stand that guy and his daughter for three months without going stark raving mad, I'll buy you dinner at the Space Needle."

An attack of doubt swept over Evaline, but she instantly battled it back with her vow to keep Allison safe. She turned the knob. "You're on," Evaline replied, and then, pasting on a smile of confidence she didn't feel inside, she swept into the room.

No one noticed her entrance: not the girl slumped on the bed, not the agitated discharge nurse, whose back was turned to the door, and not the huge man staring the nurse down. Evaline glanced at him—a blur of red plaid, bushy dark beard, wild brown hair, and long legs covered by faded jeans.

"Everyone leaves the hospital in a wheelchair, Mr. Townsend," the nurse stated. Judging by the terseness in her voice, the nurse must have repeated the policy numerous times for his benefit.

"Not my daughter."

"Mr. Townsend, your daughter can't even walk."

"The hell she can't. The doctors said there is nothing wrong with her legs. She just doesn't *want* to walk."

The nurse sighed, and Evaline took the opportunity to step in. She strode forward, holding out her hand.

"Mr. Townsend?" she said in her firmest voice. "I'm Evaline Jaye, Allison's new physical therapist."

Gabriel Townsend turned to her and she felt dwarfed by his size. He was well over six feet, with wide shoulders and muscular arms. He gave her the impression of being a very tall, very sturdy tree, complete with a full complement of crusty bark. A scruffy untrimmed beard spilled down the front of his shirt, reaching halfway to his belt buckle, a large oval affair with the figure of an eagle molded in silver. She couldn't guess his age because of the beard, which could have belonged to a man of twenty-five or fifty. Her stare traveled up the path of hair to his face, where she found two gray eyes flashing at her. She had expected cruel beady eyes but saw instead two clear pools burning with fire and intelligence.

Slightly surprised by the look in his eyes, she kept her hand outstretched until he couldn't ignore it. Almost reluctantly, he shook her hand.

"Pleasure," he said. His eyes raked her up and down. "You're kind of tiny for the job, aren't you?"

"No, Mr. Townsend, I am not."

Her reply seemed to take him aback. He stared at her for a moment, then turned to his daughter.

"Get up now, Allison. No more playacting, girl."

Allison sat on the bed, her slender back slumped, her shoulders drooping. She wouldn't even look at him, much less make a reply. She was dressed in jeans, a black T-shirt, and stylish heavy-soled shoes. Her blond hair had been brushed and pulled back and was held with a gold clip. For all appearances she looked like a normal young woman, and a very pretty one at that, except for the dull look in her eyes and the scowl on her face.

Townsend strode forward and planted himself directly in front of Allison, but the girl still ignored him. "Are you going to let them wheel you out like some sissy?" Townsend demanded, obviously frustrated by her attitude. "Or are you going to walk out of this hospital like a man?"

"I don't think she'll ever walk like a man," Evaline put in wryly, hoping a lighter attitude might induce the girl to cooperate. "Will you, Allison?"

Townsend's head jerked around, and he glowered at her. "You said you were the physical therapist."

"That's right."

"Then stick to your job description. No room for a comedian where we're going."

Evaline flushed. She'd only been trying to defuse the situation with humor. God knew the room could use a little levity. She crossed her arms over a sinking feeling in her stomach that told her the next three months might seem like three years.

"Allison!" Townsend thundered.

The nurse shot Evaline a dark and helpless look and stepped back. Evaline moved forward, rolling the wheelchair to the side of the bed. She scooted around the chair and reached for Allison.

"Come on, Allison," Evaline urged.

"I said she doesn't need that chair!" Townsend growled.

"I'm not deaf," Evaline retorted. "But you must be. Haven't you been told your daughter is supposed to leave in the chair?"

"Then I'll carry her, for chrissake!"

Evaline glanced up at his face, then at Allison. She saw the girl's eyelids flutter.

"Do you want your father to carry you?" Evaline asked, hoping to get a response and gambling on the typical teenage defiance to put an end to the discussion.

There was a sudden silence in the room as all eyes turned toward the girl. Allison kept staring at the wall, but her voice came out in a raspy monotone.

"I'd rather die first."

Evaline saw Townsend flush. It served him right. He didn't deserve a kind response, not after his boorish behavior. She glanced back to the girl. It was then she saw the second vision, much more startling than the one in the conference room. Out of the corner of her eye, she caught a glimpse of a crow sitting on the headboard of Allison's bed, just beyond the girl's shoulder. What was a bird doing in the hospital? she wondered. The teachings of her childhood flooded her memory. She remembered the meaning of the appearance of a crow: *Help will be needed to discover a betrayal.*

Alarmed and amazed, Evaline blinked, and the bird disappeared. When she looked at the headboard again, she saw nothing but the cold shining bars of stainless steel.

Shaken, Evaline issued a terse command for Allison to slide into the chair, her voice strident, and having the effect of squelching any protests the girl might have made. Evaline guided Allison into the chair, supporting her back and legs as the girl slid from the bed to the seat of the wheelchair. Then she deftly maneuvered the wheelchair across the floor, instructed the nurse to grab Allison's purse, and rolled the chair into the hall. With each rotation of the shiny wheels taking her closer to the van, Evaline wondered what lay in store for her in the wilds of Washington State. Were the spirits trying to tell her something? Warn her?

Unlikely. The spirits had abandoned her years ago.

Why would they come to her now? Only Sea Wolf, ruler of the underwater world of lost souls, had responded to her prayer long ago, granting her a new life as a new person with a new people. And here in the world of white medicine she would stay, for she was as good as dead to those of her childhood.

Evaline shook off such thoughts and rolled the wheelchair out the hospital doors.

2

Obstruction Bay, Washington

"You can stay in the house," Gabriel stated, turning off the engine of his pickup. He hadn't spoken since they'd left the ferry. "Or you can bunk in the boat tonight. Doesn't much matter to me."

"All right." Evaline peered into the darkness on the other side of the truck windshield, trying to make out the details of the house, but the property was bereft of lights, and she could see nothing but the hint of a steep roofline and the jagged edge of an exterior stairway. "Allison will have to have the bathroom adapted for her, though, and—"

"I've already installed handrails," he put in. "And built a ramp so she can get in and out at the back of the house."

"Oh, that's good."

"The house's musty this time of year, though," he added.

Mustiness was usually a sign of disuse. "You don't live in the house?" she asked.

"Never have. Never will."

Evaline glanced at him, wondering why he would buy what had to be expensive beachfront property and then not live in the house. But now wasn't the time to question his real-estate purchases. Instead, she looked at the bay where some type of vessel rocked next to a long dock. Night shrouded even that view, painting everything she saw in hazy charcoal and impenetrable ink. Still, she remembered the last time she'd been on a boat, and the thought made her shudder involuntarily.

"I'm not crazy about boats," she said. "I vote for the house. How about you, Allison?"

As usual, the girl made no response. During the entire trip, Allison hadn't uttered a single word, and seemed to have turned inward, closing her eyes during most of the journey. Evaline had thought the girl might have been afraid of being on a ferry. Once the large vessel had docked, and they transferred their gear to Gabriel's pickup—which had been parked in the marina of a small but picturesque village—Evaline had expected Allison to perk up and take an interest in the spectacular scenery. Instead Allison had leaned her head against the frame of the truck and closed her eyes again, letting the emerald cedars and sparkling bays drift past the window unseen.

Evaline couldn't believe it, and attributed Allison's behavior to exhaustion, or being jaded by seeing too much of the world too soon. The girl had been in the hospital for over a month, and it was likely she was too weary to care about her surroundings. Evaline, on the other hand, couldn't help but feel an undeniable catch in her chest as she slid out of the pickup on the driver's side and sucked in a deep breath of air, sweet and moist with the fragrance of cedar and pine—the smell of her childhood, the smell of home.

Her memories were cut off by Gabriel's gruff voice. "I'll carry Allison, Miss Jaye. You go on ahead and open the door."

"Okay, but do you have a flashlight?"

"Why?" He glanced down at her as he reached for the passenger door.

"I can hardly see."

"City folk!" he snorted in contempt. "Your eyes'll adjust."

"You might try leaving a porch light on next time."

"And run down my generator for nothing? There's plenty of light left." He pulled open the door. "Let's go, Allison."

The girl stiffened.

"You want to stay in the truck all night?" he asked tersely.

Allison didn't even look at him. Evaline pressed her arm against her own hip, where the small .38 snub-nose weighted the bottom of her purse. There was no way to predict what turn Gabriel Townsend would take, so she had to be prepared to defend Allison and herself.

"Fine." Gabriel turned. "You want to sit in the truck? Go ahead."

He stomped to the shell that covered the bed of the pickup and opened the door with a hard jerk.

"Mr. Townsend!" Evaline exclaimed, following at his heels. "You can't leave her out here!"

"The hell I can't."

"It's cold! She'll freeze!"

"She's a big girl. I'm sure she's aware of the temperature."

"But Mr. Townsend!" Evaline sputtered as he tossed a bag toward her. She caught it involuntarily and gasped as it knocked her breathless. She straightened and glared at him, even though she knew he couldn't read her expression in the darkness, no matter how acute his night vision.

Gabriel scooped up four big bags, two under each arm and the others in his hands, and effortlessly carried them across the gravel lot toward the house. Evaline stopped to assure Allison she'd be right back, then marched after Gabriel, lugging one of Allison's suitcases and aware of a strange runaway anger rising inside her, an odd response for her. She considered herself a calm, easygoing person, slow to burn and quick to explain away most people's shortcomings. She rarely got angry, rarely raised her voice. Gabriel Townsend, however, seemed to have found a crack in her good nature and had wedged one of his big feet right into it.

Gabriel clumped up the wooden stairs, and Evaline struggled after him, staring at his large back, and wondering how such a big man, loaded down with such weight, could move so easily. He carried the bags as if they were cotton balls. Without unlocking the door, he pushed it open and passed into the house. Evaline paused on the porch, surprised that he'd left his home open. Gabriel Townsend didn't seem like the kind of man to trust people enough to leave his property unsecured. Then he flipped on an interior light and her question was answered immediately. Evaline's heart sank at the sight before her.

What person would *want* to break into such a hellhole?

Covering all but a narrow path through the living room were stacks of books, newspapers, cardboard boxes, and mismatched pieces of furniture. Parkas, boots, and wool shirts had been flung helter-skelter over the boxes, and cartons of empty beer cans teetered precariously near the front door. The house looked like the kind of attic that inhabited nightmares and horror movies.

Gabriel made no comment or apology as he barged through the piles, unaware or inured to the mess, and passed down a short hall to the first room on the right. He dropped the bags on the floor between a black garbage bag stuffed with unidentifiable lumps and a dusty pile of stereo equipment. Then he straightened, his head nearly reaching the top of the doorway.

"I'll get the rest of the things," he stated. "You can unpack."

"Mr. Townsend!—"

Her protest was cut off by his quick retreat and smothered by the loud stomp of his boots as he strode down the hall and back out the door.

Evaline's shoulders drooped as she let out a long sigh. How could anyone be expected to live in such a mess, let alone find a place to sleep for the night? Was the man crazy? She sniffed, and frowned at the definite odor of mildew in the air. Most of the stuff in the cabin was probably coated with mold and festooned in spiderwebs. The Northwest, especially out in the woods like this, was inhabited by wolf spiders, huge dark brown arachnids the size of quarters. She had no desire to wage war with such creatures and was sure a young woman like Allison, accustomed to a pampered lifestyle, would be repulsed by most of the denizens found in the surrounding cedar forest. Evaline was only too familiar with earwigs, centipedes, and the four-inch slugs common to the area, for she had kept house and done yard work for her elderly father most of her life.

The thought of her father sent a stab of desolation and loneliness through Evaline. She had no father now—at least not the father she had believed in for her first twenty-three years. She had lost that icon of her childhood to betrayal and murder. To face the reality of her father, to be forced to accept a flawed shadow of the man, had shattered her faith and sent her running from the reservation. Now she no longer had any contact with him and had no idea where he had gone since his escape from prison.

"I'm putting your equipment in the back bedroom," Gabriel told her in his booming baritone. His bearded face popped into view briefly, then disappeared.

Evaline snapped to her senses and hurried after him. "Wait a minute. Allison and I can't stay here!"

"Why not?" he countered, depositing two boxes on the pine floor. "The place is built like a rock."

"The place," she retorted, hands on her hips, "is a pigsty!"

Gabriel glanced around in surprise, as if he hadn't noticed the mess. "Nothing a broom and dustpan couldn't fix."

"You can't sweep in here!" she exclaimed. "There's too much junk piled everywhere!"

"It can be pushed to the side. Stacked up."

"It's a health hazard, Mr. Townsend. I'll bet you have mice. Or worse, rats."

"No rats out here, City Girl." He dusted his hands on his jeans. "And a few field mice never hurt anything."

Evaline scowled and fled from the room, uncertain what to do. She should leave right now. She should tell Stephen Durrell to give his educational grant and this impossible mission to someone with a higher level of desperation. But fleeing back to Seattle immediately was out of the question. It was dark outside. Even if she could find her way in the gloom, it would take hours to walk to the ferry terminal in the little village. Allison couldn't make the journey in her condition. And Evaline couldn't leave her. She *wouldn't* leave Allison. Not with the likes of Gabriel Townsend. She'd never met anyone more upsetting.

Evaline was still standing in the hallway, rigid and seething, when Gabriel came up behind her.

"What's your problem?" he demanded.

"I am a physical therapist, not a bulldozer driver, Mr. Townsend. Cleaning up this . . . this . . ." She waved her hand, frustrated that she couldn't find a word to describe the disorder. ". . . this . . . landfill is not part of the agreement."

"Listen." He moved to stand in front of her, his shoulders and torso dominating her field of vision like a stone wall. "You said you wanted to stay in the house, not on the boat. Now do you, or don't you?"

"I don't know!" she retorted, surprised at how angry she sounded. She could just imagine what the interior of his boat would look like: a floating trashbucket. Added to that vision of disarray would be bad dreams, prompted by the rise and fall of the tide. Though the currents of the sea were part of her heritage, part of her blood, they were also part of her past, and she couldn't allow her memories to swell up and swallow her, to transport her once again to the night she had last been on a boat. If a stranger hadn't intervened then, hadn't said exactly the right thing at the right time, she might not have survived.

That past was better left unexamined, however, and the depth of blackness in her own soul better left unvisited. She knew how far down she had traveled once, and now she ran from that shadowy flood like a ship scudding before a squall.

"Well, I'll tell you one thing," Gabriel said. "I'm not hauling the suitcases up here just to have to turn around and take them down to the boat. Now what'll it be?"

Evaline crossed her arms, hating the fact that she had to choose at all, and hating the choices. "The house," she replied at last.

Gabriel shook his head and strode back to the truck. Evaline returned to the first bedroom and glanced around the littered chamber. Even if they stayed here only a day, Allison would have to have a bed or at least a chair in which to sit once Gabriel brought her in from the truck. Perhaps under all the junk she would find useful furniture.

Evaline picked up a cardboard box labeled "Twyla" in sloppy strokes of a black felt-tip marker and carried it out to the living room. Four more boxes bearing the same name joined the first one. Evaline dragged out the heavy garbage bag, which clanked like a collection of cheap pots and pans. Next came a pile of women's clothing, mostly dresses made of big bold flowers in primary colors, a thin red wool coat, and a box of shoes. Evaline picked up a pump and rotated it. Twyla had tiny feet, size five, and she favored spike heels and straps—not the shoes of the type of woman Evaline expected would hang around with Gabriel Townsend. But the previous occupants of the cabin were none of Evaline's business. She dropped the pump into the box and took it out to the living room just as Gabriel came back with the last of the bags.

She saw him glance at the Twyla collection she'd piled near the door, saw his right eye narrow at the corner, and then he walked by without a comment. Perhaps the love affair or marriage had gone sour. Perhaps Twyla had broken his heart. Evaline usually wasn't vindictive, but in this case, she hoped Twyla had brought Gabriel to his knees.

Evaline followed Gabriel up the hall. "Allison has to have a bed," she began, wondering if he was listening. He put down the suitcases and shot a quick glance around the bedroom.

"There's a couch in here," he replied. "Beneath those laundry baskets. See it?"

"Allison shouldn't be sleeping on a couch," Evaline countered. "Not in her condition."

"It won't kill her to sleep on a couch for a few days," Gabriel growled.

"How do you know?" Evaline countered. "You're no medical specialist."

"There's nothing wrong with Allison that a little discipline won't cure."

"I don't believe discipline is the answer in this case."

"Well, you're not her parent." He ran a hand over his hair in a tense gesture of frustration. "And it's the couch or the floor tonight."

Evaline was so upset she couldn't look at him. "Have any sheets or blankets?"

"I'll bring a couple of sleeping bags up from the boat."

"Fine. I'll clear these away, then." Evaline reached for two of the tattered pink laundry baskets. She deduced that the jumble of clothing in them belonged to Twyla, for a woman like Twyla would naturally have a pink bathroom and laundry with plenty of fluff and flounces. Stacking the baskets one on top of the other, Evaline carried them to the doorway. "What about Allison?" she asked.

"She's probably cold enough now to want to come in."

"What about heat? Is there a furnace that can be turned on?"

"No. A fireplace. But it's too blocked off."

"Mr. Townsend, your daughter has been in the hospital for over a month. Her body is not accustomed to wide swings in temperature. For her own physical—"

"A little chill never hurt anyone," Gabriel snapped. "And she'll be plenty warm in a sleeping bag." He jerked a thumb toward the front door. "That girl's been spoiled. Spoiled rotten. And I'm going to put an end to it."

He turned on his heel and left. Evaline decided to go with him in case Allison needed her protection. She scurried down the hall, shoved the laundry baskets out of the way, and hurried across the deck and down the stairs to the parking lot. Allison was still sitting in the cab of the pickup, hunched up with her back to the door.

"All right, Allison," Gabriel announced. "Time to quit playing games."

She didn't move a muscle.

Gabriel pulled open the door. "You can either walk in or get carried in."

Allison remained still.

"Pretty damn cold out here at night," Gabriel observed out loud. "Just wait until midnight, when the wind picks up. Comes right off the bay, colder than shit."

"Mr. Townsend!" Evaline protested. "You're talking to an impressionable child—"

Gabriel glared down at her. "This impressionable child can spout a string of cusswords even sailors haven't heard."

Allison scrunched into a tighter ball.

"And that silent treatment isn't going to get you anywhere around here, young lady," Gabriel continued.

Evaline stepped closer. "This isn't the time for—"

"It damn well is," he exploded. "It's high time Allison learned she's responsible for her own self. No one's going to baby her out here. And that includes you!"

"She's my patient, Mr. Townsend. It's my job to see that she isn't put at risk."

"It's my job to turn her into a decent human being."

Evaline almost laughed out loud. "What would you know about that?"

Gabriel's head snapped around, and for a long moment he glowered at her.

Evaline stared right back. Did the boor actually consider himself a shining example of humanity, or even capable of instilling decent values in a young girl? The nerve of the man!

"In September, Allison will be evaluated," Gabriel said, his voice constrained with intense emotion, "by a doctor hired by her mother's parents. If a certain level of progress hasn't been made, Allison will be taken away from me and put in an institution."

"An institution?" Evaline repeated.

"That's right. An institution." His eyes glittered in the darkness. "So don't go telling me what my job is and what it isn't. I know damn well what needs to be done. And there isn't much time to do it."

Without waiting for a reply, Gabriel turned back to Allison. "Are you coming?" The words grated through his clenched teeth. At her silence he leaned closer to the cab. "Where are your things?" He snatched Allison's large purse off the floor of the pickup.

"Here." He tossed the bag to Evaline.

The open purse tipped in her hands, spilling a pile of cosmetics at her feet, onto which tumbled a small stuffed animal. Evaline picked up the bedraggled toy bear, worn bald by years of use, and marveled that a caustic teenager like Allison would carry around such a sentimental item. Allison's sophisticated looks and abrasive personality had made even Evaline forget that in many ways she was still a child.

"What's that?" Gabriel demanded.

Evaline shot a glance at Allison, saw the wide-eyed but quickly doused alarm in her eyes, and decided to keep the girl's secret. "Nothing much," Evaline replied, quickly stuffing the bear into the purse and grasping a handful of lipstick tubes. "Just female stuff."

Her answer apparently satisfied Gabriel. He turned back to his daughter. "Let's go, Allison."

She didn't respond.

"All right, Allison," he said. "You've made your decision. See you in the morning."

He slammed the door, skirted around the front of the truck, and walked down the dock toward his boat. Evaline remained by the side of the pickup, put off by Gabriel's high-handed behavior, and quite perplexed regarding her next move.

Quietly she opened the door of the truck. "Come on, Allison," she urged. "He means it. You don't want to spend the night out here, do you?"

Allison edged closer to the center of the seat and away from the door.

"You'll freeze out here, Allison. I'd like to help you, but I can't carry you. Only your dad can do that." She paused, hoping her words would convince the girl to give in.

"Come on, Allison."

Allison's limp blond ponytail swept across her back as she turned her head slightly. Evaline felt a surge of hope that she had gotten through to the teenager, that her gentle words had more effect than Gabriel's harsh ones.

"What do you say, Allison?" she asked softly.

"Fuck off, bitch."

Evaline froze. Never in her wildest dreams had she expected such foul language to come out of the mouth of the pretty fourteen-year-old girl. And no one, not even the people who had once turned away in disgust from Evaline's scars, had ever said such a thing to her. She blinked and quickly collected herself, while her face burned.

"Good-night to you, too," she answered, determined to remain civil. She wouldn't allow Allison the satisfaction of seeing her shock. And she refused to react in anger.

Carefully she closed the door and walked back to the house, consumed by self-doubt. The job suddenly seemed daunting, far too complicated for her skills. She'd never had any children, and had been an only child herself. She didn't know the first thing about raising kids or dealing with their problems. She should have told Stephen Durrell she lacked the skills to handle a difficult teenager. All she had was her common sense, but she wasn't sure it would be enough in this case.

"I'm not a quitter," Evaline mumbled under her breath as she headed toward the bedroom.

Oh, yes you are, whispered the little voice in her head.

Evaline ignored the voice and set to work cleaning, making sure to keep her weapon close at hand. Gabriel came and went quickly, dropping the sleeping bags in the hall and informing her that he'd be up and about before seven o'clock. Evaline didn't mind starting the day early, but she was certain Allison would object to being disturbed at the crack of dawn. She took a sleeping bag and the wheelchair down to the truck. She set the chair up, in case Allison changed her mind during the night about staying in the truck, and then put the sleeping bag on the seat beside her.

Evaline returned to the house and worked long past midnight, moving boxes away from the fireplace in the living room. She took a quick survey of the main floor by poking her head over and around piles. If the house were clear of debris, it would be considered spacious, with its high cathedral ceiling above the living room and kitchen. Three bedrooms and two baths flanked the central hall, and she had the feeling that some kind of basement area was down below, since the house was built up off the ground and surrounded by a deck. Evaline also got the feeling that the house was built on some sort of promontory, but in the darkness she couldn't be certain. She left the front door open and the outside light burning, hoping Allison would change her mind and call to her. But as the night wore on, nothing but silence descended upon the bay.

Tirelessly Evaline worked, finding boxes marked "Debby" and then "Sharon." How many women had lived here? she wondered. By the appearance of their possessions, they all had tastes similar to Twyla's, favoring fancy shoes and frilly clothes, ultrafeminine attire that Evaline would never wear. She couldn't imagine a ruffle-loving woman living in this remote place, stuck with a bear of a man who probably couldn't read, much less fox-trot.

By the looks of the clothes, these ladies liked to dress up and go out for an evening, and didn't like spending too much time in the house. They were the type of women who didn't know a spatula from a sponge, and whose idea of cooking was ordering takeout Chinese. Evaline couldn't imagine such a woman would be interested in Gabriel.

By one o'clock, Evaline had managed to clear a wide path to the fireplace. Near the hearth, she found a wood-box containing some dried logs and pieces of kindling, much of which was crisscrossed by spiderwebs. How long had it been since someone had lived here? What had happened to Twyla, for instance? Had she gotten too close to the flames so that her hairspray and chiffon ignited? Evaline couldn't help but smile at the mental picture of a pile of pink ashes on the hearth.

Her smile turned to a grimace, however, as she forced her hands into the woodbox to get some kindling and logs. Two spiders scuttled out of the way, and she shuddered as she gingerly lifted the wood. She piled them on the grate, found some matches in a tin on the mantel, and soon had a fire crackling on the hearth. Evaline rose and brushed her hands on her twill slacks. Building fires was something she knew, something as basic to her nature as eating and sleeping. Satisfied, she watched the flames leap higher. This house was in desperate need of heat to dry out the dankness that permeated the place.

When at last she retired, Evaline grabbed the second sleeping bag and carried it out to the truck. She looked in at Allison still sitting in the cab. The girl was asleep and still hadn't moved.

Evaline shook her head at the girl's senseless stubbornness, then rolled out the sleeping bag on the grass beside the drive. She wasn't about to let Allison spend the night all alone in the truck.

Years had gone by since Evaline had slept outdoors. In vain she tried to find a comfortable spot, but felt each pebble, each lump of sod, beneath the heavy cotton bag. She tossed and turned until her long day caught up with her and she fell asleep, not waking up until a gruff voice broke into her dreams.

"Miss Jaye!"

3

"Miss Jaye!" a deep voice called again from the deck of the house. "Breakfast!"

Evaline blinked and rose up on an elbow, squinting into the recognizable shape of the hulking figure which loomed in the distance. Gabriel Townsend waved at her to come up to the house. She could see someone sitting at a patio table near the corner of the house, and the shining metal spokes of the wheelchair glinting beyond the deck rail. Evaline glanced back at the truck in alarm. The cab was vacant. Some guardian she'd been!

Evaline scrambled out of the sleeping bag, her frantic movements making the task even more difficult.

"Get a move on." Gabriel waved at her again. "Food's almost ready!" Then he turned and walked around the corner of the house.

Evaline scowled, aware that the expression would soon forge permanent lines on her face. Stiff and sore, she snatched up the sleeping bag and shoved her feet into her loafers. Then she stumbled toward the house, cranky and tired, mumbling under her breath about Townsend's rude personality. Seven o'clock had arrived far too soon, and she was in no mood to share morning pleasantries with him, not that he'd offer any. At the front door, she realized how chilly the morning air was, and went in to get a windbreaker from her suitcase. As an added precaution, she stuck the gun in her purse and took it with her.

Evaline stomped out the front door, pulling on the light jacket and glancing around. The front deck was wider than she had expected, having seen it only in the dark. Off to the right, on the outside of the kitchen wall, was a wooden patio set arranged to take advantage of both the magnificent view of the bay and coastal islands and the cheerful rays of the early morning sun.

Allison sat at the small table, with the wheelchair folded up and leaning against the railing at her elbow. Evaline wondered if Allison had decided to leave the truck on her own or had been coerced by her father, but didn't feel like bringing up what might be a touchy subject with them.

Walking forward, she zipped up her windbreaker, glad to smell coffee brewing. "Good morning," Evaline greeted, forcing herself to be upbeat for the sake of the girl. Allison didn't look up, and Gabriel didn't respond. His back was turned to her, and he seemed preoccupied with cooking something on the outdoor grill.

"Pour some juice, would you?" he said, throwing the words over his shoulder.

"Sure." Evaline yawned and reached for a large plastic container sitting on the table. She poured the drink into the mismatched plastic glasses and gave one to Allison. Gabriel's notion of juice wasn't real orange juice, but an orange-flavored blend of sugar and water. Evaline wondered if he was aware of the lack of nutrition in the drink, and made a mental note to talk to him about it. Allison needed all the vitamins and minerals she could get.

After pouring the juice, Evaline took a seat and glanced at Allison. "How are you feeling, Allison?" she asked.

The teenager didn't say anything. Before Evaline could continue the one-sided conversation, she was interrupted by Gabriel, who motioned for her plate. She gave it to him, and he scooped up breakfast from the grill, a concoction of scrambled eggs cooked in bacon grease, with bacon on the side—if the strips of alternating charred flesh and half-cooked fat could be called bacon. He plopped down a second spoonful of eggs on Evaline's plate and she struggled to hide her disgust at the sight of the yellow lumps tinged in green. She had a strong stomach and had learned early in life not to be picky, but she wasn't sure she could choke down this particular breakfast.

"More?" Gabriel asked.

"Thanks, no," she replied hastily. "I'm not a big eater."

She accepted the plate and set it carefully on the wood table, contemplating a strategy for the disposal of the eggs without offending the cook. Where were the Twyla boxes when a person needed them?

Gabriel served Allison, who stared at the food with a disgusted expression, and then he piled the remaining eggs on his own plate.

"Toast?" Gabriel boomed.

Allison kept staring at her plate.

"Please," Evaline answered. By the looks of the meal, she might have to survive on bread and coffee. Toast would be safe. What, to toast, could he possibly do to make it unpalatable?

Her question was answered when he provided her with two triangles of cold charred toast topped with smears of congealing butter. Evaline tried to smile. Obviously, the recipe for toast was beyond his culinary skills as well.

"Thank you," she murmured.

He nodded and sat down, unaware of the wry edge to her voice, and quickly consumed the huge breakfast in front of him. Evaline picked at the edges of her eggs and noticed that Allison didn't touch hers.

Gabriel eyed their plates. "Something wrong with the food?" he demanded.

"No," Evaline replied. "I'm just not that hungry this morning. All that traveling—"

He gave her a sharp glance, and she felt the hard stare of his gray eyes slice through her, as if he saw her excuse for what it was. Then he glared at Allison.

"Why aren't you eating?" he said.

"Because"—Allison stabbed a fork into the under-cooked mound of egg—"it looks like shit."

Evaline nearly choked on her orange drink. She watched Gabriel's face flush, from his cheeks up to his hairline. She put her hand on her purse, ready to grab her gun. When Gabriel didn't lash out immediately, she decided to try to diffuse the situation. Evaline jumped to her feet. "How about some coffee?" she blurted. "Allison?"

"Yeah."

"Hold on," Gabriel raised his left hand. "Allison shouldn't be drinking coffee."

Evaline paused.

"Says who?" Allison glared at her father with narrowed eyes. "I drink it all the time, mister."

Gabriel clenched his jaw. "What did you call me?"

"Mister."

"I'm your father."

"All of a sudden, huh?" Her chin rose and she fired a stare full of belligerence at him. "What do you want, a medal?"

"Respect."

"Respect?" She cocked her head while both of her

eyebrows raised. "You treat me like crap and think I should respect you? You fucking bastard!"

Gabriel stood up so abruptly that he knocked his chair backward. Without picking it up, he strode across the deck and thundered down the stairs, leaving Allison with a sour smirk on her face and Evaline holding the coffeepot.

She bent down and righted the chair while she watched Gabriel storm toward his boat. Then she glanced at Allison and didn't see a single flicker of remorse on the girl's face. She might agree with Allison that Gabriel was a boor and a pig, but that didn't mean she approved of the way Allison had spoken to her father. Trying to frame her words so they would be received in a positive way by the girl, Evaline poured a cup of coffee and slid it toward her.

"You know, Allison," she began, filling a cup for herself and purposely not looking at the girl, "your father is probably just as scared as you are."

"I'm not scared."

"You know what I mean. You haven't seen each other for a very long time."

"And was that my fault?" Her scathing words revealed more hurt than she probably intended to let on.

Evaline sat down. She could see why people might suspect Allison of matricide. The kid was unbelievably caustic. "Allison, your father might have had no choice."

"He could have come to see me." She slurped her coffee. "Not that I would have wanted him to, though. What an asshole."

"But didn't you live in Greece?"

"Only at the last." She looked down. "We lived all over the world. Everytime my mom got a new boyfriend or a different religion, we moved. Foreign men were her specialty, and the weirder the religion, the better."

Allison stirred her coffee and lapsed into a bitter

silence while Evaline let the last few comments sink in. Perhaps Allison wasn't as spoiled and indulged as Gabriel thought. Perhaps she was the type of child forced to move over and over, from boyfriend to boyfriend, at the expense of her childhood. Perhaps Allison was more lonely than spoiled, and harbored a deep grudge against the father and mother who had allowed such a fate to befall her.

Allison set the spoon aside. "I bet *your* mother didn't run off every six months and forget to tell you where she was going."

Evaline concealed her shock at the revelation, for no one had informed her that Meredith had been remiss in her maternal duties. She wondered what else she hadn't been told. Evaline glanced at Allison, pretty sure the girl hadn't been dealt with honestly, and realized she needed to be answered in a meaningful and truthful way. Evaline guessed that Allison's childhood—apart from the financial and social arenas—had been similar to hers, lonely and full of lies. This child needed to hear the truth from someone who knew what she was going through, someone who could do more than just claim to understand. Then and there, Evaline decided to reveal part of her own past, the life she never spoke about to anyone.

"You're right, Allison," Evaline answered softly. "My mother didn't run off every six months. She only did it once, but that was enough."

"What do you mean?" Allison actually looked up at her.

"She left my father and me when I was two and never came back."

Allison gaped at her, too surprised to conceal her reaction by hiding behind her usual mask of bored indifference. Evaline, somewhat flustered at hearing her own admission, so long buried, rose suddenly and glanced at the grill.

"What do you say I make us edible eggs?" she asked, her voice cracking. "I see your father left all the stuff out."

"Sure," Allison replied. "Why not?"

"Go ahead and crack the eggs in this bowl while I clean out the skillet." Without waiting for the girl to refuse to help, Evaline put the bowl on the table in front of her and set the egg carton beside it.

"It's a wonder your father hasn't died of heart failure," she continued, "cooking with all that bacon grease."

"I thought I'd hurl." Allison opened the carton.

"Me, too!" Evaline smiled, glad to change the subject from errant mothers to breakfast. Out of the corner of her eye she saw the girl pick up an egg and then pause.

"They say I killed her, you know," Allison declared, throwing her a hard glance. "My mother, I mean."

Evaline kept working, hoping to keep the conversation casual so the girl might continue talking. "I've heard that."

"Do you think I did?"

"I only know what people have told me." Evaline reached for the skillet and turned. "And people often misjudge what they see with their eyes, then claim what they've seen is the truth."

Allison squinted at her for a long moment and said nothing.

Evaline stared right back. "I'll wait until you tell me what really happened, Allison. Then I'll decide."

"Don't hold your breath."

After a decent breakfast, Evaline unfolded the wheelchair and rolled it to the table.

"Why don't you hop in, Allison?" Evaline suggested. "We've got a lot to do today."

Allison ignored the request. "Is there a phone somewhere?"

"I haven't seen one."

"I want to call my grandparents."

"Why?"

"I can't stay here. I'll go crazy."

Evaline sighed and glanced at the shimmering water beyond the wide stretch of beach. "Allison, I don't think you have a choice. Your father has custody of you."

"Don't I have a say?"

"Not much of one until you're eighteen."

"Jesus!" She sank back in her seat.

"Unless he's judged to be unfit, I'm afraid you'll have to stay here."

"God!"

"I know it seems awful," Evaline commented. "But give your father some time. Circumstances might change. He might find out he can't handle raising a daughter and decide to let you go back to Seattle. Or you might find you like it out here."

"As if!"

"Give it a chance. I was raised in a place like this." Evaline let her gaze wander over the cedars and back out to the bay. "There's a certain freedom living in a place like this."

"Yeah, and that freedom is spelled B-O-R-E-D-O-M."

"Think of it as a summer vacation," Evaline urged. "Because one way or another, when fall comes your father will have to do something about your education. Maybe when you get better, he'll agree to send you to a private school in Seattle. You might try cooperating."

"I'm not going to cooperate with that bastard. He treats me like an animal!"

"He's just a bit stubborn, don't you think?"

"Stubborn? The man's a fucking asshole!"

Evaline wanted to say something about Allison's language, but she refrained. The girl didn't need two adults criticizing her. In Evaline's Native American community, she'd seen children raised with firmness but never corporal punishment or cruel words. Such children grew up unspoiled and loving. Evaline believed her gentleness and genuine interest in the girl would be the most effective behavior-modification device for Allison, and a welcome foil to Gabriel's harsher methods of childrearing and Meredith's apparent disinterest.

"Let's do these dishes, and then we'll work on your legs."

"Dishes?"

"Yes. We eat, we do dishes." Evaline glanced at the house behind her. "I assume there's running water in the kitchen."

"I don't do dishes," Allison continued, her nose in the air. "We always had a maid."

"Well, I'm not a maid," Evaline answered. "And I doubt one is going to magically appear."

"I shouldn't have to do dishes. I'm sick."

"A little work won't hurt you."

"Oh, yeah? My father might have dragged me out here, but he isn't going to turn me into a slave."

"Oh, for goodness sake, Allison." Evaline grabbed the pile of dirty dishes and opened the backdoor beside the grill. It swung into a room still full of more boxes. Gabriel had cleared a path to the kitchen sink, however, and she walked through the narrow corridor and set the dishes on the sideboard. Then she searched through the cupboards until she found the necessary equipment to clean the dishes. She rinsed them alone, not insisting upon help, for Allison couldn't have squeezed the wheelchair past the boxes anyway, and then she loaded the dishes into the dishwasher.

The window above the sink looked out upon a green lagoon that looped into a narrow glen far below the house. Evaline could see a deer and two spotted fawns eating tender grass near a stream that trickled into the small inlet. Whoever had designed this house and situated it on the site had taken advantage of every stunning vista. She marveled at the peace and quiet the site afforded, the kind of tranquillity she'd lost to her new life in the big city.

Peace, fashioned from such gossamer nothings as light filtering through pine boughs and the distant chirping of sparrows, began to pool deep inside her. She felt her spirit renewing slightly. She could stay here. And perhaps she could help Allison see the healing advantages of living close to nature. With a little work and a whole lot of patience, she might be able to help turn the girl's life around.

Evaline pivoted and leaned against the counter, drying her hands on a towel as she surveyed the kitchen. She could find peace here all right. But not until she threw the boxes out and cleaned the place from top to bottom.

When Evaline returned to the deck, she was surprised to find Allison sleeping in one of the patio chairs, her legs propped up on the seat of the wheelchair, her arms crossed over her torso, and her head slumped down to her chest. At first, Evaline was sure Allison was trying to fool her into thinking she wasn't awake, but after a few moments, Evaline realized the girl was really fast asleep. Poor thing. She probably hadn't gotten a decent hour's rest out in that truck all night.

Deciding to let Allison sleep while she cleared out the bedroom, Evaline plunged into the job of making a decent place for her and Allison to stay. Two hours flew by during which Evaline moved all the boxes out of the bedroom, leaving a couch and an overstuffed chair, and then took down the dusty curtains. She found a bucket and soap in the kitchen, both of which appeared to have never been used, and carried them back to the room to wash down the walls and floor. Noon arrived by the time the task was completed, and her stomach growled fiercely. Yet she could only hope that Gabriel did not intend to serve lunch to them. It might be best to head him off before he could get the chance. She could just imagine what disgusting concoction he might whip up: peanut butter and bologna or tuna fish and cheese spread.

Evaline smoothed back a stray hair and let herself out the front entry, hoping to find Gabriel down at the boat. Before she had taken the last step of the stairs, however, she heard a loud rumbling in the lane and looked up to see a large truck rolling toward her. The horn blasted, sending a flock of ravens flapping into the trees, and somebody waved from the driver's window. Evaline waved back, then spotted Gabriel loping up the dock. She glanced over her shoulder and was surprised that the loud noise hadn't even fazed Allison. The poor girl must be exhausted. The sooner they got her into a decent bed, the better.

Evaline walked across the gravel parking lot as Gabriel strode up to the truck. A slight, brown-haired man dropped to the ground, grinning, and slapped Gabriel on the back.

"How the heck are you, Gabe?"

"Toler'ble," Gabriel answered. "How come you're so late, Skeeter? You were supposed to be here last week."

"Things came up." The man winked at Evaline, then wiggled his eyebrows at Gabriel. "And I mean came up!"

"Did you remember the beds?"

"Beds?" Skeeter echoed. His carefree grin faded, and a sheepish smile crept across his face.

"You forgot them?"

"Gosh darn, Gabe, I had a lot on my mind! You know

how some women are—they just kind of take over your every waking moment?"

Gabriel shook his head and planted his fists on his hips. "Skeeter, when are you going to learn that women are trouble?"

"I don't know, but I can't say it ain't fun while it lasts. Know what I mean?" He poked his head around Gabriel's shoulder. "And who's this? Not your daughter!"

"Hardly." Gabriel ignored his leer and nodded toward Evaline. "She's Allison's physical therapist."

"Howdy!" Skeeter stuck out his hand. "I didn't catch your name."

"It's Evaline." She shook his hand. "Evaline Jaye. Nice to meet you."

"Evaline." Skeeter whistled. "Shoot. That's a pretty name. French?"

"I think so."

"Mighty pretty gal to go along with the name, too." His gaze traveled down her figure and eventually returned to her face. His eyes sparkled with raw appreciation and the same predatory gleam she had noticed in so many men's eyes—with the exception of Gabriel's hard-edged glances. "If I'da known a pretty thing like you was at the house, I'd have been here yesterday! And I sure would have remembered the beds!"

"Skeeter!" Gabriel grabbed Skeeter's elbow. "Don't mind him, Miss Jaye. He's woman crazy. That's what happens to men left in the woods too long."

"What about you, Gabe? You don't—"

"And he's got some packing up to do, don't you, Skeeter?" Gabriel pulled him toward the house.

Skeeter turned and tried to wrench free, appearing more like a mischievous imp than a man when hauled up by one of Gabriel's massive hands. "You mean to tell me you aren't going to help?"

"I told you to *bring* some help."

"Nobody wanted to come."

"I don't blame 'em."

"Aw, Gabe!" Skeeter wrestled free and shook his arm. "It'll take me days to load that truck."

"Well, it should. There's over five misadventures of junk in that house. It'll give you something to think about."

Evaline glanced at Skeeter in surprise as Gabriel's words sank in. So, the boxes belonged to Skeeter. Had Twyla and Sharon and Debby been Skeeter's women, not Gabriel's? It certainly made sense. Evaline surveyed Skeeter's slight frame, his clean twill pants and light leather jacket. There was an air of fastidiousness about him, from his neatly parted brown hair to his small feet. He looked like the kind of man who enjoyed doing the two-step with an overly perfumed, ruffle-enveloped woman in his arms. Certainly a tiny woman with dainty high-heeled shoes would complement Skeeter much more readily than she would Gabriel.

"Shoot, Gabe, you mean to just stand there and watch me haul all that junk out?"

"Well, no, actually. I might have a beer while I watch." Gabriel crossed his arms. He had rolled up the sleeves of his blue chambray shirt and Evaline noticed the corded muscles on his forearms, in stark contrast to his friend's slender arms and legs.

"Real funny, Townsend. Some friend you are."

"Oh, yeah? I could have charged you storage fees, Skeeter," Gabriel replied. "And retired in style."

"Style?" Skeeter gave him a scathing glance. "What would you know about style? You haven't even shaved off your winter growth. Do you even know what month it is? June!"

Gabriel touched his beard almost absently, as if he *had*

forgotten his appearance and perhaps the time of year as well.

"He loses track," Skeeter remarked in an aside to Evaline. "Man lives in a time warp. If it weren't for me, he'd lose track of his own shadow. He might know fishing and hunting better than any man around, but most of the time, he's in another world."

"Really?" Evaline smiled politely but didn't know what else to say in response to such a comment.

"Pull down the damn ramp for the truck," Gabriel instructed, saving her from making conversation with Skeeter. "Damn procrastinating windbag. Let's get this show on the road."

"So you'll lend a hand?"

"Dammit, yes!" Gabriel glared down at his friend. "If I don't help you, you'll be here for days, and I don't like you that much!"

Gabriel turned, but Evaline stepped into his path. "What about lunch, Mr. Townsend? Allison is probably hungry, and so am I."

He glanced at the house and then back at her. "I'll bring some fixings up. There's also more supplies in the pantry under the house. You can make sandwiches while I help this good-for-nothing load boxes."

"I'd be happy to." She was more than willing to take over the cooking responsibilities.

"I'll be back in a minute," Gabriel said to his friend. "And don't just stand there shooting the breeze with Miss Jaye. Get your dirty mind back in neutral and your ass in gear."

"No need to get so grouchy," Skeeter called after his retreating shape. "And I don't mind saying, you sure know how to take the fun out of things!"

Gabriel waved him off and strode away, while Evaline watched him. She had believed the mess in the house belonged to Gabriel, when all the time he had been storing the boxes for his friend. She'd thought of Gabriel as a pig, as a womanizer, and as physically abusive. What else about him had she misjudged?

4

"*So where are you from,* Evaline?" Skeeter asked as he strolled toward the house with her.

"Seattle."

He nodded, and she could feel his stare race down her figure and back up to her face again. After her surgery, she had discovered many people couldn't pinpoint her racial background and often attributed her dark looks to Hispanic roots. One elderly patient had always greeted her with, "Ah, there's my Iberian princess!" She didn't mind and usually let strangers make their own suppositions, because race and heritage had no place in her life any longer. She now thought of herself as Evaline Jaye, an individual with no ties, no past, and no particular place to call home. She even tried to convince herself that her new life was enough to satisfy her, that she could make of herself anything she wanted—but she missed community ties, and sometimes suffered bouts of aching loneliness.

"How about you?" she asked Skeeter.

"Born and raised in nearby Port Angeles. Wouldn't leave it!"

"This is a lovely area."

"God's country." Skeeter chuckled. "Except for this little patch of ground. The devil owns *this* place."

Evaline wondered if he referred to the actual devil or to Gabriel. She had a few comments to make about Gabriel Townsend, and a number of questions as well, but she kept them to herself.

"That's his daughter?" Skeeter asked, nodding toward the sleeping girl at the patio table.

"Yes. Allison. She's quite a handful."

"How old is she now?"

"Fourteen."

"She looks plumb tuckered out."

"The past few days have been hard on her," Evaline explained, as Gabriel came up the stairs behind her. "Would you mind helping me get her into the house?"

"I'll do it," Gabriel put in. He deposited the lunch supplies on the table while Evaline awakened Allison with a gentle shake of her shoulder. Allison jumped nevertheless, and her eyes flew open.

"We're just going to move you, Allison," Evaline explained to the startled girl. "Where you'll be more comfortable."

Allison blinked and stared briefly at the three adults as if unsure who they were, and then tilted her head back to glance up at her father as he reached for her. She made no effort to help him when he lifted her into his arms, but help wasn't necessary, for Gabriel's strength was more than adequate for the task.

"I'll get the door," Skeeter volunteered, jumping into action.

Gabriel glanced at Evaline over the top of Allison's head. "Where do you want me to put her?"

"In the first bedroom on the right." Evaline picked up Allison's large purse and followed close at Gabriel's heels as he walked around the corner of the house. He headed for the front door while Allison bounced around like a rag doll in his arms.

Skeeter threw open the door, and Gabriel passed over the threshold, appearing much like a groom carrying his bride into their new home. Apparently Skeeter thought the same thing, for he clucked his tongue and said, "Never thought she'd be the one you carried into the house like that, huh, Gabe?"

Gabriel didn't answer and continued his brisk walk through the living room, his concentration focused on the hallway in front of him.

"At least somebody's using the place, though," Skeeter added brightly, apparently trying to lift Gabriel's dark mood. Still the taller man didn't respond. Skeeter shrugged his right shoulder and smiled as Evaline passed him.

She hurried after Gabriel, wondering about his past and questioning the fact that no one had ever lived in this house. Even in its cluttered, dirty state, the house showed potential for being a well-designed haven, one she would certainly appreciate after having lived in a tiny, noisy apartment for the last four years.

Gabriel set Allison on the couch, then straightened her legs while Evaline stood nearby, studying the girl's drawn, pale face as Allison drifted back to sleep with a sigh. She worried about Allison's unusual lethargy. Normal teenagers did not sleep through the day like this, unless they had stayed up all night. She wondered if Allison had spent the entire night wide-awake in the truck. Or if her medications were interfering with her sleep. Evaline planned to keep track of just how much Allison slept over the next few weeks. Perhaps more was going on here than just amnesia and psychological paralysis.

Evaline stowed the purse at the end of the couch, within easy reach of Allison. Then she ambled around Gabriel to the other end of the couch.

"She shouldn't sleep all day," Gabriel stated, rising and planting his hands on his hips. "Otherwise, she'll be up far too late tonight."

"I'm sure she'll straighten out in a day or two. The trip probably tired her." Evaline reached down and took off Allison's shoes.

"She's got circles under her eyes."

"I noticed that."

"From being stuck in a damn hospital."

"A number of things could cause the circles"—Evaline spread a light wool blanket over the sleeping girl—"lack of sleep being one of them."

"Well, we'll keep her out in the fresh air. That'll do the trick." Gabriel turned and left the bedroom just as his friend trailed through the doorway and gave a low, appreciative whistle.

"Shoot, haven't seen this room look so clean in years!"

"It was a mess," Evaline said. "The whole house is."

"Wouldn't call it a house, Evaline. Nobody's ever actually lived here."

Evaline glanced at him. "Why not?"

"Well." Skeeter shrugged and suddenly appeared uncomfortable. "You know how things don't work out like you expect sometimes? Such was the case in this situation."

Evaline nodded but was perplexed by his explanation. Was he referring to himself or to Gabriel? Evaline studied him, searching for answers, but didn't press him for more information. She'd been raised in a culture that didn't ask probing questions, but instead relied on silence, patience, and understanding for truth to be revealed at the proper time. Though she was no longer a part of that society, she could no more slough off her upbringing than she could discard her habit of concluding everyone found her scarred and ugly.

Skeeter crossed his arms as he gazed down at Allison. "Spitting image of her mother, that one."

"Is she?" Evaline's gaze swept over Allison's delicate profile, a beautiful line no surgery could improve upon. "Did you know Meredith?"

"You could say I did. But some people are just plain hard to get close to. Either they aren't friendly, or they don't have much to offer other folks." He shoved his hands in his pockets. "Some people run deep, like Gabe, but some don't run at all, if you know what I mean. And I always got the feeling that Meredith—"

"Hey, Skeeter!" Gabriel called from the front door, interrupting him. "Let's get going!"

Skeeter rolled his eyes. "Oh, keep your pants on, Townsend. I'm comin'!" He flashed a smile at Evaline, then turned away, pulling off his leather jacket and reaching for a Debby box in the hallway.

Evaline watched Allison sleep for a moment and left the bedroom, closing the door softly behind her. She squeezed into the kitchen and out the side door, to avoid getting run over by the two men, and surveyed the food Gabriel had set out on the patio table. Bread, peanut butter, and a carton of milk. She frowned. Was Gabriel one of those people who eschewed fruits and vegetables? She'd have to change his diet and his grocery list for the sake of his daughter's health, not to mention his own. Wondering what was in the pantry on the lower level, she hurried down the stairs and around to the side of the house, where she thought she'd find an outside door.

Her supposition was correct. She opened the door and felt along the left-hand wall for a switch, which she found a few seconds later. A bank of lights came on, revealing a veritable treasure trove of food, from what appeared to be home-smoked salmon, to fruit—fresh, dried, and canned—and a wall of wine bottles covered with dust. Evaline pulled a slender amber bottle out of the rack and wiped the grime off the label to reveal a 1975 French Bordeaux. What, she wondered, was a man like Gabriel Townsend doing with fine wine?

The pantry also contained numerous shelves of canned goods and a large freezer full of vegetables, breads, and meat, and a second refrigerator, larger than the one she'd seen in the kitchen upstairs. Evaline collected some apples, dried fruit and nuts, celery, mayonnaise, and a tin of tuna. She also selected a can of chicken noodle soup and a box of crackers, thinking something light might appeal to Allison. Then, juggling the items in her arms, she managed to make it back to the stairs without dropping anything.

As she climbed the stairs, she saw Gabriel coming down the steps with a large carton, but he didn't even make eye contact. Though he was puffing and sweating in the moderate heat of early afternoon, he worked like a whirlwind, striding swiftly from deck to truck. In comparison, Skeeter sauntered out to the deck with a box and gave her a big grin.

"Oh, good!" he exclaimed, eyeing her load. "Looks like lunch is on the way." He set his box on the deck.

"Only if you clear out the kitchen," she countered.

"Done!" He smirked and gave her a mock salute. He held open the screen door for her, and she walked into the house, heartened to see that the hall had been cleared as well as part of the space between the living room and kitchen. As she cleaned and cored the apples, Skeeter set to work on the boxes in the kitchen, and by the time she'd whipped up a Waldorf salad, the room was nearly free of junk.

Evaline glanced around, pleasantly surprised at the spaciousness of the area and the sight of a dining-room table emerging from a former pile of cartons. The table was still half-buried by boxes of Sharon's belongings, but at least there would be a place to eat inside the house once the move was completed. Evaline could visualize a warm homemade meal spread out on the table, with a fire crackling in the living room, and maybe a summer storm blowing outside to heighten the coziness of the house. How nice that would be, even if she would have to share the moment with a foul-mouthed teenager and a boorish man.

Evaline had spent the last four years eating alone, with no reason to go to any trouble to fix anything special. She missed cooking, missed breaking bread with her father on the last few occasions they had eaten dinner together. She had always wanted to share a big dinner with a boisterous family, the kind she'd seen portrayed on television and read about in books. But she had never known such a pleasure, for she and her father had been the only members in the Jaye family, and after the age of twelve, she'd never taken a meal outside her home because she'd been too embarrassed to let anyone see how difficult and unappetizing it was for her to eat with her scarred lips.

Then she heard Gabriel bark something at Skeeter, and she broke from her daydream with a start. Who was she kidding? An agreeable meal with the likes of Gabriel Townsend? Quiet conversation? Impossible. His idea of talking was shouting out orders heavily laced with profanity.

Evaline made tuna sandwiches and a few peanut butter ones, and then put everything on a tray and carried it out to the patio. Gabriel trotted up the stairs, wiping his forehead with a folded bandanna.

"Lunch?" Evaline inquired.

He glanced at her, glanced at the table, and then back

at her. "Skeeter?" he called through the screen door. "It's lunch!"

Skeeter came running, showing more energy than he had all day. He sat at the table and helped himself, while Gabriel leaned against the banister and wolfed down three sandwiches and two helpings of fruit salad, washing it all down with two glasses of milk. Skeeter made light conversation about one bar in the nearby town that was a great place to dance, while Gabriel listened but never once added a single word to the discussion. Often he looked out toward the bay as if lost in his own thoughts. Evaline caught herself staring at his bushy profile once or twice and wondering what went on in his head, completely forgetting to pay attention to Skeeter's chatter.

"That's mighty tasty salad, Evaline," Skeeter commented as he finished his last bite. "It really hit the spot."

"Thank you."

"No finer thing than a woman who can fix a good meal." Skeeter sat back and patted his stomach, obviously enjoying the chance to relax. "Well, almost, anyway!"

With a dark expression, Gabriel straightened as if disgusted by Skeeter's sexual innuendo or his propensity for gabbing, or maybe both. He slammed his empty glass on the table with a loud clunk. "Well, back to work."

"Aw, Gabe! What a slave driver!"

"We don't have all day."

"Why?" Skeeter rose, a sullen expression on his face. "What's the dang rush, anyway?"

"Miss Jaye and my daughter can't get settled until everything's out."

"We'll get it out. It's not like there's a deadline or anything."

"I don't care to spend the whole damn day sitting around yapping," Gabriel replied. He put his empty plate on the table. "There's too much to do."

Skeeter pushed in his chair. "Okay, okay."

Gabriel shot a glance at Evaline. "Thanks for lunch."

"You're welcome." She smiled, but he turned away before he could see her expression.

By early evening, Evaline had the kitchen spotlessly clean and the entire house had been emptied of boxes. The sun sank into the bay as she checked the chili bubbling on the stove. She'd thrown the stew together earlier, knowing they'd all be hungry after such a busy day, and now the fragrance filled the house. As Evaline watched the deer once again come down to graze near the lagoon, she sliced cheese and more apples. From around the corner came Skeeter's cheerful greeting when Gabriel stomped up on the deck. Evaline glanced out the window to see a six-pack of beer hanging from Gabriel's big hand. He pulled off a can and tossed it to Skeeter. Then the two men sat down, Skeeter in a chair and Gabriel at the top of the stairs, with one of his long legs spanning the width of the steps and his broad back propped against the banister support.

Evaline returned to her work, but the thought of what she'd just seen kept drifting through her consciousness. Gabriel and Skeeter were complete opposites, from body shape to temperament, and she marveled that they could be friends. Yet as she listened to them trading insults back and forth, she realized they'd been buddies for years.

Evaline arranged the fruit and cheese on a plate and tried to ignore a pang of jealousy. She'd never had such a friend. No long-term bonds tied her to anyone. She'd never tossed a beer to a friend and grinned at her, knowing every nasty thing she'd said to her would be received as a good-natured gibe. Because of her scars, she'd never

developed a knack for forging friendships, and now that
the scars were gone, she didn't know how to go about
making lasting connections. Her quiet nature made the
task even more daunting. She envied Skeeter and Gabriel
their enduring camaraderie, however mismatched.

Before she asked the men if they wanted dinner,
Evaline checked on Allison and found her awake and sitting up, listening to music through her headphones.

"Allison?" Evaline called, trying to get the teenager's
attention.

Allison didn't respond and instead tapped her hand on
her thigh in rhythm to an unknown melody, her eyes
focused on the far wall. Even in the doorway Evaline could
hear the tinny vibration of the song and knew that Allison
was probably damaging her hearing by listening to the
music at that high a volume. She walked into the room and
stood in front of the girl, making her presence known.
Allison stared up at her but didn't remove the headphones.

"Do you want dinner?" Evaline asked.

Allison glared at her and bobbed her head in time to a
song that sounded mind-numbing to Evaline.

Evaline pantomimed the motions of eating with a
spoon.

Allison shrugged but still didn't remove the earphones.

Frustration swept through Evaline, and she wondered
if Gabriel experienced the same distressing emotion when
he'd confronted his daughter over the course of the last
few days. The girl didn't have the decency to turn off her
music when being spoken to. Evaline decided that if
Allison were hungry enough, she'd ask for food. Until
then, Evaline wasn't going to turn somersaults to get her
attention. She pivoted on her heel and walked out of the
bedroom.

Just as she made it to the hall, she heard Allison call
out.

"Hey, wait."

Evaline paused, laying a hand on the woodwork and leveling an impassive gaze at the girl.

Allison dragged off the headphones. "What do I smell?" she asked.

"I don't know," Evaline replied. "What do you smell?"

"Are you cooking something for dinner?"

"Yes. Join us, won't you?"

"Like what are you making?"

"Chili."

Allison curled her lip, and at the petulant expression Evaline turned to leave. She was tired and hungry and had no patience to deal with Allison's disdain.

"Wait!" Allison called.

Evaline looked back over her shoulder.

"I'm starving," Allison said. "No one gave me any lunch."

"You slept through lunch." Evaline crossed her arms over her chest. "So how about it, Allison, do you want to join us for dinner?"

"Not really. Bring it in here."

"I might be coerced if asked politely."

"Politely?" Allison sneered. "Give me a fucking break!"

"Okay, then, forget it. If you want dinner, come out and serve yourself." Evaline turned to leave.

"I can't," Allison replied hastily. "I can't get in that chair by myself. You know that."

"Then walk."

"I can't!"

"Then it looks as if good manners are your only recourse."

"I didn't ask to be brought here, you know!" Allison shouted.

"That has no bearing on your manners, Allison." Evaline glared at her, struggling to remain calm and waiting for the girl to make the next move.

"Go ahead, then, leave!" Allison shouted, throwing her headphones on the blanket. "You don't care if I starve. No one cares what happens to me!"

Evaline gazed at her in silence, hoping the girl would recognize the ridiculousness of her last statement if given a few minutes. Unfortunately, Allison apparently had no such powers of rational analysis.

"I could starve to death in here, and no one would even notice!" she added.

Evaline shook her head. "That's not true, and you know it."

"Besides," Allison sputtered, "I don't have to be nice to you, not when it's your job to take care of me."

"Oh?" Evaline's anger mounted, and she realized her reaction to Allison was alarmingly similar to the way she reacted to Gabriel. "So if I'm hired help, you think you can treat me like dirt?"

"You're being paid to be nice to me." Allison tossed her hair. "And I don't see anybody giving me money to be nice to you. So why should I?"

"Human decency, perhaps?" Evaline put in, arching an eyebrow.

Allison glared at her.

Evaline's hand slipped down to the doorknob. "Now do you want some supper or not?"

Allison heaved a loud sigh and rolled her eyes. "Oh—fine." She grimaced again, as if the effort to be nice was too much to bear. "That is, if you would be so kind."

Evaline decided to accept her request, even if it had been served up with a good deal of sarcasm, and gave her a brief nod. She turned for the kitchen, heartened by the fact that she'd overcome a major hurdle with Allison. But her newfound sense of success was shattered by Allison's voice behind her.

"But don't go thinking I'm going to beg for food all the time!" she yelled. "Like some goddamn dog!"

Evaline strode to the kitchen, wondering how long she could take such an attitude. Could she last another week with the girl, another day even?

You're a quitter, the little voice inside her head taunted her. *You don't know how to deal with people. You'll fail and fail miserably, just like your father. You might as well give it up now because you're going to mess it up anyway. You are your father's daughter and your mother's child—doomed to fail, destined to run.*

"No, I'm not!" Evaline whispered to herself through clenched teeth. She wouldn't run this time. This was her battle, her proving ground. This was the moment in her life when she would prove to herself that she was everything she pretended to be: a calm, strong woman with a courageous heart. She stopped in the middle of the kitchen and spotted Gabriel on the deck as he shook his head at something Skeeter had said, then gulped down his beer.

"They will not get to me," she vowed, thinking back to the days when she had to shield herself against the horrified stares of people and their less than human treatment of her. She had endured years of rejection. She could outlast the Townsends, no matter how self-centered and uncooperative they were.

Working through her anger so she could put it behind her, Evaline fixed Allison a tray and carried it to the bedroom. Allison didn't say a word, not so much as a thank-you, but Evaline didn't press her. She knew not to ask for too much all at once. Then Evaline went back to the kitchen, ladled out a small bowl of chili, and slipped through the side door.

The lively conversation between the two men broke off as she appeared, and both of them looked at her expectantly.

"There's chili and fruit in the kitchen," she informed them as she walked toward the stairs. "If you want to help yourselves."

"Aren't you going to join us, Evaline?" Skeeter asked.

"No, thanks." Evaline put her hand on the stair rail. "I need some peace and quiet."

She continued down the stairs and across the parking lot toward the beach, aware of an intense stare on her back and not sure if the gaze belonged to Skeeter. She kept walking, glad to have a moment to herself and fairly sure Gabriel wouldn't threaten Allison while Skeeter was visiting.

A half hour later she returned to the house to find Gabriel and Skeeter out in the back with air pistols shooting beer cans off a stump. Evaline walked into the kitchen, expecting to find a pile of dirty dishes and dribbled food on the counters. Instead she was surprised to see someone had cleaned the dishes and loaded them in the dishwasher. Probably Skeeter had tidied the kitchen or forced Gabriel to help him.

Evaline put her bowl in the sink and headed for Allison's room. She knocked on the door and then pushed it open. Allison was once again listening to music, with the tray sitting on the floor beside her. Evaline was pleased to see the dishes were empty. She stood next to the couch until Allison took notice of her and slid aside one of her headphones.

"Would you like anything else?" Evaline inquired, keeping her voice professionally modulated even though she was certain more contention would flare between them.

"Is there any coffee?"

"I could make some," Evaline replied, bending to retrieve the tray. "But coffee at this hour will keep you up."

"I'll be up all night anyway."

"That's not a healthy schedule for someone your age."

"Like I have a choice!"

"Don't you?"

"What do you know!" Allison retorted hotly. "You think you know everything, but you don't know squat. You don't know anything about me!"

Evaline braced the tray against the small of her waist. She probably knew more about Allison than the girl ever dreamed. But she didn't know what was in the teenager's heart, and she was beginning to think that particular information was far more important than the facts she'd gleaned from Allison's medical history.

Facts and measurements were fine in some instances. And white medicine had its place. But more and more she felt it might be beneficial to augment the scientific data with the wisdom of her people and search Allison's heart and spirit instead of her body for the source of her illness. Evaline had promised herself not to revert to the old ways, because she had turned her back on that life. But she had to wonder if her vow was worth this girl's future.

"You're right, Allison," Evaline said softly. "I don't know much about you. But I'm not here to argue with you or make your life miserable. I'm here to help you."

"Yeah, to make my legs go up and down and help me to the bathroom. Big deal."

"You can make of this anything you want, Allison," Evaline continued. "I'm willing to help you in any way I can. And that includes listening to you and finding out what's troubling you."

"Give me a break! You sound like a shrink."

"Well, I sense that your medical problem is more an affliction of the spirit than of the body, and that if we can heal the—"

"Oh, roll it up tight and jam it! Now you're sounding like that idiot, Stephen Durrell."

"He might have a valid point in regard to you."

"The man's a flake. A fraud. A fruitcake. Need I say more?" She jammed the headphone back down on her ears, then just as quickly pulled it aside again.

"What's that noise?" she demanded.

"It's your father and his friend doing some target practice out back."

"His friend?" Allison straightened and peered at the window, even though it didn't provide a view of the rear property. "Who's his friend?"

"Skeeter Robinson."

"How old is he?"

Evaline glanced at Allison, then smiled when she realized the direction Allison's questions were taking. "Way too old for you, Allison. I'd say he's about thirty-five."

"God!" Allison flounced back on the pillows wedged against the arm of the couch. "It's boring here! Do you realize how boring it is?"

"No. I've been busy."

"Doing Suzy Homemaker stuff. What a drag."

"I like to cook. Don't you?"

"Me?" She laughed sarcastically. "The only time I go in a kitchen is to snitch ice cream in the middle of the night."

Evaline smiled, feeling a bit more friendly with Allison but knowing the situation could blow up in her face at any moment. "Well, there's a lot more to a kitchen than the freezer compartment of the fridge."

"Not for my mother. She was the queen of frozen food, the grand patron of caterers."

Evaline chuckled, and Allison shot a surprised look at her, as if she wasn't accustomed to making an adult laugh. "I think food made from scratch tastes better," Evaline commented. "I hardly ever cook any other way."

"You mean you didn't get that chili out of a can?"

"No."

"I thought it tasted different." Allison threw off her blanket. "How about helping me to the bathroom? I really have to go."

"Okay. But then I need your help."

"For what?"

"The mess out there." Evaline nodded in the direction of the living room. "Maybe you'll have a few ideas about how to arrange the furniture."

"Me?"

"Yes. It'll be kind of tricky, what with the traffic areas and windows, and making room for you to get around everything in the wheelchair." She set the tray on the overstuffed chair and rolled the wheelchair to the couch. "I thought before I went to the trouble of moving all the furniture, I'd see what we could do on paper."

Evaline slipped an arm around Allison's back and under her knees and lifted her into the chair. "I need to measure the place first though, and you could help with that, too."

"What kind of help?"

"Someone to write down measurements and draw a sketch. I'm a pretty good cook, but lousy with spatial stuff."

She steered Allison toward the hall, hoping her idea would encourage the girl to participate in something. Anything. She rolled Allison into the bathroom. "If I make coffee, will you have a look at the front room and see what you think might work?"

"I guess," Allison replied. "It's like I have to live here, too."

"And get around easily."

Allison glanced at the silver arms of her chair and then at her slender legs. "Yeah," she responded in a quiet voice. "In this stupid chair."

Evaline gazed at her for a moment, wishing she could

wave a magic wand and solve the girl's medical problems. "Do you want me to help you in the bathroom?"

"No." Allison pushed open the door. "I can handle it."

Evaline watched her roll into the bathroom, marveling that Allison could transfer herself to the toilet and into the bath bench in the shower. She must have strong shoulder and arm muscles, which was unusual for a patient who had spent a month in a hospital and had never used a wheelchair before. Could Allison be hiding the fact that her legs were stronger than she let on?

Evaline left the girl to take care of herself and returned to the bedroom for the tray of dishes. She hoped Allison would roll out and join her and take a small but positive first step.

5

Evaline's second morning at the Townsend house began as a repeat of the first, with Gabriel calling her to breakfast by banging on the door a few minutes before seven. This time, however, she was already up and dressed, with her black hair brushed and braided into a long plait, which she left hanging down her back.

Before Gabriel could bang on the door again, Evaline opened it, forcing a smile. "Good morning," she greeted.

Gabriel stared down at her, neither smiling nor frowning, and Evaline was suddenly struck by the realization that she'd never seen a smile in the man's eyes, the place where true smiles belonged.

"Where's Allison?" he asked.

"Still asleep." Evaline slipped out the door and closed it behind her. A light mist fell beyond the roof of the deck, shrouding the bay and surrounding hills in a curtain of fog.

"She'll miss breakfast," Gabriel protested.

"She can eat later."

"No, she can't. I'm not going to fuss over her," Gabriel said as he turned and walked toward the patio area. "I don't have the time."

"Allison doesn't sleep well at night." Evaline followed his long strides, hurrying to keep up with him. "I could hear her down the hall last night."

"Doing what?"

"Talking in her sleep. Or shouting, to be more precise."

"That's because she doesn't do a lick of work during the day. If she did, she'd be tired enough to sleep at night."

"I don't believe that's the root of her problem."

"Oh?" Gabriel picked up a pair of tongs and flipped over a strip of bacon in the sea of bubbling fat. "What do *you* think her problem is—that she's a psychopath?"

"She's emotionally troubled. From what I can tell, she's got a lot of issues to resolve, both with her mother and with you."

"That's a bunch of crap," he replied. "The only issue that child has is a severe case of boredom, brought on by too much time on her hands and nothing to do."

Evaline sighed. "I don't disagree with that point, but there is considerably more than boredom bothering Allison."

"If I was accused of killing my parent, I'd be upset, too."

"She was never formally accused."

"Might as well have been."

"I still think she needs to be treated gently right now."

Gabriel didn't respond, and Evaline surmised that for now the subject was closed. She glanced at the parking lot. "Where's Skeeter?"

"He never eats breakfast."

"Oh." Evaline watched Gabriel poke at the sizzling

meat in a black skillet. She pointed to the pan. "You know, if you turn down the heat just a bit, Mr. Townsend, the bacon will cook more evenly."

"What?" He glared at her and down at the skillet.

"See the way the bacon's burning on the edges but isn't cooking near the center?"

He poked the bacon with the tongs. "It's cooking just fine."

"You must like charred meat then."

"Food's food," he answered. "If a person's hungry, they eat, and they should count themselves lucky to have something *to* eat."

"But what they eat doesn't have to be unpalatable."

"Don't tell me—" His eyebrows lowered over his piercing gray eyes. "You're a therapist *and* a food critic?"

"As a matter of fact, I'm a fairly decent cook." She raised her chin. "I don't make fancy dishes, but what I do cook tastes good."

"Implying . . ." His voice trailed off as if he expected her to finish the sentence.

"That food should be more than just a means to survive. It should be enjoyed."

"Right." Gabriel clutched the knob of the burner and turned it down with a dramatic flourish. "There! Is that low enough for you?"

At his sarcastic display, she lowered her eyes and shook her head, despairing that a conversation with this man would ever be more than a confrontation of wills.

Gabriel grabbed the carton of eggs and yanked the box open. "Next thing I know you'll want an espresso machine."

Evaline had suffered enough of his grating personality. She couldn't help but goad him. "A breadmaker would be nice," she commented in a breezy voice behind him, "and maybe a juicer while you're at it."

His head whipped around, and he glared at her for a long, dark moment. Evaline wasn't sure if he would smack her with the spatula or crush the egg he held in his big fist. She shouldn't have made a smart-ass remark, no matter how upset she was with him. She'd gone too far and had forgotten Gabriel's proclivity for violence. Yet she couldn't back down now, or even so much as avert her stare, in case he might conclude she was afraid of him.

Where was his sense of humor? She knew he enjoyed a good joke. She'd heard him carrying on with Skeeter. Apparently Gabriel saved his foul humor and rigid behavior for his dealings with women. He'd told Skeeter not to place his trust in females. Did his distrust color his view of all women, no matter the character and strength a particular woman might possess? Did his distrust stem from a real dislike of women, or was he just slow to accept strangers?

During her years at college and her experience at the medical center, she'd learned how to get through tough situations with a gentle manner and a delicate sense of humor. Sullen patients responded well to her easygoing humor and her sincere interest in their conditions. Her ability to read people, keep the tone light, and coerce her patients into compliance with good-natured common sense had served her well.

Yet, here she was, seemingly unable to coerce Gabriel Townsend into doing more than frying his bacon at a reduced heat. She hadn't so much as coaxed a smile out of him, let alone convinced him to go easy on his daughter.

Evaline couldn't figure him out, couldn't seem to reach him. Could he possibly see through her facade? Could he see past her calm humor and reconstructed face to the scarred little girl still lurking inside—a child who distrusted most people, especially men? Did Gabriel's distrustful nature recognize a similar character trait in her?

Maybe he knew her for what she was, someone running from her own wounded shadow. Yet he didn't seem that perceptive or even that interested in other people.

"You're a real comedian," he growled at last. Then he picked up a strip of bacon and held it in the air as it dripped into the pan below. "Does this meet your standards, City Girl?"

The bacon had been cooked to a decent hue of brown, marred only by a light strip of black on one edge. "Much better," she replied.

Gabriel turned back to the stove to remove the rest of the meat. Evaline scanned his broad back, over which was draped a navy and gray plaid shirt. His dark brown, almost black hair brushed his collar, and the ends of his hair were wild and untrimmed. He was like a big bear, gruff and strong, and cutting a big swath wherever he went. Had his personality been less grating, she might have found his undeniable masculinity and strength of character attractive. She wondered what drove him to live so far from others and to cling to such a stern outlook on life, and what harsh circumstances had molded his worldview.

"May I pour you a cup of coffee?" she asked, hoping to get past the difficulties between them.

"All right."

"Milk and sugar?"

"No. Black."

Evaline poured two mugs of coffee while Gabriel cracked six eggs into a bowl. She watched him beat them with a fork, and then she slid his mug to the edge of the stove in front of him.

"You know," she ventured, "I wouldn't mind taking over the cooking detail."

He picked up the bowl. "What's that supposed to mean?"

"I think I enjoy cooking more than you do, Mr. Townsend."

"What you really mean to say is that you think you're a better cook."

"Well—"

"If that's what you mean, City Girl, say it. I can't stand pussyfooting around."

She blushed. "Pussyfooting?"

"Yes. If you've got something to say, say it, dammit."

"Okay." Evaline put her mug on the table and raised her chin. "I'm a better cook than you, and I would prefer to prepare the meals—for all of our sakes."

"What do you mean, for all of our sakes?"

"Too much fat will have us dead in a year from clogged arteries."

"Nonsense," he countered. "I'm as healthy as a horse."

"No doubt you are." She glanced at his towering form, his brawny arms and long lean legs, and found herself believing him. She'd never met a man who possessed as much blazing virility as Gabriel. "You're probably active enough to burn off the fat. But Allison and I will be chubettes by Labor Day if we eat your breakfasts every morning."

"Hmph," he replied.

"I'm sure you have enough to do without worrying about meals," she continued, "and I wouldn't mind teaching Allison how to get around a kitchen. It will be good for her. Why don't you give me a trial run?"

"Trial run?"

"Yes." She reached for the bowl of eggs. "Starting today."

He paused and studied her face for a moment. Then he shoved the bowl into her hands. "All right. I've got a lot to do on the boat this week, not to mention the house."

"Fine." She stepped in front of the stove and gladly

assumed control of the breakfast preparations. "Why don't you pour the juice while I finish up?"

She drained the bacon grease from the skillet, looking forward to a decent meal and a way to involve Allison in something constructive. In minutes she was piling fluffy scrambled eggs and warm toast on a plate. She set the dish in front of Gabriel, then served herself. Evaline sat down at the table, mildly surprised to find that Gabriel had waited for her to join him before beginning to eat. She honestly hadn't expected him to possess good manners.

"Make up a grocery list then," he commented, lifting a forkful of egg. "I'll be going into town with Skeeter today."

"We won't need much. You've got plenty of food in the storeroom down below."

"I'll be using a lot of that. I've got some charter trips scheduled for the boat."

"Soon?"

"Yeah." He sipped his coffee and squinted as the steam rose up in his face. "Sportfishing and diving mostly. I take out city slickers like you who want to catch prize salmon to hang on their walls, or dive for abalone."

Evaline turned her attention to her plate and stabbed a mound of egg. "And what gives you the impression I'm a city slicker?"

"A person only has to look at you. Plain as the nose on your face."

Evaline fought back a flush, wondering if he could detect signs of her plastic surgery. She swallowed her mouthful of food, but it stuck in her throat.

"Noses can be deceiving," she replied.

He made a muffled noise that sounded suspiciously close to a derisive snort. "I know a city girl when I see one," he said, leveling his gray eyes upon her. His glance was so direct and smoldering with such challenge that she felt another blush creep up her neck. "And you're a city girl through and through."

"You think so?" She rose. To set him straight would entail revealing her personal history and place of birth, information she didn't care to share with anyone, especially him. The best policy was to remain silent and let him jump to his own conclusions, however wrong they were. She pointed at his empty plate. "May I take that for you?"

"Yeah." He slid it toward her. While she collected dirty dishes, Gabriel gulped down the last of his coffee, thanked her for breakfast, and clumped away. He spent most of the morning under the protection of the trees splitting logs and stacking the wood at the side of the house. Evaline cleaned more of the house, while the steady thud of Gabriel's ax punctuated the air. About ten-thirty, just as Allison woke up, Evaline heard Skeeter talking to Gabriel outside, and soon afterward the two men drove off in the large truck, without so much as a good-bye.

Evaline watched the truck roll up the drive, marveling that Gabriel hadn't even popped in to see his daughter before leaving. He was accustomed to living a solitary life, without responsibilities and without having to think of other people. He probably wasn't even aware that his behavior might hurt Allison's feelings. She'd have to encourage him to make an effort to foster a better relationship with his daughter.

Over the course of the day, the light mist hanging in the air had turned into a full-fledged storm. Gusts howled down the chimney, startling Allison, who sat near the hearth in her wheelchair watching Evaline iron the newly washed curtains. Rain hammered the bare panes, and wind screamed around the corners of the house and whipped through the trees.

Allison glanced at her watch. "Two hours before midnight. Think my father will make it back before then?"

Evaline looked in the direction of the long driveway, but darkness and rain hid everything from view.

"I'm sure he will," she answered, pulling at a hem to straighten it before she pressed it with the steam iron. "I've seen worse storms. Your father probably has, too."

Allison returned her regard to the ironing board. "Don't you ever stop working?" she inquired.

"Of course. But there's a lot to be done before I can relax."

"Why don't you just make my dad pay for someone to clean this place?"

Evaline surveyed the homey living room, whose orderliness gave her a feeling of satisfaction. The design of the house afforded a sense of coziness and peace, attributes she had only suspected it might posess when it had been stuffed full of boxes. Now, with a fire going and the furniture in place, the room had an appeal straight out of a home and garden magazine. The cleaning task had also provided Allison and her an opportunity to work together and find some common ground.

"A little work never hurt anyone," Evaline finally replied with a quiet smile. "And I don't think any designer could have arranged the place as well as you and I did."

Allison gazed at the rust-colored couch and chairs, the well-beaten rug woven in the Northwest Salish tribal design of whales, and then placed her hands firmly upon the arms of her wheelchair. "I guess not."

"You've been moving around all afternoon with ease. I haven't seen you bump into a thing."

"I haven't." Allison tossed back her unruly mane of blond hair. Evaline could see dark roots along the part of the girl's hair and suspected that Allison's hair might be as dark as Gabriel's.

"I just wish there was a TV or something around here." Allison heaved a sigh. "I'm so bored I could scream!"

"You could help me iron."

"Me? I don't know how."

"You're never too old to learn."

Allison raised her nose. "No way!"

Evaline smiled again and held up the perfectly pressed curtain. She had grown up in a house decorated with cheap fabric and cast-off furniture. To iron this expensive, well-made drape was a genuine pleasure. She snatched its mate from the dining-room table. "I'm going to hang these in your room. Want to help?"

"Do what?"

"Slide the metal hangers in the slots on the top."

Allison glanced at the drape and shrugged. "Might as well. There's nothing else to do."

"Great!" Evaline grabbed the bowl of hooks and handed it to Allison. She showed the girl how to slip a hanger into the reinforced portion at the top of the drapery, and then sat in the nearby chair to work on the mate.

Evaline was just finishing hanging the curtains when she heard the front door burst open.

"Miss Jaye!" a harsh voice boomed, but there was an urgency in Gabriel's voice that she'd never heard before. "We need you."

She stepped off the stool she'd been using to reach the drapery rod and hurried out to the living room, not surprised that she hadn't heard the truck above the gale-force wind. She *was* surprised, however, to find Gabriel naked from the waist up, his hair wild and windblown, and a strange lumpy bundle wrapped in plaid in his arms. Evaline recognized the blue-and-gray fabric of the shirt he'd been wearing that morning.

"Gabe!" Skeeter exclaimed, rushing through the door after him. "I thought you said you were going to shoot it!"

"I changed my mind."

"Shoot what?" Evaline swept forward.

"We need your help," Gabriel replied calmly while he struggled to hold the bundle in his arms. A pitiful bawling noise emanated from the plaid package as something within it fought against its bonds.

"What's in there?" she asked.

"A cub," Skeeter answered, poking his head around Gabriel's wide shoulder. "A cub that's going to grow into a whole pack of trouble, that's what."

"A bear cub?" Out of the corner of her eye, Evaline saw Allison slowly roll toward the dining room in her wheelchair and stop halfway.

"He's been hit by a car," Gabriel explained in a terse voice. "Do you have some medical supplies?"

"Like what?"

"I don't know. You're the medical expert around here."

"Gabe!" Skeeter pointed at the bundle. "You can't keep that wild animal! What'll you do with it?"

"Build an enclosure for it. Feed it. It'll be old enough to release at the end of the summer."

Evaline was less interested in the future of the bear than in its present state. "What's wrong with it?"

"I think it's got a broken leg."

"Oh, poor thing!" Evaline put a hand to her mouth.

"You ever set a broken bone, Evaline?" Skeeter inquired, still no closer to the wrapped beast.

"No," she answered.

"Great," Skeeter wailed. "A novice. I tell you, Gabe, we should—"

"She can do it," Gabriel stated, walking to the dining-room table. "Now come on."

Evaline was surprised by Gabriel's faith in her. "What about a vet?" she asked. "Isn't there one nearby?"

"The nearest vet is hours away even if the ferries were running in this weather," Gabriel answered. "I didn't think the cub would make it, wrapped up like he was. So it's you or nothing, Miss Jaye."

"All right. I have my first-aid kit. I'll get it."

She dashed to the rear bedroom, rummaged around in her equipment, and ran back to the dining room as fast as she could. She glanced at Allison and found the girl gaping at her with a worried expression.

Evaline rushed to the table. "How are we ever going to work on him?" she asked, eyeing the undulating bundle. Gabriel had securely wrapped the cub, using the sleeves of his shirt like the bindings of a straitjacket. But once freed, the cub would be difficult, if not impossible, to handle. Bear cubs had sharp claws and teeth, almost as deadly as their adult counterparts. Having been the victim of an animal attack, she knew better than anyone the kind of damage claws and teeth could inflict. "He'll tear us to shreds."

"Skeeter and I will hold him down." Gabriel carefully set the creature onto the table. "Are you ready?"

"Which leg?" Evaline asked. Beads of perspiration popped out at her hairline as she forced herself to approach the wild animal. Her heart thumped, choking her.

"The left hind one, from what I could tell."

"Okay." She opened the first-aid kit and took a deep breath, as Gabriel struggled with the cub. In order to help, she had to overcome her fear, but she wasn't sure she could stop her hands from trembling enough to set the broken bone.

"This is crazy!" Skeeter sputtered.

Evaline ignored his outburst and concentrated on the plight of the bear, focusing on that one thought and banishing all others. "Maybe if he could see out, he wouldn't be so frightened," she suggested.

Gabriel didn't answer, but he managed to unbutton the top of the shirt. Immediately a dark brown snout appeared and then a large head popped out. Evaline stared into the white-rimmed eyes of the cub and knew the bear was terrified. Their gazes locked, and in the space of a single moment her heart went out to him and her own fear vanished.

"It's okay, little brother," she crooned, looking him directly in the eyes and trying to convey her goodwill. "We're going to help you."

The cub bawled again and tried to wriggle out of the shirt, never taking his eyes off her.

"Hold him down, Gabriel," Evaline instructed in a calm voice that surprised even herself. "But not too hard. Skeeter, keep his back leg pinned up by his haunch."

The men did as she requested. Evaline unbuttoned the lower portion of the shirt to expose the legs of the bear, and then very gently put her fingers on the injured limb. The cub yelped.

"Quiet now, brother bear," she said, returning her gaze to his. "Don't struggle so."

The cub stared wildly at her, unable to move because of Gabriel's firm grip, and then suddenly, as if recognizing her intent to help him, the cub lay still, panting.

Carefully she inspected the break with her fingertips, until sure of her course of action. "Okay, now Skeeter, hold both haunches."

"He'll rip off my hide!"

"No, he won't. Get him up high." She wiped her forehead with the back of her hand and tried to ignore the sight of the cub's long black claws, so similar to the wild animal claws that had slashed her arms and face years ago. "I'm going to pull his lower leg now. He'll probably struggle, but don't let him move. Everybody ready?"

"I think so," Skeeter answered.

Gabriel grunted an affirmative.

"Okay." Evaline set her jaw and slowly pulled the cub's foot until she felt the bone lock together. Then she quickly splinted the leg, making certain to knot the bindings tightly, for she was sure the bear would try to chew through them.

"Keep holding him," she said. "I need to get something."

She sprinted to her suitcase, snatched up a pair of athletic socks, and returned to the dining room. Carefully she slipped the sock over the bear's injured leg and splint, hoping that the sock would impede an attempt to remove the dressing.

By the time she was finished with the bear, the cub lay on the table panting and staring at her. Lightly she stroked the top of its head between his ears. His hair was surprisingly coarse. "You did well, little brother."

The cub mewled and jerked away from her hand.

"Now what in the heck are you going to do with him, Gabe?" Skeeter scratched the back of his head.

"Put him in the storeroom down below," Gabriel replied.

"In the house?" Skeeter blurted. "A bear?"

"We can't leave him outside to die."

Evaline nodded. "He might go into shock."

"So what are you going to do with a cub? What are you going to feed him?"

Gabriel glanced at Evaline as if soliciting ideas. She

folded her arms over her chest, wondering herself what Gabriel had in mind.

"What do bears eat?" Gabriel shrugged. "Fish and bugs and roots? It shouldn't be hard."

Skeeter waved his hands. "He's a wild animal, Gabe!"

"Wild or not"—Gabriel carefully picked up the bear, still pinned in the shirt—"he'll starve to death without our help."

Evaline's heart softened a little toward the man who'd become the cub's unlikely champion. How, she wondered, could a person rescue wild animals and then turn around and hurt women and children? It didn't seem possible. Could Stephen Durrell have been misinformed about the alleged abuse?

Perplexed, she turned her attention to the bear cub. "What happened to his mother?"

"The same car must have clipped her," Gabriel explained. "She was dead when we found her, of a head wound. The little guy was sitting at her side, crying."

"Oh, poor thing!"

"He'll be fine." He turned toward the door and strode past Allison, but then suddenly stopped. He held out the bear. "Want to see him, Allison?" he asked.

Without replying to her father or looking at the animal, Allison pivoted her wheelchair and propelled herself away toward the hallway.

Gabriel scowled, and carried the bear to the kitchen.

"Wait, Gabriel," Evaline called. "If you take him downstairs, no one will be able to keep an eye on him. And it will be cold down there tonight."

"What are you saying?"

"I think we should keep him up here, where it's warm."

"And do what with him?"

"How about putting him in the bedroom across from Allison?"

"Isn't that where you're staying?"

"I can sleep in the living room until we figure something else out."

Gabriel glanced down the hall as though weighing her words. Then he stepped away from the door. "All right. But you'd better clear everything out of that room. Knowing bears, this one will probably rip up anything he can get his claws on."

Evaline tried not to shudder at Gabriel's words. She headed for the hallway to make room for an additional, and just as difficult, patient.

6

Within minutes, Evaline had cleared the room of her belongings. She'd been living out of her suitcase anyway since she hadn't had time to clean her own sleeping quarters. As she removed the last of her clothes, she almost collided with Gabriel coming the other way. For a moment she stood mere inches from him, her eyes at the level of his powerful bare chest. She could smell his warm male scent and see the robust pulse of life in his throat.

For a startling instant she stood mute, transfixed, highly aware of Gabriel as a man and herself as a woman.

Gabriel swallowed. "Pardon me," he muttered.

"Sorry," Evaline responded, snapping back to her senses. She felt as if she had just plunged into a sea of warm water and had to struggle for air.

Gabriel strode into the room, checking the closet and master bathroom before he put down the bear cub. He closed the door to the closet but left the bathroom door open. As she watched him explore the bedroom, Evaline couldn't help but run a second appreciative glance down the man's bare torso. Though she still couldn't guess his age from looking at his bearded face, his body was that of a young man—smooth, sleek, and well muscled, with a nice set of shoulders and a trim waist, a body honed by hard work, not built at a gym. Then she saw the red welts where the bear had clawed him, both on his chest and his back.

"Your chest," she began, nodding toward him. "You should clean those scratches."

"Later," he said, gently putting the cub on the floor. "Don't untie him until I get back."

"Where are you going?"

"To get some things. I'll be right back." Gabriel glanced over his shoulder at his buddy. "Skeeter, come on in here and keep an eye on this bear."

"Oh no you don't," Skeeter protested, backing away with hands held up in front of him. "Not this cowboy. No sir! No bears for me!"

"I'll stay," Evaline said.

Gabriel's hard gaze glittered over her, assessing her. "Think you can handle him?"

Evaline glanced at the rolling bundle on the floor. The cub was nothing like the full-grown wolf that had attacked her. He was not much more than a baby, and just a bit larger than a spaniel. "I'll manage," she answered. To back up her brave words, she gave a bright smile to Gabriel and reached for the doorknob.

"Okay." Gabriel stepped into the hall. "While we get the bear settled, why don't you bring in the beds and the groceries, Skeeter?"

"Aye aye, Captain."

"Set up the bed for Allison wherever Miss Jaye wants to put it."

Skeeter gave him a salute and ducked out of the house.

"I'll be right back," Gabriel repeated, glancing once

more at Evaline. Again his gaze bored into her eyes. She said nothing and stared right back, conscious of their difference in height and peeved that he seemed to doubt her abilities, or at least her opinion of her own strength.

Then without another word he broke off the stare and headed down the hallway to the front door. Evaline closed the bedroom door and leaned against it, watching the cub's persistent efforts to free itself.

"Patience, little brother," she said. "You'll be released soon."

Minutes later, Gabriel knocked on the door. Evaline opened it for him, surprised to see him carry in a sleeping bag, pillow, blanket, and plastic dish. He tossed the sleeping bag and pillow into a corner by the window and thrust the plastic dish at her. "Would you get some water for him?"

"Sure." Evaline filled the dish at the sink while Gabriel stuffed a tattered old blanket near the end of the bathtub. She put the water dish just inside the door of the bathroom.

"I'll corner him in here for the night, so he won't mess on the wood floor," Gabriel said.

"Good. That's a smell that would be hard to get rid of."

"No kidding."

They returned to the center of the room. Gabriel knelt on the floor and tried to unbutton the plaid shirt, but the cub's struggles made the job impossible. Evaline dropped to her knees across from Gabriel.

"Let me do that while you hold him," she suggested.

"Okay." Gabriel pinned the creature down while Evaline deftly unbuttoned the shirt, aware of the smallness and delicacy of her fingers next to Gabriel's long, powerful hands. After the shirt was completely unfastened, Gabriel rolled the bear to one side to allow Evaline to untie the sleeves. As soon as the sleeves fell away, the bear bawled. Gabriel let up the pressure of his hands, and the cub scrambled to his feet. He lumbered to the door, limping on three ungainly paws and crying pitifully.

Evaline remained crouched by Gabriel, as they both watched the animal sniff the perimeters of the room, including the doorway of the closet. Neither of them spoke or made any sudden moves, aware that their voices or actions might frighten the small bear. The cub waddled to the bathroom, poked his snout into the plastic water dish, snorted in surprise and tried to rear up, but lost his balance and rolled onto his back.

Gabriel's shoulders shook as he suppressed a chuckle at the creature's antics, and Evaline stole a quick glance at him, surprised by this new version of the man she'd pegged as being hard-nosed and grumpy. Then Gabriel sensed her regard and turned to her. Evaline quickly looked away. She stood up, and he rose to his feet a moment later.

"Looks like he's making himself at home," she said, brushing her hands together. "You're going to stay with Ursa Major there?"

"Yes." He smiled at her reference to the constellation of the bear and nodded toward the sleeping bag. "Until I get something built to corral him."

The bear stretched up and tried to look out the window, but the sill was a few inches too high, and his injury gave him trouble when he put his weight on his rear legs. He dropped back down and paced the room again.

"I'll clean up the mess in the dining room and put away the groceries," Evaline said. "Do you need anything?"

"No." Gabriel combed a hand through his unruly bangs and Evaline couldn't help but notice the similarity between the thick glossy pelt of the cub and the dark lustrous waves of Gabriel's hair. He had a lot of hair on his head, but curiously enough, not much on his torso. In fact, his bare chest had appeared enticingly smooth and supple. She wouldn't have minded seeing more of his naked torso, but unfortunately he'd pulled on another shirt before returning with his sleeping bag. "Ursa Major and I will be just fine."

"I'll see to the beds, then. Good night."

"Good night." He shot a glance at her. "Thanks for your help, City Girl."

"The name's Evaline," she replied. "And I was happy to oblige."

Eleven-thirty arrived by the time Skeeter and Evaline had removed the couch to the rear bedroom and set up Allison's bed. Skeeter even helped put on the sheets and blankets while Allison sat nearby, watching them, but affecting a good deal of disinterest.

"What about your bed, Evaline?" Skeeter asked. "I wouldn't mind helping you with that." He wiggled his eyebrows at her and grinned.

Evaline smiled. "Sorry to disappoint you, Skeeter, but I'm bunking on the couch for the time being."

"You might get cold out there all by yourself," he teased.

"There's always the fire."

"What's a fire in comparison to a hot-blooded American man like me?" Skeeter dipped slightly to thrust his face in front of hers. "Would you mind telling me that?"

"Fires don't steal all the covers," Evaline retorted, although she'd never slept with a man to know if that rumor were true. She'd only heard complaints from other women regarding their bedmates.

"Ouch!" Skeeter laughed. "You're a tough cookie!" His

eyes twinkled as he swung around to lean close to Allison. "I'll wear Hard-Hearted Hannah down yet, Allison, you just watch."

Allison rolled her eyes and said nothing, although Evaline was fairly sure the girl had enjoyed the last few minutes, for she had seen a wry smile quirk the corner of Allison's mouth once or twice.

Evaline smiled to herself. The thought of Skeeter's scrawny body conjured up a vision of a barnyard rooster—all show and cockiness, with bright feathers and a raucous voice—not her idea of a fitting companion. If she could choose a farm animal to represent her ideal, she'd select a draft horse—a huge, loyal, steady creature of quiet but unrelenting strength. Suddenly the vision of Gabriel's solid torso flashed through her mind, surprising her. Evaline blinked it away and turned to Allison, reminding herself that no man could be counted on, even those of outwardly apparent strength. She had learned the hard way that strength of character could be as much an illusion as anything else.

"Well, since I can't talk you into bed," Skeeter commented, "I'll say good night."

"Why don't you come up for breakfast?" Evaline asked.

"I don't like breakfast, especially Gabe's."

"I'm cooking now. Why don't you give my pancakes a try?"

Skeeter tilted his head. "Pancakes?"

"The fluffiest pancakes this side of the Cascade Mountains."

Skeeter laughed. "Maybe I will come up."

"Good."

"See you, Twink," Skeeter said, mussing up Allison's hair.

She batted his hand away and scowled.

"Good-night, pretty lady," he called, heading for the door.

"Good-night."

Evaline stepped behind Allison and clutched the wheelchair handgrips. "Do you want to take a bath or anything before you go to bed?"

Allison glanced at her watch. "A bath."

"All right." Evaline pushed her into the hall and saw Allison staring at the closed door of the bedroom that housed Gabriel and the bear cub.

"Is my father going to stay in the house all night?" she asked.

"Yes."

Evaline saw Allison's shoulders sink in relief, and thought the movement was odd. Why would Allison be relieved that her potentially abusive father was going to spend the night across the hall? Allison didn't say anything more, however, and Evaline didn't ask any questions. Not enough trust had been established between them to share confidences.

After Allison had showered and Evaline had said good night to her, she knocked on the door to Gabriel's temporary bedroom. He came to the door, with his shirt still unbuttoned and his hair tousled.

"Is the cub settling down any?" she asked.

"Somewhat." Gabriel glanced over his shoulder. "He drank a lot of water."

"That's good."

Evaline held up a tube of ointment. "Here's some antibiotic cream for those scratches of yours."

"Thanks." He took the offered medicine. Then he paused. "I know this is going to sound like a come-on," he began, "but would you mind checking the scratches on my back? They hurt like a sonofabitch. And I can't get a good look at them."

"Sure. Come down to the kitchen, where the light is better, and I'll examine them."

He shut the door behind him and followed her down the hall, silent as usual. She carried a chair from the dining room into the kitchen and motioned for him to sit down on it. Then, while she washed her hands, he removed his shirt and straddled the chair. Evaline stepped up behind him.

"Did you have a chance to wash the scratches?" she inquired.

"The ones on my chest," he replied. "But I had a hard time reaching around the back."

"I'll get a warm cloth." She opened a nearby drawer, took out a clean cloth, held it under the tap, and lathered soap on it. Then she gently applied the cloth to his wide muscular back, letting the soap and water seep into the crimson lines.

Gabriel sighed.

Evaline was careful to touch him only with the warm cloth, although she let her appreciative gaze run wild across the contours of his shoulders and rib cage.

She rinsed the cloth and applied it again to the scratches on his back. Then she squeezed salve out on a fingertip and gingerly drew it along the scored flesh.

"Am I hurting you?" she asked.

"No." He leaned his forearms on the back of the chair and bent forward, and when he did so, the muscles near his shoulder blades bunched and rippled. Evaline watched the play of his flesh, fascinated by his male physique.

"That should do it," she remarked when the last scratch had been attended to. "Want me to do the ones on the front?"

"Sure. Why not?"

He turned in the chair and faced her, his back straight, and his eyes riveted to the far wall where the fireplace rose between two windows. Evaline traced ointment over the powerful planes of his chest but had trouble ignoring the nearness of his mouth and eyes. Harder still was ignoring the sharp, unfamiliar thrill that coursed from her fingertip to a place deep inside her belly. Flustered, she glanced at him and found him regarding her thoughtfully.

She reached for the ointment and capped it, commanding her hands to remain steady even though the rest of her body was fluttering dangerously out of control.

"Thanks," he said quietly, rising to his feet.

"You're welcome." She stepped to the sink. "You should put more ointment on those scratches tomorrow."

"Okay." He snatched his shirt off the counter. "Good night, Evaline."

"Good night."

She watched him walk away and wondered if he had felt the same unusual flutterings she had just experienced. It had been years since she'd been touched by anyone in care and gentleness, and sometimes she hungered for a simple hug or a light caress. She wondered if Gabriel's single life kept him as isolated and insulated as hers did, and if her touch had any effect on him.

Later that night, Evaline awakened to the sound of a scream. She jerked upright, heard the scream again coming from Allison's room, and bolted out of her makeshift bed on the couch. Though her brain was sluggish with sleep, she had the presence of mind to remember to arm herself. She grabbed the gun out of her purse and dashed down the dark hallway. Allison's bedroom door stood ajar and a strange bluish light filtered through the crack. Alarmed but cautious, Evaline halted at the threshold to assess the situation before rushing in.

Gabriel was in the room, towering over his daughter, and blocking the girl from view. He hadn't turned on a light, and in the gloom he appeared larger and more menacing than ever, a huge dark shape in the shadows. The blue light she'd observed moments before had paled to a cerulean film that hung over the bed. Evaline's blood turned cold at the sight. How long had Gabriel been in the room? And what had he done to Allison to make her cry out and to cause the odd blue light? Without a thought to her own safety, Evaline kicked the door open and spread her feet wide.

"Hold it right there!" she shouted, bracing herself to shoot.

Gabriel spun around and stared at her in astonishment. All he wore were unbelted jeans, revealing his powerful torso and arms that could easily dispose of Evaline should her shot miss its mark.

"What in the hell are you doing?" he demanded. A raven's wing of dark hair swept across his forehead but did nothing to shade the cold glitter in his eyes.

Just then Allison cried out behind him and thrashed in her bed, flinging her arms in front of her, as if to ward off something or someone.

"No!" she screamed. "No!"

The terrified sound twisted through Evaline, bringing her old memories up in a roar. For a moment, Evaline stared at the girl as she writhed and then glared at Gabriel. "What have you done to her?" She sighted down the gun. "Tell me or I'll shoot."

"Not a goddamn thing!" He waved her off. "Now put that gun down before you hurt somebody."

"No way." She settled her weight more firmly on the floor. "Step back from the bed, Mr. Townsend."

His eyes burned into hers, riveting in their glinting rage. She might have a single chance to get off a shot if he lunged for her. And if one bullet wouldn't stop him, he'd probably choke her with his bare hands.

Neither of them had made a move when a pile of cassette tapes fell off the nightstand and clattered to the floor around Gabriel's feet. At the sudden sound, Evaline's heart leapt in her chest and then pounded furiously as she watched Gabriel stoop to collect the plastic containers. The sound and movement had caught her off guard, and she'd nearly reacted by pulling the trigger.

Gabriel stacked the boxes in two smaller, more stable piles on the nightstand, and in doing so, gave Evaline a broader view of the bed, enough to see Allison's face.

"No!" Allison wailed. "You can't!"

Allison wasn't even awake. Her father hadn't been abusing her; she was having a terrifying nightmare. Chagrin coursed through Evaline as well as a surprising amount of relief that Gabriel wasn't guilty of hurting his daughter. Evaline noticed that the blue film had disappeared from the vicinity of the bed. She caught flickers of lavender above the nightstand, but then decided the light must be caused by a crack in the drapery, allowing the shifting lights of the storm outside to flash into the room, and that Gabriel had nothing to do with the strange pale glow. She lowered the gun and stepped forward, ready to make an apology, when Gabriel sat down on the bed and grabbed Allison's shoulders.

"Allison!" he exclaimed, shaking her. "Wake up!"

Allison's head lolled about on her shoulders, but she didn't open her eyes. Fear contorted her features, and she cried out again, pushing against Gabriel's chest.

"Allison!" he shouted, as if the volume of his voice would reach into her nightmare.

"No!" she yelled, pummeling his chest. "Get away!"

"Gabriel," Evaline rushed forward. "She's terrified, and you're only making it worse."

"I'm trying to wake her up!"

"This might not be a normal dream. Allison might be suffering a psychological relapse of some kind."

"Let me go!" Allison screamed.

"Psychological relapse?" Gabriel scowled and grabbed Allison's wrists, which only intensified her distress. "She's having a nightmare, that's all. Allison!"

"I don't agree," Evaline replied. "I'm no psychologist, but I think Allison might be subconsciously reliving the trauma she suffered, the same trauma she can't consciously remember."

"There is nothing wrong with my daughter!" Gabriel stated through clenched teeth. He shook Allison again. "Now wake up, Allison!"

"Shaking will only hurt her neck." Evaline reached out to stop him, and was shocked when Gabriel turned to her, his face flushed with anger.

"Goddammit!" he swore. "Stay out of this! Allison is my daughter, and I'll decide what to do!"

Evaline stood her ground, galvanized by Gabriel's sudden burst of anger, but too focused on Allison's welfare to remain immobilized for more than an instant. She felt a flush of anger rise up her neck and spread over her cheeks as her eyes locked with Gabriel's.

"Allison is my patient," she countered, forcing her voice to maintain a normal level, despite the wet knot of anger lodged in her throat. "It's my duty to protect her, even from her own family."

"No one gave you that right."

"I took an oath," Evaline replied. "And I won't violate it just because you shout and swear at me." She raised the gun. "Now take your hands off that child and step away from the bed."

"I don't respond well to guns pointed at my head," Gabriel retorted.

"Oh?" She arched a brow. "What do you respond to, Mr. Townsend?"

Before he could answer, the bedroom door slammed shut with a loud bang. Evaline gasped and jerked backward.

"What was that?" she exclaimed.

Gabriel leapt to his feet and dashed across the room, his bare soles making no noise as he ran. He yanked open the door and lunged into the hall. Evaline hurried after him, gun in hand and ready to defend all three of them against an intruder. Every nerve in her scalp bristled, and she felt her hair stand on end as she ran through a pocket of much cooler air.

"See anything?" she asked.

"No."

"It must have been wind from the storm." But as she put forth the rational explanation, a much more irrational theory came to mind. *Spirit visitation.* The blue light, the noise, and the temperature change were all signs of the presence of a spirit. Evaline tightened her grip on the gun as she reined in such a fantastic thought. Her childhood had been full of stories about spirits, power animals, and supernatural intervention, but her medical education had made her question everything she'd learned on the reservation. Not until this moment, thrust back into a far corner of northwestern Washington, had she realized that someday she'd have to decide which belief system to adopt as her own. And that someday might be soon.

"Are there any windows open?" Gabriel asked, interrupting her troubled thoughts. He glanced up and down the dark hallway.

"No."

"Then it couldn't have been a draft."

"Maybe from the fireplace." Her voice sounded distant and detached, even to her own ears.

"Unlikely." He swung around and looked past her shoulder to Allison. "But whatever it was, it seemed to have snapped Allison out of her bad dream."

Evaline turned to glance at the girl and was relieved to see her lying on her side, sleeping more peacefully, although her eyes twitched beneath her lids, a sign she was still involved in a dream. As Evaline watched Allison sleep, a number of questions surfaced. If a spirit had been in the room with Allison, what kind of spirit had it been? And what did it want with a fourteen-year-old girl? Yesterday Allison had accused Evaline of not knowing what she was going through. Was Allison aware of the spirit? Did she see an entity in her nightmare? Evaline reeled in her runaway thoughts with a heavy dose of logic. No proof existed of a spirit visitation, and if she examined the facts hard enough, surely she could find a reasonable explanation for everything that had occurred in the last few minutes. Yet she couldn't explain the visions she'd seen at the medical center days before—the ram shape surrounding Stephen Durrell and the crow sitting on the hospital bed. No logic she was aware of could explain those manifestations.

Gabriel walked back to the bed and carefully pulled the covers up around Allison's shoulders while Evaline looked on, sure that she'd alienated Gabriel forever by pulling a gun on him. But what alternative had there been?

He seemed to have read her thoughts, for he turned and pointed at the weapon in her hand. "Carrying a loaded gun around is dangerous and unnecessary."

"Perhaps."

He faced her and planted his hands on his lean hips. "You have some problem with me, Miss Jaye?"

His direct question took her by surprise. She paused, taking a moment to marshal her thoughts. Her problems with Gabriel were numerous, but this wasn't the time to expound a list of grievances, so she picked an item from the top of the list. "Yes. I don't trust you."

"Do you draw a gun on everyone you don't trust?"

"No, but I was warned about you."

"Oh?" Gabriel's eyes glittered again. "By whom?"

"Just some people."

"And what did they tell you about me?"

"That you might become violent."

Gabriel snorted in contempt. "Violent enough to hurt my only child?"

"I couldn't take the chance of finding that out."

Gabriel crossed his arms, and his glance flashed over her, more in an assessing capacity than in an accusatory fashion. Then he said simply, "Your sources are full of shit," uncrossed his arms, and brushed past her.

Evaline stared after him as he returned to the bedroom across the hall and shut the door. Unnerved, unsettled, and unsure of what to believe, Evaline lowered herself into the overstuffed chair next to Allison's bed. She put the gun on the nightstand next to the stacks of cassettes and leaned back against the cushions.

Before the wolf attack, before ugliness and seclusion had become the hallmarks of her life, Evaline had often seen spirits during the ceremonies at the tribal center and in the forest around her home. Her father had told her she had been born with an ability few in the tribe possessed. After the attack, which had come on the heels of the onset of her menses, she'd lost the ability to "see."

She'd never been certain if the loss of trust and childhood had been the cause of her loss of power, or if she'd lost her ability because she'd lost faith, for the wolf attack had shattered her belief in the spirit world. Surely her guardian spirit, had such a thing truly existed, would have protected her from the wolf. She had never understood why the spirits had abandoned her that day and had never accepted her father's explanation that powerful shamans often had to undergo a harrowing, life-altering experience to come into their full power. Since the day of the wolf attack, her faith had wobbled, and in the last few years, had nearly disappeared.

Why then had she seen the crow in the hospital room, the filmy vision over Allison's bed? And if the blue light wasn't a spirit, what was it? In the morning she planned to ask Allison some questions and find out just what the girl had been dreaming of this night.

7

Shortly after breakfast, Gabriel and Skeeter set out to build an enclosure for the bear cub on Allison's side of the house near the place Gabriel had split wood the previous day. Allison slept most of the morning, leaving time for Evaline to clean up the breakfast dishes and attack the third bedroom, which housed her rehabilitation equipment. All the while she worked, she tried not to listen to the bear cub wailing for his mother. There was no way to tell the little bear that his mother would never return, and no way to comfort the poor animal beyond providing him with food and shelter. Gabriel had left a bowl of sliced fruit and raw hamburger for the bear early that morning, but the creature hadn't touched the food.

Just before noon, Evaline knocked softly on Allison's door to see if she was awake.

"Come in," Allison called.

Evaline pushed open the door and surveyed the room, a cheerful place in the middle of the day and far from the frightening shadowy chamber of the previous night.

"How are you feeling?" Evaline asked, breezing into the room.

"Okay."

Evaline walked to the window and pulled back the drapes. Sunlight poured through the east window and slanted across Allison's bed, where the girl sat with tousled hair and rumpled T-shirt.

"Jesus!" Allison squinted at the sudden burst of light and shaded her eyes. "Did you have to do that?"

"Light is good for you. Fresh air, too." She unfastened the latch of the window and slid it open. Balmy air, sweetly laced with cedar, drifted through the screen. The storm during the night had left the forest lushly damp and fresh. Evaline turned back to the bed. "It's a gorgeous day, Allison. Do you want to go out on the deck?"

Allison curled her lip. "It's boring out there. Just a bunch of trees."

"It might be more interesting than staying in here all day."

Allison shrugged and glanced around the room. "You've got to make my father get a TV."

"I doubt the reception would be decent."

"He could get cable."

"It would cost a fortune, Allison."

"Yeah, and my father isn't rolling in money. What a loser."

Evaline frowned. "Why do you say that?"

Allison rolled her eyes. "You only have to look at him. I wouldn't be caught dead in public with him! He looks like a wild man!"

"I think it's the beard."

"No, it's just him!" She tossed her hair and craned her neck to look out the window to the side yard. "What's he doing out there anyway?"

"Building a cage for the bear."

"He's going to keep it?" Allison snorted. "What an idiot!"

"I think his decision is commendable." Evaline heard herself defending Gabriel and almost laughed at the preposterous notion. She looked up to find Allison intently staring at her. Flustered, Evaline grabbed the wheelchair. "How about a ride to the bathroom?" she asked.

"Okay." With Evaline's assistance, Allison half slid off the bed into the chair. Evaline noticed a tattered ear of the teddy bear sticking out of the jumble of sheets and blankets, and was surprised the girl still slept with a stuffed animal.

Allison settled into the seat and glanced up at Evaline. "Where's the bear now?"

"The cub? Across the hall."

"I thought I heard it crying earlier."

"He was. For his mother. But I think he fell asleep, poor little guy."

Allison nodded, and Evaline noticed that the girl's hands clutched the arms of the chair so hard that her knuckles turned white.

"Allison," she began, hoping the girl wouldn't retreat into her usual caustic shell. "Do you remember what happened last night?"

"Yeah. My father came home with that bear."

"No, I meant afterward. When you were sleeping."

Allison's head shot up. "What do you mean?"

"You don't recall anything unusual?"

"No. Why should I?"

"You had a terrible nightmare. Don't you remember?"

Allison brushed back her unruly hair in an impatient gesture. "Not really."

"You screamed so loudly that you woke up your father and me."

"I did?"

"Yes. You seemed to be terrified."

Allison shrugged.

Evaline pushed her toward the hallway. "Have you ever seen anything unusual?" She hoped the girl would talk to her more readily when not confronted face-to-face. "In your dreams or perhaps when you're awake?"

"What are you talking about?"

"Have you noticed anything peculiar? Like a light, for instance, out of the corner of your eye?"

Allison fell silent. Evaline didn't press her and rolled her toward the door of the bathroom, wondering why the girl wasn't spouting one of her smart-ass replies. Could Allison have *seen* something but was reluctant to discuss it with someone she didn't trust? Was there anyone Allison *did* trust?

"Why would I see anything unusual?" Allison countered after a long pause.

Evaline considered telling Allison about the strange lavender and blue light, and then thought better of it, because such information might frighten her. She looked down. "Just asking, that's all."

"Sometimes people see stuff in the dark." Allison's voice was more brusque than ever. "Stuff that isn't really there."

"Things do appear different at night."

"Yeah," Allison agreed. "I hate the dark."

Evaline tried not to show the surprise she felt at the girl's confession. Not many teenagers would admit to such a fear. "Why is that?"

"I just do. It gives me the creeps."

Evaline paused at the doorway to the bathroom, anxious to talk more with Allison, but aware that she shouldn't press for too much conversation. "Well, here we are. I'll leave you now." Evaline turned to go but Allison's voice stopped her.

"Is that why you stayed in my room last night, because you saw something?"

"Yes. I was concerned."

"About what?"

"About you."

"Oh." Allison placed her hands on the wheels of her chair. "I wondered why you were there. I woke up once and saw you sleeping in the chair."

"If you prefer to be left alone during the night, I won't do it again."

"That's okay," Allison answered quickly. "It didn't bug me that much."

Evaline couldn't help but smile to herself. In her own roundabout way, Allison had taken a small step toward accepting her. But the smile soon faded when she thought of Allison as a child, probably left to endure many terrified hours in the dark with no one to comfort her. No one deserved to be abandoned to their own fears in the middle of the night. Daylight could seem a lifetime away to a frightened child. She knew that better than anyone.

"When you're done in there, Allison," Evaline said, "come out to the kitchen. I'll make you some iced tea and a sandwich."

"Okay."

"Then we'll get you out for some sun and sea therapy."

"What kind of therapy?"

"Sun and sea. It's a new type I've designed just for you."

Allison wrinkled her nose. "Sounds like torture."

The bear enclosure took most of the day to complete, and the men didn't put their tools away until sunset. They trudged up the stairs, sweaty and dirty. Gabriel's beard and hair were frosted with sawdust, and Skeeter's twill pants showed dirt stains on the knees. Evaline was just pushing Allison in through the front door as the men came up the steps behind her.

"Gosh, that smells good," Skeeter said, sniffing the air. "What are you cooking in there, Evaline?"

"Chicken and dumplings."

"Chicken and dumplings?" Skeeter's eyes grew wide. "Really? My mother used to make that way back when."

"Allison claims she's never heard of the dish."

"Oh?" Skeeter tousled the girl's hair. "Poor darlin', you've had a deprived childhood!"

Allison batted his hand away.

"Would you two like to join us?" Evaline asked, directing her words at Skeeter but glancing at Gabriel.

Skeeter rubbed his hands together. "If those dumplings are as good as your pancakes, you're darn tootin' I'll join you!"

"Gabriel?"

"We shouldn't impose," he answered. "We're filthy."

"You've got time to wash up. Allison and I still have to set the table and make a salad."

At the mention of work, Allison's head whipped around, and she tried to catch Evaline's eye, but Evaline refused to look at her, knowing very well what was on Allison's mind.

Gabriel shifted his weight. "If it won't be too much trouble—"

"It won't. Besides, I told you I'd take over the cooking detail."

"Fine. I'll take The Major out to the cage, then we'll get cleaned up."

Gabriel clumped through the living room, passed into the bedroom, and came back with the bear wadded up in a blanket, kicking and bawling, and trying to bite Gabriel's wrists. Allison watched them pass by her wheelchair while Evaline observed the girl. Allison pretended not to be interested in her father's business, or to even recognize his presence, but sometimes she forgot herself. Evaline wished she could think of a way to bring the two together, but suspected that only time would bridge the gulf between them.

"Let's see what happens with the bear," Evaline suggested to Allison as the two men walked toward the newly built enclosure. The cage looked much like a dog run, with a long fenced area and a small wooden box for a shelter at one end.

"Why?" Allison retorted.

"I want to see what The Major does."

Evaline approved of the name Gabriel had given the bear, a shortened version of the constellation Ursa Major. The military title would fit a male bear, especially when fully grown. With hope, the bear would thrive in their care and have a chance to mature once it was released at the end of the summer. "Come on!"

Without waiting for an answer, she turned the wheelchair and rolled Allison back onto the deck and around the corner at the front of the house. Allison heaved a big sigh, as if the prospect of watching her father and the bear was utterly boring, but she didn't protest. They watched Gabriel free the bear into the cage and place the food and water dishes near the little house. The cub ambled around the perimeter of the cage, sniffing and bawling.

"Think he'll ever quit crying for his mother?" Allison asked. "I can't stand that noise."

"He'll settle down once he gets accustomed to us and this place."

Evaline watched the bear rise up and push against the wire fence, but Gabriel had built it with sturdy materials meant to take abuse and wear. She doubted the cub could chew through the wire or rattle the cage loose.

"Did you ever have a pet?" Evaline asked.

"No. My mother said animals were filthy."

"I had a dog once. He was great."

"My mom hated dogs. She said they had fleas."

"Sometimes they do."

"I want a horse really bad, but I'll never get one."

"If you like horses, maybe we could go riding someday." Evaline felt Allison's scathing glance on the side of her face but didn't say anything more in hopes the girl would volunteer some conversation. When the conversation didn't come, Evaline continued to gaze across the yard, all the while wondering what had happened to Allison to make her so bitter, withdrawn, and susceptible to such terrifying nightmares. She waited until she saw Gabriel close the cage door behind him, then she wheeled Allison back into the house. Allison seemed to want to chat, for she trailed after Evaline as she walked into the kitchen.

"Were you serious?" Allison asked, accepting the pile of plates and silverware that Evaline gave to her. The kitchen had been completely stocked with everything from wineglasses to napkin rings, and all the items appeared to be brand-new. Again, Evaline wondered why no one had ever moved in and what kept Gabriel from living in this delightful house.

She glanced down at Allison. "Serious about what?"

"About going riding?"

"Sure. I love to ride."

Allison almost broke into a grin before she caught herself. "But what about my legs?"

"If you work hard, you'll be strong enough to ride a dependable mare. I bet Skeeter would know of a stable nearby, or someone with a few horses."

"You think so?" Allison put the dishes on the table.

"Forks go on the left," Evaline instructed. "On the napkin."

"Okay." Allison struggled to maneuver around the table in the dining room, but after a few minutes she finished the task and rolled back into the kitchen. "How long do you think it would take, really?"

"To get in condition?" Evaline pursed her lips and smiled down at Allison. "Probably a few weeks." She saw Allison consider the answer and could almost see her counting the days off a mental calendar. "Should we plan on it?" Evaline asked. "As a goal, say just after the Fourth of July?"

"Sure," Allison replied. Then her expression darkened.

"Why the long face?"

"Oh, you'll probably forget when the time comes. My mother made promises all the time and always forgot. Conveniently."

"We won't forget it if we put it on the calendar." Evaline pulled out a drawer by the stove and rummaged around for a pen. "Here, circle the seventh of July, on that calendar by the bulletin board."

Allison glanced over her shoulder. "You mean it?"

"Of course I mean it. But it also means that you'll have to work really hard at strengthening your leg muscles."

Allison circled the date on the calendar and wrote "Riding" in fat round letters. "I didn't mind sitting on the dock and hanging my legs in the water like we did today."

"Good. More of that and exercise and you'll be walking in no time."

"Yeah, right." Allison's voice took on the all-too-familiar sarcastic tone, and Evaline wondered if she'd ever completely break through the girl's wall of bitterness.

* * *

Evaline was amazed at how quickly the chicken and dumplings disappeared. Both Gabriel and Skeeter had seconds, and Allison managed to consume a large portion. A similar fate befell the chocolate pudding she'd whipped up for dessert. During the meal, Skeeter tried to draw Allison into conversation, but she replied in mumbled monosyllables, defeating his commendable attempts. Finally he gave up and asked Evaline questions about her life in Seattle, and shared some of his adventures as a bush pilot. Gabriel said very little, and once or twice Evaline caught him surveying his daughter across the table, his eyes searching and troubled. Again she wished she could come up with a way for them to find common ground, but didn't know either of them well enough to be aware of any similar interests they might possess.

When Evaline rose to get more coffee, Gabriel leaned back in his chair. "Have you heard the weather report for tomorrow, Skeeter?" he asked.

"Blue sky and seventy-five degrees, if you believe the weathermen."

"Good. Just what we need for tomorrow."

"Why? Taking out a party I don't know about?" Skeeter asked, referring to Gabriel's livelihood of charter boat fishing.

"Nope. The deck needs weatherproofing."

"Love to help," Skeeter said, smiling up at Evaline as she poured him a cup of coffee. "Thanks, Ev." Then he turned to Gabriel. "But I'm going back to Port Angeles tomorrow."

Gabriel pushed his cup toward her. "I didn't intend to ask you, Skeeter."

"Oh." He grinned. "Whew!"

"Allison's going to do the job."

Allison's mouth fell open in astonishment.

"Weatherproofing isn't too hard," Gabriel continued, turning to his daughter while Evaline poured his coffee. "You should be able to do it in a couple of days."

"You've got to be kidding!"

"A roller and a brush will be all you'll need. You can handle them."

"In case you haven't noticed, genius, I'm in a wheelchair!"

"So you are," Gabriel replied evenly. Evaline watched him struggle to contain his anger at Allison's insulting reply. She sat down, impressed by his temperate tone of voice.

"How do you expect me to paint?"

"There's a pole on the roller. I'll put a long handle on the brush, too."

"I'm not doing it!" Allison yelled, throwing her napkin on the table. She jerked the wheelchair away from the table and tried to roll past her father, but he grabbed an arm of the chair and stopped her. Allison glared straight ahead, refusing to look at him.

"You *will* weatherproof the deck, young lady," Gabriel declared in a voice that was deadly calm in its control. "And from now on, you will dispense with the name-calling and the swearing."

"I don't have to do anything you say!" she blurted.

Evaline, uncomfortable at witnessing such a confrontation, stirred her pudding with her spoon while Skeeter, equally distressed, traced the edge of his plate with his fork.

"You do and you will," Gabriel countered. "Not just because I am your father, but because you need to work on respect for people, including yourself."

Allison's pale face turned to stone.

"We all work around here. Miss Jaye never stops working.

Skeeter goofs off sometimes, but for the most part he more than earns a meal at my table. I have more work than I can handle. But what do you do to deserve to eat?"

"I don't have to do anything!"

"Think you get a free ride, Allison?"

"You have to take care of me. You're my father!"

"I thought you said I was a fucking bastard." He tilted his head to look her in the eyes. "Isn't that what you called me the other day?"

Evaline flushed and stared down at her plate. She would have never dreamed of holding such a conversation with her father.

"Isn't it, Allison?" Gabriel added.

She raised her chin and refused to answer.

"Until you decide to pitch in and show a little respect, you can forget the chow line."

"Gabriel!" Skeeter exclaimed, jumping halfway out of his chair.

"Shut up, Skeeter."

Skeeter sank back in his seat.

"I'm serious." Gabriel turned his attention back to his daughter. "No work and no respect means no food. It's your choice, Allison." He released his grip on the arm of her wheelchair.

"Go to hell!" she exclaimed, and jerked away.

Complete silence fell over the dinner table.

8

The next evening, as the sun sank into the bay, Evaline wiped her hands on a towel and ambled toward the side window of the living room. She stood close to the glass so she could see Allison sitting in her wheelchair on the deck at the east side of the house. The girl had been out there since noon, parked in the same place, with the painting tools untouched leaning against the wall behind her, and a stormy pout on her face. Evaline wondered how Allison could maintain such a sour expression for so many hours, but if anyone were capable of the feat, it would be a Townsend. She had come to realize that Allison had a stubborn streak which equaled if not surpassed her father's. Worried that neither father nor daughter would give in, Evaline glanced at the treetops, where the sky faded to the orchid and steel bands of dusk. Soon it would be too dark to work. And then what would happen? She wouldn't let Allison go to bed hungry.

The front door opened behind her, and Evaline turned slightly to face Gabriel, who had just stepped into the house.

"Is dinner ready yet?" His voice was unnecessarily loud for the question. Evaline paused, surprised he'd shown up on his own without Skeeter to serve as a social buffer and perplexed by his strange tone. Then she realized what Gabriel was up to.

"Dinner? Yes, it's ready," she replied. "But what about Allison?"

He ignored her question. "What's on the menu?" He nearly shouted out the words. "Smells like pasta."

"Spaghetti and meatballs."

"Great! Let's eat then!" He walked over to the table and looked down at the simple setting of place mats and stoneware which she had set for two, not expecting Gabriel's company at the evening meal. "Want me to set anything out?" he asked.

"All right, but I think you should let Allison—"

Gabriel waved her into silence. "Allison is fine."

"But she hasn't eaten all day."

"She'll live." He glanced at the living-room window and lowered his voice to a more normal tone. "She's got to learn who's boss around here before we can get anywhere with her."

"But starving her is cruel!"

"It's her choice, Evaline. She doesn't have to go hungry." Gabriel lifted up the large bowl of pasta, and Evaline noticed he took a deep breath of the fragrant aroma of garlic and oregano. Gabriel glanced at her. "If she so much as paints a square inch of that deck, I'll let her come in. But as long as she sits there scowling and doing nothing, she doesn't deserve dinner."

"I think you're being far too hard on her," Evaline remarked, setting the tossed salad on the table.

"And I think you're being far too easy."

They glared at each other until Evaline broke off her gaze and sat down. Gabriel pulled out his chair and took his place at the head of the table, on her left. He put his napkin in his lap.

"Lucky for me, you could smell this spaghetti cooking clear down at the dock. I'll bet Allison is going crazy out there, trying to stick to her guns."

"Then let her come in," Evaline urged, watching him mound loops of noodles on a plate. "I won't be able to eat a bite thinking about her out there alone and hungry."

"You can and you will," he countered. "And I want you to put a smile on your face while you're at it, and pretend we're having a grand old time in here."

Gabriel offered the plate to her, and, as she accepted the dish, she suddenly realized that Gabriel, in trying to cook for her and now dishing up food for her, was the first man to ever "do" for her. She had always been the care-taker—first with her father, then with her patients. A for-eign but lovely warm feeling surged through her.

"Thank you," she said, her voice unusually husky. Odd, how this gruff bear of a man could amaze her with his unexpected manners.

Gabriel nodded and served himself. "Don't look now," he said, lowering his voice, "but Allison's spying on us and probably thinks no one knows she's there."

Evaline could hardly keep her gaze from darting toward the window. She forced a bright smile. "Oh?"

"I want her to think she's really missing out." Gabriel sat back in his chair and pretended to laugh, pulling at the shaggy ends of his beard in mock glee. Though the chuckle was pure pretense, the sound had an amazing effect on Evaline, who couldn't help but grin.

"You're a lousy actor," she commented through her teeth.

"And you've got a really phony smile," he retorted, leaning forward to twirl pasta onto his fork. He stuck the roll into his mouth.

Evaline watched him chew. "Do you think she'll break down?"

"Any minute now. I'll bet her stomach is growling louder than The Major."

"What if she doesn't decide to paint?"

He turned and smiled at her, persisting in the fake cheerful dinner routine. "You don't have much faith in me, do you? But I'm not surprised."

She lifted a bite of salad to her mouth. "And what is that supposed to mean?"

"You're the one who thinks you need a gun in order to deal with me."

Her pasted-on smile felt like wax lips due to the turn in the conversation. "I'm not going to apologize for that," she replied hotly. "Under the circumstances—"

"I've never hurt a goddamn soul," Gabriel retorted, smiling so hard it looked painful.

"So you say." She choked down a meatball. "But I've seen your temper, Gabriel, and I'm not convinced."

"Temper? I just like getting things out in the open."

"Oh, really?" She choked down the meat. "All that blustering and swearing and knocking over furniture is your idea of healthy communication?"

"I don't knock over furniture!"

"Yes, you do. You knocked over a chair the other morning and stomped off in a huff."

Gabriel stopped eating and glared at her. At first his gray eyes cut through her, as sharp as glass, then they softened, melting into a smoky pearl color. "So I did."

He broke off his stare and reached for more spaghetti. "Seconds?" he asked.

She shook her head and watched him heap his plate full again. Did the man have a bottomless stomach?

"The problem with you and Allison is that you're too

much alike," Evaline ventured, hoping he would listen to her theories without brushing her off.

"Alike? Ha! She's the spitting image of her mother."

"I meant in temperament. You're both as stubborn as mules. And you both have chips on your shoulders that make your lives miserable."

"Chips?" Gabriel's smile vanished. "I don't have any damn chip on my shoulder."

"Oh, yes you do." She put her fork down. "You can't stand women."

He looked away and stuffed a meatball into his mouth.

"And what about this house?" she continued, pressing for personal information, which wasn't her usual way. "Why don't you live in it?"

"I told you—I prefer my boat."

"It must go deeper than that."

Gabriel skidded back his chair and jumped up. "What are you *now*—psychic?"

"Gabriel!" Evaline struggled to her feet.

"You're here to work with my daughter, not dissect my personal life."

"I meant no—"

"Then keep out of my affairs. I like my life just the way it is. And I don't need a goddamn woman butting in and telling me what's wrong with it!"

"You just don't seem very happy."

"Happy?" He gave a short, bitter laugh, which reminded her of Allison. Yet the bitterness did not conceal a dark glinting light in his eyes as he surveyed her. Was it regret she saw there? Envy? She couldn't read the expression. Gabriel shoved in his chair. "Happiness is not an ingredient of most people's lives, City Girl."

"That isn't what I meant to say. I was referring to peace that comes from a balance in our—"

"Hold on!" He harshly interrupted her with a raised hand. "Listen."

Evaline bit back her words and strained to hear over the roar of frustration in her head. A faint thumping noise came from the direction of the deck.

"She's using the roller," Gabriel commented, cocking his head to one side. "What did I tell you?" He raised a black eyebrow.

Evaline crossed her arms and frowned. "No need to gloat."

"I knew she'd come around," he said. "Let's see how much she does before she asks to come in."

Without another word, Gabriel stacked up the dirty dishes and carried them into the kitchen. Evaline followed with the spaghetti and salad bowls.

"How about some coffee?" he inquired, glancing over his shoulder, and acting as if the terse words they'd just thrown at each other had never occurred.

"I'll make some as soon as I finish cleaning up."

"I'll do it. Where'd you put the coffee?"

"In the cupboard above the coffeemaker."

Gabriel puttered about the kitchen while Evaline cleared the rest of the table. She felt nervous having a man working in her kitchen, for her father had never helped with any of the household chores. But Gabriel, accustomed to taking care of himself, apparently knew his way around a kitchen better than he knew his way around a cookbook. She did her best to ignore his disturbing presence and was pleasantly surprised to see him wipe up a few grounds he had spilled on the counter. Maybe Gabriel wasn't as big a slob as she suspected him of being.

"Why don't you go out and give Allison a word of encouragement?" she suggested as she bent to load the dishwasher.

"Not for a few minutes. She needs to worry a while."

"She thinks nobody cares about her, Gabriel."

"Why would she think that?"

"From what I can tell, her mother didn't have much time for her. And you never made an effort to see her."

"That's not true."

"You did make an effort?"

"At first. Until Meredith did everything she could to keep me from seeing her, like moving to Paris, and then to Greece." Gabriel stared down at the brown liquid streaming into the coffeepot. "I didn't have the money to go flying around the world chasing after them, and Meredith knew it."

"Allison thinks you didn't care about her."

Gabriel scowled. "She's too young to understand everything involved."

"No, she isn't. She's bright and she's sensitive. And I think she's very angry."

"I don't blame her," Gabriel remarked quietly. He poured two cups of coffee. "You take yours black, right?" He offered her a steaming mug.

She was surprised that he'd noticed her choice in coffee. She hadn't thought he'd paid that much attention to anyone's likes and dislikes. "Yes. Thanks."

He regarded her over the rim of his cup. "You sure you're in the right business, doing physical therapy?"

"Why do you ask?"

"Because you really are a good cook. That was the best spaghetti I've ever had."

"Why, thank you." Evaline flushed at the unexpected compliment. "But I consider it part of the job. Studies are proving that good food is an essential part of the healing process."

"Well, you can take care of my stomach anytime," he replied. "Just stay out of my head."

He winked at her, then swung around and strolled out

of the kitchen, leaving her startled by the sudden appearance of charm in his manner. She had expected neither kind words nor winks from the man. She heard him sink down on the couch. Evaline put her coffee cup on the counter and tried to make sense of the last few minutes. They'd gone from pretense to tirades and then on to intense personal information, all in the space of twenty minutes. She should have felt emotionally drained but didn't. She was more intrigued than anything else. The last few moments of conversation had given her a considerably different view of Gabriel Townsend. For the first time since she'd arrived at Obstruction Bay, she'd glimpsed the kinder, more accessible side of him. She hoped she'd see more.

A half hour later, the front door creaked open. Evaline looked up from her chair by the couch, where she was slip-stitching clean pillow covers for the sofa, and saw Gabriel stiffen. He'd been idly inspecting the condition of the house while sipping coffee. Silence had hung between them, but the quiet hadn't been uncomfortable, since they had both been concentrating on their tasks, and not until the noise at the door did Evaline become aware of the absence of conversation.

Gabriel turned around as Allison presented herself at the threshold.

"It's too dark to paint any more," she announced.

"You might have started earlier," Gabriel answered.

Evaline stared at him in dismay. He could have said a hundred things other than the words he'd just uttered. Criticism of Allison would negate all the progress he'd made with her, but obviously he couldn't see that. Evaline stood up, not about to let him sabotage Allison's attempt to cooperate.

"Did you have any trouble with the roller, Allison?" she asked.

"No." Allison rolled her eyes. "Any dummy can paint."

"Did you put the lid back on the sealer?" Gabriel added.

"Yes." She frowned. "It reeked."

"Did you put the roller in the plastic bag?"

"Yes."

Gabriel paused and crossed his arms. "Okay, then. You can finish up tomorrow."

She took his statement as permission to come into the house and rolled forward. Evaline expected her to rush into the kitchen, or at least ask for something to eat. Allison didn't say another word, however, as she wheeled past her father and headed for the hallway.

"Evaline made some good spaghetti," Gabriel called after her retreating form.

"I'm not hungry," she replied.

Evaline watched shock and disbelief blossom on Gabriel's face, and she couldn't help but smile. In his own daughter, Gabriel Townsend had met his match in the pride and obstinacy department.

For a moment he stared after the girl, then he turned and looked down at Evaline.

"What are you smiling at?" he demanded.

"Am I smiling?" she countered, raising her eyebrows.

"You damn well are." He studied her expression, his male brain apparently not grasping the sublime irony of the situation.

"Females!" he sputtered at last. "Try to understand them, and you can drive yourself crazy."

"I don't have any trouble understanding," she replied smugly, knowing it would aggravate him, and returned to her needlework.

* * *

The lights in the house blinked off earlier than usual, as both Evaline and Allison turned in before midnight. Evaline wrapped up in her blankets, telling herself that she had only one more night to spend on the couch, and that the next day she'd assemble her bed and finally move in to the master bedroom. She fell asleep, only to dream about The Major breaking out of his cage, growing to a monstrous size, and trying to eat Allison. She screamed as the bear shook the girl's arm, gnawing at it with slavering jaws, then suddenly discovered it was her own arm the bear was ripping to shreds.

Evaline awoke with a start, jerking to a sitting position, her hair soaked with sweat, and realized that the screams she heard were not part of her dream, but were real, and coming from Allison's room. Then, to add to the confusion, someone turned on music loud enough to drown out the screams.

Alarmed into instant lucidity, Evaline grabbed her gun. Dressed in nothing but a long-sleeved T-shirt and underwear, Evaline sprinted down the hall, burst into Allison's room, and flipped on the light switch. Nothing happened. The lightbulb must have burned out.

"Damn!" Evaline muttered under her breath, loping forward. She could see Allison writhing on her bed again, fighting with her invisible enemy. No one else was in the room. Evaline skidded to a stop in the center of the chamber, squinting against the blare of the music, whose vaguely familiar melody was obliterated by the pulsing drums and bass. She was amazed that the girl could sleep through the cacophony.

Clamping her hands over her ears, Evaline dashed to Allison's cassette deck, fumbled for the on/off switch, and pushed it to the left. Nothing happened. The music blasted as loud as ever, rattling the cassettes on the nightstand as well as her eardrums.

"What's going on?" a male voice yelled behind her.

Evaline whirled and spotted Gabriel in the doorway, dressed in jeans and a red plaid shirt. She felt oddly relieved to see him.

"The cassette player won't turn off!" she shouted.

"Pull the plug!" He ran toward her as she turned back to the boom box and followed the cord to the outlet. Still sweating, she yanked the plug from the wall. The music continued, as loud as ever. She held up the plug and they both stared at it, confounded.

Gabriel dropped to his knees. "It must have battery backup."

"But I turned it off!" she yelled.

"The switch must be bad." He turned the black appliance onto its face and searched with his fingertips until he found the latch for the battery compartment. He opened it and Evaline hung above him, watching his progress. He tore out six batteries and threw them on the floor, desperate to stop the oppressive, throbbing music.

Just as he slid the last battery out of the boom box, the song came to an end and simply faded to nothing. Had the batteries been responsible for delivering the music, the sound should have abruptly broken off with the removal of the first one. Instead, the song drifted away like a parade going over a distant hill.

"Is Allison okay?" Gabriel asked.

Evaline leaned over the girl. "She appears to be."

"Whew!" Gabriel exclaimed, sinking back on his heels. "What a relief! I never liked that song to begin with."

"Certainly not at a thousand decibels," Evaline replied, staring at the cassette player. "But I don't understand how it could have kept running."

"There must be something wrong with the machine." He rose. "I'll look it over in the morning."

Evaline frowned. "But who turned it on in the first place?"

They both looked at Allison, who had quit thrashing and was now sleeping fitfully. Most of the signs of struggle were gone.

"When I got here, she was having another nightmare," Evaline explained, nodding toward her. "And now look at her."

"You don't think she's faking it?"

"Not at all." She crossed her arms and frowned. "At first I thought her sleepiness during the day might be caused by the medications she takes, but that doesn't explain why her sleep is so fitful, or why these strange things are going on."

"Yeah." Gabriel rose to his feet. "And I don't like it. First last night, and now this. Someone must be in the house."

"Someone or some*thing*."

Gabriel glared down at her. "What are you talking about?"

· "You'll tell me I'm crazy."

"Try me." He crossed his arms over his wide chest, and his gaze raked down her scanty outfit and back up to her face. She wished she had pulled on a pair of pants, but it was too late now to think about her professional appearance. Seeing his smooth chest through the opening of his unbuttoned shirt made her highly conscious of her naked thighs and the hard cold steel of the gun against her leg. But there wasn't time to think about Gabriel's body or how keenly petite and feminine she felt standing in front of such masculinity. More important matters had to be discussed.

Evaline looked him directly in the eyes and decided to come right to the point.

"I think a spirit might be responsible."

9

For a moment Gabriel stared at her, not saying a word. Then he slowly nodded. "You're right," he said finally. "I think you *are* crazy."

"But how else can you explain what happened?"

"Not that way!" Gabriel rolled his eyes. "Ghosts! I should have expected as much from you."

"Meaning?"

"You're one of those people who read the latest tabloids and actually believe them."

Evaline put a hand on her hip. "Have you ever stopped to think you jump to conclusions a lot?"

"Not in your case." He blew a breath of air out through his nose. "You psycho-babble people think you know all the answers. But ninety percent of you are full of shit." Gabriel held out his hand. "Now give me the gun, and I'll sit up and keep watch tonight."

"I can do it," she replied tersely.

"Didn't you stay with Allison last night?"

"Yes."

"Then I'll handle it tonight."

Evaline peered at her watch in the darkness. Twelve-thirteen. She could get a few hours of sleep and then relieve Gabriel. "Okay," she said, handing over the weapon. "I'll come back in four or five hours and spell you."

"You sure you want to sleep out there?" he asked, nodding toward the living room. "What if there is somebody hanging around?"

"I don't believe what we've witnessed was caused by an intruder. What would be the motive?"

"To scare Allison."

"Scare her?" Evaline frowned doubtfully. "She didn't wake up either time!"

"To scare you, then."

"Why me?" Evaline shrugged. "And if so, why would the noise occur in Allison's room, and not out by the sofa?"

"Good question." Gabriel glared at the cassette player. "Or it just might be a coincidence. A draft last night, and a faulty electrical circuit tonight."

"That's what you'd like to believe," Evaline commented, "but things happen sometimes that defy explanation. And I think something else is involved here, something you can't blame on air or electrical currents."

"Like a ghost?" Gabriel retorted. "No way. I don't believe in anything I can't see."

"Well, you'll never see a ghost with an attitude like that."

"I live in the real world, Evaline. I don't have the time for mumbo jumbo crap. That was Meredith's big thing, you know. Channeling, past-life regression, crazy stuff— all so she could find herself." He snorted in contempt. "From what I can tell, she only got more lost than ever, and lined some charlatan's pocket while she was at it."

"Not all spiritual teachers are charlatans, and not all of what they teach is mumbo jumbo."

"As far as I'm concerned, they are and it is."

"I see we will have to agree to differ on the subject." She turned for the door. "Good night."

"I'll walk out with you. I want to check the doors."

"Suit yourself."

She walked down the hall, highly conscious of his tall form striding behind her. While Gabriel made certain the kitchen door was locked securely, Evaline burrowed into her nest of blankets on the sofa. She watched him walk to the front door and check its lock as well. Then he yanked on the windows by the door and at either side of the fireplace to make sure they were latched. Evaline snuggled into her covers as a pleasing warmth stole through her, warmth that had nothing to do with her wool blankets. Though she didn't need a man around to feel safe, she couldn't deny there was something reassuring about the way Gabriel insisted on checking the doors and windows. She listened to his steady footsteps as he passed through every room in the house to inspect the windows. Then she sighed and lay back, thinking she'd never get to sleep. But knowing Gabriel was on guard down the hall seemed to reassure her subconscious, for she no sooner put her head on the pillow than she fell asleep.

Evaline awoke sometime before dawn, threw back her covers, and went to relieve Gabriel. Allison's door was partly open, and she peeked inside to find Gabriel asleep in the chair, with his head angled toward Allison. In sleep, father and daughter wore identical peaceful expressions, looks Evaline doubted she'd ever see on them in daylight—at least in each other's presence. She noticed that the sharpness of

Allison's nose and brow was reflected in the stronger line of her father's profile—what she could see of it above his mustache. Evaline couldn't help but wonder what Gabriel might look like without a beard, and suspected there might be a lean, sculpted face under all that hair.

Then, against the plain backdrop of the wall, she saw a faint translucent silhouette surrounding Gabriel's head. Evaline paused to study it, wanting to see the animal shape this time instead of denying its existence as she had done with the ram and crow.

Soon the form grew more evident, until she could make out a large round head, small ears, and pointed snout of a bear. *What did the bear signify?* She scanned her memory. *Natural helper and person with power.* Evaline smiled to herself. She wasn't surprised that Gabriel's spirit animal was a bear. The more she got to know him, the more she could see through his outer gruffness to his solid character and stalwart heart. A bear spirit animal would explain why Gabriel had felt such a strong urge to save the cub, and perhaps why Allison found sentimental value in her bedraggled stuffed bear. Evaline wondered if Gabriel had given the toy to Allison when she was a baby, and whether her child's heart remembered a father's love?

Instead of waking Gabriel, Evaline decided to return to the couch and go back to sleep. If Gabriel's intruder had intended to strike, he would have done so by now. Shivering from the early morning chill, she covered up and closed her eyes.

When Evaline awoke next, she was greeted by light streaming across the room and the smell of coffee wafting from the kitchen. She sat up, yawning, and glanced at the kitchen, where Gabriel moved around as quietly as possible for a man of his size.

He caught the flash of movement on the couch and looked over his shoulder. "'Mornin'."

"Hi. How's Allison?"

"Sleeping like a baby. Coffee?"

"Sure. Thanks." Before she could extricate herself from the tangle of blankets, she saw him stroll toward the sofa with two cups of coffee in his hands. Nervously she rubbed the sleep out of her eyes and hoped she didn't look washed-out and frumpy, for she wasn't accustomed to presenting herself to public view from the platform of her bed. Gabriel didn't seem to notice any disarray and handed her a mug of steaming coffee.

"Thank you," she said, smiling. "I've never had coffee in bed."

"Never?"

She shook her head. Gabriel's gaze traveled swiftly over her braided hair and then away.

"No one's ever made you breakfast in bed?" he inquired, sitting on the arm of the nearby chair.

"No." She sipped the coffee and found that her hands trembled when she raised her arms. Having a man this close, this early in the morning, threw her off-kilter, especially since the man was Gabriel Townsend.

"No need to get nervous, Evaline." He winked. "I wasn't planning to cook."

She chuckled. "That's a relief." But the chuckle was tight and came out more like a titter. She didn't admire women who tittered. She could feel Gabriel's regard on the side of her face, which increased her disquiet. Flustered, Evaline took another sip of coffee in an attempt to fill the uncomfortable silence.

"I would have thought a woman like you would have—" He broke off, squinted, and took a big slurp of coffee. "Aw, forget it."

"Would have what?" she pressed.

"Well, would have traveled, stayed in fancy hotels with room service. Had a rich boyfriend or two."

"No, never."

"Never?"

"The farthest I've ever been from Seattle is Walla Walla. And the closest I ever got to a fancy hotel was attending a seminar at the Seattle Sheraton once."

"That's hard to believe."

"Especially when you persist in thinking I'm a city girl."

"What about the boyfriend part?"

"Wrong there, too," she replied, trying to tell him as little as possible about herself or her past. Her lack of experience with men was something she preferred to keep to herself. Evaline decided it would be prudent to change the subject, before he asked anything more. She set her mug on the coffee table. "Well, I need to take a shower and get the day started," she announced, throwing off her blankets.

"Just a minute," Gabriel put in.

She paused and glanced up at him, not knowing what to expect.

He put aside his mug. "I know it's not the best timing after last night, but I have to run into town today."

"Is that a problem?"

"It means leaving you to supervise Allison's deck job and look after The Major."

"I can handle it."

Gabriel frowned. "But what about the strange goings-on with Allison?"

"I don't know about that." Evaline shot a glance toward the girl's room. "But the trouble seems to be occurring only at night."

"Then you think you'll be all right if I leave for the day?"

"I've survived for twenty-seven years without you, Mr. Townsend. I believe I can manage one day alone." She didn't tell him that ghosts and spirits were a natural facet of life for a Native American, because she didn't want to discuss her heritage or past.

He didn't smile. "You know what I mean."

She nodded. "We'll be okay."

"Keep the gun handy until I get back."

"A gun might not help."

"I'd feel better if you did, anyway."

"When will you return?"

"Late in the afternoon. I have to pick up a few things for the boat before tomorrow." He squinted again.

Evaline watched his troubled expression darken. "You're not telling me everything," she ventured.

"That's because I'm having second thoughts."

"About what?"

He frowned and stood up. "I have a group of divers scheduled for a two-day cruise starting tomorrow. And now I'm thinking I shouldn't go."

"Because of Allison?"

"Yes, dammit." He shoved his hands in his pockets. "What if something happens when I'm out at sea?"

"We'll be fine."

Gabriel's intense stare sliced across her. "Do you actually know how to use that gun you carry?"

She raised an eyebrow. "Do you have a spare beer can?"

His eyes glinted. "Out in the trash."

"Get one, and I'll meet you out in the drive in a minute."

He made a derisive snorting noise and picked up his mug. "Okay, City Girl. You're on. The gun's on the counter by the stove."

He left through the kitchen door while Evaline pulled on a pair of jeans and shoes. Then she grabbed the small handgun and headed out after him.

Gabriel stood in the gravel waiting for her as she hurried

down the steps, invigorated by the chilly morning air and the challenge of showing him that she was more than a pretty face. She crunched across the drive toward him and checked her weapon.

"Okay," she said. "Throw it up as hard as you can."

Gabriel leaned over and hurled the aluminum can skyward. A fraction of a second later, Evaline blew it out of the sky. She lowered her arm and looked over at Gabriel, who gazed at her in amazement.

"So much for your theories about me, Gabriel Townsend," she remarked, staring him right in the eyes. "A city girl I'm not."

"Hmmm." A corner of his mouth pulled down, while the other side threatened to twitch into a smile as he returned her stare. But before his expression could betray him, he swooped down and retrieved the can, which he made a big deal of inspecting. Evaline watched him, her frustration mounting with each second. The man couldn't even admit she was a good shot.

"Could have been better," he commented.

"What?" she choked in disbelief.

He pointed to the circle surrounding the logo. "Your shot wasn't quite dead center." He held up the can for her to see.

"Oh, you are absolutely maddening!" Peeved, she turned on her heel and stomped off. He ran after her, chuckling, and grabbed her arm.

"You can dish it out but can't take it, eh, Evaline?"

She pulled out of his grip and glared up at him. "What are you talking about?"

"Am I smiling?" He cocked his head as he repeated her words of the previous evening in a high singsong voice. "I don't have any trouble understanding." He batted his eyelashes for effect.

Evaline waved him off and scowled, but had a difficult

time hiding a smile. He looked ridiculous mimicking her. "Go bite yourself, Townsend."

"Now *that's* not City Girl talk."

"No, it isn't." She looked up at the sky and drawled dramatically. "It's a miracle! Gabriel Townsend is finally getting the picture!"

He chuckled. "So where'd you learn to shoot like that?"

"Out in the woods." Evaline continued her march to the house. "When I was a teenager."

"You're good." He strolled beside her, his long easy strides effortlessly matching her hurried pace. "Looks like I don't have to worry about you handling a gun."

"I told you I knew what I was doing."

"Yeah, but lots of people claim to know a lot of things, when they don't know squat." He tossed the beer can toward the trash container near the corner of the house and hit his target, which was a considerable distance away. "Ever notice that, Evaline?"

She nodded, and also noticed she wasn't the only marksman in the bunch.

"If there's one thing I can't stand, it's big talk," Gabriel added, "with nothing to back it up."

Evaline couldn't agree more. She often filtered what people said to her through a healthy screen of doubt and good sense. She hadn't filtered Gabriel's conversation simply because of his sheer lack of words. She doubted he ever opened up and really talked to anyone, not even to Skeeter. He wasn't the type of person to sit around and chat, or to make up stories to entertain other folks. He didn't seem to feel the need to impress people and apparently wasn't interested in trying to make points with her. In fact, his lack of artifice and interest in her allowed her to interact with him honestly—however grating their interaction might be at times.

They returned to the house, fixed breakfast, and then Gabriel took off for town, after saying good-bye to Allison at Evaline's suggestion. She watched his truck bumping up the driveway and felt suddenly alone, more than she had in a long time. Evaline turned and leaned her hip against the kitchen counter, worrying about what she would do if something awful happened while Gabriel was gone. She had no way to call the police, no vehicle to use for escape, and no nearby neighbors to run to, should an intruder be lurking around the house. Making sure the safety was on, she slipped the gun in the back waistband of her jeans, and knew the day ahead would be a long one.

Evaline fixed Allison a hearty breakfast of eggs, oatmeal, and toast, then went out to feed and water the bear. She tried to check his leg, but he wouldn't allow her to get close and swiped at her hand. She spent the rest of the morning supervising Allison as she did her mat exercises to strengthen her legs. As they progressed through the exercises, they talked. As usual, Allison didn't recall anything of the previous night, and was upset when Evaline told her she shouldn't use her cassette player.

"Why not?" Allison asked, brushing her hair after the therapy session. "It's the only fun thing I have to do around here!"

"Your father wants to look at it. He thinks there's something wrong with it."

"Like what?"

"An electrical problem. It wouldn't turn off last night." She glanced at the ceiling. "And that reminds me, I have to change the bulb in your light."

"How come?"

"It's burned out."

"No it isn't. I had it on this morning."

"You did?" Evaline frowned and looked up at the light fixture again.

"Yes. It's fine."

"That's funny. It didn't work last night."

Allison gave a short, sharp laugh. "Maybe you were the one dreaming last night, not me."

Troubled, Evaline rolled up the exercise mat and got to her feet. Things weren't making sense, and she didn't like it.

"What's for lunch?" Allison inquired.

"How about some spaghetti from last night?"

"Jesus!" Allison whined. "Leftovers?"

Evaline turned on her, just about at her limit with the Townsends for one day, and then caught Allison's grin.

"Just kidding!" Allison laughed and sat back in her chair, her shoulders shaking. "Boy, you should have seen your face just then!"

"I thought you were serious," Evaline replied, slightly miffed. "You've complained before, you know."

"That look was perfect!" Allison sputtered, still chuckling. "You were just about to flip out!"

"Try dealing with your father on a daily basis," Evaline said. "And see how long it takes you to 'flip out.'"

"You have a point there." Allison wheeled to the door of her room. "Actually, that spaghetti smelled great yesterday. I wouldn't mind trying it."

"That's more like it." Evaline followed her out to the hall. "And don't forget your father wants you to work on the deck this afternoon, you know."

"I know." She made a face.

"It would really surprise him if you were done by the time he got back. I bet he thinks you don't know how to work."

Allison frowned. "What's there to know about weatherproofing a dumb deck?"

"Mostly just getting at it and getting it done."

Allison shrugged. "I guess I *could* go out there after lunch. There isn't anything else to do around here."

Evaline stowed the exercise mat in the equipment room and followed Allison out to the kitchen. Progress was being made with the girl, but it looked to be a slow and painful process.

Gabriel didn't return until dark. Evaline heard the truck in the drive while she was putting the last of her clothes away in the bureau of the master bedroom. Allison's shower sprayed in the bathroom next door, a comforting sound. Evaline appreciated the presence of other human beings in the house, having lived by herself for years and never really liking the silence of a lonely apartment. All the while she worked, she listened for the sound of Gabriel's footsteps in the hall, expecting to hear his voice any minute. She smoothed the last wrinkle from the comforter and made certain her alarm was set and the clock in position on her nightstand. Then she straightened and glanced around the room, now spotlessly clean and arranged to her satisfaction.

If the house had belonged to her, and she had the freedom to do what she liked, she would wallpaper this bedroom in forest greens and wine, and buy an oak bed frame and matching dressers. She'd drape the bed in an opulence of ruffles and mound it with pillows, just as she'd seen in magazines, and hang watercolors in brass frames on the walls. But she'd never owned a house, never had the opportunity or money to decorate her living quarters to match her dreams. Evaline sighed. Maybe someday, after medical school, she could afford her own place.

Curious that Gabriel hadn't at least poked his head into the house yet, Evaline slipped out of the house and down the stairs. The lights on his boat glowed bright in the early evening, throwing rippling squares of silver onto the water of the bay. She could see him carrying a carton up to the side of the boat and handing it to someone on board, probably Skeeter. Then Gabriel stepped into the boat and disappeared. His silhouette looked a little different, but from such a distance she couldn't tell why.

Evaline walked across the drive and down the beach to the dock, planning to ask the two men if they cared to sample a slice of apple pie she'd made that afternoon. Her loafers clunked a dull rhythm on the heavy timbers of the dock as she approached. She'd never walked all the way out to his boat before, having lost her interest in such vessels after her brush with death four years ago, when she'd nearly frozen to death in a boating accident that really hadn't been an accident. Gabriel's boat was a good-sized craft, larger than her father's, and looked to be over forty feet long. In the darkness, it appeared clean and well maintained, and its metal trim gleamed.

When she came alongside, she paused for a moment, thinking she heard a woman laugh somewhere in an aft cabin. Then she decided the noise must have been Skeeter's high-pitched chuckle.

"Gabriel?" she called, her voice sounding small against the vast emptiness of the bay. She waited, expecting Gabriel to appear any moment, and let her gaze wander over his boat. The ship rocked gently in the water and a glint of light caught her eye, drawing her gaze to the painted script on the bow. Idly, she viewed the rounded shapes until the flowing letters registered as a name. Then she sucked in her breath, hardly believing what she'd just read.

Sea Wolf.

She'd seen that name once before, looming above her as two hands reached out to pull her frozen body from a snow-covered rowboat, reaching into her tomb of despair and literally dragging her back into life.

Though most of the events of that terrible night were a blur, certain details had burned themselves into her memory. She didn't remember being carried to the cabin of the man's boat, but she vividly recalled the bands of his strong arms and the heat of his chest. She couldn't remember how he had managed to strip the ice-encrusted clothing from her stiff limbs, but she would never forget the way his blazing skin had melted her frozen flesh as he wrapped his nearly naked body around hers in his bed, giving of his heat to save her life.

She couldn't remember what his bunk or cabin looked like, for all the time he held her in his arms, she hadn't allowed herself to think about what she'd done, or what would happen to her. She could only stare straight ahead, ignoring her present emotional state, knowing if she didn't put it out of her mind, she would go crazy. Given her advanced hypothermia at the time, it hadn't been hard to do. She riveted her attention upon a line of books on a shelf at eye level—old, well-used books by the appearance of their tattered bindings—books bearing the names of Byron, Keats, Tennyson, cummings, Sandburg.

When she had begun to thaw and had melted against the furnace of the man who surrounded her from behind, she remembered word for word the poetry he had murmured in her ear, his baritone voice rumbling against her back. Perhaps he had recited the verses to pass the time, to amuse himself while he waited for her to recover, or to occupy her thoughts with something other than her trauma. Regardless of his intent, his deep voice offered a strange comfort to her wounded spirit, like a lullaby sung by a loving parent to a child who'd suffered a nightmare. Her improving body temperature first showed in the hot tears that rolled out of her eyes and soaked the pillow beneath her cheek, as she accepted this stranger's kindness and wept silently in the dark. She cried for all that she had lost and for the abysmal stretch of solitude she would have to endure if she returned to the world, where living for her was an unending series of rejections.

Yet his words had pulled her out of that fear, made her look at the beautiful spirit behind her hideous facial scars, and set her upon the path toward life again.

Sea Wolf. She had prayed that night for the Sea Wolf to come to her, to take her to its world of death, where her ravaged face and her shameful past wouldn't matter any longer. But instead of a supernatural being coming to her rescue, she had been saved by a very real man. Now she knew his name: Gabriel Townsend. And now, for some unfathomable reason, she had been thrown into his world again. Why? Perhaps her destiny was linked to his in a way she had yet to understand. Perhaps she was here to repay her debt to him.

Evaline stared at the name of the ship as tendrils of her long black hair blew around her shoulders in the slight breeze. She couldn't move, couldn't tear her gaze off the graceful blue letters.

"Evaline?"

She heard Gabriel's voice, heard her name, and knew she should have recognized the deep baritone from long ago. And yet she hadn't made the connection, for Gabriel's shaggy hair and beard had concealed the face she knew from before. She couldn't believe the coincidence. She couldn't believe it *was* a coincidence. She was practically living with the man who had given her a second chance at life four years ago.

"Evaline?"

She jerked out of her memories and looked up, shocked a second time by the sight of Gabriel leaning over the rail, just as he had leaned and reached for her years ago. The same boat, the same man, the same face.

Gabriel had shaved off his beard and had gotten a haircut. In doing so, he'd dropped at least fifteen years from his face. Instead of appearing like a middle-aged man, he now seemed only a few years older than she was. But even more surprising than the age difference was the visage that had emerged from the hair. Gabriel's face was as taut and sculpted as she'd imagined, with a sharp jawline and prominent cheekbones. He was more handsome than she had suspected or remembered—ruggedly handsome, to be sure, but undeniably good-looking. His dark hair, trimmed just above his ears, was brushed up and off his forehead, thick and glossy, the kind of hair that begged to be touched. He could have been a model for an outdoorsman catalog.

Evaline stared at him, speechless.

"Do we have a visitor, Gabe?" a stranger called behind him.

Through the fog of her shock, Evaline heard a female voice. She blinked, thinking her ears must be playing tricks on her as thoroughly as her eyes had fooled her into viewing Gabriel Townsend as handsome. Then she saw a figure step up behind Gabriel. The figure came into focus, materializing into a pretty young woman with brown hair and round face. She wore an apron and held a full coffeepot in her hand—the very picture of Suzy Homemaker domesticity. Evaline gaped at the woman, more confused than ever, while an undeniable shaft of disappointment dragged through her. Gabriel had a housemate?

10

Before anyone could detect Evaline's dismay, she quickly pulled herself together. "Gabriel," she greeted, forcing her lips into a smile. "I thought I heard your truck."

"Had to unload some things before I checked on Allison."

Evaline glanced around his shoulder to find herself being equally inspected by the woman in the apron. Apparently Gabriel realized both females wanted an introduction, for he stepped aside and motioned toward his companion.

"This is Mandy Bayer. She helps out on dives."

I'll just bet she does, Evaline thought to herself. She held out a hand and increased the wattage of her smile, feeling phony and rigid, and uncharacteristically jealous. That she was jealous of anyone, especially a woman connected to Gabriel, annoyed her.

"Mandy, this is Evaline Jaye, Allison's physical therapist."

"Hi," Mandy said, shaking Evaline's hand. "Gabe's been telling me about you."

"Has he?" Evaline replied. "I hope it wasn't all bad."

"As a matter of fact, he was raving about your cooking." She looked up at Gabriel. "Actually, Gabe, I could take that personally!"

He smiled at her. "You have nothing to worry about."

Mandy turned back to Evaline, her expression open and happy. "Want to join us for some coffee?" she asked. Her tone was light and rose at the ends of her sentences. "I just made some."

"No, thanks. I should be getting back. I just came down to see if everything went all right in town."

"I'll come up in a few minutes," Gabriel put in. "Allison is still awake, isn't she?"

"She's taking a shower but should be out any minute." Evaline turned toward the house, wishing she had never walked down to the boat, and sure she'd interrupted Gabriel's private time with his cute young friend.

Gabriel glanced at Mandy, then back at Evaline, which only confirmed her suspicions.

Evaline gave a short wave, too uncomfortable to hang around any longer. "Well, see you later, Gabriel. Nice to have met you, Mandy."

"Sure. I'll probably see you in the morning."

Right. If you can still walk after a night with Gabriel. Evaline imagined that Gabriel would be more than most women could handle, being such a large man. Not having any experience in the romance department, she theorized that someone as large as Gabriel was probably not the gentlest of lovers. But that theory was immediately dashed by her memory of him murmuring poetry in the darkness, treating her with more kindness and generosity than anyone had ever done. She had reason to suspect there was much more to Gabriel Townsend than met the eye. He might well be a most satisfying lover; how lucky for Mandy, she mused. Then Evaline chided herself for such thoughts and forced a smile over her shoulder at the woman. "Good night."

She walked briskly to the house, shoulders back and head held high, questioning the strange feelings rolling one on top of the other inside her. Why should she care who stayed with Gabriel on his boat? Why should she be bothered by the fact he had a lady friend? And what did it matter that Gabriel was younger and more good-looking than she had ever dreamed? He was still the same frustrating, obstinate man he was before the haircut. He just wasn't as isolated from the world as she had surmised or as lonely as she had thought.

It seemed she was the only isolated one.

Evaline pushed through the door and strode across the living room, out of sorts with herself. She'd had no reason to believe Gabriel was a kindred spirit, and she would never have jumped to that conclusion had her thinking been clear and logical. She vowed to remain more rational from now on, especially in regard to Gabriel. "I am the master of my fate," she muttered, remembering a line from "Invictus," a poem he had whispered in her ear four years ago and had never forgotten. "I am the captain of my soul."

Allison rolled her wheelchair into the hallway, startling Evaline out of her thoughts.

"Is he back yet?" she asked.

"Yes. He said he'll come up pretty soon."

"Where does he get the idea that I want to see him?" Allison scowled. "He's so full of himself."

"He's your father, Allison."

"So?" Allison adjusted the towel on her head. "What about Skeeter? Did he come back?"

"No. Some woman named Mandy Bayer came back with him."

"A woman?"

"Yes. A brunette, about twenty-one or so."

"A girlfriend?" Allison tilted her head. "My dad has a girlfriend?"

"I don't know about that," Evaline answered, even though she'd drawn the same conclusion. "He didn't say."

"Who would ever like my father?"

Evaline shrugged. "Probably lots of women."

"You've got to be kidding! He looks like a caveman."

"Not anymore he doesn't." Evaline pushed Allison into the bedroom, simply to get out of her range of sight. She didn't wish to subject herself to Allison's discerning regard, afraid that her expression might lead to questions she'd prefer not to answer. "He shaved off his beard."

"He did?"

"Wait until you see him. I think you'll be surprised."

"Nothing surprises me," Allison replied.

Evaline didn't doubt it. From what she'd gathered about Meredith's love life and pursuit of self-awareness, she suspected that Allison had seen a lot of the world, perhaps too much for a girl her age.

Allison twisted around to look at Evaline. "Do you think you could get some dye for my hair?" she asked.

"Why?"

"My roots are really starting to show. It's gross."

"Why do you want to dye your hair?"

"Haven't you heard?" Allison retorted. "Blondes have more fun." She frowned and looked down. "At least blondes out of wheelchairs do."

"You'd be a cute brunette, Allison. Why don't you try the natural look for a change?"

"No way!"

"Just let it grow out. Who will see you this summer?"

"I hope *some*body!" She pulled the towel off her damp

hair. "But I'm not holding my breath. It's like really boring around here."

Evaline sat on the end of the bed. "Before the accident, were you used to having a lot of friends—boyfriends?"

"Yeah. Just like dear old mom." Allison combed the snarls out of her hair with agitated strokes. "Not that I was crazy about any of them, but they did help to pass the time."

"There are many other things to do to fill your day than fritter your time away with boys."

"Yeah? Like what?"

"When I was your age, I liked to paint, to sew, do target practice—things like that."

"Target practice?" Allison stopped combing in midair. "You?"

Evaline nodded. "Would you like to try it sometime?"

"Yeah." She placed her comb on the nightstand. "That is, if you trust me with a gun."

Evaline thought back to the rumor that Allison had started the fire which had killed her own mother. The more she got to know the girl, the less she thought her capable of such a horrible crime. Allison needed to feel trusted, and this was an opportunity to display just that.

"Of course I trust you," Evaline replied. "And you know why?"

Allison craned her neck to look at Evaline. "Why?"

Evaline cocked an eyebrow. "Because I know if you shoot me, you'll have to go back to eating Gabriel's cooking."

"Yuck!" Allison laughed. Then she broke off and glanced sidelong at Evaline. For a moment their gazes met. Then Allison quickly looked away and scowled, obviously having caught herself conversing animatedly with the enemy.

"We could start tomorrow."

"Okay." Allison picked up her cassette player. "Here, would you ask my father to look at this?"

"You can ask him yourself when he comes up to say good night." Evaline rose. "Is there anything else you need before I turn in?"

Allison looked at her watch, then up at Evaline. "Is anyone going to stay in the room tonight—like, you know, with me?"

"Do you want someone to?"

"Why would I?" Allison rolled toward her dresser, avoiding scrutiny just as Evaline had done when she'd ducked out of view a few minutes earlier. "I'm not a baby."

"Maybe your father will stay."

"Fat chance," Allison blurted, "with Miss Twenty-Something on his boat. Knowing him, he'll probably forget to come up to the house."

Evaline couldn't predict what Gabriel might do, but for Allison's sake she hoped he'd remember to consider more than himself and Mandy this evening.

"Do you think he'll notice the deck?" Allison asked.

"It's rather dark. He might not. Would you like me to mention it if I see him?"

"Naw. It doesn't matter." Allison pulled her nightshirt out of a drawer.

Evaline watched her, certain that a lot of things mattered to Allison, but the girl had never been important to anyone, not even to her parents as far as she knew, so she hid her disappointment and vulnerability behind a tough facade.

"I'm sure he'll be surprised that you finished," Evaline remarked.

"He probably won't even notice."

"Yes he will, by the smell alone." Evaline wished she could put her arm around Allison's shoulders and give her a big hug, but knew the gesture wouldn't be tolerated. "Well, I'll say good night, now. Do you want help getting into bed?"

"I can do it."

"See you in the morning then."

"'Night."

Evaline closed Allison's door and strolled down the hall just in time to see the front door open.

"Is she decent?" Gabriel asked, nodding toward Allison's room.

"Knock first."

"All right." His glance swept swiftly down her figure and back. "I need to talk to you tonight. You're not going to bed yet, are you?"

"I have to bank the fire and tidy up the kitchen."

"I won't be long." He turned for the hallway, and she noticed he carried a paper shopping bag.

"Gabriel," she called out quietly. He stopped at the corner of the living room and looked over his shoulder.

"You did notice the deck, didn't you?"

"Yes. Didn't want to walk on it, as a matter of fact." His dark eyebrows raised. "Did she do the whole thing?"

Evaline nodded. "She worked on it from noon until dinnertime."

A pleased expression blossomed on Gabriel's face, which only served to heighten his newly acquired attractiveness.

"She's sure you won't have noticed."

He shook his head and continued up the hall.

"Say something nice," she called after him, knowing he could be insensitive.

Evaline fussed over the fire and wondered what was being discussed in the room up the hall. A few minutes later, Gabriel returned, carrying the bag in one hand and Allison's cassette player in the other. He set the machine

on the dining-room table and put the bag on the floor.
Then he pulled a plastic container of small screwdrivers
out of his back pocket and sat down.

"What do I smell?" he asked, sniffing and peering into
the darkened kitchen.

"The deck oil?"

"No. Something kind of cinnamony."

"Oh, that's the apple pie I baked this afternoon."

"Smells good." He slipped a screwdriver out of the
case.

"Would you like a piece?" she asked.

"Yeah." He glanced at her. "If it isn't any trouble."

"Not at all. That's why I came down to the boat, to ask
you and Skeeter if you wanted pie, and then I saw that
Skeeter wasn't with you." Her voice trailed off, and she was
grateful for a reason to leave the table and his presence.

"Mandy probably would've liked a piece of pie."

"I thought you and she"—Evaline reached for a plate—
"were busy."

"We were. But I'll always stop for pie. That's something you can count on." He grinned as she carried a plate
to him. She didn't quite know how to interpret his words
or his expression. He seemed to have made himself at
home in the dining room, and didn't appear to be in a
hurry to leave.

"Want some milk to go with it?" she asked.

"Sure. Thanks."

Gabriel managed to unscrew and remove the back of
the cassette player before she returned. Though he was a
big man, his fingers were deft and slender, obviously
meant for fine work. She put the glass on the table and sat
down as Gabriel lifted a forkful of pie into his mouth. He
chewed and shook his head.

"Damn, that's good," he commented. "Melts in your
mouth."

"Thanks. The secret is putting a little butter in the crust."

He took another bite and sipped his milk, regarding her over the rim of the glass, squinting slightly, which she had deduced was his usual expression when he wasn't sure of what to say.

"Did Allison mention your haircut?" Evaline inquired.

"No, but she sure stared."

"You do look really different."

"I forget sometimes about the beard and all," he commented, "living alone like I do." He tipped the cassette player to the light. "Hmm. Everything looks all right. I'll have to check for bad connections."

"Did you tell her you noticed the deck?"

"Of course." He peered at a voltmeter as he tested the circuits of the machine. "Gave her a reward."

"You did? What?"

"Got her some magazines to read and a couple of novels."

Evaline was pleased. "Good," she said. "I'll bet she'll enjoy them."

"Got you something, too." He threw a sidelong glance at her.

Evaline paused. She was totally unaccustomed to receiving gifts. "You did?" she stuttered.

Gabriel reached into the bag and pulled out a magazine which he kept rolled up. He gave it to her, his eyes twinkling mischievously. Evaline accepted the magazine, but seeing the devilish gleam in his eyes, she prepared herself for a prank. Slowly she let the cover uncurl in her hands while she read the banner.

"*Guns & Ammo* magazine?" she exclaimed, cocking an eyebrow and than batting her lashes. "Why, Mr. Townsend, you shouldn't have!"

He sat back in his chair while he gazed at her, his gray eyes turning to quicksilver in merriment.

"Thought you might find some pointers in there to improve your aim."

"How thoughtful of you!" She made a big show of flipping through the glossy pages. "And look! Rifle cartoons!"

Gabriel laughed again and reached down into the bag once more to bring out a cardboard box, which he set on the table in front of her.

"Here's what I really got for you," he said, sobering.

Evaline surveyed the carton. "A phone?"

"A cellular phone." He pushed it closer. "Go ahead, open it. You can use it in case of emergency, or to contact me when I'm out with my clients. I was told the range would extend that far if you go out on the deck away from the trees."

"This is great!" Evaline said, pulling open one end. "I'll feel much safer with a link to the outside world."

"I arranged for service weeks ago, but never had time to pick up the phone."

Evaline held the small black receiver in her hand. "This is perfect."

"Great. I'll feel better knowing you and Allison won't be stuck out here without being able to call for help."

"Me too."

"Not that I expect anything will happen when I'm gone. But just in case."

Evaline nodded and inspected the little buttons of the sleek new phone. Just knowing she could call the police took a load off her mind.

"Thanks, Gabriel," she said.

He nodded and reached for the pie, finishing it in a few gulps.

"I just hope Allison doesn't find out about this," she remarked, "and decides to call some boy in Greece."

"She has a boyfriend in Greece?"

"I believe we should talk in plurals when mentioning boys."

"Boyfriends?"

"Yes." Evaline gave him a wry smile and held up the phone. "This little present could cost you."

"Keep it our little secret then."

"What about her grandparents?"

Gabriel frowned. "The less she talks to them, the better."

"But they're her relatives."

"That doesn't mean diddly-squat."

Evaline thought of her father, committing crimes and lying for years about his complicity in a murder. She looked down, letting her silent agreement speak for itself.

Gabriel picked up the back of the cassette deck. "I'll give you a list of important numbers in the morning before I leave."

"Okay."

"You think you can handle it?"

"You mean Allison and The Major?"

"Yes."

"For two days? Certainly."

"Good. I've lost quite a bit of business in the last few months. I'd be hurting financially if I turned this bunch away."

"Don't worry, Gabriel." She gave him what she meant to be a brave, confident smile.

He studied her, his serious eyes boring into hers. Not many men had looked at her in such a fashion. Other men had been more flirtatious than sincere, and she hadn't taken them seriously. With Gabriel, however, the situation was different. They had Allison's welfare as a common worry, and affairs regarding the house to discuss. Their link was more practical and real than she had ever experienced with a man. She'd never shared a day-to-day existence with a man other than her father, had never cooked for a man outside her family, and had never known the satisfaction of seeing people consume and relish the dishes she created in her kitchen. In fact, she'd never felt as close to a human being as she did at this moment, sitting at the table with Gabriel, talking while he puttered with fixing Allison's tape deck.

Evaline had the strongest urge to reach across the space between them and touch the side of Gabriel's face, to see if his lean cheek felt as smooth as it looked. She had a compelling desire to tilt her face up to his and see how warm his lips would feel pressed against hers and to discover what it felt like to be surrounded by his capable arms again. No man had ever kissed her, except for a guy in the reservation casino who had forced himself on her. And she tried not ever to think about that incident.

Gabriel was different than other men she'd met. He'd treated her honestly, almost fraternally, as if he didn't perceive her as an attractive woman. He called her City Girl, as though her good grooming and good looks counted against her in his world. Odd how she'd reacted to his disinterest and disdain, for instead of pushing him away, she was contemplating kissing him. A delicious ache fanned out in her belly at the thought of touching him, confounding her, for it wasn't like her to succumb to a man so soon or so easily. And in Gabriel's case, succumbing wasn't a good idea, for he had Mandy to consider, and she had her professional reputation to uphold. Being attracted to the father of her patient while living in close quarters with them was not something she should choose to act upon, if she had any sense. And Evaline prided herself on her common sense.

"You know, Evaline," Gabriel remarked, still studying her, his eyes narrowing. "I get the feeling I've seen you somewhere before. Do I look familiar to you?"

His question startled her. She wasn't ready to discuss how they'd met years earlier. "Where would we have ever met?" she asked, rising to grab his empty plate off the table. Quickly, before he could ask anything else, she headed into the kitchen. She lingered over cleaning his dishes and putting away the pie, and by the time she was finished, she saw Gabriel screwing on the back of the cassette player.

She returned to the dining room. "Find anything wrong?" she asked, guessing that he hadn't.

"Nope. Works fine." He scowled and stood up. "But I wish I *had* found something wrong."

"Me too." She picked up the cellular phone. "Well, I'm going to turn in. Good night."

He glanced down at her. "I'm going to check on The Major." He grabbed the tape deck. "Then I'm going to crash on the couch, in case Allison has another bad night."

"You mean the couch here in the house?"

"Where else?" His eyebrows raised. "Do you have a problem with that?"

"Of course not," she replied hastily, more perplexed than ever. What about his plans with cute little Mandy on his boat?

11

Evaline's alarm rang at six o'clock the next morning and she shut it off, amazed to have slept through the night without an incident in Allison's room. She rose, took a shower in the master bath, and walked back into the bedroom, naked. A full-length mirror on the closet door caught her eye, and she turned sideways to view herself. Small-boned and trim, with silky black hair that reached to her waist, Evaline knew she had an attractive figure—as long as the lights were off and the purple-blue scars on her upper torso and arms couldn't be seen.

She pivoted slightly and glanced at her breasts, which were small but firm. Her gaze traveled down her body to her waist, which curved in at her slender hips. Many Saquinnish women had large torsos and short legs, but she'd been blessed with fine shoulders, a willowy body, and long, shapely legs. She framed the top of her hips with her hands and wondered what it would be like to feel Gabriel's fingers splayed there. His fingertips would probably meet at her navel, since she was so small in comparison to him. She flushed at the thought of him standing behind her, holding her against his body, and glared at her face in the mirror.

"No more, Evaline Jaye," she warned herself. "Don't be a fool."

The wolf attack had been directed at her father, who had been cursed by the wolf clan for stealing artifacts from an ancient village. But something had gone terribly wrong, and she had been the one to suffer the nearly fatal assault and resulting horrendous disfigurement. For eleven years she'd faced a world that had averted its eyes whenever she appeared, had endured the awful hush when a crowd took notice of her, had known the frustration of seeing the questioning eyes of children who wanted to learn what happened to the lady, but whose mothers hustled them away before she could explain. Such reactions had taught her to remain in the shadows, to avoid public life, and to forget the idea of ever having a physical relationship with a man.

She tore her gaze from the reflection and her thoughts from Gabriel, and hurriedly dressed in jeans and a red T-shirt. Then she pulled on a University of Washington sweatshirt to ward off the summer-morning chill, braided her hair, and slipped out of her room.

Gabriel lay on the couch in the living room, still asleep, his bare shoulders half-covered by a blanket. Evaline paused for a moment to study him while he slept. Already a shadow of beard darkened the lean planes of his face, but the stubble only served to increase his raw masculinity, which Evaline was discovering had an undeniable appeal to her. His lashes, much fuller and longer than hers, brushed the top of his ruddy-colored cheeks, and his hair, almost as dark as hers, fell over his forehead in a thick fringe. She wished she could reach out and smooth his hair back with her fingers, but knew she must keep her hands to herself.

Instead she quietly built a fire, careful not to wake him, and then noiselessly replaced the fire screen.

She left him sleeping and moved into the kitchen to prepare breakfast: thin slices of ham, hash browns, bran muffins, and boiled eggs. Just as the coffee was done brewing, and she was reaching into the cupboard to get two mugs, she heard a step behind her. Evaline glanced over her shoulder to find Gabriel padding through the doorway of the kitchen, his jeans riding low on his lean hips, and his shirt hanging from his right hand. His hair was tousled, and his eyes were clouded with sleepiness, but Evaline found his morning look endearing, and wondered if he had thought the same of her yesterday when he brought coffee to her bed.

"'Mornin'," he said, running the palm of his hand down the rippled plane of his muscular abdomen.

"Hi." She set the mugs on the counter. "You're just in time for coffee."

"Good. I need something to jolt me into consciousness."

"Have a bad night?" She offered a cup to him.

"Thanks." He accepted the steaming mug. "Yeah, that couch isn't designed for a guy like me. But Allison didn't have any problems last night, did she? I didn't hear anything."

"Neither did I."

"Good." Gabriel sipped his coffee. "Maybe it *was* just coincidence the other times."

"Maybe." Evaline checked the hash browns frying on the stove and was startled when Gabriel stepped up behind her to peer over her shoulder, almost as though he'd read her thoughts earlier that morning and had decided to fulfill her fantasy.

"Mmm," he said. "Those look great."

"They're almost done." Nervously, she pushed at the

edges of the golden patty, trying to ignore the way her back tingled at his nearness. Her spine and shoulders felt incredibly rigid. Evaline knew if she turned to face him, she'd see his spirit–aura of the bear. Her need to act as a proper hostess took over, however, so she remained still. "Do you think Mandy will want to join us?"

"I'll ask her." He moved away, taking his seductive warmth with him. "I'll check on The Major, too, if I have time."

"I'd say ten minutes for everything to get done."

"Great." He set his empty cup on the counter and pulled on his shirt. "Why don't you wake Allison up while I'm down at the boat? I'd like to see her before I go this morning."

"Okay, and don't forget to jot down those telephone numbers."

"Right." He buttoned the front of his shirt. "Skeeter should be here about nine with the divers."

"He flies them in on his seaplane?"

"Yeah." Gabriel unzipped his jeans and deftly stuffed the tails of his shirt in his pants. Evaline averted her gaze, suddenly flushed from the heat of the stove or the casual intimacy of his behavior, she wasn't certain which. She snatched off the lid of the eggs and checked to see they were simmering gently so none of the shells would crack, thankful to have a necessary distraction to keep her busy.

"I'll be back," he said behind her.

"All right."

She heard him walk through the living room and go out the front door. Only when she heard his last footfall on the stairs did she relax. For her sake, she was glad that Gabriel would be gone for the next few days. His absence would give her the opportunity to put him in a more realistic perspective, for certainly both her imagination and her appetite were running dangerously out of control.

*   *   *

Two hours later, Evaline watched the divers carrying their tanks and gear to the *Sea Wolf* as she rinsed the dishes in the sink. Allison sat in her chair near the dishwasher, loading it without having been asked.

"Gabriel said he brought you some reading material," Evaline commented. "What novels did he get?"

"A mystery and that autobiography by Katharine Hepburn."

"Do you like mysteries?"

"They're okay." Allison reached for a pile of silverware and carefully arranged them in the plastic holder, separating the forks, knives, and spoons without being told.

"What kind of books do you really like?"

"I don't know. Historical ones, I guess."

"I do, too. I brought a few if you'd like to borrow them."

"Great."

"I'll bring them in when we finish your exercises."

Allison nodded and closed the dishwasher. "That Mandy is sure an airhead," she remarked.

"She's young, that's all."

"I don't know what my father sees in her."

"She's cute."

Allison shrugged. "I guess she is. But I still don't like her."

"We might be wrong in assuming they're interested in each other."

"Get real!" Allison rolled her eyes. "Didn't you see the way she looked at him? She wanted to jump on him."

Evaline knew exactly what Allison meant. Breakfast had been difficult for her to bear, with Mandy chattering through the meal, trying to coax Allison into talking, just as Skeeter had done. Mandy's perky personality was the type that dominated conversations and ran roughshod over reserved people like Evaline. Gabriel seemed content to sit there as Mandy rambled on, and he actually smiled at her a few times. As usual, Allison showed little interest in talking, just like her father, although Evaline caught her intently surveying Mandy across the table. The girl had shown up for breakfast mainly to check out her father's girlfriend, and had admitted as much to Evaline as she rolled down the hall to the dining room. That she didn't approve of her father's companion secretly pleased Evaline.

"Do you think your father likes Mandy?" Evaline asked casually, wiping down the counter.

"Men always like cute women," Allison answered. "Haven't you ever noticed men will go after just about anything with boobs and a smile?"

"Allison!" Evaline chided, trying not to grin.

"It's true! Men's brains are in their pants! And One-Eyed Willy does all the thinking."

"Allison!" Evaline sputtered, turning crimson. Never having had a close female friend, she'd never engaged in such ribald talk, and was embarrassed by the turn in the conversation.

"You're blushing!" Allison exclaimed, rolling closer, a crooked smile on her lips. "God, Evaline, you'd think you'd never heard the word penis before."

"Of course I have." Evaline rinsed the dishcloth, hoping her flush would subside. She rarely thought about men's reproductive organs, much less talked about them. It wasn't a subject she'd ever broached with her father in her youth or to anyone in her adult years. And never having had a lover, she hadn't grown accustomed to talking about such male attributes.

"Penis. Penis. Penis!" Allison chanted beside her, then giggled and sputtered until tears rolled out of her eyes.

Evaline turned and planted her hands on her hips. "That's enough, young lady," she said but couldn't keep from grinning. "Now go on, get out of my kitchen! Shoo!"

"Penis! Penis! Penis!" Allison repeated, rolling toward the living room, still laughing.

Evaline watched her go, pleased at how far she and Allison had come in the past few days. Three days ago, she wouldn't have dreamed she and Allison would ever laugh together. A warm flood of satisfaction poured through her, accompanied by a deeper glow of connection. As unbelievable as it seemed, Evaline was beginning to care for the girl and to appreciate her spirited if stubborn character. More than ever she doubted Allison was capable of killing anyone.

Before Evaline had recovered from the barrage of new sensations, she heard a knock on the kitchen door that led to the deck. She wondered if Gabriel had come to say good-bye, but then eliminated the possibility, for he would have come in without knocking. Evaline passed through the kitchen and opened the door, surprised to see a small, middle-aged redhead standing on the deck.

"Yes?" Evaline asked.

"I have a message from Stephen Durrell," the woman said, glancing over her shoulder at the boat, as though worried about being spotted at the house.

"What is it?"

"He wants you to call him. Today. This number." She thrust a piece of paper into Evaline's hands. "I have to run," she said. And before Evaline could ask her anything more, the woman turned and hurried across the deck to the stairs.

Evaline glanced at the paper in her hand, wondering why the woman was so anxious not to be seen. What was there to hide? Then she thought of Stephen Durrell's suspicions that Gabriel was a violent man, and the woman's odd behavior made sense. She slipped the telephone number in the pocket of her jeans and smiled. Stephen would be relieved to hear that Gabriel Townsend was proving to be a decent guy, and not the monster everyone thought he was. So far, the only potential danger he presented was to her wavering self-control.

Hours later, after the *Sea Wolf* was long gone and the mat exercises were completed, Evaline left Allison on the deck. Allison was eager to start reading one of her historicals in the sunshine, so Evaline returned to her room to use the phone. Much to her surprise, she learned that Stephen Durrell was in the area and wanted to pay a short visit. Allison invited him for dinner. He declined, having urgent business in Seattle that night, but said he could drop by in midafternoon. Evaline baked chocolate chip cookies and brewed sun tea on the deck rail in preparation for his visit.

A few minutes after two, she heard The Major wailing stridently, and rushed out onto the deck to see what was wrong, just in time to spot Stephen getting out of a white Jaguar sedan. The bear cub, apparently distressed by the appearance of a stranger, paced his enclosure and clawed at the fence, desperate to break free. Evaline hadn't seen him exhibit such unusual behavior when Mandy or the divers arrived. *Why now?*

Evaline strolled to the top of the stairs as Stephen walked through bands of light blazing between the cedars. At two o'clock, the temperature of the late June day had climbed to nearly eighty degrees, subduing the chattering animals in the forest behind the house, except for The Major, who continued to bawl.

"Hi," Evaline greeted.

"Good afternoon," Stephen replied, glancing over his shoulder. "That's a bear over there, isn't it?"

"Yes, he's an orphan Gabriel rescued. He has a broken leg."

"Noisy little fellow."

"Only sometimes." She opened the door. "Come in."

"Thank you." Stephen passed into the living room, took off his sunglasses, and discreetly inspected the surroundings while Evaline closed the door behind them. He was dressed in off-white trousers and a salmon-colored shirt with the cuffs folded neatly upon his forearms. He wore a gold bracelet on one wrist and an expensive watch on the other, and she noticed that his nails were perfectly contoured, most likely manicured. As if conscious of her regard, he slipped his hands into his pockets. "Ah, it's nice and cool in here."

Evaline nodded. "Yes. The house stays fairly decent on hot days." She motioned toward the couch. "Won't you sit down?"

"Thank you." He sank to the seat cushion.

"Would you like some iced tea?"

"That would be marvelous." He sighed and sat back, stretching his right arm along the top of the couch. "Where's Allison?"

"In her room, listening to music, I believe." Evaline glanced down the hall toward the bedroom. "Shall I have her come out?"

"I'd like to see her."

Evaline took a step toward the hallway but paused when Stephen rose to his feet and held up his hands.

"Oh, don't bother getting her, Evaline," he said. "I'll just look in on her while you get the tea."

"All right."

Evaline walked to the kitchen, where she arranged cookies, sugar, and tea on a tray, taking her time so that

Stephen would have a few minutes alone with Allison. Outside, The Major cried louder than ever. Worried that a wild animal might be trying to molest him, Evaline craned her neck so she could see the bear at the side of the house. Nothing out of the ordinary caught her eye—only trees and bushes and grass. Still the bear paced and cried. Whatever was bothering The Major was really starting to bother Evaline, for his voice carried well in the still heat, setting her nerves on edge.

Wondering how she'd ever be able to concentrate on a conversation with Stephen while The Major carried on, she picked up the tray and headed for the living room. She set the tray on the coffee table, then ambled down the hall to see if Allison wished to join them for a snack. Allison's door stood open, and Evaline walked into the bedroom, hoping Allison's behavior would reflect the progress they'd made in the last few days. But when it came to either of the Townsends—Allison or Gabriel—Evaline could never predict what path their mercurial natures would take.

Her hopes were dashed immediately when she took in the scene before her. Silent as a statue, Allison sat in her wheelchair by the window, mostly shielded by Stephen Durrell, who stood in front of the girl, inclined at a strange angle toward her, seeming to whisper a secret in her ear. His right elbow hung in the air, as if he held something in front of Allison's face. Evaline paused, struck by the peculiar attitude and even more so by the misty animal shape which quickly materialized and surrounded Stephen's body. Evaline's chest tightened with unease.

Against the white wall of the house, the shape was even more distinct than before and rose above Stephen's head and shoulders in the unmistakable curled horns of a ram. Then he turned at the sound of her step, and the vision vanished.

He straightened at once and smiled at her in a golden expression of peace and goodwill, his figure still blocking her view of Allison. He slipped his right hand into his trousers. Evaline wondered if he was hiding something in his pocket. The gesture was a familiar one for him, so Evaline pushed back her suspicions and returned his smile, knowing hers was a pale rendition of the jaunty expression on his face.

"Is everything all right?" she asked.

"Of course."

Before she could move, Stephen strode toward her.

"How about that iced tea?" he asked cheerfully.

Evaline craned her neck to see around him to Allison. "What about you, Allison?" she asked. "Care to join us?"

Allison stared at her blankly, her unused headphones like a thick collar around her neck.

"Allison," Evaline repeated. "Did you hear what I said?"

Allison blinked, but the dreamy look in her eyes remained. Evaline's unease deepened, and she lurched forward, but Stephen detained her.

"She's okay," he explained with a well-practiced chuckle. "She's just rummy. I'm afraid I woke her up from a nap."

"Oh."

"I'm not even sure she knew who I was for a minute, there."

A small amount of relief passed through Evaline. Stephen had probably been bending close to get Allison's attention. Nothing to worry about, surely. Stephen was a decent man, evidenced by his solicitous visit to a remote area, just to check on Allison's well-being. *How many people*, she asked herself, *would go to such trouble?* Still, her intuitive sense told her the undercurrent was at odds with what her eyes were seeing.

Evaline decided to put on an amiable front. "She does tend to nap during the day."

He guided her out to the hall and shut the door behind them.

"She still isn't sleeping well?" he asked.

"No." She led him back to the living room.

"Other than her sleeping problems, how is everything going?" Stephen waited for her to sit down. Then he took a seat, as she bent to the tray on the coffee table.

"Better than I expected."

"Townsend is behaving himself?"

"He's obnoxious but hasn't threatened Allison or me in any way."

"That's a welcome bit of news."

She gave him a tall glass of tea. "In fact, I can't see Gabriel hurting anyone. He might yell once in a while, but he doesn't strike out."

"I wouldn't trust him, though," Stephen replied, sipping his drink. "He's probably just deceiving you."

"I don't think so." Evaline frowned and stared at the hearth, where last night's fire had long since burned itself out. She knew if she were prudent, she should continue to distrust Gabriel, but each day she spent in his company chipped away at the notion that he was physically violent.

"He's a wily one," Stephen added. "That's what Meredith told me."

"He seems to have Allison's best interests at heart."

"I wouldn't trust that either."

"Maybe he's changed from the time Meredith knew him. That must have been years ago. Twelve or so, right?"

"Yes. But a leopard can't change his spots, Evaline. If a man grows up violent, chances are he'll remain violent as an adult."

"I'll keep an open mind," Evaline remarked. "But I think you might be wrong about Gabriel."

"As long as you remain on your guard."

"I will."

Stephen reached for a cookie. "What about your medical progress with Allison? How is she doing?"

"Physically not much has changed. Emotionally, she's beginning to open up to me. But as I said, she's having trouble sleeping at night."

"She's still taking her medication, isn't she? The doctors assured me the pills would help her sleep."

"They do in a way. But then she's drowsy during the day." Evaline took a drink of her tea. "Personally, I'd like to take her off the tricyclic antidepressant and see what happens."

"I don't think that would be wise. Allison is a high-strung girl, Evaline, and she's been through a considerable trauma."

"Sometimes an antidepressant like the one she's taking can interfere with a patient's ability to recover their memory loss."

"If that's the price we have to pay in Allison's case," Stephen put in, "so be it. I would much rather have her remember the accident when she is mentally capable of dealing with it, than do so prematurely and to her detriment. It would be best for her to keep taking the prescribed medication, I'm sure."

Evaline paused in thought. Allison was far from being emotionally stable. Still, she wondered why Stephen wouldn't consider a new approach. She sighed. "Perhaps you're right."

Stephen patted her forearm. "We must have patience in this matter, Evaline. With time, perhaps Allison will get better. But I dread to contemplate what might happen to her state of mind if she is pressured into remembering too much too soon. It might destroy her. Even I have trouble facing the days sometimes, knowing Meredith is gone."

His voice trailed off, and he looked down as though hiding raw emotions from her.

"I understand," Evaline answered softly. She waited a moment to permit him to regain his composure.

Stephen put down his glass and stood up, his back to the fireplace. "I hate to run off so quickly, Evaline, but I have an important meeting tonight that I have to get back for."

"That's all right."

"Why don't we make a date to meet in about two weeks—say July tenth, so you can update me on Allison's progress."

"Okay."

"I'll meet you at the end of the drive at two P.M. There's a pull-off there by the main road. Try not to let Gabriel see you. Heaven knows how he might react."

"It would be just fine for you to come to the house."

"No." He held up a hand. "Let's keep this between ourselves for a while longer, Evaline. I think it would be best for Allison's sake."

Just then a sudden gust of air roared down the chimney and blasted a flurry of ashes and soot onto the back of Stephen's pants. He whirled around, horrified, while Evaline pointed at his legs.

"Mr. Durrell!" Evaline gasped, jumping to her feet. "Your pants!"

He twisted at the waist to assess the damage to his expensive trousers and swore under his breath.

"I don't understand it!" Evaline exclaimed, checking the damper. "The flue is closed! How could this have happened?"

"My pants are ruined!" Stephen cried. "Absolutely ruined. Look at them! The soot will never come out!"

"A dry cleaner might be able to help."

He ignored her suggestion. "Dammit!" Stephen glared

at the fireplace. "Where'd a breeze come from on a day like this?"

"We're finding there are strange air currents in this house," Evaline explained, but only half-convinced by her own words. "Doors have been shutting by themselves. That sort of thing."

"Well, Townsend had better check out his chimney," Stephen growled. "What a mess." He stomped to the door. "I should send him the bill."

"Why don't you? It would be perfectly understandable."

Stephen yanked open the front door and strode to the top of the stairs. He turned, his usually calm expression pinched with irritation. "Remember. July tenth. Two o'clock. Call me if anything changes."

"All right." She leaned on the banister. "I'm sorry about your pants, Mr. Durrell."

"So am I." He hurried down the stairs and shot a perturbed glance at the still bawling bear.

Evaline watched Stephen start his car and tear up the gravel lane, his abrupt driving betraying his anger. Then she headed for The Major's enclosure to see if the splint had shifted, causing the bear to wail.

By the time she got to the cage she could no longer hear the engine of Stephen's car, and the cub's cries had broken off.

"What's wrong with you, little brother?" she inquired softly, squatting down on her haunches. She knew from childhood stories that animals sensed things long before humans, and they were sometimes sent as harbingers of good or evil, depending upon the animal that appeared. Bears symbolized strength and protection. But how could an injured cub weighing less than a hundred pounds protect anyone from anything?

"Were you sent to us?" Evaline asked.

The bear cocked his head and stared at her, his small brown eyes glittering and his sturdy frame posed to bolt.

"I won't hurt you," she promised. "Don't be afraid." She visually inspected the splint as best as she could from her position at the fence, but could see nothing amiss, except for a frayed portion of her sock where he'd tried to chew through it.

"No more crying, Major," she admonished. "You know what happened to the boy who cried wolf, don't you?"

The bear stared at her, unmoving, his gaze unwavering, while her own words sunk in. She shivered at the memory of wolves and stood up. "Be good now, brother bear."

Evaline gave him one last look and then headed back to the house, unable to explain what had prompted the cub to raise such a fuss. What was it about this place that gave rise to so many unanswerable questions? Even though the air was hot and humid, she shuddered again, recalling the visions she'd seen in the last few days. She glanced at the house where Allison's bedroom window reflected a benign canvas of sky and trees, while something far from benign lurked on the other side of the glass.

Now that Gabriel was gone, Evaline could try any therapy she liked on Allison, and not have to defend her techniques or worry about being interrupted. Tonight was her opportunity to contact the spirits—if there were spirits in that room—and search for an explanation for the disturbances.

The time had come to go beyond white medical practice.

12

Evaline waited to perform the spirit ceremony until late that evening, when Allison was asleep, worn out by a busy day of exercises and target practice. Around eleven-thirty Evaline slipped into the bedroom with her supplies, moving quietly, so as not to disturb the girl even though Allison had slept through much louder noises during her nightmares. Regardless, Evaline worried that she would be discovered and forced to explain what she was doing. Allison wouldn't understand, and Gabriel wouldn't even try to understand. If he found out Evaline had practiced spiritual healing on his daughter, he might forbid her to see the girl. Evaline had no desire to relinquish her treatment of Allison or give up the progress they'd made.

She lit the cedar tips she'd gathered earlier that evening, waited until the flames caught and held, then blew them out. Fragrant smoke wafted from the small dish in Evaline's hand, rising in a feathery column toward the shadowed ceiling. Using the flat of her hand, Evaline gently fanned the smoke toward her face and torso. A healer from the reservation would have used a feather fan, but she had no such equipment, for she had left her childhood home carrying nothing with her but memories.

After she had cleansed the front of her body, she swept the smoke across her back and legs. Then she slowly strolled around the perimeter of the room, keeping her mind focused on the cleansing process by softly singing the sacred song of the sea otter, a song handed down through her family on her mother's side. After Evaline had smudged each corner of the room and the space around Allison's bed, she smothered the smoldering cedar tips and sat down in the center of the room.

She continued the sacred song until it was finished, and then she began a prayer to the spirits, asking her power animal, the lynx, for guidance in healing Allison. At first the phrases came with difficulty, clouded by four years of disuse, years during which she hadn't uttered a single word in her native language. The strange clicking sounds and glottal pronunciations felt foreign to her tongue and throat, and she flushed with the realization that in four years she had lost a considerable part of herself—a part which had once meant everything to her. She wouldn't have believed she could forget the prayers of her childhood, and yet they came slowly now, like hinges weathered rusty by salt and rain.

Still, Evaline pressed on, determined to help Allison in any way possible, and to pursue the source of the strange events which had occurred the past few nights at the house. More than ever she was certain Allison's affliction was of the spirit and not of the body. Modern medical practices did not reach into the supernatural world—the only place she was sure the answers to her questions could be found.

Not long into the prayer, she felt something soft, like a tuft of animal fur, brush past her cheek. Evaline opened her eyes to find teeny sparkling dots near the wall by the window, the first evidence that spirits had arrived. During ceremonies at the tribal center she'd seen such small lights before. Other people who were present had felt the whisper-light touches and had seen the lights as well, but for most that was all they'd experienced. Only a handful of people, those with a special link to the spirit world, were granted stronger visions. Evaline had been one of the select few who had seen power animal shapes enveloping both the men and women of her people.

Shutting her eyes again, she intensified her concentration and the strength of her conviction, asking for the spirit in the house to make itself known to her. If there was a reason for the spirit to attach itself to Allison, she asked that the reason be given. Then Evaline fell silent, listening intently for music in the air. Sometimes a shaman could hear the song of a foreign spirit, and if so, could repeat it and bring the spirit forward. Once the spirit appeared, a shaman could communicate with the being and in doing so, cure his patient by finding out why the spirit was troubling the mortal or by convincing the ghost to go somewhere else, through the use of persuasive words or force.

Evaline had little confidence in her ability to hear a spirit song, much less to dispel a malicious ghost, for she was no shaman. Her people had been without an official shaman since the death of Carter Greyson's great-grandfather more than fifty years ago. All she knew of shamans were the stories told to her by her father and the tales she had read in books.

Many shamans had been born into the Wolf Clan, her family clan, including some powerful female shamans, and she had often wondered if she possessed the heart and mind of a shaman. Evaline had known all her life that she was different, as most shamans were, and the wolf attack which had left her scarred and broken, had only increased her isolation from the rest of humanity. Perhaps if she had found a mentor in her childhood, she would have developed her innate shamanic skills. But she had grown up relatively alone and untutored. All she could do now was work with scraps of memory and bits of information she'd gleaned over the years and hope that her innate talent would make up for her lack of formal training.

Evaline remained seated in the center of the room, listening intently, but as the minutes ticked by nothing happened. Perhaps her eardrums had suffered damage the previous night during the loud music incident, because all she could hear was a faint echo of the rock 'n' roll ballad that had blared out of Allison's tape deck.

"If I could go back to a time," the male singer crooned, *"the time I spent with you—"*

She tried to block out the song, but it persisted in her thoughts until she gave up trying to hear anything else. Finally, Evaline decided to give up the ritual altogether. She sighed, then smiled at her own silliness. She'd been a fool to think she could perform a ritual and contact a ghost, especially after such a long, self-imposed hiatus from attending any sacred ceremonies. During her college years in Seattle, she hadn't prayed or fasted at all. She wasn't worthy of success. And it was glaringly obvious she had failed to make contact. No spiritual being she had ever heard about had been represented by a modern song.

Shaking her head at her own naïveté, Evaline opened her eyes, and instantly froze in shock. Directly in front of her, not more than two feet away, floated a column of shifting blue light about five feet high. Evaline stared at the undulating shape, too flabbergasted to move backward and too overwhelmed by the thunder of her heart pounding inside her chest to think of getting away. She had an unshakable feeling that the being made of light was studying her, intently staring at her, considering. Considering what? Reaching out and killing her?

Evaline tried to scream, but her jaw wouldn't unclench, and her dry tongue stuck to the roof of her mouth. She thought of rolling to the side and scrambling out of the way, but her jeans seemed to be glued to the pine floor. All she could do was gape at the flickering blue cloud and wonder how she could tell whether a spirit was bad or good. Surely the color emanating from the being had some significance. What did blue mean? Good? Wouldn't an evil spirit have a dark or muddy aura?

Uncertain and terrified, Evaline stared, until the adrenaline rush passed through her, leaving her arms and legs wobbly.

"Who are you?" she gasped, finally able to form sounds with her parched lips. "What do you want?"

The shape shifted at the top, flaring wider for an instant, then dropping back to a narrow column, and spreading wider again, as if a bellows pushed it in and out. Evaline heard a muffled sound, like a voice from another room carrying through the wall. She could hear the tone and the inflection of a female voice, but couldn't make sense of the words. The spirit was speaking to her, but the words couldn't translate through the supernatural world.

Evaline's initial fear of the being eased slightly, and she leaned forward. "Please, try again," she said. "I can't understand what you're saying."

The figure's shape billowed and flared at the top again, and once more the muted voice droned haltingly from a great distance and with considerable effort.

Evaline rose to her feet. "I can't understand the words," she declared. "What are you trying to tell me?"

The blue light hung in the air for a moment, flickering quietly. After a moment, it moved toward the nightstand, rolling and sparkling over the small piece of furniture.

Then, just like the first night of disturbance, the pile of cassettes fell to the floor. Evaline stared at them in alarm. The spirit had pushed them to the floor that night as well, in an effort to get their attention, only she and Gabriel hadn't realized the significance of the gesture.

She walked the few steps to the pile of cassettes, frightened by how weak she felt, and worried that her shaky knees would collapse under her. In her clumsy shuffle, her foot kicked one of the small plastic boxes, sending it spinning toward Allison's bed. Evaline reached down for the box and picked it up. She turned it over in her hands, to see if the title or artist bore any significance to the current situation. To her amazement, she'd picked up a tape containing the very song she'd heard echoing in her head a few minutes ago.

Her legs grew even shakier. How much more blatant did the spirit have to be until she made the connection? The rock 'n' roll ballad, "Time and Place," was the spirit song of this particular ghost. This spirit wasn't an ancient being. This spirit was a modern entity. And only one modern entity would have an obvious reason to haunt Allison.

"Meredith?" Evaline gasped, glancing up at the blue light.

Immediately, the cassette box grew warmer in her hands. Evaline gaped at the plastic container, hardly believing the sensation in her own fingertips. The cassette box was definitely warmer, almost hot, now. The words on the label swam before her eyes, as if melting from the heat. They swirled into spiral shapes that snagged her thoughts and dragged her into a world of dizzying circles and throbbing, ear-shattering drumbeats. Evaline watched the shapes, aware of being hypnotized but slowly succumbing to it and unable to stop herself. She staggered backward, feeling drunk or drugged, or both. She could no longer see, and her hearing was swiftly being obliterated by the deafening rhythm of hundreds of drums.

Then she heard the all-too-familiar sound of a wolf snarling. She cried out, flailing her arms, trying to ward off the creature, but her feet were rooted to the ground. There was no escape. She fell, crashing through the drums and careening into the spiraling shapes, whirling around and down and around and around, until everything went black.

"Evaline?" a voice called.

Evaline tried to move, but her body wouldn't respond. Her flesh seemed to have been melted and poured onto a hard surface, left to congeal into a flat, powerless shape.

"Evaline!" the voice repeated, more stridently.

Evaline managed to open one eye and was sorry she did, because a bright light blinded her, stabbing a shaft of pain through her head. She groaned and tried to move again, and had just enough strength to raise her cheek a few inches off the floor. Her neck was so stiff, she thought her spine would crack if she turned her head toward the voice.

"Evaline! What's wrong? What happened to you?"

She heard a frantic rustling noise and a soft creak, and not long afterward, Allison's wheelchair appeared at her elbow. Evaline gazed numbly at Allison's long bare feet and slender ankles, glad to see the girl was unharmed, and uncommonly relieved to be in the company of a flesh-and-blood human being. She'd definitely gone too far as an untutored shaman, and had entered a land not meant for the uninitiated. Wherever she'd been in the last few hours—and by the looks of the sunlight pouring into the room, she'd spent the entire night on the floor—the journey had been completely draining.

Evaline pushed at the floor with the palm of her right hand and wedged herself onto her side, feeling unusually enervated. Each movement sent a tremor of exhaustion through her arms.

"Are you okay?" Allison questioned, bending closer.

"I think so."

"What happened?"

"I'm not quite sure." The statement wasn't a lie. She had no idea what had transpired for the past few hours. "What time is it?"

Allison glanced at her alarm clock. "Nine."

"Nine?" Evaline grimaced. More than nine blank hours had flown by. "I must have fallen asleep!"

"On the floor?"

"I must have been more tired than I thought." Evaline rose to an elbow, but her shoulder muscles were so shaky she couldn't maintain the position long. She struggled to sit up, and Allison reached out to assist her. "Boy, am I stiff!" Evaline sputtered, hoping Allison didn't detect how her limbs were trembling.

"Are you sure you're okay?" Allison asked again. "You don't look so great."

"I just need to sit down for a minute," Evaline replied. "In the chair."

She rose on shaking legs and propelled herself to the chair by the nightstand, which was only a few steps away. But those few steps made her sweat with the effort. She collapsed into the soft cushions and lolled her head back, gasping for breath.

"You look like you could use some coffee," Allison stated, rolling past her.

"I don't think I can walk to the kitchen just yet—"

"I'll make it." Allison headed for the door.

Evaline didn't question whether Allison knew what she was doing. She had only enough energy to remain upright in the chair. She closed her eyes and fell into a state of semiconsciousness, and didn't wake up until Allison rolled back into the bedroom with a tray across her knees.

"Evaline?"

Evaline opened her eyes and focused her vision on the pale, worried face of the girl, wishing she could say something to allay Allison's fears, but not sure what was going on herself.

"That smells wonderful," she murmured. Her lips felt like rising bread dough, too large for her mouth to be able to form words properly. She let her weary gaze slip down Allison's torso to the tray, where the coffee carafe and two cups were balanced on top of Allison's knees. She watched as Allison carefully poured her a cup of coffee and held it out, grateful that the self-centered teenager had decided to take care of her.

"Thank you, Allison," she said. The cup was almost too heavy for her to hold. She took a small sip and then lowered the mug to her thigh and held it there while the beverage cooled.

Allison stirred her coffee, having put sugar and milk into her cup before coming back to the bedroom. She put the spoon down and looked over at Evaline. "Do you think you're sick?" she asked.

"I don't know. I'm just weak. I'll be all right soon. Just give me a minute."

Allison nodded and took a drink of her coffee. Then she noticed the small plate on the floor and pointed at it. Evaline followed her gaze and her heart sank. She wouldn't be able to keep Allison from learning what she'd been doing in her room during the night, not with evidence of the ritual in plain sight.

"What's that?" Allison asked.

Evaline licked her lips. "Some tips of cedar."

"Why are they in here?"

"I was smudging your room last night."

"You were what?"

"Smudging. It's a cleansing process."

"Never heard of it."

"It's something my people do before certain ceremonies."

"Your people?" Allison tilted her head. "What are you talking about?"

Evaline sipped her coffee, but her strength was not returning as quickly as she'd hoped. She had no energy left to keep secrets about herself from Allison. "I am a member of the Saquinnish tribe, Allison. And last night, I performed a Saquinnish healing ceremony, hoping it might help you."

"You're an Indian?" Allison's eyebrows raised.

Evaline nodded.

"I never would have guessed. I thought you were from the Philippines or something."

"Many people do."

"Where do the Saquinnish come from? Montana or somewhere?"

"No, Washington. Northeast of here across the water."

"So that's why you like riding horses and living out in the forest."

Evaline might have smiled at Allison's uninformed generalization about Native Americans, but she was too tired to do much more than put her coffee mug on the nightstand.

Allison cocked her head. "Do you always perform ceremonies for your patients?"

"No."

Evaline thought she detected a pleased flush passing across Allison's face. She sighed.

"Any better?" Allison asked.

"A bit. I'm just going to sit here for a few minutes." Evaline closed her eyes.

"Well, I'm going to take a shower."

"Fine. Holler if you need me."

She heard Allison move away, heard the clink of the ceramic mugs on the tray, and then she slipped into nothingness, exhausted.

When Evaline woke up again, she was startled to find herself still in the chair in Allison's room, sitting in the golden glow of late afternoon. She glanced at her watch to double-check the time, not believing she could have slept the entire day. But the hands on her watch indicated four-thirty. Gabriel would be home in a few hours. What if he found her incapacitated? Worse yet, what if something had happened to Allison while she'd been sleeping? Evaline had assured Gabriel that she could handle everything while he was gone, and if Allison had been hurt, she would never forgive herself.

Evaline swallowed and scrambled to her feet, thankful that her legs held her weight, slight as it was. She ran her palms over the sides of her head, testing the strength in her arms. The strange weariness had passed, much to her relief. She took a step toward the door, and found that her knees had returned to normal.

"Allison?" she called, hurrying to the open doorway.

No one answered. Desperate, fear gripped her. What if Allison fell in the bathroom and she hadn't heard her cries? Evaline lunged for the bathroom door and stuck her head into the shadowed room. No one was there.

"Allison?" she called, louder this time. "Allison, where are you?"

Evaline staggered down the hallway, damning herself for subjecting Allison to danger by attempting to contact the spirit world. She barreled across the living room and flung open the front door.

"Allison?" Her cry echoed in the cedar glen at the west side of the house, and carried into the forest.

"Evaline?"

Evaline whirled in the direction of the voice and spotted Allison at the door of The Major's cage. Utter relief poured over her like a warm shower. She stumbled across the deck and down the stairs, so happy at seeing Allison safe that she grinned like a fool.

"Allison!" she exclaimed, hurrying across the yard. "Are you all right?"

"Of course I'm all right. What do you think?" Allison stared at her, with a crooked smile of incredulity on her lips.

"Thank God!" She glanced at Allison's lap, where a metal bowl filled with apple slices perched on her thighs. "How did you get all the way out here?"

"Down that ramp." Allison pointed to the back of the house. "The grass was kind of hard to get across, but I made it."

"Why did you come out here?"

"The Major was bawling his head off." She glared at him, but not in an unkind way. "I had to do something!"

Evaline flushed. She hadn't even heard the bear. She wondered what else had gone on without her being aware.

"So I cut him up some stuff and brought it out here," Allison continued. "He likes to be fed by hand."

"You're kidding!" Evaline stared, astonished.

"I'm serious. He likes it when I hold out the food to

him." Allison pushed an apple slice through the wires of the cage. "See? Isn't he cute?"

The Major edged closer, never taking his eyes off Evaline. Then, warily, he stretched his neck out, just far enough to snatch the slice out of Allison's fingers.

"Wow!" Evaline exclaimed, making sure to keep her voice soft. "That's really something."

"I think he likes me."

"I think you're right."

Allison peered up at her. "Are you okay now?"

Evaline nodded. "But you shouldn't have let me sleep all day."

"You seemed to need it."

"But we didn't get to your exercises."

"So?" Allison laughed. "I got tons of upper body stuff just getting across the yard!"

"What about the rest of the day? Did anything else happen while I was asleep?"

"Nope. I mostly read."

Evaline heaved a sigh of relief, but was still concerned that she had blacked out while Allison was in her care. "Shall I help you back to the house?" she asked. "I'm going to start dinner."

"No, I'll stay out here for a while."

"Okay." Before thinking twice about the response she might get, Evaline patted Allison's shoulder and turned back toward the house.

The rest of the early evening was spent eating and cleaning up after the meal, and worrying about how she would approach Gabriel with a report of the last few days. She would have to find a way to relay everything, including Meredith's spiritual manifestation. Leaving out a single detail might put Allison in danger, and that was the last thing Evaline wanted to have happen.

Just as Evaline gave the counter a final wipe down, she heard two short blasts of a horn in the bay and looked out the window. The *Sea Wolf* motored toward shore, its running lights filtering through the deepening dusk.

13

"You did what?" Gabriel thundered.

Evaline jumped at the sound of outrage in his voice and instantly wished she had been able to control her reactions better. She'd get nowhere by cowering before his wrath. She turned from the sink, where a pile of abalone rested in a pail of water—a gift to Gabriel and Allison from the divers before they left earlier that evening—and faced him squarely.

"I performed a ritual."

"What kind of a ritual?" He planted his hands on his hips and glowered at her.

"A healing ritual."

"That damn voodoo crap? Is that what they taught you at school?"

"No. But as I said before, this thing going on with Allison isn't a medical problem."

"How do you know?"

"I sense it." She stood her ground and raised her chin. She had no other defense than a born-again faith in her intuition.

Gabriel stared at her. Deliberately he paced the floor around her, raking her with his disdainful regard. "You sense it!" he exclaimed. "Dammit, Evaline, you could have burned down the house—with you and Allison in it!"

No matter how much she wanted to look away, she kept her eyes leveled on his face. "The cedar tips posed no fire hazard."

"How do you know? You weren't even conscious!"

"I had no way of predicting I would lose consciousness. It never happened before."

"You told me you were responsible, you told me you could handle everything, and I come home to find out you slept half the time I was gone, like some . . . some . . . !"

"Gabriel, you know very well I'm not a slacker."

He glared at her, his right eye squinting at the outer corner, and she knew he was searching for something else to throw at her. "Well, that was damn poor judgment on your part!"

"I thought I could help her."

"If I'd wanted a quack's help, I would have hired that idiot, Stephen Durrell!"

"You can criticize me all you want," she countered, "but the fact is, I saw an entity in that room!"

"Now you're talking like Meredith again!" Gabriel swung away. "I thought you were different, Evaline. I thought you'd see through the hocus-pocus. But no—you're into the same kind of shit!"

"I don't know what Meredith was *into*, Gabriel," Evaline retorted, holding on to the last shreds of her composure. "But she's in this house now. And I think we should find out why."

"Bullshit."

"I saw what I saw."

"You were half-asleep."

"I was not. She tried to communicate with me."

"Why hasn't anyone else seen this ghost—me or Allison or Skeeter?"

"Because you won't even admit such a thing is possible!" She rolled her eyes. "You wouldn't believe in a ghost if it hit you over the head!"

"That's right." He punctured the air between them with his finger. "Because ghosts don't exist. And I don't want you practicing any more of your crazy rituals on my daughter. You got that?"

"I intend to try any kind of treatment that might help Allison."

"I told you before, Evaline, all that girl needs is some discipline."

"And I told you before that I don't agree." She crossed her arms over her chest. "And if you don't trust my judgment in treating her, Gabriel, maybe you should hire someone else."

He returned her heated glare with one of his own. "Maybe I will."

"All right then. I'll leave in the morning." She turned on her heel and marched down the hall toward Allison's room, with her pride stung and tears close to the surface.

"Where are you going?" Gabriel demanded behind her.

She stopped in her tracks but didn't look back. "I'm not leaving Allison alone in there."

"She's not your concern anymore." Gabriel stomped up behind her. "I'll take her down to the boat."

"Fine."

Evaline walked back to her room and shut her door with more force than necessary. For a moment she stood in the dark room, trying hard to collect herself. She didn't want to leave Obstruction Bay, but she couldn't stay if Gabriel doubted her. More importantly, she didn't want to leave Allison in danger, not from Gabriel so much, but from the spirit world. Yet there was nothing else she could do but leave. The only way she could help Allison was to tap into her Saquinnish knowledge and find a way to talk to Meredith's spirit, but Gabriel had made it clear he wouldn't allow it. Under such a restriction, it would be useless for her to stay.

A few minutes later, Evaline heard Gabriel's voice in the hall, talking tersely to Allison. Evaline listened in the darkness, waiting until their voices faded from the house. Then she fell into bed, exhausted, shattered, and feeling very much alone. Hot tears welled up in her eyes, but she brushed them away and refused to give in to disappointment. Gone was her chance to draw out a bitter lonely girl, gone was her hope of uncovering the deeply buried poet in Gabriel Townsend, and gone was her dream of medical school.

Flopping onto her side, Evaline buried her cheek in the pillow and stared blearily at the door. No more frustrating dealings with the Townsends. No more tense meals shared in the cozy dining room. Tomorrow she would return to her well-structured urban life. The question was, could she bear to live in the city again, after having tasted the challenging but oddly satisfying life at the Townsend house?

In the morning Evaline packed her bags and carried them out to the deck. Then she lugged her equipment outside and placed it near her bags. Still upset, but resigned to leaving, Evaline watched the pale summer sun color the eastern sky pink above the treetops, the rays of dawn not quite reaching the waters of the bay, which lay motionless and black beyond the dock. She'd miss the stupendous views from the house. Her gaze traveled down the dock to the boat moored alongside. Lights in the forward cabin of the *Sea Wolf* glowed yellow in the gray dawn, and Evaline expected Gabriel to appear any moment.

She returned to the kitchen to brew a cup of coffee. The chill of the morning and her upcoming departure made her feel tense, and a warm cup of coffee might alleviate the tightness inside. Evaline thought of making breakfast, but had no appetite or desire to share another meal with Gabriel. If Allison got hungry on the road, he could stop and buy her something.

Just as the coffee finished brewing, a sudden movement outside caught her attention. She looked out of the kitchen window and saw Gabriel pushing Allison down the dock toward the drive. The time had come to leave.

"So much for a soothing cup of Java," Evaline muttered to herself, trying to keep her spirits bright, if only for Allison's sake. Evaline switched off the coffeemaker, grabbed her windbreaker from the back of a dining-room chair, and slowly took a final look at the homey house she had enjoyed for the past week. Then she pasted on a brave smile, opened the front door, and stepped out.

Gabriel and Allison rolled toward the truck as Evaline crunched across the drive. When she appeared at the front corner of the truck with her bags in her hands, she saw Allison's expression change.

"Wait a minute!" Allison said, arching around to peer up at her father. "What's going on? Evaline's got suitcases."

Evaline stood there, her heart as heavy as her bags when she saw the confusion in Allison's face. Gabriel hadn't told his daughter about his decision to find a new physical therapist. Where was the man's common sense? The last thing Allison needed was to be abandoned again by an adult she had come to depend upon. Even worse was to be abandoned without being forewarned.

Gabriel didn't look at Evaline. "We're taking Evaline to the ferry."

"The ferry? You said we were going into town for breakfast."

"We are."

"But why is Evaline going to the ferry?"

"She's going back to the hospital in Seattle."

Allison jerked around to stare at Evaline, her face contorted with hurt she made no effort to conceal. The expression opened a raw wound in Evaline's heart, a gash that had been there since she was a child herself. She realized there was nothing she could say to this fourteen-year-old kid to explain why she had to go. No explanation would be good enough. All Allison would believe was that yet another person didn't care enough for her to stick around.

"Your father and I have a difference of opinion regarding your treatment, Allison," she said gently, avoiding Gabriel's gaze. "I thought it best that he find a different therapist for you."

"Why?" Allison's hands clutched the arms of her chair. "You're doing just fine."

"It's your father's decision, Allison. I have to abide by it."

The girl turned back to face her father, her eyes darkening. "You told her to go?"

Gabriel squinted and clenched his jaw. "She wasn't doing her job."

"That's a bunch of crap!" Allison blurted. "Evaline's the best!"

"She put you in danger yesterday during that idiotic ritual."

"The heck she did!" Allison would have vaulted out of her chair in anger had she possessed full control of her legs. As it was, she pushed herself up with her arms, lifting her body off the chair to accost her father. "I wasn't in any danger!"

"That's for me to decide." Gabriel pushed the chair down the ramp to the drive, forcing Allison to return to her seat.

"What a minute!" Allison shouted, grabbing onto the rubber wheels of her chair and using her hands as brakes. "You can't make her go just because of that!"

"That isn't the only reason."

"But, Dad, she's my friend!" Allison sputtered. "Evaline listens to me! She's the only one who's ever really talked to me!"

Evaline stood there, mute with astonishment, the bags hanging unnoticed from her hands, and her heart breaking with agonizing swiftness.

"You can't do this!" Allison swiped at her face, trying to hide the fact that tears popped from her eyes. "Evaline understands me!"

"It's for the best, Allison," Gabriel answered brusquely. He pushed her toward the passenger side of the pickup.

"Why?" Allison yelled. "Why, Dad?"

Gabriel looked down at her and Evaline saw his shoulders shift, as if he wanted to sigh and give in to his daughter's tearful entreaty but wouldn't allow himself to yield. "Because Evaline has some beliefs that I can't accept."

"Like what?" Allison rubbed the tip of her nose with the back of her hand.

"Like thinking there is a ghost in your room."

Allison blinked and glanced at Evaline, her lashes blobbed with tears.

Gabriel opened the truck door. "And I won't have your head filled with such ideas."

"You think there's a ghost in my room?" Allison asked, swallowing, as her hot, vulnerable stare bored into Evaline.

Evaline nodded.

"Then I'm not the only one?" Allison's hand shook as she brushed her blond bangs off her forehead.

Gabriel's hand slid off the door handle. "What have *you* seen?"

"A blue cloud in my room. I've seen it ever since I woke up in the hospital. It scared me, but no one would listen. No one believed me. So I quit telling anyone about it. But I had trouble sleeping after dark, knowing it would show up at night."

"Allison," Evaline exclaimed, dropping her suitcases and sinking to her knees in front of the girl. "Why didn't you tell me?"

"I thought you were like all the others!" she replied. "I thought you'd pat me on the head and tell me there are no such things as ghosts."

"I'd never do that!"

"How was I supposed to know?" Allison sniffed. "Then it wasn't so bad when I knew you were in the room with me, keeping watch."

Gabriel stared at them, uncharacteristically quiet.

Evaline grasped Allison's hands firmly, knowing this might be her last chance to help the girl. "Allison," she said, squeezing her fingers, "you don't have to be afraid. This spirit we've seen is a ghost that means you no harm."

"How do you know?"

"Because it's . . ." Evaline glanced up at Gabriel. He shook his head almost imperceptibly, warning her not to divulge the identity of the spirit. For once, Evaline thought he might be right to withhold that particular piece of information, especially since she wasn't absolutely certain the ghost belonged to Meredith. ". . . It's something I sense."

"But why is it bothering me?"

"It's hard to say. Some ghosts don't realize they're dead and have to be convinced to go somewhere else. Some ghosts have unfinished business they need to resolve. There are many reasons."

"But why does this one show up just before midnight all the time?"

"I don't know, Allison. That's something I wanted to find out by doing the ritual."

"If you go, what will happen to the spirit—and me?"

Evaline couldn't bring herself to spout unfounded reassurance. "I don't know, Allison."

"Oh, hell," Gabriel blurted. He slammed shut the door of the truck and snatched up Evaline's suitcases. "Forget the ferry. We've missed it by now anyway."

Evaline slowly rose to her feet, hardly believing her ears, while a flicker of hope fluttered in her chest.

"She can stay?" Allison asked, beginning to grin.

"On one condition." Gabriel shot a hard dark glance at Evaline.

She raised an eyebrow. "Which is?"

"That you do your hocus-pocus stuff only in my presence and after you convince me it has a shred of credibility in it."

"All right." Evaline felt Allison reach for her hand and give it a hard squeeze. Then, instead of releasing her, the girl remained holding her hand, her fingers clutched around Evaline's. At the silent gesture of support and camaraderie, a hot burst in Evaline's chest made it difficult to retain her composure.

Gabriel's gaze dropped to their hands, then he quickly looked away. "Come on then. The day is wasting."

He turned toward the house and strode away. Evaline walked around to the back of Allison's chair.

"Thank you, Allison," she said softly.

"For what?"

"For everything you said."

"It's the truth."

"I know." Evaline laid a hand on the girl's shoulder. "And that's the best part."

Allison looked down, and without saying anything more Evaline pushed her to the house.

Late that evening, as Evaline knelt at the hearth and banked the small fire she'd built to ward off the evening chill, she heard the front door open behind her. She looked over her shoulder to see Gabriel standing in the doorway. He'd kept busy all day and hadn't shown up for dinner, which led Evaline to believe he planned to avoid her as much as possible. She was surprised to see him, and even more surprised to see him carrying two cans of beer. He held one up.

"Join me in a brew?" he asked.

Evaline rose and brushed her palms on her jeans. "Okay," she said, wondering why he had waited all day to come to the house. She accepted the can he held out to her. "Thank you."

Gabriel snapped the ring on his can and ambled to the window, his back to her, as she opened her beer and took a tentative sip. Gingerly, she sat down on the couch, feeling nervous and high-strung, and wondering why he created such tenseness in her. She wrapped her fingers around the can and stared at the silver ridges on the top while she waited for Gabriel to speak.

"You care a lot about Allison," he said at last, turning at the shoulders to glance at her. "Don't you?"

"Yes."

He nodded. "I didn't realize how much she liked you until this morning."

Evaline gave a small laugh. "Neither did I."

"Do you always care this much for your patients?"

Evaline considered the question while she rotated the can between her palms. "I care, but in a different way. Allison is special to me."

"How's that?"

Evaline glanced up at Gabriel, wishing she felt safe in sharing her thoughts with him, wishing she could tell him that she cared for Allison partly because she was his daughter, and that she had begun to care for him just as much. But she said nothing, still wary of Gabriel's volatile nature and knowing she should get to know him more fully before she revealed her feelings.

"She reminds me of myself at her age," Evaline replied at last. "I try to do for Allison what I would have wanted someone to do for me when I was fourteen."

"Did your parents split up when you were a kid?"

"You might say that." She stared at the beer can and didn't offer anything more.

"Well, something you're doing is right." He turned all the way around to face her. "Did you hear what she called me this morning? Dad."

Evaline nodded and smiled. "That *is* a good sign."

He took a drink and regarded her while he slowly swallowed his mouthful. Then he cleared his throat and shoved a hand into his front pocket.

"Look, Evaline," he said, "I'm sorry about yelling at you last night."

She gazed at him, astounded at the words she was hearing coming out of his mouth.

"Sometimes I fly off the handle," he continued. "When I think the old days might be coming back, it makes me crazy."

Evaline rose to her feet. "I don't know what went on between you and Meredith," she said. "But I am not her."

He nodded. "Yeah."

"And I would never do anything—*anything*," she repeated vehemently, "to hurt your daughter."

"I know."

For a long moment their eyes locked and held. In that moment Evaline saw again the man who had rescued her and murmured life back into her heart. In that moment, she realized she would never do anything to hurt Gabriel either. In fact, more than ever she wanted to discover what had happened to him to seal him inside such a gruff shell.

After what seemed like forever, Gabriel broke from her gaze. "What about Allison's ghost?" He turned his wrist to the light and peered at his watch. "It's nearly midnight."

"Do you honestly want to see it?"

"Yes," he answered, cocking one eyebrow. "And no. Because I still don't believe things like that exist."

He stood in front of her, staring at her again, their bodies only inches apart, and the air full of a scintillating awareness. Evaline didn't know what to say but didn't move a muscle, afraid that if she raised her hand, it would reach up to him on its own accord and stroke his face. After Gabriel's recent behavior, however, she didn't know if she should caress him or turn away once and for all.

"You'll believe it when you see it, eh?" she murmured.

"You got that right, ma'am." He nodded at her empty beer can. "Want me to throw that away, or are you saving it for target practice?"

She grinned. "You can have it."

He carried the cans to the kitchen. Evaline regarded his wide back and lean hips as he bent slightly to throw the cans in the trash under the sink. She didn't often look at a man and imagine what it would be like to touch him. But for the past few days, she'd wondered such things about Gabriel far too often for her own good. When he straightened to return to the living room, she pivoted abruptly, hoping he hadn't caught her staring.

Evaline headed down the hall, knowing more than ever that it behooved her to concentrate on her work and forget Gabriel. She turned her thoughts toward the ghost in Allison's room and prayed that of all nights, the spirit would appear this evening.

14

Evaline repeated the smudging process while Allison slept and Gabriel sat in the chair and watched, his face an impassive mask. Evaline tried to ignore him. For the ritual to be successful, it was best if all participants believed in the spirit world. Doubters and their sarcasm only hindered the process. To Gabriel's credit, he kept his doubts well hidden.

Even so, she was highly aware of Gabriel's gaze on the back of her head as she sat on the floor and sang the Sea Otter song, then began her prayer to the spirits. After a while she forgot everything but the melody spilling out of her heart, taking her to a place far beyond her childhood, as she tapped into an ageless oneness with another world.

As the prayer drew to a close, she felt a light touch on her shoulder and opened her eyes. Gabriel gently squeezed her shoulder and left his hand on her either in a gesture of solicitousness or out of sheer shock—she wasn't sure—for there before them floated the blue spirit, undulating in the darkness.

"Meredith?" Evaline whispered.

The cloud billowed near the top.

"Jesus!" Gabriel exclaimed behind her, his voice hushed with awe.

"Meredith," Evaline pressed onward. "We want to help Allison. Is that why you are here?"

The distant voice moaned through the night again. Evaline strained to make out the words, but as before the muted inflection wasn't clear enough to be understood.

"Meredith, I can't understand what you're saying," Evaline said, wondering if Meredith had a similar problem in comprehending mortal speech. "Is there a way you can tell us what you want, why you are here?"

The faint strains of the ballad drifted toward them. Evaline felt Gabriel's grip tighten.

"That damn song again," he commented under his breath. Evaline squeezed his knee, warning him to keep his observations to himself. However, he did have a point. Why, she wondered, did Meredith persist in playing the same song over and over again?

"Are you trying to tell us something with the song?" Evaline queried.

The blue cloud flared immediately. Evaline took the movement as a yes. She glanced at Gabriel, who raised his index finger, which she interpreted as a sign that he had something to say but would wait until later to tell her.

She turned back to the spirit. "Meredith, do you realize you have died?"

The blue cloud billowed slightly.

"You are free to leave this place. It isn't natural for you to remain. Allison doesn't understand why you are here, and your presence frightens her."

The spirit hung motionless in front of them, as though considering Evaline's words. Gabriel had become so still and silent that Evaline wondered if he'd quit breathing.

"Meredith, Allison is safe here. Gabriel will see to her safety. And I am here to help her get better. There is no need for you to remain."

The blue cloud grew faint, and Evaline heard the sound of a woman weeping. Though muted, the sobs were unmistakable. Evaline paused, worried that she'd made a grave mistake in telling the ghost she had no reason to remain in Allison's world. What mother wanted to hear that she was dispensable? Yet, from what Evaline had learned about Meredith, the woman hadn't provided much nurturing to her daughter. Why start now, Evaline thought, when it was nearly impossible to reach the girl? Still, she worried that her words had been thoughtlessly cruel. She'd only sought to reassure Meredith, hoping the ghost might move on to another plane if she knew Allison was safe.

Then, to Evaline's surprise, she saw the cloud moving toward her.

"Meredith," Evaline gasped, rising to her feet. "Don't—"

The spirit passed by her, sweeping through her hair and clothing like a cool, dry breeze. Evaline had never experienced such close contact with the spirit world and gaped in alarm as she watched the cerulean glow envelop Gabriel and settle around his figure in the chair. He sat with his back rigid and his hands clutching the arms of the chair, his eyes locked with Evaline's as they both tried to make sense of the sudden action of the ghost.

The weeping continued, pitiful and persistent, as the nimbus around Gabriel arced and ebbed. Evaline could see Gabriel's patience shredding as the sobbing continued. After a few moments, he jumped to his feet.

"Damn you, Meredith!" he swore vehemently. "Leave me alone!" He staggered toward Allison's bed. Instantly the spirit vanished, along with the plaintive weeping and the haunting refrain of the ballad.

Evaline stared in shock as Gabriel stood near Allison's

slumbering form, his eyes stormy and his face uncharacteristically drained of color. She didn't have to ask if he had changed his mind about the existence of spirits, for it was obvious the man had literally seen a ghost.

Then, just like the last time when Evaline had performed the ritual, she felt a sudden and overwhelming lassitude pulling her down. Gabriel's white face blurred against the far wall as her vision narrowed and grew black around the edges. She tried to call out to him, but her mouth wouldn't obey. Instead, she felt herself dropping to the floor, unable to break her fall.

"Evaline?"

Her eyelids were heavy cedar planks.

"Evaline?"

A warm hand brushed back the tendrils of hair on her forehead.

She struggled to rise out of the pool of muck her mind and body had fallen into, but she hadn't the strength to drag herself out of the sticky goo.

"Evaline, are you all right?"

The voice was deep, full of concern, familiar. She let the tone sweep through her, felt the warm palm gently but insistently pat her cheek, and absorbed the caring touch, drawing strength from it.

"Evaline, wake up for a minute."

"Wha—?" she managed to mumble.

"Wake up, so I know you're all right."

Gabriel. The voice was Gabriel's. She swallowed, finding her throat dry and raspy, and with the last remnants of energy, willed her eyes to open.

Gabriel's worried face hung above hers. His gray eyes glowed dark with concern and a deep furrow creased the space between his brows. His hand remained cupped around her left cheek.

"Evaline, are you okay?"

"I think so," she replied, her voice not much louder than a whisper. More than anything, she wanted to drift off to sleep.

Gabriel leaned closer. "Let me have a look at your eyes," he said, gently forcing apart her lids to check her pupils, one at a time. "They don't look abnormal. No concussion."

"Concussion?"

"You hit your head on the wood floor."

"Oh." Evaline licked her lips.

"I was afraid to leave you, in case you'd suffered a head injury."

Evaline paused and let the condition of her body register, now that she was fully conscious. She squinted at the pain throbbing in the back of her skull. "I just have a headache, that's all."

"I'm not surprised."

She glanced around. They were in her bedroom, and she was lying in her bed, and he was sitting on the edge of the mattress beside her. Though the ritual had drained her, she felt a surge of energy that had nothing to do with the spirit world and everything to do with the physical plane and the nearness of Gabriel, who, as he had done many years before, now leaned over her protectively. His scent, fresh with the outdoors and laced with his own light musk, bathed her in both comfort and desire.

"Is Allison all right?" she asked weakly, trying to direct her thoughts away from Gabriel's arousing proximity.

"She's restless, but sleeping." Gabriel ran his hand over her hair, brushing it back from her left temple. "Don't worry, Evaline. I scared off Meredith for the evening."

"She does seem to make a single appearance and then vanish."

"I'm not worried about her right now," Gabriel put in, his eyes glinting in the darkness. "I'm worried about you."

Evaline's heart flopped in her chest. "I'll be fine, Gabe."

"You sure?" His thumb traced the arc of her brow. Evaline longed to close her eyes and savor his deft, gentle touch, but couldn't allow her feelings for him to show. Instead, she gazed up at him, never taking her eyes off his face. Then, to her astonishment, she saw his elbow bend near her ear as he slowly dipped closer, his fingertips splayed in her hair.

Before she could move, she felt Gabriel's mouth closing upon hers, warm and firm and questing, asking for something she wasn't certain she should give. His kiss plunged her back to an altered state of consciousness where time hung suspended and unnoticed. She heard a ragged sigh and realized with a blush that the sound had come from her.

"Evaline," he murmured against her lips.

She wondered if he could feel the teeny lines around her lips, where a plastic surgeon had repaired her disfigured mouth. She wondered if he had noticed the altered lid of her eye, where streaks of silver scars had once pulled half of her face into a fright mask.

Evaline couldn't accept this man's kiss—any man's kiss—without the fear of discovery robbing the moment of its rightful abandon. She raised her hands to push him away before he could get any closer and see her for what she was—a patched-up child masquerading as a beautiful grown woman. Then she felt the wall of his chest sinking onto her breasts, his solid male torso pressing into her soft womanly contours, trapping her desire for him between them and leaving no avenue of escape. His weight was like a drug that fired her hunger and immobilized her limbs at the same time. The thought of his tall, powerful form descending upon her petite, slender frame made her ache with longing, and she prayed that the cover of darkness would hide all that she was from him. Evaline closed her eyes and moaned into his mouth as her body flushed with an undeniable, driving need she'd never felt before.

"Evaline," he repeated urgently, and kissed her neck, just below her ear.

Her mouth felt swollen, her breasts ached, and something deep inside her throbbed and flared, making her moan again. An urge to arch upward and press her hips to his swept over her, but she fought the desire, sure that it would set them on a path of no return. Evaline knew if she reached for him—gave him the slightest sign of acceptance—he would pour himself over and into her. And she would drink him up greedily, every ounce of him. But she knew making love this soon with Gabriel would be a mistake. Neither of them were ready for such intimacy, for neither of them had been honest enough with each other to share such closeness and have it mean anything. Evaline did not intend to have meaningless sex with any man, especially Gabriel.

Not knowing how to express herself in words, Evaline froze, her hands in the air, fingers curled slightly, in a gesture of abdication that Gabriel read instantly, just as she expected he might.

"Shit!" he exclaimed, his voice hoarse. He jerked up and rolled off her in a fluid movement. His sudden reaction shocked her.

"Gabriel!" She hadn't meant for her silence to translate into rejection. But obviously he had interpreted her reluctance as a slap in the face. "Gabe, please don't think—"

"Forget it, Evaline," he retorted, cutting her off. "I was

out of line." Without saying another word, he turned and walked out of the room.

Evaline rolled onto her side and watched him leave, her eyes hot and dry.

All the next week, Evaline's thoughts kept returning to Gabriel's hasty retreat from her bedroom. She constantly mulled over the scene in her head, searching for the right phrase to explain her behavior, because she knew, by his absence from the house and the dinner table, that he had taken her rejection as a personal affront. He probably thought she had no feelings for him, when nothing could be farther from the truth.

Evaline assumed the strain between them would gradually ease, but as the last days of June melted into July, and the weather grew warmer, her relationship with Gabriel grew more chilly. She realized the tenseness had increased, and something had to be done about it. But what could she do? Any explanation she came up with was immediately discarded, for only the truth about her plastic surgery would suffice, and she wasn't willing to divulge that part of herself to him. Each day she rose with a new resolve, determined to break through the wall that had risen between them, spent the day working with Allison, then crawled into bed, frustrated by yet another day of silence. Each time she got the rare opportunity to speak to him, she was interrupted, either by Allison, The Major, or by her own cold feet. The silence ate at her, driving her toward a confrontation or an ulcer, she wasn't sure which.

Even Allison was more subdued, as if she sensed the tension between the two adults but didn't want to ask any questions.

The tension didn't let up until the Fourth of July, when Skeeter showed up unexpectedly with Mandy and a request that Gabriel take them out to watch the fireworks display offshore of Port Angeles.

Skeeter's gregarious personality was a welcome change from the cold atmosphere at the house, and Evaline was happy to see him. Gabriel, on the other hand, seemed equally happy to see Mandy, who spent most of the morning in his company down at the boat. Evaline kept busy cooking potato salad and pie for a picnic dinner aboard the *Sea Wolf,* and tried not to envision what Mandy might be doing with Gabriel.

In midafternoon, they set out and remained in two camps for most of the day: Evaline and Allison on one side of the deck and Mandy and Gabriel on the other, with Skeeter playing the part of go-between/bartender. The leisurely cruise across placid water on a clear warm day would have been perfect except for Gabriel's obvious avoidance of Evaline and his lack of eye contact, and Evaline's old memories of the first and only time she'd been aboard the *Sea Wolf.* Evaline fiddled with her gin and tonic—the second one she'd had since the start of the journey hours ago, and kept her mind occupied by helping Allison complete a crossword puzzle, while the sun baked through her long-sleeved cotton shirt. Though Evaline suffered from the heat, she never wore short-sleeved clothing, never swam in a public pool, or undressed in anyone's presence, for fear of showing her scars and having someone remark on them, or, worse yet, stare.

Over the course of the afternoon, Evaline had discovered Gabriel was a tidier housekeeper than she was. His boat was spick-and-span, from the bilge to the bridge, and she realized once again that she had misjudged him, having assumed he was a slob because of the condition of the house when she'd first arrived. Now she knew the truth:

the mess had been the making of Skeeter and his last girl-friend.

At ten-thirty that evening, they sat in deck chairs, drinking wine and watching the glittering poofs of fireworks explode in the sky, like gigantic dahlias in red and yellow and blue. Mandy was already well on the way to being drunk, and exclaimed in dramatic oohs and ahs whenever a firework burst above. Once or twice Evaline saw her grab Gabriel's upper arm, feigning surprise and draping herself halfway across him. Evaline sipped her wine, wishing Gabriel would shrug her off, but he seemed to possess an unusual amount of patience when it came to Mandy.

Occasionally Allison caught Evaline's eye and gave a knowing smirk, finding Mandy's condition and behavior an additional source of entertainment.

After the fireworks display was over, Gabriel told Allison it was time for bed. She didn't complain, tired by the long day and fresh air, and allowed her father to carry her below.

"Will you come and say good night?" Allison asked as they passed by Evaline.

"Of course," Evaline assured her. She hadn't missed a single night of tucking Allison in, and apparently the girl had grown accustomed to the habit. "I'll be down in a few minutes." Evaline didn't look at Gabriel.

"She's really changed," Skeeter remarked as Gabriel and Allison disappeared down the hatch. "Both of them have, as a matter of fact."

Evaline nodded. "Allison is coming around." She smiled, but inside she wasn't happy with Allison's progress. The girl might have polished her social skills, but she wasn't any closer to walking than she'd been a month ago. The summer was nearly half over, and September would arrive far too quickly.

"She even let me muss her hair," Skeeter put in.

"That's what I call real progress."

Skeeter laughed and watched as Mandy rose unsteadily to her feet. She teetered for a moment and hiccuped loudly.

"G'night, everbuddy," she announced, probably seeing twice as many people as there actually were in front of her.

"Good night," Evaline replied.

Mandy fumbled for the rail.

"Need some help?" Skeeter asked.

"I think I can make it," Mandy said, giggling and pointing to the spot where Gabriel had just walked. "'Spose Gabriel'll tuck me in if I ask him nice?"

Skeeter shot a glance at Evaline, then quickly looked away. "Now, Mandy girl, don't go causing any trouble." He stood up and took a step toward Mandy. She laughed and half slid, half fell down the companionway.

Evaline sipped her wine as she listened to Mandy call out for Gabriel in a musical voice. Skeeter turned back and pulled out a cigarette.

"That little gal doesn't know I exist," he remarked, lighting up. The end of the cigarette glowed in the dark, but left his expression shadowed and unreadable. "I keep hoping she'll come to her senses."

"She seems to like Gabriel."

"The little idiot." Skeeter took a drag of his cigarette.

Evaline didn't know how to interpret his remark, but let it go unquestioned.

"She's kind of young anyway," Evaline said in consolation. "For either of you."

"She's old enough," he retorted, and chuckled knowingly. "Don't let her fool you."

Not wanting to know more about Mandy's experience with men, Evaline got to her feet and picked up her empty wineglass. "I think I'll turn in, too. Good-night, Skeeter."

"'Night, Ev." He waved. "Any more of that pie left?"

"It's down in the galley."

"Might have a piece."

"Help yourself." She smiled at his insatiable appetite for her cooking, slowly descended the stairs and walked to Allison's cabin, located at the farthest end of the boat. Evaline rapped softly and let herself in, not surprised to discover Gabriel had already left. She could just guess where he had gone.

Evaline sat on the edge of Allison's bunk and chatted with her for a few minutes. Allison had some catty remarks to make about Mandy, which Evaline didn't add to, even though she had a couple of observations of her own. She pulled the covers up around Allison's shoulders and wished her good night.

She switched off the light and quietly closed the door, just as Gabriel slipped out of Mandy's room, stepping backward into the corridor. They bumped into each other and immediately jerked away, both embarrassed to find themselves uncomfortably close in the narrow companionway. Evaline backed against Allison's door, unable to extricate herself from Gabriel's disturbing proximity without brushing by him. He stared down at her, his hair mussed slightly. Evaline felt a sharp shaft of jealousy streak through her at the thought of Mandy being the cause of his dishevelment. At the same time, she became aware of her breasts, which had transformed into highly sensitive antennae, seeking out the warmth of his chest.

Knowing she was a bigger fool than Mandy for wanting Gabriel Townsend, Evaline decided to push past him and retreat to the safety of her own cabin. "Good night, Gabriel," she stated brusquely. She took a resolute step, but he moved to block her.

Suddenly from above came Skeeter's voice, calling for his friend. "Hey, Gabe!" he yelled. "How about a nightcap?"

Gabriel glanced toward the stairs, then back to Evaline, who hadn't moved a muscle. To her dismay, she felt her breath coming as hard as her heart was pounding in her chest, and knew Gabriel had noticed as well. His eyes glittered in the darkness.

"Gabe!" Skeeter called again, his voice closer.

Without a word, Gabriel grabbed Evaline's wrist and pulled her a few paces down the corridor. He yanked open a door and quickly urged her inside. Evaline stumbled into the dark cabin, and when he shut the door, she couldn't help but remember the way a stranger at the casino had pushed her into a dark room like this and nearly raped her. Evaline broke out in a cold sweat.

"Let me go!" she gasped, pulling at his iron grip.

"Hold on!" he protested.

She lurched away, trying to wrench free, but his fingers only clamped more tightly around her wrist.

"Calm down, Evaline," he said. "We've got to talk."

15

"Let me go!" Evaline whispered hoarsely, not wanting anyone to hear.

"What's the matter?" Gabriel asked. "You're as stiff as a board!" He released her wrist, and she immediately pulled away, rubbing her arm where he'd gripped her. Gabriel stared down at her. "You're afraid of me!"

"I am not!"

"You're frightened of something. What?"

"Nothing, I said." She paled and was glad he hadn't turned on the light.

"Your eyes tell me otherwise."

"What can you see in the dark?" she countered.

"Plenty." Without asking her permission, he tipped her chin up to see her face better. Evaline didn't pull away this time, trying to prove to him that she had courage by staring directly into his eyes. But beneath his unwavering scrutiny, she broke down and had to look away. "It's not just me, is it?" he asked.

She blinked. "I don't know what you mean."

"You're as white as a sheet, Evaline."

"I don't see how you can tell."

"I can. But maybe I should turn on the light."

"No!" She felt his probing stare on the side of her face. "I mean, it isn't necessary. I should be going anyway."

"Not just yet. We need to talk."

"About what?"

"You know damn well about what."

She fell silent, and he waited impatiently for her to respond. She turned her head enough to make him let go of her chin. At the movement, he heaved an exasperated sigh and dropped his arm to his side.

"You know," he began. "I was going to apologize again to you. But then I got to thinking about what went on between us the other night, and I realized there wasn't a goddamn thing I did that I was sorry about."

"Gabriel, you don't have to say—"

"And the more I thought about it, the crazier it seemed. You liked it when I kissed you, didn't you?"

"Yes, but I thought we should stop there."

"Why?"

"For a lot of reasons."

"Name one."

She shot a glare at him. "Why does everything have to be an argument with you?"

"We're not arguing!"

"It seems like it to me."

"I don't like pussyfooting around. I've told you that." Gabriel ran a hand through his hair. "So what is it, City Girl? Why the cold shoulder?"

"The time never seemed right to talk to you."

"What about now?" Gabriel paused, waiting again. "I'm listening."

Evaline looked down.

He crossed his arms over his chest. "Is there some reason why you don't like being alone with me?"

His question rankled her. She looked up at him. "For one thing, I don't appreciate being dragged by the hair into your cave."

"Come off it, Evaline. You know what I mean."

Evaline lowered her lashes, unsure of how to reply. She longed to touch him, but didn't know how to tell him that she was afraid to let him get close enough to see her real scars, the ones that cut bone deep.

Gabriel tilted his head. "Do I personally turn you off, or do you have some objection to men in general?"

Evaline flushed. "No," she blurted, and fumbled for the handle of the door behind her.

"No, what?"

"Just no!" She yanked at the latch, unable to turn it in her flustered state. "I need to go."

"Evaline." Gabriel stepped up behind her, and she felt his warm hand slip over hers. He didn't pry her fingers away from the latch, but instead gently squeezed her hand. His chest lightly pressed into her back, and he lowered his head next to her left ear. He was close enough to make full body contact but far enough away to allow her to break free if she chose. "Don't," he murmured in her ear.

She stared at the door in front of her face, battling the wild, soaring sensations he produced in every part of her body. She could feel his warm breath on her neck and closed her eyes to block out the urge to turn around and kiss him.

"I can't stand the silence, Evaline."

"Neither can I."

"Then why the games?"

"I don't play games."

"Then tell me what's going on."

"Nothing is going on." She hoped he would drop the subject.

"Nothing?" His left hand slid up her arm while his right arm encircled her waist and he pulled her gently against him. His jaw brushed her cheek. She tried to relax in his embrace, but was more stiff than the first time he kissed her. "I don't buy it."

"Gabe, please—"

She raised her chin, and he took the opportunity to kiss her throat. His hair tickled her, sending delicious chills coursing down her arms and legs. She pushed against his embrace.

"Gabe, this isn't a good idea—"

"Why?"

"Allison's right down the hall. Mandy's—"

"So what?"

"They might hear."

"That's just an excuse."

"No, I—"

"What's the real reason you pull away from me?"

"I don't want to go into it."

"Why?"

"I just don't." She glanced over her shoulder at his handsome face, just inches from hers. "And it isn't a reflection on you, Gabe."

"The hell it isn't."

"I wanted to tell you all week that it wasn't you, that you didn't offend me the other night—but I . . . I . . . just didn't know how to say it."

"So what is it? Is there someone else?" he continued. "I thought you said you don't have a boyfriend."

"I don't."

"Then what?"

She paused and looked down. "I don't want to go into it, Gabe."

"Why?"

"It's too . . . personal."

"I *want* to get personal with you, Evaline." He gathered her close again, and his hands moved upward to cup her breasts. Evaline sucked in her breath and hung suspended between shock and surrender as she was intimately caressed for the first time in her life. Like fruit left to sweeten on the vine, her breasts swelled in his hands, and she moaned, unable to resist his touch any longer. Closing her eyes, she let her head ease back against his chest.

"Oh, Gabe," she whispered through half-parted lips.

"Evaline." His voice cracked near her ear. "I've been half-crazy all week, thinking there was something about me that you—"

"It wasn't you," she murmured, "believe me." His hands drove her wild, made her ache for more. "It's just that we haven't been honest with each other."

"What do you mean?" He pushed his nose into her hair and took a long, appreciative breath.

"I know nothing of you," she replied, her tongue thick with desire. "And you know nothing of me."

"I know enough," Gabriel countered, easing his hands under her blouse, "to want to know more."

His hot hands cupped her breasts. Even through her lacy brassiere she could feel the heat of him. "What about you?" he asked, his lips on her throat. "Do you want to know more?"

"Yes," she exclaimed before she considered the consequences. "I mean no! Gabe—" She reached up for his forearms.

"Don't push me away." His deep voice rumbled along her spine as he gently squeezed her. "Not now."

"But—"

"Doesn't this feel right to you?" He embraced her tightly. "To be with me here like this?"

She swallowed and closed her eyes, melting against him. "Yes," she answered, certain of that truth.

"Then let's just go with that for now and forget the rest."

"I don't know if I can."

"Everybody has baggage, Evaline."

"But there are things about me—"

"That I find damned attractive." He clutched her shoulders and turned her around. "So just be quiet and kiss me, City Girl."

He raised his eyebrows, and she couldn't help but smile. Her heart surged in her chest. "All right."

"That's more like it. Complete submission." He bent closer.

"Don't bet on it, Wild Man."

"Wild Man?" Gabriel smiled slowly, and she could see good humor sparkling in his eyes. "I like the sound of that."

Gabriel growled softly, swooped her into his arms, and dipped down for a kiss. Still smiling, she lifted her chin to meet him halfway. She couldn't think of her scars now, couldn't let them be a barrier. It was dark. Gabriel could see next to nothing. And she didn't want to push him away, or deny herself the wonder of touching him and showing him how she felt. She could take the chance just this one time. And afterward—well, she wouldn't think of afterward.

Blocking out her fears, Evaline reached up for Gabriel and wrapped her arms around his wide back, totally and completely aroused by his physical girth. Beneath her hands, she could feel his power and already knew his strength, and thrilled at the thought that he was in her arms, wanting her as much as she wanted him. This was no fantasy from her old life, a dream doomed to go unfulfilled. This was a real-live experience with a very real man—a man who was far beyond any fantasy she had imagined all those years ago.

And then she kissed him, with the raw, driving hunger of someone who has been starving for a lifetime and has stumbled upon a sumptuous feast. She felt herself exploding like one of the fireworks they'd just watched, bursting into glorious colors and then shimmering down around him, enveloping him with her lips, her arms, her spirit— with her entire being.

"God, Evaline!" Gabriel swore, rising up from her kiss. "You've been holding out!"

"I have," she whispered against his mouth. "For*ever*, Gabriel."

She plunged back into the fantasy of his kiss as she felt herself being lifted off her feet. This time she didn't question what would happen. This time she wanted to journey with Gabriel to a place where only the two of them existed—far beyond the past and the present. Just this once she wanted to know what it was like to be caressed and desired, and by this man in particular. He carried her small figure easily, one arm beneath her knees and the other supporting her back, and kissed her all the way to his bed.

In his arms she lost track of time and of the outside world. She was conscious of nothing but his lips and hands as he laid her gently upon his bunk. Gabriel hung over her and gazed at her as she reached for the buttons of his shirt.

Then someone banged on Gabriel's door.

Evaline scrambled to her feet, slammed back to reality, while Gabriel glared a hole through the door behind him to whoever stood on the other side.

"Damn," he muttered.

The magic between them vanished in an instant, and the warmth between them shriveled at that single sound.

Evaline stood in the shadows, very much aware of her tousled hair, rumpled clothing, and well-kissed lips. Anyone who saw her could easily guess what she and Gabriel had been doing. To her surprise, however, she realized she didn't care if anyone knew she'd been with Gabriel. She wasn't ashamed of her feelings for him, or the fact that she'd been expressing those feelings. Except for Allison. Allison wouldn't be ready to see her father kissing anyone. It would destroy her slowly emerging sense of security. Evaline flushed, realizing how close she and Gabriel might have come to alienating Allison for good. Then and there she made a vow that she wouldn't repeat such selfish behavior.

Gabriel combed his fingers through his unruly hair and reached for the latch to pull the door open a crack.

"Mandy?" he croaked in surprise.

Evaline stuffed her shirttails back into her shorts, hoping Mandy wouldn't shove her way into Gabriel's cabin. She wondered if Mandy had ever been pinned against the door before and kissed as thoroughly as Gabriel had just kissed her. Mandy didn't seem like the type of woman to interest Gabriel, but who knew what went on late at night between two lonely people during an extended cruise? Something as equally unpredictable had nearly just happened between her and Gabriel.

"Gabe," Mandy's slurred, pouting voice carried through the opening. "Can't sleep."

"Then read something," he answered, looking at his watch. "It's midnight, Mandy."

"I don't have anything t' read."

Gabriel stepped back a pace and Evaline wondered if Mandy had reached out for him.

"Lookslike you can't slee' peither," Mandy continued, her speech nearly incoherent. "Wanna have a nigh'cap?"

"Another time," he replied. "I was just about to turn in."

"Why don't you come 'cross the hall?" she asked. "Read me a bedtime story, Gabe? You've got lots of books in there. I've seen 'em. Lots an' lots an' lots."

Evaline saw the door start to swing open, but Gabe stopped it with his hand. "Mandy, you're drunk. Go back to bed and sleep it off."

"You're no fun!"

"I'll see you in the morning, Mandy."

"Gabe—" There was a long pause, and then Gabriel jerked into action, but not quickly enough. Evaline heard a loud thump.

"Great," he exclaimed. "She's out for the count."

Evaline looked around the edge of the door as Gabriel stooped and gathered Mandy's limp body in his arms.

"Sorry, Evaline," he said, shrugging one shoulder. "Bad timing."

"Maybe it was for the best," Evaline replied.

"What do you mean?"

"What if she'd been Allison?"

Gabriel glanced down at Mandy's face, then back to Evaline. His expression sobered.

"Allison's had too much bouncing around during Meredith's romances," Evaline continued. "And she thinks you like Mandy."

"Ridiculous." Gabriel gave a short humorless laugh. "Mandy's like a daughter to me."

"That's not what Mandy or Allison thinks."

"You've noticed?"

"Gabriel, everybody has noticed. And if Allison saw you coming on to me, I don't know what would go through her head."

Evaline opened the door to Mandy's cabin and Gabriel paused on the threshold, looking back as if deciding whether or not her theory was valid.

Evaline crossed her arms, calling upon her sense of

humor to lighten the moment. She nodded toward Mandy. "Need a chaperon?" she drawled.

"I can handle her."

"Sure?" She raised an eyebrow.

"Piece of cake." He surveyed her over Mandy's dangling figure and slowly his eyes swept over her breasts and into her hair.

At his lingering gaze, Evaline felt herself longing to succumb to him all over again. For a moment all she could think about was the warmth of his lips and the strength of his arms. Then she shut out the vision. Thinking about him was senseless torture. It would be best if she cut off their fledgling relationship before it could grow any deeper. She broke from his gaze. "I should go."

His right eye squinted as he watched her move back toward her cabin.

"Good night, Gabriel."

"See you in the morning, Evaline," he answered softly.

Later that week, Evaline crunched across the gravel parking lot, her spirit renewed by a long after-dinner walk alone on the beach. Allison sat near The Major's pen, tossing apple slices to the bear, who rolled playfully in the grass. She'd discovered through a mishap that even though the cub might flee from his pen, he would return for his evening meal and pile of blankets, as dutifully as a dog.

Gabriel sat on a deck chair, tinkering with a downrigger assembly from his boat. Evaline paused at the edge of the yard and took in the quiet scene before her. Though she ached to explore a deeper relationship with Gabriel, she would not jeopardize the tranquillity that had descended upon the Townsend house since the

Fourth of July. At night when she thought of Gabriel, she didn't feel so tranquil, but knew she could get through this rough time, as long as Gabriel kept to himself.

Evaline waved to Allison and walked up the stairs to the deck. Gabriel glanced up from his work as she approached.

"'Evening, beautiful," he greeted.

Evaline flushed with pleasure. "Don't call me that," she advised in a soft tone that wouldn't carry across the yard.

"I'll call you anything I damn well please," he retorted, "beautiful."

By now, Evaline heard his crusty language for what it was: a way of masking the gentle side he concealed from the world.

"What if Allison could hear what you just said?" She brushed by him, but he reached out and snagged her fingers.

"She can't." He studied her, his gaze raking her from head to toe. "I don't know how long I can take this," he murmured. "It isn't natural, Evaline."

Evaline bit her lip and forced herself not to look down at him. If she saw the hunger she knew was gleaming in his eyes, she'd lose her resolve and sink down to his lap. She longed to embrace him again.

"I don't care what you say about Allison," he continued, "we're lying to her, acting like there's nothing happening between us."

"It's for her own good." She tried to pull away from his hand, but he gently resisted.

"It will be worth it, Gabe." Evaline darted a glance his way and her legs turned to water at the fire she saw streaming from his clear gray eyes. Immediately she looked away, focusing on Allison, who tossed another apple to the bear.

"Allison is so close to making some real improvement,"

she said. "I think she'll soon be able to deal with what happened. To remember. And maybe to have the will to get out of that chair."

His eyes lit up. "You think so?"

She nodded. "You should have seen her riding this afternoon. She was a different person!"

"She was certainly different at dinner, jabbering away," Gabriel added, gazing across the grass toward his daughter. "You should do more riding with her."

"She's making progress, Gabe. Mostly emotionally. But I'm still convinced that's the bulk of what's wrong. And I will not compromise her progress with my own selfish needs."

"What about my needs?" he teased, tugging her closer. "Don't you care about my state of mind?"

"You're a big boy, Gabriel," she retorted. "You can handle it."

"But I want you to handle it." He wiggled his eyebrows suggestively.

"Gabe!" She laughed nervously and stepped out of his grasp, just in time to see Allison look up from the yard.

16

That night the heat of the day hung over the water, refusing to dissipate, as if in chorus with the heat lingering inside Evaline. No breeze whispered through the cedars or drifted into the house, just as nothing she could do doused the fire inside her. Evaline lay awake, dressed only in a T-shirt and panties, her arms behind her head, wondering why her choice to remain separate from Gabriel seemed so wrong to her heart. Her head told her the decision to back off was logical and decent. Why, then, she wondered, did she feel so unconvinced deep down inside?

She thought she was well acquainted with solitude, but now that she'd met Gabriel, she was discovering the yawning abyss of true loneliness. It was like being hungry and standing with an empty plate, looking at a full buffet spread out before her and knowing she couldn't touch a single morsel. In the past she'd been able to turn away without too much difficulty, because she'd never tasted anything from the table. But it was different now. She'd sampled the passion in Gabriel's arms, she'd heard his voice crack when he spoke her name, she'd caressed his thick lustrous hair and felt her body melting into his, and she would never be the same. Or satisfied with anyone else.

Gabriel—her tempting, forbidden buffet—lay on the couch in the living room, a post he assumed each night since seeing Meredith's ghost a few weeks ago. Evaline wondered if he was already asleep, or if his personal demons plagued him in the stifling heat just as hers did. But she knew better than to seek answers to her questions.

He'd called her beautiful. If he only knew . . .

Just as Evaline finally drifted off to sleep, she was awakened by Allison crying out in fright, which was quickly followed by a sudden blast of too-loud music. Evaline bolted out of bed and practically collided with Gabriel, who came streaking down the hall. They burst into Allison's room as the music flared full force around them.

Allison thrashed on the bed. "No!" she screamed. "No!"

Gabriel dashed to her side and pulled her to a sitting position. "Allison!" he shouted over the music. "Allison, wake up!"

"It's useless," Evaline yelled. "She won't. Or can't."

Allison writhed in Gabriel's arms and pummeled his chest. He ignored her futile attempts to injure him as he extricated her from the tangled sheets and lifted her from the bed.

"I'm getting her out of here," he exclaimed.

"Take her to my room," Evaline suggested, thinking, as Gabriel presumably did, that Meredith's spirit might not follow them.

Gabriel nodded.

Evaline fumbled with the tape deck, hoping she could turn the machine off this time and dispense with the loud music. As she groped for the switch, she knocked something off the tape deck. A square piece of paper fluttered to the floor and landed on her bare foot. Evaline ignored it and turned off the tape deck, but the music blared on.

"Damn!" Evaline swore, having been influenced by Gabriel's raw vocabulary over the past month. There was nothing she could do but leave the room and hope the lack of human interaction would induce Meredith to give up. Evaline snatched the paper off her foot and followed Gabriel's path out of the bedroom.

Light gleamed from her chamber, and as she entered the room, she tilted the paper toward the lamp. A small snapshot of a dark-haired child with missing teeth smiled up at her. Evaline didn't recognize the kid in the photo, so she turned her attention to Allison, who lay in her bed, her hair wet with sweat.

"No!" Allison rasped. "Let her go!" She writhed again, fighting Gabriel's grip on her wrists. Evaline placed the photograph on the bureau and hurried to the master bathroom to get a cool cloth for Allison's forehead.

"Mother!" Allison screamed, terrified. "Mo-ther!"

Gabriel jerked around as Evaline ran back with the damp cloth. "Evaline!" he said. "Do something. We've got to help her!"

"Here," Evaline offered the cloth. "Dab her forehead. She looks like she's burning up."

Gabriel lowered Allison to the pillows and reached for the cloth while Allison struggled against an unseen foe.

"Does she feel hot?" Evaline inquired.

"I can't get close enough to tell!" Gabriel retorted. "She keeps hitting me!"

Evaline leaned over Allison and managed to lay her hand along the girl's hairline. "She doesn't feel hot."

"But she's never been this bad." Gabriel placed the folded cloth on Allison's forehead. "What's going on?"

"Mother!" Allison cried again.

"That does it!" Gabriel jumped to his feet. He headed for the door.

"Where are you going?"

"To Allison's room. To tell Meredith to leave us alone!"

"But, Gabriel—"

"The worst she can do is repeat her 'woe is me' performance. And maybe I can distract her enough so she won't bother Allison."

"Just be careful!"

"Don't worry," Gabriel replied. "I know Meredith's tactics—only too well." He ducked into the hall and disappeared. Evaline sank to the mattress beside Allison.

Within minutes, the girl's thrashing quieted and she slipped into a fitful sleep, her eyes rolling wildly beneath her lids. Evidently Gabriel had been successful in diverting the spirit's attention to himself, leaving Allison with nothing more than a bad dream. Evaline remained beside her, gently brushing back the girl's damp bangs and watching her closely. All the while, however, she worried about Gabriel, wondering if he'd have the same reaction to dealing with Meredith that she'd had. Would she find him sitting in the chair, exhausted? Or worse. Meredith might hurt him, in retribution for something he'd done to her in the past.

Ten minutes ticked by, each minute dragging Evaline through an hour of worry. She didn't want to leave Allison, but she was growing more and more concerned about Gabriel. As soon as Allison lapsed into a more relaxed state of sleep, Evaline slipped out of the room to check on him.

She found Gabriel on the floor of Allison's bedroom, unconscious.

"Gabe!" Evaline cried, dropping to her knees at his side. She shook his bare shoulder. "Gabe!"

He didn't respond. She patted his cheek. "Gabe! Wake up!"

Still he lay there, unmoving.

In a panic, Evaline pressed her two fingers to his throat. His pulse beat stoutly against her fingertips. At least he was alive. But she didn't know how long he would remain unconscious. She could never move him. He was far too heavy. Instead, she grabbed a pillow from the bed, elevated his feet, then covered him with a blanket. She found another pillow and slipped it gently under his head.

His comatose condition shook her to the core. Not until that moment did she realize how she depended upon Gabriel to be the vibrant, virile man she'd come to love. Yes. She loved him. She couldn't deny it. Looking down at his drawn face and closed eyes, she was overwhelmed with tenderness and concern for him. Gently, Evaline traced the lean contour between his cheekbone and jawline, darkened with the first few hours of beard. Then she passed her index finger across his firm lower lip while her love for him swelled up in a hot wave.

"Oh, Gabe," she whispered. She leaned down and tenderly kissed his mouth, but his unresponsive lips seemed like those of a stranger. Slowly, she rose, willing him to regain consciousness. But his eyes remained closed.

Frustrated, Evaline shot a quick glance around the room and glimpsed a pale lavender glow near the head of the bed, hovering in the shadows, watching her. Meredith wasn't just haunting Allison any longer. She was affecting all of them, twisting their lives.

"Leave us alone, Meredith!" Evaline shouted at the

fading entity, knowing she wasn't being very shamanic. "Just leave us alone!"

Gabriel moaned faintly, and Evaline turned back to search his face for signs of recovery.

"Gabriel!" she patted his cheek again. "Wake up, Gabe!"

His black eyelashes fluttered and his chest heaved as he took a deep breath. His eyes blinked open.

"Evaline?" he mumbled.

"Gabe! Thank God!"

He squinted and studied her face as if he didn't recognize her. "Where am I?" he asked.

"Allison's room. You fainted."

He swallowed and moved his head, but winced in pain.

"I must have hit my head," he gasped. "It hurts like a sonofabitch."

"Do you think you can sit up?"

"I think so. Give me a hand."

She stood up and reached for him, throwing her weight back to lever him to a sitting position. Gingerly, Gabriel ran a hand over the back of his head. "Ouch," he said, wincing again.

"Let me have a look." Evaline bent closer, but he waved her off.

"I'll be all right. How is Allison?"

"Sleeping peacefully."

"Good." He rubbed the back of his neck. "God, I feel weird. Drained."

"Just like I did those other times. She must feed on our energy somehow."

"Well, I'll tell you one thing. I don't like being someone's midnight snack." He held out his hand again. "Can you help me to the couch?"

"I can try. Want to use Allison's wheelchair?"

"Hell no." He grabbed her wrists and Evaline heaved at

his heavy form. Slowly he rose to his feet. As soon as he stood up, Evaline hurried forward and wrapped her arms around him to support his upper torso. She'd never felt tiny than at that moment, trying to hold up this giant of a man.

"I'm as weak as a baby," he commented. "Don't go trying to take advantage of me, nurse."

"I wouldn't think of it, sir," she retorted.

"Damn." He gave her a faint smile, and she knew he was going to be all right.

They stumbled together toward the living room. Gabriel collapsed onto the couch.

"I'll be right back," Evaline said, wedging a pillow between the arm of the couch and his torso. "I just want to check on Allison."

"Okay."

She left him feeling for the bump on the back of his skull. When she returned, he looked up, his eyes much clearer than they'd been a few minutes earlier. Relief poured over her.

"I could use a brandy," he said. "Want to join me?"

"Sure. Do you have some down at the boat?"

"There should be a whole case downstairs. Would you mind getting a bottle?"

"Not at all." She headed for the door of the kitchen which opened onto a stairway leading to the storeroom.

"You're not scared, are you?" he asked.

"No." Evaline gave him a reassuring smile. "I don't believe Meredith wants to hurt us. If she did, we'd probably be dead by now."

"You have a point."

"I just can't figure out what she does want from us."

"That's nothing new, believe me." Gabriel nodded toward the storeroom door. "But let's talk about Meredithwhen you get back with the brandy."

*   *   *

A few minutes later Evaline handed Gabriel a snifter partially full of the amber liquid whose fragrance wafted up and tickled her nose. The heat had finally vanished, leaving the house pleasantly cool. Evaline sank to the chair near the end of the couch, while Gabriel sat back, stretching his long legs the length of the sofa. He wore a simple pair of navy blue cotton shorts and nothing else. Evaline took a moment to peruse his nearly naked legs, with their powerful calves, and then upward across the muscled wedge of his abdomen and chest. Though Gabriel probably weighed close to two hundred pounds, there wasn't an ounce of fat anywhere on his lean body. She continued her survey up the supple bow of his body to the corded column of his neck, past his mouth, and up to his eyes.

To her embarrassment, she realized he'd caught her checking him out.

"What are you looking at, City Girl?" he purred over the rim of his glass, his eyes flashing in flint and silver.

She fought back a blush. "Just making a visual assessment, Wild Man."

"And what's your diagnosis?"

"Subject seems to be in good condition—"

"Subject would be in better condition after a full body massage."

"—however, there is evidence of short-term memory loss."

Gabriel chuckled. "Such as?"

"As I recall we were going to talk about Meredith, not massage therapy."

"Ah, Meredith." Gabriel swirled his brandy. "How could I forget sweet, lovable Meredith?"

Evaline sipped her drink. "You said you knew her tactics, Gabe. What did you mean by that?"

"Meredith was always predictable." Gabriel glared down at his glass, his expression darkening immediately. "Whenever she was in trouble, she'd run to me."

Evaline nodded silently, having come to learn Gabriel was the type of person most people would look toward as a source of strength and dependability.

He sighed and kept staring at his liquor. "At first I liked it. I felt needed. I liked slaying dragons for such a beautiful princess."

"She was beautiful?"

"A knockout. Tall, blond, slender—Meredith was every guy's dream."

A frisson of jealousy zipped through Evaline. She took a hasty gulp of brandy. "How did you meet her?"

"A diving trip. Her family was up here on vacation. Spent the summer nearby in their house. She was just out of high school. I was just starting my business."

"So she went out on the *Sea Wolf* with you?"

"Yeah." Gabriel squinted and took a drink. He swallowed and seemed to be considering something which disgusted him. "I should have realized what I was getting into. But I didn't want to. I wanted to see her as the perfect girl with the perfect family and perfect life. I should have known that perfect girls don't slip into a man's room the first night they meet."

"She made love with you the day she met you?"

Gabriel nodded and looked down. "Sex was the only language Meredith knew. It was the only thing we had in common." He glanced up at Evaline, his eyes hard. "When I was twenty, I thought sex was enough to base a lifetime on."

Evaline tried to keep the corners of her mouth from trembling. She hated visualizing Gabriel with another woman, hated the thought that he had considered spending a lifetime with anyone.

"I was young," he continued, "too young to know that hot sex could get cold real fast. And once it did, we had nothing to talk about. It was a nightmare."

"But you married her."

"Oh, I married her all right. She was tricky. Kept flitting back and forth to Seattle, kept me guessing, kept me chasing her, wanting her. She went off to college, and I spent those four years building this house for her, dreaming of the night I would carry her across the threshold and show her the nest I'd created for her, right down to the smallest detail."

"You built this place?" Evaline asked, indicating the living room with a sweep of her goblet.

"Yeah. On dreams and bullshit."

"Gabe, it's beautiful!"

"She didn't think so. Should have seen her face when I showed it to her. Know what she said?"

Evaline's heart sank for him. "What?"

Gabriel tilted his head and mimicked the inflection of his ex-wife's voice, "But, Gabe, you promised me a real house!" He shook his head. "Then we had one of our vicious fights, and she ran back to Daddy in a huff."

"She never lived here?"

"Never set foot in the place."

"I can't believe it!"

"Believe it." Gabriel finished his brandy. "Nothing was ever good enough for her. And you want to know what?"

Evaline raised her brows.

"I was fool enough to try to please her, even after the house fiasco. She was pregnant then, and I was determined to make a family out of us. So I moved to Seattle. I gave up my charter business and worked for her father."

"That doesn't sound like you, Gabe."

"Damn right." He snorted in disgust. "I was miserable. Each day I lived in Seattle, the city chipped away at my soul."

Evaline looked down at her glass. She knew exactly what he was talking about. Since her arrival at Obstruction Bay, she had come to realize just how much of her soul had been lost in Seattle away from her heritage. Little by little she was regaining it, but she still had a long way to go.

"How long did you work for Meredith's father?"

"About a year, until Allison was born. Soon afterward, I realized I couldn't take it anymore."

"So you came back here?"

He nodded. "Meredith refused to live out in 'the boonies' as she termed the area. She called me a quitter, a loser, all the usual stuff. She'd already found a guy to take my place, so I left. And she stayed in Seattle."

"She had an affair while she was married to you?"

Gabriel's eyes narrowed. "After Allison was born, Meredith was worse than ever. I don't think she was ready for the responsibility of being a wife and mother. She had one affair after another."

"I don't understand," Evaline murmured. "Why would she ever cheat on a man like you?"

Gabriel flushed and gazed at her face, his stare plunging into hers. Then he broke off his gaze and picked up the bottle of brandy.

"One more round?" he asked gruffly.

"Why not?" Evaline held up her glass as he poured another drink for them. "Thanks."

"You're welcome." Gabriel returned the bottle to the tray and sat back. "She might have called me a loser, but she always came back. Whenever her heart was broken, or some guy didn't treat her right, she'd call me up and cry on the phone about how much she still loved me, that she was sorry and wanted to start over again. Those first few years were a living hell—because I was naive enough to believe her."

"That she loved you?"

"Yeah. It took me a while, but I finally figured out that Meredith wasn't mature enough to know what love was. She was always talking about 'finding herself' and 'tapping into her inner spirit.' But the only thing that got tapped was her pocketbook by guys who took advantage of her. The bloodsucking bastards."

"She was well-off?"

"She never had to work a day in her life. Her daddy saw to that."

Evaline wondered what it would be like to live a life of ease. Maybe it wasn't so great, judging by the problems Meredith experienced. She cupped her goblet in both hands. "So why do you think she's bothering us?"

"She wants something, plain and simple."

"But what? And why the song?"

"'Time and Place' was her favorite song. I once thought it was our special song, until I saw her dancing with some other guy and singing it in his ear. She played that damn song so often, I wanted to break every stereo in the house."

"Do you think she's trying to tell you something? When the music plays in Allison's room, that line keeps coming up about going through time with someone. Could that be you and Allison? Could she have finally realized what she'd given up?"

"I doubt it, Evaline," he replied bitterly. "Meredith was never that deep."

Evaline watched his expression darken and worried that his emotions seemed far too raw for a man who had been divorced for twelve years from the woman in question. What if he still harbored strong feelings for Meredith? What if he would always love her, even after death? It would break Evaline's heart.

Evaline traced the rim of her glass with her fingertip.

The brandy, combined with her doubts and fears, burned like fire in her stomach. "Do you still love her, Gabriel?"

"Love her? No." Gabriel snorted again and sipped his drink. "I wanted to love her, for Allison's sake." He swallowed and looked up at the ceiling. "But I didn't know what love was any more than Meredith did."

"I doubt that."

Gabriel leveled his gaze on her again. "What makes you so sure?"

"You seem like a practical, responsible guy to me. Someone who has had a lot of time to think."

"Yeah, well, I've never had much opportunity to test my theories. If you haven't noticed, women are scarce out here."

"They don't have to be."

A small smile tugged at the corners of his mouth. "Meaning what?"

"That I don't think you wanted to look." Evaline set her glass on the coffee table. "Meredith hurt you, didn't she? And you weren't about to get yourself in a similar situation again, were you?"

His slight smile vanished.

"She's the reason you mistrust women and doubt your own judgment, isn't she?"

He shrugged. "A person learns from their experiences, Evaline. That was the lesson I learned."

"But there are so many other experiences you could have."

"I know that, City Girl." He leaned forward to put his snifter on the tray and remained posed in front of her, his left forearm draped across his knee. "But I don't want just any woman. I want something genuine and meaningful with a real person." He glanced up at her, and their gazes linked until Evaline's nerves slowly dissolved. Her mouth went dry and she scooted forward in her chair, knowing she was headed for the point of no return again.

But scooting forward only brought her closer to Gabriel. She knew she should say good night and slip past him, but her tongue was glued to the top of her mouth, and her feet seemed pasted to the floor. The chair and Gabriel's steady gaze had taken her prisoner.

Then he reached for her hands.

17

"You're real, Evaline," Gabriel said, raising her hands to his mouth. He kissed her knuckles while Evaline watched in fascination. "More real than anyone I've come across in a long time."

"Don't let me fool you," she murmured.

"Why would you?" he retorted, his words husky with emotion. His eyes were like pools of smoky quartz, drawing her in. "Neither one of us plays games." He tugged her closer for a kiss and tipped her off-balance. With a small yelp, she fell against his hard body, and he caught her in his arms, pulling her onto him as he collapsed against the couch. His lips claimed hers in an electrifying kiss.

"Gabriel!" she gasped, breaking from his insistent mouth and scrambling to sit up.

"Don't!" he whispered, urging her back down. "Please."

He caught her thighs in his hands and pulled her even closer, inducing her to straddle his hips. She gasped again when she felt the hard length of him beneath his shorts.

The only barrier between them were two thin layers of cotton—his shorts and her T-shirt and panties—and she could feel every bulging contour of his straining shaft. Unable to resist touching him, she closed her eyes and eased her hips upward, barely rubbing against him.

Gabriel sucked in his breath and held it as she moved back down. Her panties were slick and wet by the time she settled into his lap, and Gabriel had ceased to take audible breaths. He kissed her thoroughly, pushing one hand into her hair and removing the clip that held it up. Her raven hair, like heavy silk, fell upon her shoulders and down her back. He drew his fingers through her shining tresses.

"Such beautiful hair," he commented, "like women in Gauguin's paintings."

From her art history classes in college, she remembered the lithesome, raven-haired South Sea Island women painted by Paul Gauguin. Gabriel's flattery warmed her, and his knowledge of art impressed her.

"Thank you," she replied. But flattery couldn't compete with the seductive words his body spoke to her.

Gabriel's hands slid down her torso to the hem of her shirt. He began to ease it upward, but Evaline stopped him.

"Don't take it off," she murmured, her hands on his wrists, afraid he'd see the scars on her torso that the surgeons had advised were better left untouched. "Allison might wake up and come out."

Gabriel didn't say anything. Instead, he leaned forward and found her nipples, which poked against the cotton fabric like wild rose hips. He kissed her through the shirt, then gently tugged at her nipples with his teeth. Evaline thought she would burst at the sensation that streaked through her. Involuntarily she arched against him again. Gabriel groaned.

The next time he attempted to push up her shirt, just enough to expose her breasts, she didn't stop him. She watched him take her right breast in his mouth, but closed her eyes again when his warm hands cradled her torso and he sucked her hungrily. Her breasts seemed to be a conduit to her womb, and she was alarmed at her strong compulsion to connect with Gabriel, to have him fill her up as she suckled him. Her breath came hard and fast the more he kissed her, stroked her, and laved her with his tongue. Before she knew it, her hips were moving in rhythm to his tongue, and he was echoing every one of her gentle undulations with one of his own.

Then she felt his hand between them, pulling away the cotton barriers. She kissed him, trying to ignore what he was doing, trying to deny that she was allowing him to go this far. And yet, she wanted him inside her, just as much as he wanted her. Evaline kissed his jaw, then froze, her lips near his ear, as he pulled aside the crotch of her panties, and she felt his warm, blunt tip against her sensitive folds. The touch of him was like nothing she'd ever felt before. Suddenly, it was her turn to quit breathing.

Gabriel paused, waiting for her response. Evaline glanced down and saw the thick column of his manhood bridging the distance between them. Instantly, a sheen of sweat broke out under her T-shirt. He was going to put that huge curved thing inside her? Before she could react, Gabriel moved slightly and his warm tip slid downward to a more intimate spot. She ached and throbbed for him there, regardless of what she thought about the disparity in their proportions. He gave a small push of his hips and slid a fraction of the way into her. She tensed, the muscles of her thighs straining to keep him at bay, poised at her entrance.

"Jesus, Evaline," he whispered, his nose pressed between her breasts.

Evaline hung above him, rigid with worry that his body might be too large for her. In theory she knew how these things worked between a man and a woman, but in actual practice she wasn't so certain.

"Gabe, you're so"—she blushed hotly—"so big!"

"It'll be all right," he replied. "You'll see."

"I don't know—"

"Go slow, just like you're doing." He glanced at her, his cheekbones pink.

She flushed again, worried that he might guess she hadn't the faintest notion of what to do and was proceeding purely on instinct. She caressed his cheek with the palm of her hand and leaned forward to kiss him. The tips of their noses brushed, and she discovered even her nose had become an erogenous zone.

Then Gabriel moved his hips again, stroking her back and forth and dipping the tip of his shaft into her, but letting her control the depth of penetration. He must have known his rhythm would eventually overpower her misgivings. Slowly, Evaline sank lower and lower, and with each dip he eased in more and more of himself, gritting his teeth with the effort of holding back. His hands swept down the sides of her torso and encircled her waist as he concentrated on the gradual but unbelievable perfection of their joining. Each of them watched the process, entranced by the sight of one another and breathless with pleasure.

Evaline thrilled as he pushed in farther, but still only halfway. Then something painful tweaked her momentarily, like a stitch in her side, and she flinched upward. "Ow!" she gasped.

Gabriel paused. "Am I hurting you?"

"No, it's just that for a moment I—"

"Wait a minute!" Gabriel exclaimed, straightening. "My God, Evaline!" He slipped out of her and held her hips away from him. "Goddamn, you're a virgin, aren't you?"

"Yes." Evaline reached for his shoulders, urging him to return to her. "Is there something wrong with that?"

"How old are you?"

"Twenty-seven."

"Goddamn!"

"It doesn't matter, Gabe—"

"The hell it doesn't." His fingers squeezed her waist. "We're not going to do it like this, half-dressed and falling off the couch—not your first time."

"It'll be all right, Gabe. Really!"

She leaned forward, pressing her breasts against him and wanting more than anything to lose her virginity to Gabriel now, half-dressed or not. She tried to wriggle closer, but his arms remained outstretched, keeping her at a distance.

"No. Let's make it special," he continued, kissing her neck. "Let me make it special for both of us, Evaline. As it should be."

"You're making me crazy, that's what you're doing," Evaline moaned against his temple, her lips in his hair. "Hot and cold, cold and hot."

"There's nothing cold about either one of us," he retorted. "And there never will be." He slipped his hand between them and explored her with his middle finger, finding her hard, aching nub.

"Gabe!" she gasped, closing her eyes against the sudden swell of desire he unleashed.

"That's right." He stroked her, leaning forward to kiss her navel. She thought she'd surge so powerfully, she would turn inside out. "Just go with it, Evaline," he urged.

The sound of his rich deep voice speaking her name sent a warm shimmer through her. Evaline tensed her legs and arched up, her breasts thrust outward as she chased the riot of heat flaring inside her. How could she have lived for so many years without knowing what it felt like to do this? Yet would crossing this threshold have been the same without Gabriel? Evaline knew the answer without thinking. The time for lovemaking had come at long last, and the time was right with this man. But with this man only.

"Ah, Evaline!" he breathed. She knew he was watching her and enjoying the sight, which only heightened her escalating pleasure.

She writhed against his hand and within moments burst into a glorious climax, and it was unlike anything she had ever felt. Her eyes flew open in astonishment as his name burst through her lips.

"Jesus!" Gabriel swore, still framing her hip with one hand. "Jesus, Evaline!"

She hung in a state of shocked ecstasy, barely able to contain the shooting waves of her climax, sure that she would burst into flames. Then she collapsed on his chest, totally sated.

Evaline knew by the look on his face and the incredulity in his voice that their interlude on the couch had been extraordinary. She'd guessed as much, but in her inexperience, she had nothing on which to base her opinion. She couldn't help wondering what true lovemaking would be like with Gabriel. She couldn't imagine anything more special than what he'd just given her.

"Gabe," she whispered, her lips thick with passion. "That was wonderful!"

She could feel him smile against her cheek. "There's plenty more where that came from, beautiful."

Gabriel held her close until she caught her breath, and then he kissed her long and hard, sealing her love of him forever.

"I want to take you out on the boat," he murmured,

"where we can have complete privacy. As soon as this Meredith business is over."

He rose up to gaze at her face and lightly traced the edge of her mouth with his index finger. Instantly Evaline froze, worried that Gabriel might try to explore the rest of her body. She didn't trust their new relationship enough to allow him to stare at her openly and at such close range.

"Evaline?" he asked, straightening. "Are you all right?"

"Yes."

Evaline drew away and struggled to get to her feet.

"What's wrong?" Gabriel asked. "Is it about Meredith?"

"No." Evaline smoothed her T-shirt. "It's late, Gabe. We should get some sleep."

His brows drew together, slashed by a deep crease. "Did you hear something?"

"No. But I should go." She bent down and gave him a quick kiss before he could ask any more questions. "Good night," she said softly. Then she hurried out of the living room and stumbled to her bed.

To Gabriel's credit, he didn't allude to their changing relationship the next day and remained quietly reserved. After dinner, he sat on the couch and read the daily paper, as was his custom, careful to keep his eyes and his hands to himself whenever Allison was present.

Although Gabriel had no television, he did receive the newspaper, which he picked up each day with his mail by driving down to the end of the lane, where a minor highway passed by, about two miles away. Each evening after dinner, Gabriel drank a beer on the deck and read through the paper, or if it was raining, he sat on the couch and slowly flipped through the newspaper sections while

Evaline puttered in the kitchen, cleaning up for the night or getting ready for the next day. Sometimes Allison snatched the classified section, sat at the dining-room table, and completed the daily crossword puzzle. None of them said much to each other, but the silence was no longer sharp with hard feelings.

Evaline loved those quiet times when they relaxed together at the end of the day. She didn't care whether there was conversation or not. The simple presence of other human beings was enough for her.

"Well, would you look at this," Gabriel remarked, folding back the front page of the newspaper with a loud snap.

"Look at what?" Evaline drifted toward the couch, wiping her hands on a towel.

Allison looked up as Evaline peered over Gabriel's shoulder at the newspaper article.

"Stephen Durrell is building a retreat north of Seattle."

"Oh?"

"There's a drawing here." He held up the page. "Look, it's huge!"

"What do they say about it?" Evaline inquired, leaning closer.

Gabriel lowered the paper to read the article. "'Dr. Stephen Durrell, well-known guru of New Agers all over the world, has chosen LaConner, Washington, a small town north of Seattle, as the site of his research and retreat center. Dr. Durrell has gained international attention for his much-touted personal growth system dubbed "The Path" and has an estimated following of three million disciples, mostly comprised of baby boomers and generation X-ers. The construction of the new center, already known as Trailhead, will be completed in the fall of next year, and will be comprised of a thirty-thousand-square-foot research center, six lodging facilities, four pools, several sports courts, and situated on twenty wooded acres.'"

"Sounds like a great place to vacation," Evaline commented, shaking her head. "How much do you think the place will cost to build?"

Gabriel scanned the article. "Thirty-six million, it says here."

"Thirty-six million?" Evaline whistled. "Boy, Durrell must have sold a ton of inspirational tapes."

"Or has some flush friends," Gabriel muttered. He fell silent, and a familiar scowl darkened his expression.

"I wonder why he's building in the Northwest?" Evaline mused, strolling back toward the kitchen. "Seattle is quite a distance from Greece."

"He never liked Greece," Allison put in, surprising Evaline, for the girl rarely talked when all three of them were present. "He was always bugging Mother to move back to the States."

Evaline glanced down at Allison. "How long did your mom live in Greece?"

"Only a year. But she was going to stay there longer. She told me so, before"—Allison fumbled with her pencil—"before the fire."

"Is Stephen Durrell from the Seattle area?"

"I don't think so." Allison frowned. "Come to think of it, I don't know where he's from."

"Fourth roadapple from the sun," Gabriel quipped from across the room.

Allison almost laughed at his remark, but disguised her slip by coughing, and quickly returned to her puzzle.

Evaline patted her shoulder and walked on to the kitchen. She wondered what type of people would follow a man like Stephen Durrell, and what sort of person would give him huge sums of money. Had Meredith funded part of his project? She thought about the ram's-head aura that she had seen surrounding Stephen. A person with such an aura had a tendency to misuse their talents. And though he had done nothing to make her suspect his motives, Evaline distrusted his outward charm.

Tomorrow was July 10, the day she'd agreed to meet Stephen. She wasn't looking forward to their rendezvous.

18

The next afternoon, Evaline reached the last curve in the lane and scanned the highway for signs of Stephen Durrell. She'd told Gabriel she was going for a walk, and he hadn't questioned her because taking a walk was nothing out of the ordinary for her. Still, she felt more than a little guilty. Her meeting with Stephen had taken on an aspect of betrayal, even though she was seeing him to update him on Allison's progress. Where was the harm in that? The next meeting, however, she would insist they talk at the house, in the open, no matter what objections Gabriel might make. She would rather face Gabriel's wrath than sneak around behind his back like this.

By the time she reached the turnoff, the back of her blouse was wet with perspiration, both from the heat of the July day and from her wish to get the meeting over with as soon as possible. The forest around her lay silent and dark, but she couldn't shake the feeling that someone or something was watching her. Evaline stood in the turnoff, throwing uneasy glances over her shoulder. She looked at her watch. One-fifty-five.

Moments later, a white Jaguar turned off the highway and glided to a stop in front of her. She had only to look at the vanity plate, PATHMAN, to know the identity of the driver. She stepped closer as the front passenger window slid down and Stephen ducked into view.

"Evaline," he greeted. "Get in and we'll talk."

"Okay." She slipped into the car and sank against the smooth leather interior, grateful for the cool breeze blowing from the air conditioner. The electric window closed, sealing her inside with Stephen. She glanced at him.

He was dressed in a blue-and-white-striped shirt, silver jewelry, and a pair of jeans so perfectly pressed, they looked as if they'd never been worn before. She'd take Gabriel's rugged, practical clothes over this man's impeccable attire any day. Gabriel's clean scent and functional clothes complemented his manliness and strength, while Stephen's fastidious perfection detracted from what masculinity he possessed. She couldn't imagine Gabriel with his shirt collar turned up at the back of his neck, or sporting a diamond-laced bracelet, and didn't care if he ever wore anything but plaid shirts and jeans.

Stephen guided the Jaguar out onto the highway again and headed toward Port Angeles. Evaline had never been in such a luxurious car and commented on the absence of road noise.

"You get what you pay for," Stephen said with a wink.

Evaline smiled slightly. "Where are we going?"

"Oh, just down the road for a bit. I didn't want to sit and talk by the mailbox, in case Townsend catches sight of us. He doesn't know you're seeing me, does he?"

"No, but I'd like to talk about that."

"What do you mean?"

"I don't like sneaking around on him."

"You're not sneaking around, Evaline," Stephen replied. "Why would you think that?"

"I feel like I'm spying on him and reporting to you."

"For Allison's sake." He glanced at her. "We're doing this for Allison's sake, remember?"

"Gabriel doesn't pose a threat to her. I'm sure of it."

"Still, it won't do any harm to be discreet."

"Gabriel wouldn't see it that way."

"And why do we suddenly care what Townsend thinks?" Stephen shot a penetrating glance at her.

Evaline gazed straight ahead, willing herself not to blush.

"What he thinks is of no concern," Stephen added. "You and I are here to see to Allison's health and future. And the sooner we get her away from him the better."

"I'm not so sure that's true."

Stephen shot her another sharp look. "What are you saying?"

"Allison has made a lot of progress."

"In what way? Is she walking?"

"No, but she's calmed down considerably. Soon I think she'll be ready to talk about the fire."

Evaline watched the play of tendons on Stephen's hands as he suddenly gripped the wheel more tightly.

"I urge you to approach that subject with much caution, Evaline," he warned in a slow, measured tone.

"I'm not about to rush her." Evaline studied the side of Stephen's face. Unlike Gabriel, whose emotions flared uncensored and mostly unchecked, Stephen kept his expression under complete control. She wondered if he ever responded with anything but a charming smile. And she was beginning to wonder if she should trust him.

"Surely you don't attribute her progress to living with Townsend."

"I believe a number of factors are involved, including

being isolated from negative influences, and being forced to interact with her father and me. She's learned that if she doesn't share in the work, she doesn't eat."

"That's barbaric!" Stephen exclaimed.

"But effective."

"You mean Townsend is starving her into submission?"

"He isn't starving her." Evaline frowned. "Why must you always suspect him of cruelty?"

"From what Meredith told me, I thought it was a logical conclusion to draw."

"Well, from what I've heard about Meredith, she might not have been the best judge of character."

"Where'd you hear that?" Stephen laughed mirthlessly. "Let me guess—from Townsend?"

"From Allison, as a matter of fact."

Stephen's smile hovered on his thin lips. "When it comes to Meredith, I wouldn't believe either of them, father or daughter. Poor Allison has had difficulties with her mother for years. Surely you wouldn't take the child's view of her mother as truth."

"A child's view is sometimes clearer than most."

"In Allison's case, I think not." He looked at his watch, then pulled into a gas station and slowly turned around. "Would you like anything before we head back? A soda? Mineral water?"

"Nothing, thanks."

Stephen guided his sleek car back onto the highway. "What about Allison's nightmares? Are they still recurring?"

"Yes."

"But you've continued the medication?"

"Yes." Again Evaline wondered why Stephen was so adamant that she continue to administer drugs.

"Good." He set the cruise control. "When Allison is

evaluated and returned to her grandparents' care in the fall, we'll have her see a specialist about those dreams of hers. We'll get to the root of that problem right away."

"You seem certain that Allison will be taken away from Gabriel."

"Why shouldn't I be?" Stephen replied with a smile. "I can't imagine she'll get better in the time allowed—unless a miracle occurs."

Evaline stared at him, hating the smugness in his tone. He was so assured, so confident, and seemingly insensitive to the fact that his plans to take Allison away from her father might destroy Gabriel. She wondered why he was set on separating father from daughter. She guessed it was purely a male power play in one-upmanship, using Allison as a pawn. The thought of toying with a child's welfare for personal satisfaction disgusted her.

"Surely you believe in miracles, Mr. Durrell," she remarked coolly, crossing her arms over her chest.

He glanced at her and gave a short laugh. "Of course I do, Evaline. And if Gabriel Townsend can work a miracle in the month and a half he has left, the more power to him."

"The best way to handle this is with all of us working together."

"I don't agree."

"You don't know Gabriel, Mr. Durrell."

"And I don't intend to."

Evaline frowned and turned to him. "Then perhaps we'd better discuss our options, because I am not going to meet you alone like this again. In fact, I plan to tell Gabriel that I have been making reports to you."

"Toward what purpose?" he asked.

"To get things out in the open."

She watched Stephen squeeze the wheel tightly, but never once did his calm expression change. He swallowed, and she saw his Adam's apple rise above his perfectly pressed collar and sink back down.

"May I remind you, Evaline, that you are working for me?"

"I know that."

"May I also remind you that a generous scholarship has been offered to you in payment for your cooperation?"

"I still don't see why being aboveboard would jeopardize anything."

"Let's just say silence is my preference in the matter," Stephen replied. "And leave it at that."

Evaline glared out the side window. The scholarship to medical school suddenly didn't seem so important when weighed against the possibility of hurting Gabriel. The longer they talked, the stronger her feeling of disquiet became, and the more she distrusted Stephen. She felt the prickling of his gaze on the side of her face and turned.

"Why the silence?" she asked, studying him for the slightest reaction. "What are you hiding?"

He merely smiled. "I told you, Evaline. It's because of Townsend."

"I don't believe you."

He gave a small light laugh, but she wasn't fooled and heard instead the tenseness behind the sound.

"There's something going on," Evaline continued. "You have an agenda you haven't told me about, don't you?"

"And if I should, what of it?" he replied. "I am your employer. I don't have to tell you everything." He pulled off the road.

Evaline glanced out of the car. They had arrived at the lane leading to Obstruction Bay. Stephen rolled up to the mailbox and parked, but didn't turn off the engine. Evaline put her fingers on the handle of the door, anxious to get out of the car, but she paused when he turned to her.

"Do I have your word, Evaline, that you won't speak to Townsend of our affiliation?"

She considered his question for a moment. Her future career might ride on her answer. Still, she knew without a doubt what her response would be. "No," she replied, "I can't promise that." She pushed her shoulder against the door.

"Even if your cooperation might ensure the safety of your father?"

Evaline jerked around to face him. "What?"

"Your father. I know all about him. I know where he is."

"You know about my father?"

Stephen rolled his eyes. "I told you, Evaline. I made it a point to find out everything about you, including the fact that your father was charged with murder and is a criminal at large."

She gaped at him, unable to speak, her mind reeling with questions. She hadn't seen her father since he had escaped from jail. Where was he now? Mexico? He certainly couldn't have returned to the reservation he betrayed.

"I could make it easy or hard for old Reuven. And he *is* quite old, is he not?"

"Yes." Her voice was barely a whisper.

"It would be a shame to spend one's final days in a federal prison."

"It would kill him."

"Yes, it probably would. But that's what cooperation is all about, Evaline. You cooperate with me, and I will see that he remains unmolested by the authorities.

"Now"—he smiled one of his most charming smiles—"what about our agreement?"

"All right! I won't say anything!" Evaline jumped out of the Jaguar. She slammed the door and hurried down the lane toward the bay without looking back. The bastard had blackmailed her into submission. If she said anything to Gabriel and Gabriel took action, she was sure Stephen would retaliate by turning in her father. The longer she reviewed the discussion in the car, the angrier she became. She vowed she'd do everything in her power to make a miracle happen to keep Allison away from Stephen. He didn't have the girl's best interest at heart. There was something else motivating him, but she didn't know what it was. And until she did, she wouldn't trust the man or follow his advice, especially his views on keeping Allison medicated. Perhaps, she thought, there was a reason Stephen didn't *want* Allison to regain her memory or her ability to walk.

Evaline strode down the lane, her pace driven by her racing thoughts. The first thing she'd do was wean Allison off the pills. Immediately.

Evaline returned to the house just after three o'clock, checked on Allison, then started dinner. Gabriel didn't show for the evening meal and skipped his habit of reading the paper. He left in his pickup shortly after seven and didn't return by the time Evaline retired for the night.

She stretched out on the sheets, worrying that once again something had gone awry with Gabriel. She knew him well enough now to realize that he remained at a distance when he didn't feel capable of handling his strong emotions. But he would soon come forward to confront her. Had she hurt his feelings by drawing away too quickly on the couch the other night? Surely that wouldn't be the cause for this latest silence. Evaline sighed and rolled onto her side, listening in vain for the sound of Gabriel's truck returning.

The next morning, just after the breakfast dishes were done and Allison was in the shower, Evaline heard the front door slam. She looked up from her stance by the kitchen sink to see Gabriel and Skeeter standing in the living room.

"Hi, Ev," Skeeter greeted with a nod, but his usual grin looked green around the edges.

"Good morning, Skeeter."

She glanced at Gabriel, who jabbed his thumb in the direction of the bedroom.

"Pack your things," he said. Then he stomped through the living room and down the hall.

Evaline trailed after him. "I beg your pardon?"

"I said pack your things, Miss Jaye."

He was back to addressing her formally. What was going on? Evaline took one look at his grim expression and knew whatever was wrong this time was much worse than the abrupt ending to their lovemaking.

"Gabe! What's going on?" She reached for his sleeve, but he yanked away.

"Get your clothes together," he grated between clenched teeth. "Skeeter, take her equipment out to the truck."

"Sure thing." Skeeter ducked out of sight, obviously happy to be out of the range of Gabriel's anger.

Gabriel strode to the bedroom closet and snatched Evaline's two suitcases off the top shelf. "Here," he said, throwing them on the bed. "Pack up!"

Evaline stood in the center of the room, galvanized. "Why?" she exclaimed. "What's going on?"

Gabriel glared at her again and crossed the room to the dresser. He pulled the top drawer so hard it nearly fell out of the frame. He grabbed a bunch of her underwear and threw it on the bed.

"Gabe!" Evaline shouted.

He turned, his face and neck red with rage. "I saw you yesterday. With Durrell."

Though she had nothing to be ashamed of, Evaline flushed deeply. Her sense of being watched yesterday had been correct. Gabriel must have followed her from the house and saw her get into Durrell's car. "So?" she blurted.

"What is it with him?" Gabriel blurted. "First Meredith and now you!"

"It isn't like that—"

"I don't want that bastard having anything to do with Allison. I don't trust him." He threw another handful of socks and brassieres on the bed. "And I see now that I can't trust you!"

"You're jumping to conclusions, Gabe!"

"Am I? I gave the benefit of doubt to Meredith a hundred times. Where did it get me? Nowhere."

"I told you before, I am not Meredith."

"You might as well be, goddammit." Eyes blazing, he threw more clothes. "Now get over there and pack your bags."

Caught in a numb zone between rage and tears, Evaline stumbled to the bed and flung her belongings into the nearest suitcase without bothering to fold them. She knew better than to try to explain herself to Gabriel right now. He was in no mood to listen to reason, and if she told him of her initial purpose for coming to the house—to protect Allison from an abusive father—the information would only inflame him more. Her clothes blurred on the bed as a shimmer of hot tears burned her eyes.

"And what's this?" Gabriel demanded.

Evaline looked over her shoulder and recognized the small square of paper in his hand as the photograph she'd found in Allison's room.

"A photo," she replied tersely, returning to her packing.

"So you've been snooping around my boat, too. Spying on me. Why? What's Durrell want?"

"Oh, for goodness sake, Gabe!"

"Then where'd you get this picture?"

"In Allison's room, after the last incident with Meredith."

"Why didn't you show it to me?"

"Because I forgot." She yanked the zipper shut around the suitcase.

He stepped closer. "Why were you keeping it?"

Evaline turned and stared at him, her tears flash-dried by anger. "I told you I forgot about it. I don't even know who the hell it is!"

"It's Allison."

"With dark hair?"

"Allison at seven. This was the last photograph of her that Meredith ever sent to me."

Evaline returned to her packing, not as interested in the photograph as Gabriel. She could hear the shower still running and worried that Gabriel would hustle her out of the house without permitting her to say good-bye to Allison. The girl took extraordinarily long showers and spent at least a half hour doing her hair and makeup afterward. They'd be halfway to Port Angeles before Allison was out of the bathroom.

"So you've gone through my stuff on the *Sea Wolf*," Gabriel continued. "Why? You're working for Durrell, aren't you?"

"I have not gone through your things!"

"Don't bother to lie." Gabriel held up the photograph. "This shot of Allison is from an album I have on the boat."

"Maybe it's a duplicate."

"It isn't." He glanced at the back of the snapshot. "To Dad," he read, "Love, Allie."

Evaline heaved an exasperated sigh. "I don't know

how the photo got in Allison's room. But that's where I found it."

"Can't you be more imaginative than that?" he goaded. "Make that lying, cheating bastard Durrell proud of you!"

"Go to hell, Townsend!" She flung open the second suitcase and threw in her jeans and slacks. The noise of the shower thundered in her ears.

Gabriel stuffed the photo into the chest pocket of his shirt. After a long tense silence, he said, "I trusted you."

Evaline turned slightly to look at him. "No, you didn't." She straightened. "You don't know how to trust, Gabriel."

He flushed but said nothing.

Still staring at him, she dragged her luggage off the bed. "I'd like to say good-bye to Allison."

"Not a good idea."

She shook her head in exasperation at his relapse into gruffness and bad communication. Evaline trudged to the door of the bedroom. Then she stopped. "But what about the September deadline? What's going to happen with her?"

"That's none of your business now." He brushed past her. "Skeeter, you got Miss Jaye's stuff loaded?"

"Aye aye, Captain." Skeeter held open the front door for them.

"Good. I'll be back as soon as I can." Gabriel hurried down the steps toward the waiting pickup.

Evaline set her suitcases down. "I guess this is good-bye, Skeeter," she said.

"I can't believe he's doing this, Ev." Skeeter's brown eyes were more serious than she'd ever seen them. "You're the best thing that ever happened—to the both of them!"

"Miss Jaye!" Gabriel called. "Hurry it up!"

Evaline fumbled in her purse and found her case of

business cards. She handed one to Skeeter. "If Allison wants to talk to me, please have her call me, Skeeter. There's a phone in the nightstand in the master bedroom. Would you tell her that?"

"Sure will, Ev."

"And if something happens—" She broke off, her voice suddenly choked by emotion, forcing her to look down so Skeeter wouldn't see her tears.

"Don't worry." Skeeter patted her shoulder. "This can't be the end," he said. "Gabe'll come around, I know he will."

"He doesn't trust me. He won't listen to a word I say."

"He's like that sometimes. But it won't last, Ev. You'll see."

"No, I won't be coming back. Not when he doesn't trust me."

Gabriel tooted the horn, impatient to leave. Evaline glared at the truck, then picked up her bags. "Well, so long, Skeeter. And would you please tell Allison good-bye for me?"

"I'll do that, Ev." He looked down at her card, then quickly back up. "You take care now."

"I will. 'Bye!" She hurried down the steps and across the driveway, hardly able to see through the tears welling in her eyes.

That evening, at her apartment in Seattle, she finally got through on the telephone to Stephen Durrell to explain what had transpired at the house.

"He did *what?*" Stephen exclaimed.

"He saw us together and kicked me out."

"This complicates things."

Evaline could hear his frown over the phone line.

"We had a deal, Evaline," he said at length. "You have to go back."

"I can't. Gabe was really angry. He'll never let me set foot on his property again."

"Why didn't you talk to him and smooth things over?"

"I couldn't. He wouldn't let me get a word in edgewise. I told you we should have met at the house, out in the open."

"Honesty is not always the best policy, Evaline."

She paused, struck again by the duality of Durrell's nature. An evangelist should embrace honesty in everything, not practice selective truth. "Honesty would have been better in this case, believe me."

Stephen clicked his tongue, then said firmly, "If you don't go back, Evaline, we'll have no choice but to rescind the scholarship offer."

Evaline's heart sank, but she wasn't surprised at his threat. Still, she wouldn't go back to Obstruction Bay and lie to Gabriel for the sake of an educational grant.

"Evaline?"

"I heard you," she retorted.

"And I can't promise your father will remain out of the hands of the authorities either."

Evaline's heart surged with pain. Yet her father had made his own choices, dug his own grave as they say. With a swell of certainty filling her chest, Evaline realized she could no longer choose her father over Gabe and Allison. Reuven Jaye would have to take his chances.

"I understand," she replied evenly.

"Evaline, I am very disappointed in you." Stephen sighed. "And I am very concerned about Allison's future. As are her grandparents."

"So am I."

"Then let's work together."

"No, thanks," Evaline said, squaring her shoulders and

knowing she was doing the right thing. "I'm through working with you. Good-bye, Mr. Durrell."

She hung up the phone before he could say anything more, and worried that he'd call back immediately to threaten her with more information about her father. But the telephone remained ominously still. Evaline kept glancing at it as she prepared for work at the medical center the next day. She had a detailed report to write about the Townsends and didn't look forward to explaining her reasons for quitting the job.

19

"*So, dinner at the Space Needle is off, eh?*" Patty Johnson chided, reminding Evaline of their bet concerning Gabriel Townsend. She leaned on the admitting counter and grinned. "Couldn't take it, eh?"

"Nope." Evaline faked a smile. A week had passed since Gabriel had dumped her off at the ferry terminal, and the wound of separation was still as raw as ever. Allison hadn't called her either. She hoped Skeeter had told Allison it wasn't her fault that she'd left, but she had no way of knowing how Allison had taken her sudden departure.

"How about lunch at the cafeteria?" Patty continued. "I'm starving. And I want to hear all about your adventures with Mr. Personality."

Evaline watched the bubbles in the fish tank rise in a sparkling column from the blue rocks to the green plants floating on the surface. She wasn't ready to discuss Gabriel and Allison yet, and perhaps never would be. "I'd like to, Patty," she replied, "but I've got a killer schedule today."

She sensed Patty's regard.

"Is there something wrong?" Patty asked at last. "You look awful, Evaline."

"Thanks a lot!"

"Maybe you should take some vacation time."

"I'll be fine." Evaline picked up a file and headed for her next patient. She had to work. She'd been working like a fiend ever since she got back from Obstruction Bay. Her job was the only thing keeping her sane.

July passed in a blur of days seeing patients at the hospital and nights donating her time to soup kitchens and free clinics downtown. Sometimes she fell asleep on the couch in her living room, unable to face the questions that plagued her whenever she lay in bed. How had Allison's photo traveled from Gabriel's boat to Allison's bedroom? Surely Allison hadn't retrieved it. And why was Meredith's spirit haunting the girl? Why was Stephen Durrell so concerned about Allison's health? And would Gabriel ever have faith enough in a woman to be able to trust again? No matter how hard Evaline tried to convince herself that the Townsends and their problems were no longer her concern, she couldn't stop worrying about them.

Evaline thought life would become easier to bear as the days passed, but more and more she felt the need to outrun, outwork, and outwit her memories of Obstruction Bay. She missed Allison's quirky sense of humor and Gabriel's strong arms. She wondered if Allison was making any progress and worried that Meredith's entity might make more trouble. She longed for the quiet forests, the sparkling bay, and the cozy fire of the house. There was no one to cook for, which made her apartment kitchen more bleak than ever. The noise and bustle of the city irritated her, and the heat of the bare sidewalks made her yearn for the cool cedar groves. She didn't belong to the cement and steel of the city. She never had. But most of all she missed Gabriel, with an ache that wouldn't go away. She missed his quiet company, his slow smile, his melting eyes and warm lips. And nobody called her City Girl anymore.

August was a repeat of July, broken only by a staff picnic on nearby Lake Washington, and a visit by Carter and Arielle Greyson, friends from her reservation days. Once she had considered Carter the most handsome man she'd ever seen, and had harbored a secret desire for him for years. But now, looking at Carter leaning against the doorway of her kitchen, she was struck by the memory of Gabriel coming into the kitchen half-dressed that one morning, and how attractively mussed he'd appeared. She sighed.

"What's the sigh for?" Carter asked, tilting his head and grinning. "Tired of us already?"

"Oh no!" Evaline replied immediately. "I was just thinking."

"Of what?"

"Of—" She broke off and glanced around. "Of what to serve with the coffee."

"Don't worry about that." Carter laughed and swept into the kitchen, his tight, athletic body remarkably graceful. She remembered that about him from the old days, and the way his black hair fell over his forehead in a thick fringe. "We're going to dinner soon. I don't think Ari'll want anything before we go. I know I don't."

Dr. Arielle Greyson was relaxing in the bathtub after an international flight from Peru to Seattle. Evaline made coffee, glad for the company of her friends, and was looking forward to an evening spent hearing about their latest medical jaunt to South America.

Carter watched her grind the coffee beans and pour them into a filter. He leaned his hip on the counter beside her. "Boy, Evaline, I've got to say, those surgeons did an amazing job on your face." He folded his arms over his chest. "You're a knockout. You know that?"

She blushed and smiled at him. Once she had longed for Carter to give her a second look and see the woman behind the scars. Now, his presence did little but warm her with a sense of enduring friendship, for she had learned the difference between having a crush on a man and coming to truly love someone.

"Thanks, Carter."

"You must have a hundred guys chasing you," he remarked. "Got any good prospects?"

"Why?" she teased, confident now of his place in her life. "Are you interested, Mr. Greyson?"

"And have Ari come after me with a scalpel?" He laughed. "No thanks!"

Evaline grinned and reached for coffee mugs, and when she did, the sleeves of her shirt pulled back to reveal a few blue scars. Carter glanced at them.

"Couldn't they do anything about your arms?" he asked.

"No." Evaline set the cups on the counter. "I only had so much skin for grafts for my face and neck, and each of the grafts left scars themselves."

"Still, it's amazing." He watched as she poured freshly brewed coffee for them. "I bet no one on the reservation would recognize you."

"I wouldn't know. I never go there."

"Yeah. I heard about your father turning his back on you."

"He did it to protect my honor, now that I look back."

"Yeah." Carter lifted the steaming mug and took a sip. He squinted and reminded her again of Gabriel. Her heart squeezed together, aching anew, and she looked down, absently tracing a scar near her wrist.

"Carter," she began. "Can I ask you something?"

He glanced up. "Sure. What?"

"It's personal. And I need you to be honest with me. Really honest."

"I've learned some lessons about the truth." He gave her a slow, endearing smile. "So shoot."

"Do you think . . ." she paused and nervously picked up her coffee cup. "I mean, would a man be—" She blushed and stared out the window at the cluttered alley two floors below, uncertain how to continue.

"Go on," Carter urged. "I'm listening."

"It's kind of embarrassing."

"It can't be that bad, Evaline."

"Well, it's kind of personal." She took a gulp of coffee.

"You're talking to a man who's been bald, bloated, and had tubes stuck up every orifice of his body when he had cancer. I know embarrassing *and* personal, Evaline. Believe me."

She couldn't help but smile. Of all the people in the world, Carter would be the one to understand. His experience as a bone-marrow recipient had given him an appreciation for life and a deep compassion for the human condition.

"Okay." She swallowed. "Do you think if a man cared for me, that my scars would repulse him?"

"Jesus, Evaline!" Carter exclaimed. "Is that what you're worried about?"

She nodded, her eyes searching his face.

"Evaline"—Carter reached for her hands—"any man who is lucky enough to be loved by you wouldn't even notice the scars on your arms."

"But what about my chest? Don't men like women's . . . um. . . women's breasts?"

"Sure they do. But, Evaline, if a guy loves you, he'll love all of you, whatever's on the surface and everything inside."

"That's the theory, but is it really true?"

"Absolutely." Carter squeezed her hands. "Do you have someone in mind?"

"Not any longer. I was afraid to let him see the real me."

Carter squeezed her again. "That's how I was until Ari made me see that the real me wasn't who I was on the outside, or the person I'd been in the past, but the guy I'd become inside."

"Well, I panicked. I didn't know what he'd think."

"And he let you go?"

"Yes." She looked down. He'd not only let her go, he'd sent her packing.

"Then he wasn't worthy of you." Carter released her fingers and tipped up her chin with his left hand. "But the next time, don't let those scars stop you. They're nothing. Believe me."

She nodded and gazed at him. "Thanks, Carter."

But she didn't share Carter's confidence in her character or his statement about Gabriel either. Perhaps she was the unworthy one. Perhaps she'd been guilty of the very thing she'd accused Gabriel of—a lack of trust. She hadn't trusted him enough to reveal herself to him. If she had trusted him enough to share from the very beginning, she and Gabriel might have had a strong enough friendship to weather the misunderstanding about Stephen Durrell. But she had withheld almost everything about herself from Gabriel. And now she was paying for her lack of trust. She was miserable and alone.

*   *   *

The last week of August baked the Seattle area in a record heat wave. Evaline had Saturday off and sat down after breakfast to pay some bills. She dabbed a napkin to her forehead and reached for her iced tea just as the phone rang.

"Hello?" she said, looking up at the ceiling.

"Ev?"

Evaline straightened immediately. "Skeeter?"

"Ev, something's happened. Something real bad. You've got to come out here. Gabriel's out of his mind!"

"What?" Evaline shrieked. "What's happened?"

"You just got to come out. Can you, Evaline?"

"Of course." She glanced at the calendar, knowing she had to see patients on Monday but instantly putting off that concern until later. Patty could take over for her. "But, Skeeter, what's wrong?"

"You know that air harbor at the north end of Lake Washington, where float planes land?"

"In Kenmore?"

"Yeah. Meet me there at noon. I'll pick you up."

"Skeeter!" Evaline exclaimed, hoping he wouldn't hang up in his rush. "Tell me what happened!"

She heard Skeeter make a choking sound on the other end of the line. "Ev—" he blurted. "Ev, Allison's been kidnapped!"

Golden light filtered through the forest as Evaline and Skeeter got out of the plane and jumped onto the dock. Evaline glanced in the direction of the house. None of the lights were on. She glanced over her shoulder at the *Sea Wolf*.

"He's probably on the boat," she remarked. "Come on."

They sprinted down the dock. Just as they came alongside the ship, a large dark shape rose up on the deck in front of them, startling Evaline.

She cried out and stepped back.

"It's just The Major," Skeeter assured her, clutching her arm to steady her.

In shock, Evaline gaped at the bear. Over the course of a month and a half, he'd grown considerably and was now the size of a rottweiler. When he reared up on his hind legs, his big head was almost level with hers, and his shoulders were easily twice the size of hers. He weaved his head back and forth and roared, his upper lip curling to expose a line of huge pointed teeth. Evaline was glad she knew he was as tame as a dog, for his display of bravado would frighten anyone who thought he was a wild animal.

"Hi, Major," Evaline greeted, allowing him to sniff her hand. She'd remembered to bring him an apple, which she pulled out of her pocket and held out. The Major took it from her fingers with his snout, amazingly gentle for a beast his size. She noticed a bandage on his back flank and pointed to it.

"What happened to him?" she asked.

"Somebody shot him," Skeeter replied. "Whoever took Allison winged him pretty good. We found him in the woods behind the house."

"Any idea who it might have been?"

Skeeter shook his head.

"Poor Major. That leg of his seems to be jinxed."

"Yeah." Skeeter stepped onto the boat. "Gabe?" he called. "You here?"

No one answered. Evaline followed Skeeter below. She braced herself for Gabriel's anger as they approached his door, but she wasn't prepared for the sight of him.

He sat against the side of his bunk, unshaven and unkempt, wearing a pair of jeans and a dirty T-shirt. His hair stood in spikes on his head, and his eyes were bleary and red-rimmed when he glared up at them. Beneath the veneer of his tan, the ridges of his face glowed an unhealthy white. He must not have slept since the kidnapping occurred.

"Gabe," Skeeter said, stepping past her, "I brought Evaline."

"So?"

"She can help."

"Like hell!" Gabriel flopped out his arm in an uncontrolled gesture of disgust. He wouldn't look at her, which sent a shaft of dismay through Evaline.

"Gabe," Skeeter commented, "you got to get ahold of yourself."

"Leave me alone."

Evaline stepped into the room. "Skeeter, would you go make some coffee?"

"Sure thing." He left, obviously relieved to let Evaline take over.

She took another step closer to Gabriel and gazed down at his dark head, wishing he would accept her embrace, but knowing better than to attempt to reach out to him.

"Gabe," she said softly. "What happened?"

"Why should I tell you?"

"Because I'm worried sick about Allison!"

"Bullshit," Gabriel retorted. "You're here to spy on us."

"No, I'm not. I don't work for Durrell anymore."

"Think I believe you?"

"Gabe, you never let me explain—"

"You don't have to." He turned away. "I know your kind."

"No, you don't." She leaned closer. He reeked of perspiration. "You don't know me. I never let you get to know the real me."

He didn't reply, but she could tell he was listening, and perhaps wasn't as disinterested as he pretended to be.

"Gabe, I was hired by Stephen Durrell, but I came here to protect Allison, not hurt her."

"I told you to get out." He gave her a sidelong glance, his bloodshot eyes more scathing than ever. "I don't want your help."

"For Allison's sake, let's put aside our differences," she suggested tersely. "And concentrate on finding her. What happened?"

"None of your business, City Girl. I don't want you here."

"I don't care what you want," she retorted in exasperation. She put her hands on her hips. "I'm not here for you. I'm here for Allison. I care about her. And I'm going to stay until she's safe and sound."

He glared at her, squinting his right eye.

"Look at you," she continued, "You're exhausted. How are you going to help her when you can't think straight?"

"I *can't* help her!" Gabriel dropped his head in his right hand and his big shoulders sagged. "These last few weeks have been a nightmare. She's hardly talked to me. I couldn't find anybody to help with her. And now this. I don't know where in the hell else to look for her!" He kneaded his forehead with his fingertips and hunched forward. "I'm not even sure she was kidnapped, Evaline. She might have run away or had an accident. I found her wheelchair on the dock."

"The dock?" A shudder passed through her at the thought of Allison falling into the deep water of the bay and not being able to save herself.

"Yeah." He sighed but didn't look up. Evaline thought he might be covering his face to hide his tears, and her heart twisted inside her chest. She sank to her knees in front of him and placed her hand on his shoulder.

"Gabe!" she said softly.

"Gone, just like that!" he said, his voice cracking with emotion. Evaline guessed it was the first time he'd admitted defeat to anyone, perhaps even to himself. "No note, no good-bye, no clue to what happened."

She slid her hand from the base of his neck to the back of his head and gently stroked his hair. He made no indication that he felt her touch.

"Skeeter said you found The Major wounded behind the house. Do you think he was with Allison when she disappeared?"

"Yeah, but we searched the woods and didn't find anything." Gabriel raised his head slightly. "I've spent hours looking for her, Evaline. I've put up posters, canvassed the area, got divers to look for her, everything. There's no trace of her. No vehicle tracks. Nothing."

"She couldn't have just vanished."

"Well, she did. And it's been raining, making tracking goddamn impossible."

Evaline frowned and bit her lip.

Gabriel straightened a bit. "What about that ghost of yours? Meredith's spirit? Could she have something to do with this?"

"Ghosts don't shoot animals. Humans do."

"Yeah." He sighed heavily.

Evaline tilted her head. "Has Meredith's spirit been making an appearance?"

"Just the music part." Gabriel ran a hand through his thick, unruly hair. "Between Meredith playing that blasted song and The Major bawling his head off, we haven't been getting much sleep around here."

"The Major has been noisy?"

"Noisy as hell."

Evaline recalled the way The Major had fussed during Stephen Durrell's visit to the house weeks ago. She wondered if the bear had sensed a dangerous presence then and during the days before Allison's disappearance. There must have been someone lurking around the house, watching and waiting for an opportunity to snatch the girl.

"When did she disappear?"

"Two days ago, when I went to get the mail."

"Obviously someone knew your schedule."

"And I'll bet it's someone we know," he growled. "Stephen Durrell."

"To ensure that you're judged as incompetent when the time comes for Allison's evaluation."

"I hope to God that's the only reason he's got her."

Gabriel's bleary eyes met hers, and Evaline stared back at him in sudden shock. His burning gaze spoke the unspeakable. The thought that Stephen might do bodily harm to Allison had never entered her mind.

At that moment, Skeeter strode into the house. "Java's ready," he called softly, holding up two mugs.

"Thank you," Evaline said, taking one and handing it to Gabriel. "Here, drink this," she instructed. "I'm going up to the house and make something for all of us to eat. Come up in a half hour when you've showered, and bring a map."

"A map?" Gabriel asked, raising his eyebrows above the rim of the mug.

"Yes, a map. I've got a plan."

20

White shreds of clouds raced over the face of the full moon as Evaline and Gabriel broke into the clearing, half-trotting to keep up with The Major. Skeeter brought up the rear, complaining all the way. Evaline's plan had been to use the bear to track the scent of the kidnapper, and so far her idea seemed to be working.

Across a field stood a dilapidated summer home which had been built decades ago and was slowly rotting under a cloak of moss. The branches of an ancient oak tree, out of place among the cedar, hung over the sagging roofline.

Behind Evaline, a low growl rumbled in The Major's throat, and she glanced at him. He rose up on his hind legs and sniffed the breeze, his snout poking the air as if snatching clues from the sky. His keen sense of smell had brought them this far, just as Evaline had suspected it might. But she couldn't imagine there would be anyone staying in the decrepit structure.

"Allison can't be in there," Skeeter said quietly, echoing her thoughts. "Can she?"

"Naw," Gabriel replied, stepping into the lush grass of the meadow. "Only an idiot would keep her within walking distance of her own house."

Gabriel had showered, shaved, and dressed, and looked like his old self, capable and in command. He slipped his gun out of the back of his jeans and grasped it firmly in his right hand.

"Let's check out the house anyway," Evaline suggested. "We've followed the trail this far. The Major's still getting a strong scent, so let's keep going."

Gabriel nodded and led the way to the old cottage. They approached it cautiously, peering through the grimy broken windows and finding nothing but an overturned chair and a tattered mattress.

"Gabe, look." Skeeter pointed at the young bear, who was waddling toward the water, his nose close to the ground. Evaline trained the flashlight beam on the grass. Two lines of crushed vegetation showed where a vehicle had driven recently, the first real sign of success they'd found.

"Car tracks," she exclaimed.

Gabe followed The Major, letting the bear lead them through a sparse copse of alder, which opened onto a beach, a rickety dock, and a boat launch. The tracks went all the way to the water. The Major waded in, then rose up on his hind legs again, bawling plaintively as if calling to his missing companion.

"That's how they did it," Gabriel declared, scanning the water. "They took her through the woods to this old dock, where a boat was waiting for them."

"They've got two days on us," Skeeter added. "She could be anywhere. She could be in Canada for all we know."

"She could." Evaline ambled up to the men. "But what do you want to bet she's somewhere near LaConner?"

Gabriel turned to her. "Trailhead?" he asked, remembering Durrell's construction project north of Seattle.

She nodded.

"Good guess," Gabriel put in, "but I've already checked it out."

"What are you guys talking about?" Skeeter demanded.

Evaline ignored Skeeter's question. "What about another summer home in the area?" Evaline thought back to the things Gabriel had told her about Meredith and Allison. "Didn't you tell me once that Meredith's family vacationed around here?"

Gabriel studied her for a long moment, and even without the flashlight beam illuminating his face, Evaline could see a bright gleam of appreciation lighting his eyes. "Yes," he said, his voice trailing off in thought.

"The Delaneys?" Skeeter put in, eager to be part of the discussion. "They still own that place near Sequim."

Gabriel leveled his eyes on him. "How do you know?"

"Shoot, I know where everything is in these parts."

"Hmm. The Delaney's summer home," Gabriel spoke his thoughts aloud. "As I recall, it was surrounded by a lot of land."

"A hundred acres." Skeeter bobbed his head. "Huge spread. Real remote-like."

"And from what Durrell says, he's still pretty thick with Meredith's parents," Evaline put in. "I'll bet he's there."

Gabriel nodded. "All right." He returned his gun to the waistband of his jeans. "Back to the house. Time for a moonlight drive."

Hours later, at the Delaney property, Evaline slipped from Gabriel's truck and waited for him to let down the tailgate so The Major could jump out of the back. They were counting on his sense of smell to lead them to Allison, and his nose would soon tell them if they were on the right track.

"Looky here," Skeeter commented in a low tone as he pointed to the ground. "Looks like tread marks."

Evaline trained the flashlight on the dirt lane. Fresh tire tracks caked the moist dirt and gravel into a faint pattern. Gabriel stepped up behind her and looked over her shoulder. She longed to sink back against him, to feel his arms around her, but she didn't move.

"I'll bet they're here," Gabriel said. "So no talking after this. We'll have to walk about a half mile, if I remember the place correctly. Evaline, turn off that flashlight. We can't take the chance of its being seen."

"Okay."

She flicked off the light. Soon her eyes adjusted to the cool blue glow of the moon.

"The house is an A-frame, facing the water. It's all windows in the front, so don't go around that way or you'll be seen for sure. There's a master bedroom on the first floor, and then more bedrooms upstairs. If Allison is here, she's probably upstairs."

Skeeter stuffed his hands in his pockets. "How are we going to get upstairs?"

Gabriel frowned and looked down the road, which disappeared into the gloom.

"They're probably all asleep. We'll try the doors first. If nothing's open, we'll check the windows."

"What if they're awake?" Evaline asked.

"Then we'll create some kind of diversion."

"Have The Major knock over the garbage," Skeeter suggested.

Gabriel smiled tensely. "Not a bad plan."

"He might get shot again," Evaline protested.

"We're all in danger of getting shot." He touched her arm. "You know that, don't you?"

Evaline nodded and gazed up at him, totally committed to helping Allison. She wished he would believe in her and realize she was nothing like his first wife, but there was nothing she could do except trust that her actions would prove what her words could not.

"Skeeter and I'll try to get into the house," Gabriel said. "I want you to keep out of sight and stay with The Major. If anything happens, run back to the truck and call the police on the cell phone."

"All right."

"Okay." Gabriel grabbed The Major's collar. "Let's go."

They walked in silence through the tunnel of tree branches that arched over the lane. Soon the A-frame house materialized in the gloom, lit by a single bulb at the back, where a dark sedan was parked. Gabriel relinquished his grip on the bear and silently motioned toward a grove of hemlock at the left of the house. Evaline looped her fingers around The Major's collar and urged him to accompany her to the trees. Though the night was balmy, she felt a sudden chill as she backed into the shadows, while the Major snuffled around her. A few feet behind her was a sheer drop-off to the sound, and she could hear the sigh of deep water relentlessly shouldering the cliff. Breeze from across the bay blew through her hair and ruffled the legs of her slacks, sweeping her with unease. The Major, sensing danger, slowly lowered to a sitting position, panting, his small brown eyes intent on Gabriel and Skeeter as they crept around the house, checking the doors and windows.

The men paused at the side of the house, and Evaline guessed they'd found an open window. Soon, Gabriel was boosting Skeeter into the opening. Just as the last of Skeeter's body disappeared, a light blinked on at the front

of the house, illuminating the living room and the huge
deck that jutted over the cliff. Evaline jerked to attention
as the sliding glass door slid open and a dark figure rushed
out of the house.

The Major lunged forward, and it was all Evaline could
do to hold him back. She prayed he'd obey her command
to stay, and that he wouldn't make a sound, for they
would surely be discovered, and she was the only backup
Gabriel and Skeeter had. When she glanced up from her
struggles with the bear, she saw the stranger had already
surprised Gabriel and was frisking him for weapons.
Dread poured over her. Skeeter had probably been cap-
tured inside, and Gabriel was being taken prisoner. It was
up to her now. But one thing she knew for sure: Allison
was in that house. All Evaline had to do was run for the
truck, get the police, and hope no one got hurt before the
authorities arrived.

Evaline waited in the shadows until the stranger jostled
Gabriel around to the front of the house and in through
the sliding door. With the lights on in the house, she could
see everyone plainly. Two men pushed Skeeter and
Gabriel into chairs, then tied their hands and feet.
Afterward, one of them picked up a phone and made a
call. *To whom? Stephen Durrell?* Evaline tugged at The
Major's collar. "C'mon," she said.

He wouldn't budge.

She pulled harder, but her weight was no match for
his, and he seemed determined to stay where he was.
"Come on, you big lug," Evaline whispered.

He shook his huge head, easily dislodging her hold on
his collar. There was no way she could get him to go with
her if he didn't want to. She was no match for his brute
strength.

"Okay," she replied, brushing her hands. "But stay out
of trouble."

The bear glanced at her, as if he comprehended her words. He rolled back his upper lip in response, either sneering at her puny efforts to command him or giving her a farewell grimace, she wasn't sure which.

Carefully Evaline picked her way around the yard to the back of the house, staying outside the periphery of light. Blackberry bushes snagged her clothes and hair, but she barely took notice. Her entire focus was on getting back to the lane and dashing for the truck. The yard narrowed at the rear of the house, forcing her to creep close to the side of the house. Fortunately, there were no windows at the corner. Evaline hurried toward the back of the house, hoping no one could hear her strident breathing and pounding heart, and watched the ground with each step so she wouldn't betray her presence by stepping on brush.

Just as she cleared the corner and made for the road, a voice behind her stopped her in her tracks.

"And just where do you think you're going?" a man asked.

Evaline whirled around. A tall, thin man stood beside the car, with a gun in his hand.

He chuckled. "We don't get much company out here," he drawled. "Why don't you step on in and join the fun? We're having ourselves a little party tonight."

"I'm not the party type," Evaline replied, looking around for an avenue of escape. Somebody had to get away and call the police, or they'd be in deep trouble. "Some other time."

"Sorry. Attendance is mandatory." The man waved the gun and grinned. He had a rack of big, square teeth. "Now get over here."

Evaline had no alternative but to obey. She trudged to the back door, with the man close behind her pushing the barrel of his gun into her left shoulder blade. She could sense he was still smiling as he checked her out from behind. She paused at the door, and he came up against her, dipping close to her hair.

"Maybe you and I'll have a private party," he commented, nuzzling her neck, "a little later on."

"Don't chill any champagne," she retorted, arching away from him.

He laughed and unlatched the back door, pushing it open. "Get inside," he said, and gave her a rough shove. Evaline stumbled forward, rotating her arms to maintain her balance. He closed the door and grabbed her upper arm to drag her into the living room.

"Look what I found, Herb," her captor crowed to his companion. He flung her forward, and she fell headlong to the floor at Gabriel's feet. As she rose on her hands and knees, she looked up at Gabriel and saw the concern in his eyes. "Another visitor."

"Put her in that chair," Herb instructed, pointing at the straight-backed seat they'd dragged from the dinette set.

"Sorry, Gabe," Evaline said, as she was jostled to her feet. She'd failed. She wondered what would happen to Allison now? To them?

"Are you okay, Ev—"

"Shut up," Herb barked, cutting off Gabriel's inquiry. "No talking!"

They didn't tie her hands and feet. They might not have had anymore rope, or they might not have felt threatened by such a small female. Evaline sank into the chair, worried that Allison would be in more danger than ever, owing to their botched rescue attempt.

The group fell silent. Gabriel glowered at the two thugs, Skeeter slumped in his chair and tapped his foot, while Evaline unobtrusively looked around the room, searching for signs of Allison. Above their heads was the banister of a second-floor loft, but she couldn't see anything beyond the railing. Herb paced the floor by the bank of windows, his squat frame reflected in the black glass, while Evaline's captor sat on the arm of the couch, gun in hand, resting his wrist on his knee. They apparently were waiting for some- one, because Herb kept glancing at his watch.

The Major appeared at the sliding glass door, stretch- ing to his full height to look in. Then he paced the deck, back and forth, until Herb pounded on the glass.

"Damn bear!" he shouted. "Get outta here!"

The Major paused, then roared, throwing back his head in anger.

"I'm going to shoot that animal!" Herb threatened.

"Don't," Evaline pleaded. "He's our pet."

"Some pet." Herb glowered at the bear, as if worried the animal would break through the glass.

Gradually The Major quit pacing and lumbered off to the shadows. An hour passed. Evaline shifted in her chair and uncrossed her legs, wondering how long they would have to sit in the uncomfortable seats. The long, stressful day had worn on her, sapping the last of her energy. She found it hard to stay awake.

Herb must have suffered from the same problem, because he eventually paused in front of the sliding door and yawned. Afterward he pointed his gun at Evaline.

"You," he said. "Get over there and make some cof- fee."

"Me?" Evaline pointed to her chest.

"Yeah. You." He waved the pistol in the direction of the kitchen behind her. "And no funny stuff, or I'll shoot both your boyfriends."

Evaline rose, grateful for the opportunity to move about and possibly do something to get them out of the spot they were in. She slipped into the kitchen and searched through the cupboards until she found the coffee and filters. Every move she made was carefully observed by Herb. She opened a drawer to find a spoon, and wished she could palm a small knife to slip to Gabriel.

"I said no funny stuff!" Herb shouted.

She glanced over her shoulder. "I'm just looking for a coffee measure." She waited until he lowered his gun. Then she turned back to finish the task, her mind racing for a way to free Gabriel and Skeeter. As she reached for coffee cups in the cupboard, an idea struck her. Evaline considered the plan while she waited for the coffee to finish brewing. She was a healer, and ordinarily wouldn't condone physical injury of another person, but in this case she saw no alternative.

"Do either of you take cream or sugar?" she asked, keeping her tone light.

"No," Herb answered. "Just black."

Evaline grabbed two mugs and lifted the heavy pot of coffee, carrying it across the room, and hoping no one would question her serving methods. She could have just as easily poured the mugs full in the kitchen and left the carafe behind.

"Here you go," she said, setting the mugs down and pouring coffee into one of them. Just as she'd hoped, the men drifted closer. She finished pouring the coffee and picked up the mug. Just as Herb reached for it, she dashed the scalding liquid into his crotch. With a howl, he yanked backward, dropped his gun and tore at his belt to drop his pants, while Evaline whirled around and threw the coffeepot at the other man's hand. The spray of burning coffee hit his right arm. He screamed, and his gun slipped out of his fingers. The coffeepot shattered on the floor, and the gun spun in circles to Gabriel's chair. He trapped the weapon with his foot while Evaline pivoted and grabbed Herb's discarded weapon.

"Bitch!" Herb seethed, standing in his sodden briefs

and holding the drenched fabric away from his body. "You goddamn bitch!"

She ignored him and backed toward Gabriel to untie his hands, struggling to unfasten the rope with one hand.

"Good going, Ev," Skeeter declared, grinning, while Gabriel bent for the rope at his ankles, freed himself, and picked up the gun.

The tall man held his burned hand to his mouth.

Evaline turned to him. "Get your friend some ice," she instructed. "There's probably a bag of frozen veggies in the freezer."

She kept her weapon trained on him as he fumbled in the freezer and brought out a bag of peas.

"Hurry it up, idiot!" Herb cried. "My dick hurts like a sonofabitch!"

By the time the bag of peas had exchanged hands, Gabriel had untied Skeeter.

"Who has the car keys?" Gabriel asked, glaring at the injured men.

"I do," the tall man whined.

"Give them to Evaline."

The tall man rummaged in his pants pocket and brought out a ring of keys.

"Sit down," Gabriel demanded. He tied the man up, roughly pulling his arms back behind him.

"Ow!" the tall man cried. "Take it easy, will ya?"

Gabriel ignored him. When he was done with the first guy, he ordered Herb to sit down. Herb minced over to the chair.

"Call 911," Herb pleaded. "I'm seriously burned here."

"You've got your frozen peas," Gabriel retorted. "Now sit down and shut up!"

Ruthlessly, he tied Herb to the chair, and then he pounded up the stairs, shouting for Allison.

Skeeter glanced over at Evaline and grinned. "Nice

going, Ev," he said. "I admire a girl who can sling a good cup of Java."

Evaline smiled back, but her attention was riveted on Gabriel's progress above. She moved sideways to the base of the stairs.

"Is she up there?" Evaline called.

"Yeah. Oh, God!"

Evaline's heart sank when she heard Gabriel's voice. What had been done to the girl? She kept her eyes and gun trained on the men tied to the chairs, but every other sense strained for the faintest noise coming from upstairs. Moments later, Gabriel appeared, carrying a dark-haired girl, her arms and legs dangling loosely. For a moment Evaline was confused by the girl's appearance, but then realized Allison must have dyed her hair to her natural color, which was identical to her father's hair.

"Oh, Gabe!" Evaline cried, her heart breaking. "Is she—"

"She's drugged," Gabriel said, coming down the stairs. "I can't wake her."

"Bastards!" Evaline swore, though her anger was laced with relief at finding Allison alive. She faced the men in the chairs. "What'd you give her?"

"Didn't give her nothin'," Herb shrugged. "The boss takes care of that kind of stuff."

"What did Durrell give her?"

"I don't know—some kind of shot."

Evaline and Gabriel's dark gazes met over Allison's limp form.

"Get her out in the fresh air," Evaline suggested.

"Right." Gabriel walked toward the couch. "Here, Skeeter, take my gun." He held out the weapon. "Evaline, get the car and pull around to the side. I'll meet you at the edge of the deck."

"Okay." She headed for the rear hallway while Gabriel

hurried to the sliding glass door, leaving Skeeter to stand guard. Evaline hopped into the sedan, put the gun on the seat, found the ignition key, and started the engine. Deftly, she backed it out of the carport and pulled along the east side of the house. Skeeter stepped onto the deck, keeping his gun aimed at the bound men, while Gabriel walked toward the car, the bear trailing after him, sniffing solicitously at Allison's limp hands and feet. Evaline got out to open the passenger door for Gabriel and anxiously scanned Allison's pale face as he stooped to put her in the car.

Just as he straightened, a familiar voice rang out.

"Going somewhere, Townsend?"

21

Surprised, Evaline jerked up, hitting her head on the doorframe of the car, but barely taking notice of the pain blossoming in her skull. She rubbed her scalp as Stephen Durrell stepped away from the corner of the summer home, a pistol in his hand.

Gabriel rose up from the car and faced him. "What have you done to my daughter?" he demanded.

Durrell didn't answer his question. "Drop the gun," he said, glaring at Skeeter, "or I'll shoot your buddy."

Skeeter let his weapon fall to the deck with a loud thump. The Major jerked around at the sound and sniffed the air, apparently forgetting about Allison lying on the backseat of the car. His eyesight was weak, especially at night, but his excellent sense of smell compensated for his poor vision, and he was definitely smelling something that disturbed him. Evaline wondered if the scent of Stephen Durrell was familiar to the bear, or whether he could pick up the scent of a bad apple much the same way a dog could detect fear and cowardice in a person. And it was apparent that Stephen Durrell was not just a bad apple, but an entire barrel of rotting fruit.

"I asked you a question, Durrell!" Gabriel shouted, striding toward him.

"Back off, Townsend!"

Gabriel kept walking, immune to threats regarding his own safety, which forced Durrell to raise his weapon even higher. "One more step, Townsend, and your precious therapist gets it."

"You bastard." Gabriel ground to a halt, glowering. "What did you give Allison?" he demanded. "Tell me!"

"Something to relax her."

"Relax her? We can't even wake her up!"

"She'll be fine, Townsend. She was just a bit excited. I thought it best to medicate her."

"You're going to jail for this."

"Not if you and your friends die in a tragic fire."

"Oh?" Gabriel glanced at the house. "Just like the fire in Greece—the one that killed Meredith?"

Durrell narrowed his eyes. "I wouldn't jump to any conclusions, Townsend."

"It's not much of a leap."

Durrell smirked and turned his attention to the henchmen guarded by Skeeter. "You there," he remarked to Skeeter. "Untie those men."

Skeeter didn't move until Durrell stepped closer. "Must I shoot someone?" he asked. "Believe me, I wouldn't mind."

"Okay, okay," Skeeter replied. "Don't go getting your britches in a snit." He turned to Herb and his companion and slowly unfastened the ropes that bound their hands.

Evaline didn't move from her place by the car and watched The Major's body tensed as Durrell's men rubbed their arms and sauntered away from the glass doors where they'd been trapped. Her gun lay on the front seat of the sedan, but if she reached for it, she'd probably be shot by Durrell.

"Get the girl out of the car," Durrell instructed them.

Herb headed for the car, but The Major growled at him menacingly. The deep liquid sound rumbled across the clearing, making even the hairs on Evaline's neck stand up. Herb paused, his face white against the night sky and his wary stare riveted on the animal.

"I said, get the girl out of the car!" Durrell repeated tersely.

Herb raised his hands in the air, as if he were acting in a Western movie and someone had just poked him in the back with a six-shooter. "Nice bear," he crooned in a shaky voice. "Nice boy—"

To avoid confronting The Major, Herb took a small step toward the passenger side of the car, but the instant his foot moved, the bear lunged at him.

Herb screamed and staggered backward, while his companion dashed for the relative safety of the forest at the edge of the property. Evaline heard a loud crack and whipped around to discover Durrell had fired at The Major. The bear turned toward Durrell and bellowed, and the roar was so loud that Evaline felt a reverberation in her bones. She froze, unable to act or speak, as she watched The Major stand on his hind legs and roar again—transforming from a lumbering good-natured pet into a slavering, enraged, five-foot-tall beast. She could see a dark patch growing on his right shoulder where Durrell's shot had hit him. Had Durrell been the one who had shot The Major in the back leg? If so, he was in dire trouble. Bears not only had a keen sense of smell, they had prodigious memories.

Durrell fired another shot, but The Major did little more than flinch. Then the bear bellowed and dropped to all fours in a heavy movement that sent his pelt rippling over his powerful haunches. As The Major charged, Durrell scrambled backward, firing round after round until the pistol clicked, empty of bullets. When he realized the gun was useless, he flung it at the animal and dashed sideways, back to the deck, where he'd have a better chance of getting to the house or car. The Major swiped at him as he ran by, slashing Durrell's expensive trousers, and knocking him to the ground.

"Gabriel!" Evaline cried, as her childhood trauma rushed back to her in full force. The periphery of her vision darkened, and she worried that she would faint, just like the other times when the memory of the wolf attack overwhelmed her. "Do something!"

Gabriel glanced at her, his face nearly as pale as Durrell's, but he said nothing, and Evaline realized there was nothing anyone could do. No verbal command would check The Major now during his blood frenzied attack on Durrell. And no human being could match the brute strength of an injured and angry male black bear. She watched The Major swipe at Durrell again and remembered with sickening clarity the lightning hot pain of claw slashing through flesh. Nauseated and half-blind with fear, Evaline stumbled forward, but Gabriel grabbed her and pulled her back.

"Don't!" he yelled. "You'll be killed!"

Then he stepped in front of her, a stout branch in his hand. "Keep back!" he barked.

Evaline wavered between consciousness and insensibility as she watched Gabriel stab the bear's chest to force him to retreat. But The Major disregarded such a puny attempt to stop him.

"Major!" Gabriel yelled. "Back off!" He whacked the beast across the shoulders with the branch, but the bear didn't take notice.

"Oh, God!" Durrell cried, scrabbling on his hands

and knees, his clothes and flesh in bloody tatters. "Help me!"

The Major lunged again, his paws clawing the air as Durrell staggered backward to the edge of the deck. He careened into the railing and wildly looked behind him. He'd trapped himself between the bear and the sheer drop-off of the cliff, his only choice dismemberment or drowning.

"Townsend!" he screamed.

Evaline's eyesight darkened as the sound of Durrell's scream ballooned in her head. She fought the blackness, concentrating on Gabriel's valiant effort to stop the bear.

Gabriel lunged forward and grabbed a handful of hair on the bear's back just as The Major hurtled forward. The animal pulled out of Gabriel's grip, clutched Durrell with his forearms, and locked him in a fatal bear hug.

"Major!" Gabriel thundered.

A sharp cracking sound ripped through the bear's roars. Frantically, Durrell kicked his feet, struggling for purchase on the blood-slick deck. And then as Evaline watched, frozen in horror, she saw the railing give way and both man and bear plunge out of sight.

For a stunned instant no one moved. Then Gabriel glanced over the shards of railing to the dark water below. Evaline stood at the other edge of the deck, shaking and sweating, unable to control the trembling of her hands and knees. Gabriel looked back at her, and she felt his hard gaze rake over her. Then all she could see were sparkling shapes as the echo of The Major's bellow swelled in her head. The deck tilted beneath her feet, and she flung out her arms, determined to retain her balance and her sanity.

"Evaline!" Two arms caught her and held her up, giving her the strength and support she needed to maintain her fragile hold on reality.

"Evaline!" Gabriel repeated. "Are you all right?"

Evaline flung her arms around him, holding the tragedy at bay by embracing him with every ounce of her strength. She felt Gabriel's strong right arm surround her as his left hand stroked her hair and back, and for a long moment they held each other, immobilized by shock. After she stopped trembling, she heard his voice rumble in his chest.

"Skeeter," Gabriel said, his breath in her hair, "find a phone. Call the police."

Then he pulled away, and Evaline reluctantly stepped back, wondering if their sudden and hard embrace would be the last time she'd ever touch the man she had come to love.

Dawn filtered through the cedars as Evaline followed Skeeter up the steps of the Townsend house. They had spent a good two hours waiting at the Delaneys' for the police and explaining what had happened, and Evaline was tired and hungry. She held open the door for Gabriel, who carried his daughter through the living room and back to her bedroom, where she could sleep off the effects of Durrell's drugs. Skeeter flopped down in one of the chairs and sprawled back, while Evaline waited in the center of the living room, rubbing the backs of her arms and wondering what the arrangements would be for her return to Seattle. After a few minutes, Gabriel strode back down the hall.

Evaline glanced over her shoulder at him, and for a brief moment their gazes met, then he looked away, leaving her body humming with a painful ache she knew she must ignore.

"Anybody want breakfast?" Gabriel asked.

"No. I'm beat," Skeeter replied. He stood up. "I'm going down to the boat and crash for a few hours."

"What about you, Evaline?" Gabriel inquired, glancing at her again. His gaze swiftly surveyed her body as well as her face.

"I should be getting back to Seattle soon." She crossed her arms over the dread she felt at the prospect. "I've got patients to see tomorrow."

"I need some shut-eye before I fly you back," Skeeter put in. He looked at his watch. "How about we leave around three or so? That'll give us time to catch some winks."

"Fine." She gave him a quick smile, even though her heart was far from happy.

Skeeter snapped a comical salute and let himself out the front door, abandoning her to the wall of silence behind her. Evaline didn't want to turn around and face Gabriel. They'd worked together to find Allison, but now that the girl was all right, they had nothing left between them but their hard feelings.

"You can use the bed in the master bedroom if you want," he said gruffly.

Evaline turned slightly. "What about you?"

"I'm going to stay with Allison."

She glanced at his ruggedly handsome face, made more intensely masculine by the dark shadow of beard on his sharp jaw. She doubted he'd gotten any sleep in the last few days, and marveled that he could still be on his feet. Her heart surged with love and tenderness for him, but she didn't let her reaction show in her eyes.

"If you want to take a shower"—he cocked his head toward the hall—"there's clean towels and stuff in the bathroom cupboard."

"Thanks. I think I will. But I'd like to look in on Allison first, if it's all right with you."

He nodded and stuffed his hands in the pockets of his jeans. For a long, tense moment he gazed at her, slightly squinting his right eye, which accentuated the lines of fatigue in his face. "Thanks for your help, City Girl," he said at last.

"I'm glad we found her."

Gabriel nodded again, and she realized he was too distraught or exhausted to make a reply. She didn't know what else to say, or if her words would comfort him anyway, so she decided not to say anything.

"I'll see you in a few hours," she said, turning for Allison's bedroom.

Clean and relaxed, Evaline closed her eyes and listened to the sound of the shower down the hall as Gabriel washed away the worry of the last few days. Naked, she snuggled into the nest of blankets, which smelled faintly of his scent, and breathed in deeply. She couldn't help wondering how different life would have been had he trusted her and she him.

Had they been able to trust, she would have known what it was like to be held by him, to be surrounded by his heat and his love. She might still be living at Obstruction Bay, sharing the days and nights with Gabriel and Allison, learning how to laugh and love again—all three of them.

A sharp ache of despair twisted in her chest and brought quick tears to her eyes. But Evaline refused to cry for what-might-have-beens and willed herself to empty her thoughts of Gabriel.

Just as she drifted off to sleep, she heard a knock at the door.

"Evaline?" Gabriel called softly from the other side. "Are you still awake?"

"Yes," she replied, her voice husky. "Just a minute."

"No need to get up," he said, pushing the door open. "I just wanted to check on you."

Evaline struggled to sit up and pulled the blankets around her shoulders as Gabriel crossed the room. His hair was still wet from the shower, and he wore only a pair of jeans—no socks and shoes. For a long moment he stood above her, surveying her face and hands, until she couldn't stand the silence.

"What?" she asked.

"I wanted to make sure you were all right." He cocked his head. "You were a wreck this morning. You had me worried."

"I'm okay now." She scrunched the blanket against her naked breasts.

"It wasn't just the bear attack, was it?"

Evaline's heart skipped a beat. "What do you mean?"

"You nearly fainted. That isn't like you, City Girl."

Evaline looked down, unable to answer without evading the question or lying, and she didn't want to do either. Before she could come up with a decent reply, she felt the bed shake as Gabriel sat down on the edge of the mattress.

"You've been hiding things from the very first." He reached for her right arm. "Like these scars on your wrists and arms."

Evaline tried to pull away, and when he wouldn't release her, she glanced at him, expecting to see his face full of pity and disgust. Instead, he tipped her forearm to the light that filtered through the crack of the drawn drapes and studied her scars, as if he saw the marks as separate from her spirit.

"How'd you get these, Evaline?"

She swallowed. He traced the silvery lines up the tendons of her wrist, leaving a path of tingling awareness in the wake of his fingertip. And then he looked at her, his gray eyes melting with tenderness, as he drew her wrist to his mouth and kissed her skin.

Evaline's breath caught in her throat at the gesture.

"You were attacked by a wild animal," he murmured. "Weren't you?"

"A wolf," she whispered at last.

"How long ago?"

"When I was twelve."

He lifted her arm away from the blanket and surveyed its length from wrist to shoulder. "You've got scars all over your body?"

"Mostly."

"I'd like to see them." He cupped her cheek and gazed into her eyes. "Evaline, let me look at you."

"Gabe, they're—"

"Let me see them."

He leaned forward to lightly kiss her mouth. She closed her eyes and sighed as he gently eased the blanket off her other shoulder. His hand curved around her upper arm as the kiss deepened, until Evaline could not resist him any longer and gave in to his embrace. He felt her surrender and slowly urged her forward against his wide warm chest. The rest of the blanket fell away as she came up against his solid flesh with a gasp of wonder.

"Is that why you wouldn't take off your shirt before?" he asked, his mouth at her ear. "Because of the scars?"

"Yes."

He squeezed her tightly and kissed the hair at her temple. Then he slowly drew away, sliding his hands down her torso. Without another word, he bent closer and kissed her streaked flesh, from navel to fingertip and back again. Evaline lay against the pillows, awash in heartbreaking pleasure. That he could accept her wounds, and pay such sweet homage to them, made her heart burst with joy. Never in her wildest dreams had she expected such acceptance from him.

Then he kissed the tips of her aching breasts, and she knew she was lost to whatever he wanted to do with her. She pushed her fingers into his soft dark hair and urged him back for more, loving the way the damp spikes of his hair brushed her skin.

"Evaline," he whispered against the soft round side of her breast. In his voice she heard more than desire, and in his embrace she felt his need of her, not just to slake his thirst for a woman, but to share in the sweet relief of finding Allison, and to seek shelter from a world that had been a harsh landscape for both of them for too many years.

She knew what he was asking for, and it was something she wanted just as much as he did. She reached for the button of his jeans and unfastened it, not quite daring enough to unzip him and stroke him.

Gabriel left her breasts for a moment, long enough to yank off his pants. Then he slipped under the covers with her and pulled her close. His arms encircled her, pinning her to his torso, and one of his long legs drew up and over her thigh while he dipped to kiss the top of her shoulder. He felt incredibly warm and supple, and smelled of soap and talcum powder and a clean scent all his own.

Evaline melted in his arms, remembering the way he had held her just like this on his boat, giving of his body and his spirit to heal her. And now he was here in her bed, needing the same kind of support from her. She would not refuse him. She wouldn't worry about her scars, or Allison, or the future. Gabriel hadn't come to her out of lust, but out of a basic human need to be loved and comforted. She wanted to be the one to give him both things, and finally trusted enough to realize these gifts would also be hers in the exchange.

Now that Allison had been found and Stephen Durrell was no longer a threat, Gabriel didn't have to be a pillar of strength. Apparently he felt he could allow himself a moment of sweet relief. Evaline sighed as he cupped her breasts in his big hands. She would concentrate on the here and now with him, and go with him where their passions led. She'd learned the hard way that trust involved appreciating the present and being confident that the future would take care of itself.

Slowly Evaline turned in his arms, her breasts pressing into the glowing heat of his chest. Something hot and glorious unfurled inside of her, and she knew it for what it was: joy. She loved Gabriel, and she was finally coming home to the place she belonged.

"Oh, Gabe!" she breathed against his jaw. She wrapped her arms around him and embraced him, gently at first, then with a strength fired by her love of him. For a long while their silent embraces were enough to slake the loneliness of their solitary years. They traveled the silken contours of one another's body with lips and hands, never speaking, never needing to speak. Then their caresses became tight with urgency, their kisses deepened, until at last Gabriel urged her onto her back and slipped his long hands around her hips.

Evaline raised her knees slightly, offering herself as she had to no other man.

He sighed and dipped his head, and as his mouth sank upon hers, he pushed into her. Evaline let out a low moan of pleasure. At the sound, she felt him swell inside her. Then he began to move upon her and with her, and she gave herself up to him, creating with him a safe haven where he could pour out his doubts, despair, relief, and hope. His lovemaking was as intense and relentless as she suspected it would be, for this was not a time to savor one another, but a coupling of much-needed release.

Evaline embraced his muscular back and closed her eyes, stroking him until he gave a hoarse cry and flooded her with his seed. She clutched his rump, keeping him against her for a few precious moments more while his warmth spread deep inside her. Then he kissed her, his mouth lingering on hers, until she felt him slipping away from her most intimate part. With a sigh, Gabriel rolled onto his back and collapsed, sated and exhausted.

She gazed down at him and smiled when he opened his eyes and looked up at her, his pupils large and dark in his light eyes. She thought he was going to say something. Instead, he reached up and slipped his hand around the back of her neck to urge her down for another long kiss.

"That was worth waiting for, beautiful," he said softly against her lips.

"Yes," she answered, meaning it with all her heart. "It was."

He caressed her back with the palms of his hands, and she slowly collapsed upon his chest, amazed that she could find such comfort in the firm planes of his torso.

Evaline watched him fall asleep. She brushed back the hair at his temple and surveyed his face from the side. He looked so boyish when he slept—one of the few times he ever relaxed. His neck and jaw looked so vulnerable, his mouth so tender, that she lightly placed a kiss in the hollow of his cheek and then again at the corner of his eye. Slowly, she slipped an arm across his smooth chest and snuggled against his side. Gabriel responded by stirring and sliding his palm across her thigh. Even in his state of exhaustion he was conscious of her presence, enough to forge a link between them. Strangely satisfied by the gesture, Evaline closed her eyes and fell asleep, her head on his shoulder.

* * *

Evaline woke up to a crack of thunder and a flash of lightning that lit up the master bedroom. Rain hammered the cedar shakes on the roof and poured off the eaves in a torrent. What had begun as a clear day had transformed into a severe summer storm. She sat up with a start and was surprised to find Gabriel's side of the bed empty. Disappointed, she threw off the light covers and walked to the bathroom, checking her watch as she went. Four-thirty! She was shocked to find she'd slept nearly all afternoon. Skeeter had probably waited hours for her to get up. And now they wouldn't be able to leave until the storm passed.

Grimacing at her lapse, Evaline quickly freshened up at the sink, then stood by the dresser and pulled on her shirt and jeans, wondering why Gabriel had left the room without saying anything. Had he not wanted to wake her? Maybe he'd thought twice about what they'd shared and didn't want to embarrass her with a scene. Had he been disappointed in her? Evaline bit her lip and discarded the notion before it had time to worm its way too deeply into her thoughts. She knew he'd appreciated her body and her companionship as much as she'd enjoyed his.

When she zipped up her jeans, she happened to glance at the top of the nightstand. For some reason, Gabriel had left the small snapshot of Allison there, the one he'd accused her of taking from his private album. The mysterious appearance of the photograph still bothered her. Gabriel hadn't left it in Allison's room on the cassette deck, and neither had she. Allison couldn't walk to the boat by herself, so she couldn't have gotten the photo out of Gabriel's album. That left Skeeter. Evaline shook her head, sure that Skeeter had no reason to involve himself with the snapshot. Only one other person might have retrieved the photograph. *Meredith.*

The more Evaline thought about it, the more certain

she was that the spirit had somehow managed to leave the photograph out in the open so they would see it. But why? And what was she trying to convey with the loud music? Evaline frowned and pursed her lips as a sudden idea struck her. Then she snapped her jeans and left the bedroom, anxious to speak to Gabriel—for more reasons than one.

22

Evaline followed her nose to the kitchen and stood in the doorway, watching as Gabriel reached for a spoon lodged in a pot of bubbling tomato sauce. When he touched the metal utensil, he swore and jerked back his hand, obviously burning himself. Then he rushed to the sink, turned on the tap, and thrust his hand under the stream of cold water. The burner under the pot glowed red-orange, and Evaline smelled the acrid odor of tomatoes just beginning to scorch. She couldn't help but smile. Gabriel's culinary skills hadn't improved since she'd been gone.

A bag of frozen manicotti sagged against the microwave door. Skeeter stood beside Gabriel, drinking a beer and leaning on the counter, and behind him the sky glowed an ominous purple. Both men looked up as she appeared in the kitchen doorway. Skeeter smiled at her. Gabriel flushed and immediately returned to the saucepan and turned down the burner.

"There she is," Skeeter greeted. "Rip-lene Van Winkle."

"Sorry, Skeeter," Evaline replied. "I guess I was more tired than I thought. Someone should have wakened me."

Gabriel shot her a quick glance, and Evaline felt a flush brand her own cheeks. She swept into the kitchen, trying to act casual in front of the man she'd just made love to a few hours ago.

"That's okay, Ev," Skeeter put in. "With this storm, we're not going anywhere anyways." He took a sip of beer.

Gabriel put a lid on the sauce. "You might want to call the hospital and tell them you're going to be waylaid a day."

Her heart skipped a beat at the prospect of remaining overnight at the house and perhaps sleeping in his bed for an entire night. Sleeping in Gabriel's arms had been more satisfying than anything she'd ever known. Evaline longed to wrap her arms around him again and wished Skeeter was anywhere else but in the kitchen with them. With Skeeter around she also couldn't broach the subject she wanted to discuss with Gabriel. She kept her tone even. "So you think the weather will stay like this?"

"Yeah." Gabriel looked out the window. "Usually it takes a while for a storm to blow over. And after it does, it'll be dark. I don't want you flying at night around here."

"Why not?" Skeeter put in. "Don't trust me, Gabe?"

"Not in the dark," Gabriel retorted. "And not with a woman as pretty as Evaline."

She flushed again, knowing his words weren't empty flattery. A few hours ago, he'd found her attractive. In fact, he'd made her feel downright beautiful.

Skeeter inclined his head toward Evaline. "Are you going to take over dinner, Ev, or do we have to be subjected to another one of Gabe's burnfests? I'm kind of sick of cajun blackened macaroni and cheese."

Evaline grinned. "Well, I don't know, Skeeter. I'm not on Mr. Townsend's payroll anymore."

"You never were," Gabriel interjected, pretending to be crotchety. "And I don't burn food that often either."

"Only when I'm around," Skeeter retorted. He turned back to Evaline. "I'll *pay* you to make dinner, Ev," Skeeter continued. "It'll be worth it to have some good home cookin' again. What do you say?"

"Sure, if Gabriel doesn't mind."

"Go ahead." Gabriel waved her toward the stove and stepped aside. "I'll go see if Allison is awake yet."

Evaline brushed past him, her senses on fire, and made herself concentrate on dinner. While Gabriel was gone and Skeeter made a salad and chattered away, she whipped up a quick Bolognese sauce, full of fresh garlic and onions. Soon the house was filled with the fragrance of the simmering meal. Gabriel returned and built a fire, and by the time Evaline set the table, a cozy ambience had settled, made more intimate by the raging storm outside. She watched the play of muscles beneath Gabriel's shirt as he poked at the fire, and drank in the scene before her, knowing she was viewing one of those precious moments when everything in her world came together in all the right ways. Such times were so fleeting and so rare, she had learned to appreciate them as they occurred, storing them away for her long stretches of solitude.

"Was Allison awake?" Evaline asked as Gabriel rose to his full height.

"Yeah. But I don't think she feels up to eating at the table."

"Does she know I'm here?"

Gabriel shook his head. "She took it pretty hard when you left before. I don't know how she'll react if she sees you. You know how she is."

"Did you tell her why I left?"

Gabriel frowned. "I told her we didn't see eye to eye on some things."

"But you didn't tell her it was your decision that I leave."

"Not exactly. But I think she knew."

Evaline crossed her arms. "You have been known to jump to conclusions."

"That may be true."

"In more ways than one."

He studied her, and Evaline was highly conscious of Skeeter standing to the side, watching them. Finally Gabriel sighed and nodded.

"Yeah. Especially about Durrell."

His words warmed Evaline's heart, but they didn't surprise her. She had expected all along that Gabriel would come to his senses about her relationship with Stephen Durrell. Gabriel might blow up at first and jump to conclusions, but she had learned that when they argued, he would stomp off, consider what he'd said, and then be man enough to come back and admit he was wrong. To react spontaneously was integral to his passionate nature, and she didn't want him to change that part of himself.

"I'll take a tray to Allison," Evaline suggested, nearly overcome by the spontaneous urge to throw her arms around his neck and kiss him for all she was worth. "I can't wait to talk to her."

"I'll go with you," Gabriel remarked, following her into the kitchen. "There's no telling how she'll react."

"Don't be long, that's all," Skeeter put in. "I'm starving!"

Gabriel shook his head and opened the refrigerator for the milk. He poured Allison a glass while Evaline fixed her a plate of pasta, bread, and salad. Gabriel carried the tray as Evaline walked ahead of him down the hall, her heart thumping in her chest. When dealing with Allison, she never knew what to expect.

She knocked quietly before entering, and stood in the

doorway for a moment as Allison turned to see who was entering her room. The girl's face went slack in disbelief. And then with a yelp, she threw out her arms.

"Evaline!" she cried, unable to suppress a huge grin that burst upon her face. She was haggard from her experience with Durrell, and her complexion was pale in contrast to her newly dyed hair, but the circles under her eyes were nearly blotted out by her smile.

Evaline's heart soared with joy at the radiant expression, and she rushed forward to sweep the girl into her arms.

"Allison!" she exclaimed, hugging her tightly, and amazed at the strength and heart in the girl's answering embrace. "Allison! It's so good to see you!"

Evaline waited until much later to talk to Gabriel about the photograph—until eleven o'clock, when Skeeter, sensing his company was straining the atmosphere, announced he was going down to the boat to read and turn in for the night. He left, slapping Gabriel on the back and reminding him to be good. Gabriel flushed and glanced at Evaline, who sat near the fire while the storm continued to blow. She felt a blush heat her cheeks and quickly looked down at the newspaper article she'd been reading about the death of Stephen Durrell, New Age guru, whose dark side had been hidden from most of the world. He'd not only been involved in kidnapping and fraud, he was now suspected of killing his fiancée.

She heard the door close and slowly raised her gaze from the paper. Gabriel stood near the dining-room table, studying her, his face solemn. When he realized she was looking at him, he smiled.

"I thought he'd never leave," Gabriel declared, striding closer.

Evaline chuckled softly. "Me neither."

He reached out a hand. "Come here, City Girl." With surprising ease, he drew her from the chair and into his embrace. His large frame dwarfed her small figure, especially when they stood toe to toe. She slipped her arms around his neck as he nearly lifted her off the floor, then she tilted back her head for a slow, luxurious kiss.

"Thanks for dinner," he murmured.

"My pleasure."

"Ah," he sighed, pressing her against him. "And this is what I call a great dessert."

"Not so fast," she teased. "Are you sure you finished everything on your plate?"

"Yes, but I'm still ravenous." He squeezed her rump with both hands and bent down for another kiss, laughing. She'd never heard him really laugh before, and the sound washed over her in a delightful wave.

Before she knew it, Gabriel was tugging at her blouse, and her own hands had managed to slip under his shirt while she straddled his left thigh, blatantly pressing against it.

"Evaline!" Gabriel exclaimed, his voice husky and his breathing heavy. "Let's move this into the bedroom."

"No, wait," she replied, backing away a step. "There's something we have to do first."

"What?" His voice cracked.

"It has to do with Allison."

"What are you talking about?" He pulled back and stared down his straight nose at her.

"I think I know why that photograph was left on her cassette deck."

Gabriel's hands slipped to her elbows. "Why?"

"I think Meredith's spirit wants Allison to hear that ballad."

"Are you serious?" Gabriel retorted. "That's *all* we hear at night. Over and over again."

"*We* might hear it, but Allison doesn't. She's always caught in that weird nightmare state. Oblivious."

Gabriel paused in thought and stared at her, his brows knitted together. Evaline let the silence stretch between them until she could see the light of understanding dawn in his eyes.

"You mean to tell me that Meredith might be playing 'Time and Place' to get Allison's attention?"

Evaline nodded. "But Meredith's window of opportunity seems to be limited to a certain time frame, which occurs around midnight. And that's the time Allison usually is sound asleep and impossible to wake up—probably because of her medication."

"So you think the song has some meaning for Allison?"

Evaline nodded again. "Or Meredith thinks it might."

"But why?"

"That's what we need to find out. It might be a key to her psychological block." Evaline stepped out of his embrace. "Gabe, if Allison is still awake, let's play the song for her and see what happens when she's fully conscious."

"All right." He smiled and his warm gaze poured over her. "But make yourself presentable, madame. We can't have my daughter thinking you've been ravished by some brute."

The moment the words slipped out, he flushed. "Sorry, Evaline—" he stammered, realizing how the words might affect someone who had actually been attacked by a wild animal. "I didn't think—"

She smiled and touched his cheek. "It's all right, Gabe."

And it was. For the first time in her life, she'd forgotten her scars. Gabriel's kisses had wiped them away.

*   *   *

"You want me to listen to what?" Allison asked, crossing her arms as she sat in bed.

"To some old-fogy music," Gabriel replied, sorting through the cassettes on Allison's nightstand. "Humor us, Allison, will you?"

Allison glanced at Evaline for help, but Evaline only raised one brow and smiled.

"I get the feeling I'm outnumbered here," Allison commented with a slow grin. "You two haven't joined forces, have you?" She tilted her head, and Evaline fought to keep a blush from creeping up her neck. Allison studied her as a funny little smile grew on her lips. "That'd be the day."

Evaline fumbled with the cassette deck, turning it on and sliding it closer to Gabriel. He straightened and looked at the old clear plastic cassette.

"What's that?" Allison asked, turning her attention to her father.

Evaline breathed a silent sigh of relief at having been released from the girl's scrutiny.

"An old cassette your mother gave me."

"In my stack?" She leaned on her elbow, trying to peer around his shoulder.

"Yeah."

"That's weird. I've never seen it."

Evaline stepped closer. "That's why we're here, Allison. We'd like you to listen to a song on it."

"Which one?"

"Your mother's favorite." Gabriel held it closer so she could read the label. "'Time and Place.'"

Allison scowled. "I don't remember that one."

"She played it constantly," Gabriel said, slipping the cassette into the machine. "It was her theme song. She was always searching for everlasting love, one to last throughout time. And looking for it in a perfect man."

Allison nodded, and a shadow crossed over her features. "And she was so busy looking that she never learned how to love anybody."

Evaline glanced at Allison, surprised at the girl's insight.

"She loved you, Allison," Gabriel commented, looking down at her. "In her own way, I'm sure."

"Are you kidding?" Allison snapped out of her momentary lapse into quiet philosophy. "I was a fucking obstacle to her, that's all I was."

"Allison!" Evaline exclaimed, sinking down beside her and reaching for her hand. "Surely that wasn't the case."

"It was. I was always in the way. When I was little, she couldn't travel as much as she wanted to. And then when I got older and prettier, some of her boyfriends—" Allison broke off, pulled her hand away, and yanked the sheet up over her chest.

"Some of her boyfriends what?" Gabriel thundered.

Evaline watched a torrent of emotion pass over Allison's pale face—disgust and then shame. She had suspected Allison had experienced far too much for a girl her age, and now she was certain of it.

"Some of her boyfriends did what, Allison?" Gabriel repeated.

"Gabe!" Evaline glanced up at him, flashing a warning with her eyes. "For now, let's just play the song."

For a long moment Gabriel stared at her, his eyes glittering with outrage. Evaline held the stare, willing him to calm down, until she saw his anger diffuse around the edges. Then in a sharp movement, Gabriel broke away and turned to the cassette deck to push the play button. Evaline felt Allison's thin fingers snake back beneath hers, and she gently enclosed them in her hand. Evaline suddenly realized she had communicated on a wordless but deep level with both Gabriel and Allison, and had served as a conduit between them, a service she was glad to provide. It spoke of an understanding of spirits, a closeness she had never shared with anyone, and now shared with two.

After a moment of gravelly static, the ballad began. Evaline let her gaze drop to the comforter and prayed the words or music would trigger a reaction in Allison to help her overcome her psychological trauma. While the man's voice sang through the words about spending time with a person you love and recognizing the right person to go through life with, Evaline let her thoughts drift. She knew she'd found her life's partner, but did Gabriel feel the same way? He'd never talked about his feelings for her. He might consider her more as a pleasant interlude than a long-term companion.

While the song played, Gabriel darkly glared at the floor. Evaline couldn't guess if he was thinking about Meredith or Allison or both. Beside her, Allison sat uncharacteristically quiet. Then something warm and wet dropped on the back of Evaline's hand, and she looked up in surprise.

"Turn it off!" Allison blurted, her face pale and her eyes full of tears. "Turn the damn thing off!"

Gabriel reached down and pushed the stop button. Evaline touched Allison's arm.

"What's the matter, Allison?" she asked gently. "Do you want to talk about it?"

"I hate that song!" Allison swiped at her eyes with her free hand.

"So do I," Gabriel remarked, once more in control of his emotions. He sank into the chair beside the bed. "But Evaline thinks your mother wants you to hear it. Do you know why?"

"Why should I?" Allison glared at him through her short dark bangs.

"Sometimes a song can spark a memory," Evaline remarked quietly, reaching out to push a strand of dark hair behind Allison's ear. "Does this one have any particular significance to you?"

Allison sniffed and swallowed, but said nothing.

Gabriel leaned forward. "It didn't make you think of anything?"

She still didn't answer, but Evaline felt her trembling.

"The song made you cry. Why, Allie?" Evaline asked softly.

Allison's posture stiffened as she stared at Evaline, her bloodshot eyes searching Evaline's face. The look in her eyes was as wild and frightened as a small child's. Evaline's heart flopped in her chest, and she never thought twice about reaching out to Allison and wrapping her arms around her. At first Allison didn't move, and Evaline thought she'd overstepped her bounds. She fully expected Allison to yank back and launch a barrage of swear words at her. Instead, she felt Allison shudder, and then the girl seemed to collapse into herself, wilting into a little ball against her. Evaline held her even more tightly, knowing instinctively that Allison needed to be comforted, needed to be held until her tears passed.

She could feel Gabriel's intense stare on her back, as if to remind her that Allison was his responsibility and it was his place to deal with his child, but Evaline didn't once let up the reassuring pressure of her embrace. She'd built a relationship with this child, and she was the one who could bring her out of her trauma if anyone could.

"She's punishing me," Allison whispered.

"What?" Evaline stroked her short dark brown hair.

"My mother. She's punishing me."

"With the music?"

"To remind me."

"Of what?"

"That night."

"When the villa burned?"

Allison nodded against Evaline's shoulder. "I remember it all now. It used to be a dark spot that I could never quite see through. Or didn't want to, I guess."

Gabriel leaned his forearms on his knees. "What do you remember about that night, Allison?"

"Mother was playing that song the night of the fire. She was all messed up, crying and carrying on."

Evaline didn't ask any more questions, afraid if she pursued the topic, Allison would fall silent as usual. Slowly she stroked Allison's back, hoping the girl would continue to talk when she was ready. Suddenly Allison clutched her tightly.

"What's wrong?" Evaline asked.

"He'll find me," Allison whispered.

"Who?"

"He'll find me!"

Gabriel stood up. "Durrell?" he questioned.

Allison nodded.

"No, he won't," Evaline assured her. "Stephen Durrell is dead. The Major killed him."

"Are you sure?" Allison's voice sounded like that of a young girl. "What if he isn't really dead? He'll come after me."

"Don't worry. He's not coming after anybody," Gabriel growled. "Not from six feet underground."

"He said if I ever told what happened, he'd kill me."

"That bastard!" Gabriel looked up at the ceiling, frustrated by his inability to get to the man.

"But why?" Evaline put in. "Why did he threaten you?"

"It's a long story."

"That's all right." Evaline patted her arm. "We have all night."

Allison heaved a sigh. "Okay." She paused for a long moment, then licked her lips. "When mother found out about us," Allison continued in a distant voice that worried Evaline, "she got mad. Really mad. And drunk."

"Wait a minute," Gabriel said. "What do you mean—us?"

"Oh." Allison rolled her eyes and sighed again. "I was really angry at Mother before the accident. So I decided to get back at her."

Evaline didn't like the direction the tale was taking, especially for Gabriel's sake, but she decided to let Allison continue. The truth must be told completely, once and for all.

"How did you plan to get back at her?" Gabriel asked.

"I decided to see if I could steal Stephen away from her. I knew that would really get to her."

"And?" Gabriel urged.

"I didn't intend to actually do anything." She swallowed and looked down. "I was just going to tease him. But he had other ideas."

"Like what?" Gabriel's question hung on the air until Evaline squirmed uncomfortably.

"I think we get the picture," she said.

"What happened?" Gabriel demanded. "What did he do?"

"He almost raped me." Allison started to sob. "He—he told me I'd asked for it. That I had it coming. Maybe I did. I keep thinking that maybe I—"

"No!" Evaline held her close. "Don't recriminate yourself, Allison. He was wrong to take advantage of you. You were just a child!"

"I knew what I was doing," Allison retorted vehemently.

"You were a child."

"Damn right," Gabriel swore. "If I'd known what he

did to you, I would have strangled him with my bare
hands!"

"Mother was furious for a few days. But I don't know
who she was more mad at—me or him. She wouldn't
speak to me. Then that night she told him she was breaking the engagement and cutting him off."

"Cutting him off?" Gabriel repeated, stepping up
behind Evaline. "She was giving him money?"

"Yes." Allison heaved a big sigh. "Lots of it."

"Trailhead," Gabriel muttered, remembering the article
in the paper about Durrell's proposed retreat.

Evaline glanced up at him and nodded slightly. She had
expected all along that Meredith had supported Stephen
Durrell's construction project.

"She told him she was staying in Greece," Allison went
on. "And that he could go to hell."

Gabriel shook his head. "Bastard."

"What happened then?" Evaline asked.

"Stephen blew up. They had this huge fight." Allison
broke off and burrowed her nose into Evaline's blouse.
Evaline squeezed her tightly. "He pushed her, and she fell.
She hit her head—"

"He killed her, didn't he?" Evaline said. "He didn't
mean to, but he killed her."

"Yes."

"And then what?"

"He saw me standing there. I couldn't move. I was,
like, frozen. He pulled something out of his pocket—a
necklace or something—and the next thing I knew I
was standing outside the villa, and it was going up in
flames."

"He hypnotized you," Evaline said. She remembered
the time Stephen had come to the house and visited
Allison in her room, and the way she'd found him standing in front of the girl as if holding something in the air

between them. He must have been hypnotizing her again, to "refresh" the trance. If she'd only known!

"But what about the accident?" Evaline questioned, wondering how a traumatized child could have decided to drive off in a car.

"I don't know. I found myself in my mother's sports car that night. The brakes didn't work. I couldn't stop it. And when it hit that curve—"

"Durrell's handiwork again," Gabriel muttered bitterly. He sank to the mattress beside Evaline and put his hand on Allison's back.

"Allison," he said, his voice cracking, "if I'd known what was happening to you over there, I would have come and gotten you. You should have told me."

Allison made no reply.

"You're right." Gabriel sighed. "I should have made certain you were okay. But you and your mother were always so far away."

Allison didn't move or speak, and Evaline held her securely, knowing she should remain silent during this part of the conversation.

"Yeah." He bent his head. "That's no excuse. I was wrong to have left you solely in the care of your mother. That was a big mistake. I see that now."

Allison sniffed and turned her head to gaze at her father.

"I'm sorry, Allison. I'm truly sorry."

Evaline felt Allison pulling back and she released her, hoping Allison might reach for Gabriel. Instead the girl sat up ramrod straight. For a moment, all she could do was mouth a silent scream. Then she pointed to the center of the room, and Evaline turned to follow the gesture.

"There's the ghost!" Allison gasped.

23

Blue spots undulated in the darkness between the door of Allison's room and her bed.

"It's Meredith," Gabriel said, his tone taut with frustration and disgust.

The song began once more, but this time the melody seemed to emanate from a great distance away instead of from the cassette deck. Evaline slid off the bed and stood up, ready to protect Gabriel and Allison with her life if necessary.

"You think that's my mother?" Allison whispered incredulously.

"It's her spirit." Evaline looked at her watch. It was a few minutes before midnight. "She's been making an appearance in some fashion almost every night at just about this time."

"That's the time it happened," Allison put in. "When Stephen pushed—when she died."

Evaline nodded. She'd suspected as much. "I think she's been trying to help you in her own way by trying to get you to remember."

"I doubt it!" Gabriel retorted. "Meredith was too self-ish to make an effort like that."

Evaline touched his sleeve. "Perhaps death taught her some lessons, Gabe."

Gabriel looked down at her, his eyes flashing. But she knew she'd struck a chord.

"I saw that same sparkling light in the hospital," Allison interjected. "It scared me. I didn't know what it was."

"She had no business scaring you. And there's no reason for her to hang around anymore." Gabriel took a step toward the sparkling light. "It's over, Meredith. Leave us alone."

The light flickered lavender, transformed to blue again, and then rolled toward Gabriel. He edged backward toward the window to avoid the lights, well aware of their dangerous, enervating quality, but Meredith's spirit seemed intent on making contact with him. Evaline detected the faint sound of weeping in the distance.

"No!" Gabriel exclaimed, bumping against the wall. The sparkling glow surrounded him as the sobbing grew louder, so loud, in fact, that Evaline covered her ears. She ran forward, trying to remember what a shaman would do to dispel an unwanted spirit, but the sobbing filled her head with noise, clogging her thoughts.

"Leave us alone, Meredith!" Gabriel exclaimed, his powerful body veiled by the sparkling cloud, and his strength obviously being sapped by the spirit. He seemed to be trapped in the light.

Evaline tried to push through the cloud, but the energy was strong enough to repel her. A bone-chilling wall stood between her and Gabriel, preventing passage. Panic washed over her as she realized she was powerless to help Gabriel, at least on a physical level.

"Enough, Meredith!" Gabriel thundered. He covered his ears and flattened his back against the wall.

"Dad!" Allison threw off her covers. Evaline turned at Allison's cry, and saw the girl lunge out of bed. For a heart-stopping moment Evaline watched Allison sway as if she were about to fall on her face. Her legs trembled and her kneecaps jerked up and down. But the girl didn't collapse, and after a few hesitant steps, she careened toward her father and broke through the cloud to join him. She burst into the lights and flung herself into Gabriel's arms.

"Don't, Mother!" Allison cried, hugging her father. "Don't you dare hurt him!"

Evaline stared, flabbergasted that Allison was walking. An instant later the shock turned to amazement that Allison had not only walked, but had leapt into action to protect her father. How had the girl penetrated the cloud when Evaline could not? Evaline tried again to push through the wall, but once more she was repelled. She stepped back, perplexed and desperate to help. Perhaps the exclusion stemmed from the fact that Evaline was not part of Meredith's family. She didn't belong with Gabriel and Allison, at least not as far as Meredith was concerned.

She stood transfixed at the end of the bed, watching the light sparkling around father and daughter while she tried to block out the oppressive weeping. Then, against the light curtains, she saw the shape of a bird—a crow— just like the one she'd seen in the hospital months ago. Could the crow be Meredith's power animal, still in evidence after her death? Evaline remembered the teachings of her childhood. *Crow. Help will be needed to discover a betrayal.* They'd certainly needed Meredith's help to discover what had happened to Allison and for the girl to recover her memory. Without Meredith's intervention, Allison might never have walked another step in her life.

Then it came to her. Suddenly Evaline knew why the spirit had pursued Gabriel and Allison. Meredith didn't want to hurt Gabriel or cling to him even in death; she wanted his forgiveness. She wanted to set things right after all the years she'd spent in self-absorption. She wanted Allison and Gabriel to come together and know the truth.

Perhaps playing "Time and Place" over and over again had been an attempt to tell Gabriel she had made a mistake long ago in being blind to the depth of his character and for leaving him to search the world for a love she'd been too immature to appreciate and would never find again. Perhaps Meredith had finally grown up.

"Meredith," Evaline called out, her voice choked with emotion. She'd searched her mind for a shamanic ritual to deal with the spirit, when all the time she had possessed the tool of understanding in her heart. Evaline knew she'd just learned an important secret of spirit healing—perhaps the greatest one of all.

"I understand," Evaline declared. "You've wanted to help them. I will tell them."

The light billowed.

"You no longer have to stay, Meredith."

The weeping broke off.

Beside the bed, the cassette player clicked on. For a moment, all Evaline could hear was static. Then a faint voice whispered through the noise. Evaline hurried to the nightstand and crouched down to put her ear next to the speakers.

"Forgive," the distant voice pleaded.

Evaline glanced at Gabriel. "She asks to be forgiven."

"When pigs fly," Gabriel retorted gruffly, still holding Allison close.

Scratchy static filled the room, like the sound of an old record played by a dull needle. Evaline turned up the volume.

"Love," the distant voice moaned. "You. Gabriel."

Evaline glanced at Gabriel again. He'd turned pale behind the veil of sparkling lights.

"Allie," the straining voice whispered over the static. "Please, please, forgive."

Allison blinked furiously while tears ran down her cheeks. She'd never looked younger or more vulnerable.

"Mother?" she gasped.

"So many mistakes," the spirit voice said. Static rasped over the end of her words. And then the voice came again, fainter this time. "So tired—"

"Mother?" Allison pulled away from Gabriel's arms and stepped toward the cassette player. "Mother? Wait!" The light focused around her in a sparkling whirlpool. Allison looked up at the ceiling and then around her, as if searching for a tangible form to put to the voice.

"Forgive me, Allie—"

"I do," Allison said. "It's all right, Mom. I do!"

"Allie!"

"Mom—don't go!"

"Love—" The light swirled and glowed, changing from blue to a beautiful shimmering gold, circling Allison's legs, and then lifting her hair up in the air as the light curled to the ceiling, shrinking smaller and smaller, until it remained just a pinpoint of goldenrod.

Evaline heard a soft sigh, almost imperceptible over the static of the cassette deck, and she wondered if Allison or Gabriel had heard it. The cassette player clicked off. Then the small light blinked and vanished.

Outside a lone crow cawed in the tree near the deck— an odd sound for that time of night, when most birds were roosting. But Evaline knew if she looked out the window, she'd see a dark shape flapping upward, disappearing into the roiling black clouds of the storm, never to be seen again.

*　　*　　*

Early the next morning, a friend of Gabriel's who worked at the police station called to ask him about the disposal of The Major's body. Ordinarily they wouldn't allow a pet to be buried on personal property, but for Gabriel they'd bend the rules. They also assured him that no charges would be filed. From what Durrell's henchmen had told the police, Durrell had been responsible for both the kidnapping and the bear attack.

Gabriel and Skeeter drove into Port Angeles just after breakfast, leaving Allison in Evaline's care until they got back. Evaline was more than happy to stay a few more hours at the Townsend house, and spent the time talking with Allison and evaluating her physical state. Evaline was surprised at how strong the girl had become until Allison informed her that she'd continued exercising on her own over the last month and a half when Evaline had been in Seattle.

In midmorning they took a short walk down the beach. Evaline tried to keep her mind on Allison's chatter, but her thoughts continually drifted back to the night spent in Gabriel's arms. They'd talked and made love for hours and had finally fallen asleep just before dawn, their limbs entwined.

Still, Gabriel had said nothing about his feelings for her or his future plans in regard to her. She wondered if he saw their time together as just a pleasurable hiatus. Or did he, like she, want much more of a commitment but didn't know how to arrange it since they lived so far apart? Because of the distance, theirs could never be a typical relationship in which they gradually got to know one another over a long period of time spent dating and interacting. To sustain a real relationship, one of them would have to sacrifice their job and place of residence, which was a dangerous step to take so early. Perhaps Gabriel had doubts about the depth of their feelings for each other, and was not ready to make any sudden, serious moves.

Gabriel hadn't made their affection for each other public either, which worried her, although he might be holding back in deference to her request in July. She hoped they would have a chance to talk privately before she left for Seattle.

When Evaline and Allison returned from their walk, they saw Gabriel's pickup parked in the drive, alongside a red VW bug.

"Whose car is that?" Evaline asked, nodding at the little VW.

"Mandy Bayer's. It's new."

"Ah." Disappointment passed through Evaline. With Mandy around, she wouldn't get to talk to Gabriel, surely. "Does she come to visit often?"

"Every once in a while. She helped me dye my hair."

"Oh." Evaline tried to smile but knew she did a poor job of hiding her emotions. Though she was no longer worried about Mandy's place in Gabriel's affections, she still didn't like the idea of Mandy inserting herself into the lives of the Townsends.

Evaline slowly crossed the drive and climbed up the stairs, helping Allison up the last few steps. Allison's stamina would have to be built up over the next few months before she was anywhere near back to normal.

When they walked into the house, Evaline saw Mandy look up, then freeze in astonishment.

"Allison!" Mandy gasped. "You're walking!"

Allison glanced down at her feet, shot a grin at her father, and then back up to the young woman. "Yeah, I am."

"That's wonderful!"

"I guess all the exercise paid off."

Evaline smiled at Gabriel, glad that Allison had chosen not to discuss the spirit intervention part of her recovery.

Gabriel's glance met hers and bathed her in a warm glow, which spread from the inside out. How could she spend another night without him lying next to her? Was he so strong—or so uncertain—that he could take or leave the exquisite communication of their lovemaking?

He stepped forward. "We've got The Major out back," he said, putting his hand on Allison's shoulder. "Let's pay our last respects to him. Allison, are you up to it?"

She nodded and looked down.

Gabriel guided her toward the back door of the house, with Evaline and the rest following in their wake. When they got to the back deck, Allison asked them to hold the ceremony for a minute, and returned to the house.

Evaline strolled next to Gabriel down the couple of steps to the lawn, and they silently crossed the yard to the edge of the woods, where he and Skeeter had prepared a grave. A large wooden crate sat at the bottom of the pit, starkly white against the dark brown soil. Skeeter and Mandy stationed themselves on the opposite side of the hole and looked down.

Gabriel turned to Evaline. "When Allison gets here, would you say a few words," he asked, "before we bury him?"

"I'd be glad to." She smiled and looked up to see Allison carefully walking down the steps, holding her old tattered bear against her chest. Evaline's throat tightened, and she wondered if she would be able to speak without breaking into tears.

No one said a word as Allison walked across the grass and took her place at Gabriel's side.

After a long pause, Gabriel looked down at Evaline. "Ready?" he asked.

She nodded and took a deep breath, hoping she would find the right words to honor The Major and the fortitude to deliver them. She closed her eyes.

"Great One, we are gathered here today," she began, her voice shaking, "to honor the spirit of our brother, whom we called The Major." She broke off, her throat too clenched to continue, until she felt Gabriel's warm hand find hers. His fingers laced through hers, and he squeezed her hand gently, giving her the strength to continue.

Evaline took another deep breath. "He came to us hurt and starving, and we mistakenly thought he had entered our lives so that we could help him grow into an adult. But in our blindness, we did not see the real reason our brother came to us. There are some things in life we cannot see until we look back, until we cross the river and cast our sights on the bank behind us, and see the truth."

Gabriel squeezed her fingers again, understanding the double meaning of her words, as they pertained to Meredith and to each other as well.

"Great One, it is the belief of our people that the spirit of the bear symbolizes strength and protection. So it was with our brother, The Major. He was sent to us for a specific purpose, to protect Allison. And this he did, giving up his life to save her.

"We thank him, our brother, for keeping Allison safe from harm, for giving her joy when she was ill, and for restoring her back to us when she was in danger. We will honor his memory always, and we will not be sad, for we know he is in the Land Above, in the lodge of his people, looking down on us and smiling."

Slowly she opened her eyes. No one said a word. After a long moment, Allison bent down on one knee and let her old stuffed bear drop to the wooden box below. It bounced slightly and came to rest facedown in the middle of the crate. Then Skeeter pulled something out of the pocket of his light jacket and let it fall into the hole. An apple. Evaline felt tears running down her cheeks, but she did nothing to stop them.

Instead she reached down for a clump of soil, which she slowly crumbled on top of the crate. Mandy did the same, then turned away, following Skeeter back to the house. Gabriel draped his arm around Allison's shoulders and drew her close while he still held Evaline's hand, and for a few minutes the three of them stood at the grave, offering their private prayers for the bear who'd given his life for Allison.

"You two go on in," Gabriel finally said, his voice husky with emotion. "I'll take care of the rest."

Evaline slowly strolled back to the house with Allison, their arms around each other's waists. At the door Allison paused and stepped back.

"That was nice, what you said about The Major."

"I wasn't sure what to say. So you thought it was okay?"

"It was great." She brushed back her hair and looked over at Evaline. "Are you really going back to Seattle today?"

"Yes."

"Do you have to?"

"I have to work sometime." Evaline smiled at her.

"What about coming back and being my therapist again?"

Evaline reached for the doorknob. "I don't think you'll be needing a therapist much longer, Allison."

"I still have to go to that evaluation in a few days," Allison put in. "I might need some extra coaching."

"But if the evaluation is positive, you'll be staying with your father. I thought you wanted to live with your grandparents in Seattle."

"Not so much anymore."

Evaline arched a brow in a knowing expression. "He isn't so bad once you get to know him, is he?"

"No." Allison grinned and shook her head. "I never

thought I'd say this, but my father's all right." She walked into the house, and Evaline shut the door behind them, but not before she glanced back at Gabriel, who was shoveling dirt into the hole. She burned the vision into her memory, still not certain how long Gabriel would be a part of her life, and wanting to retain as much of him as possible in her thoughts.

She turned back, surprised to see Allison watching her.

"You like him, don't you?" Allison asked.

Evaline flushed, wondering if Gabriel would appreciate her discussing this topic with his daughter. Yet he had stood between them moments ago, linked to both of them. Anyone observing such a tableau would jump to the same conclusion Evaline had, that he saw them as a unit.

"Yes," she answered, instantly overcome with a warm sensation that gushed through her. It was a wonderful feeling to tell someone of her true sentiments at last. "Your father is a fine man."

"I mean, you *like* him. *Seriously* like him."

Evaline glanced at Allison's face, surprised to find the girl's eyes sparkling.

It was her turn to grin. She felt like a teenager with a crush. "Yes. Yes, I do," she replied, brushing past Allison, to avoid any more questions.

Allison caught her elbow. "I'm glad," she said.

Evaline looked back at her, and her blush faded quietly.

"Whatever you guys want to do," Allison added, "don't worry about me. I mean—it's all right with me if you want to"—she broke off and rolled her eyes—"well, like, you know, whatever!"

Evaline's gaze swept over the girl's face, astonished by Allison's precocious maturity. In some ways this young woman was much older than many adults, due to having lived through things some adults would never experience. "Thank you, Allison," she murmured.

Mandy had brought over a blueberry coffee cake, which they ate as they drank a cup of coffee and talked about The Major. Each of them had a special memory of the bear to share, and by the time all the tales were told, Evaline's grief had lifted and early afternoon had arrived.

She stood up and picked up her plate and mug. "Well, Skeeter," she said, knowing she couldn't linger much longer, "time to head out?"

"I guess." He pushed back his chair, seemingly as reluctant as she was to leave the circle of the table. They'd shared many meals at this table, and Evaline despaired that this chapter of her life was coming to a close. Skeeter grabbed his mug. "Don't want to be too late getting back."

Gabriel got to his feet. "Don't clean up, Evaline. We'll do it."

"All right." Was he rushing her out of the house or just being nice? Evaline wasn't sure. She found her purse near the couch and looped the strap over her shoulder while she tried to catch his eye. But he was busy taking dishes to the kitchen.

Everyone trailed out to the dock, where Skeeter's float plane bobbed in the water. Sunlight glinted off the calm surface of the bay, nearly blinding them. Gabriel shielded his eyes with the flat of his hand while Evaline gave Allison a good-bye hug.

"Come back and visit soon," Allison said. "Promise."

"I will. And good luck with the evaluation."

"Thanks."

Evaline squeezed her tightly and felt Allison's heartfelt embrace. Tears brimmed very close to the surface. She was leaving Obstruction Bay, and she didn't want to, but there was nothing she could do but go.

When she was more confident of mastering her emotions, she stepped away from Allison and turned to Gabriel. He held out his arms, and she gave him a hug, highly conscious of everyone watching them.

"Thank you, Evaline," he said near her ear. "For everything."

"You're welcome, Gabe," she answered.

"Allison wouldn't be here without you, wouldn't be walking."

"Maybe."

He squeezed her tightly and she heard him sigh. "I'm going to miss you like hell," he whispered in her ear.

Then ask me to stay, a voice inside her shouted. But she said nothing. Staying with him was out of the question. It wouldn't be right to throw her future plans in the hopper with his, unless they were married, and it was too soon to make a decision like that.

"I'll call you," he promised.

"Okay. Let me get my number." She stepped back and reached in her purse for a business card, which she gave to him. "I'll be anxious to hear how Allison does next week."

"Of course."

They stared at each other, blocking the rest of the group out of their world. Gabriel's eyes were full of troubled lights, and a crease slashed his face between his brows. Evaline's breathing became shallower, quicker, as his eyes took her back to the hours they'd shared together in each other's arms. Yet she didn't move, afraid that her strong feelings for Gabriel would be so obvious they'd put him in an embarrassing position.

"For criminy's sake, Gabe," Skeeter exclaimed. "Kiss her!"

Evaline glanced at Skeeter as a hot blush flooded her face, but before she could make a move, she felt Gabriel's arms gently fold her against his solid chest.

"Skeeter's right for once," Gabriel said with a slow smile that shot through her body. "I can't let you go without a kiss." Then he bent down to her lips, closing his eyes and surrounding her with his strong, warm arms.

Evaline surrendered to him and spread her hands over the pockets of his plaid cotton shirt, loving the way his large frame engulfed hers. Standing in his arms she felt safe, loved, and cherished.

When at last their mouths drew apart, she gazed up at him and hoped her eyes told him everything she couldn't say out loud, with everyone listening. She could feel Allison's stare boring into her back

"Good-bye, Gabe," she whispered.

"Ev—" he began, his eyes dark with an indecision she'd never seen there before. He seemed to be fighting an internal battle with himself and staring at her for answers. Evaline forced her expression to remain placid and objective.

"Yes?"

"Aw, hell." He sighed and smiled shallowly. "I'm rotten with this good-bye stuff."

"So am I." She smiled softly. "Let's just say 'until we meet again.'"

"Good. Because we will." He kissed her lightly once more, then released her. "You can count on it, City Girl."

Evaline turned from his arms, her heart breaking. Skeeter helped her step onto the pontoon and up into the cabin. She belted herself in, struggling to find the buckle while her vision blurred with tears. Then Skeeter got in beside her and started the engine. She looked back at Allison and waved. In moments, they were motoring away from the dock, heading out toward the deeper water where they would take off.

Evaline watched the three figures on the dock grow smaller until they were nothing but black specks. And as the small plane rose higher and higher, even the dock disappeared from view. Evaline sighed and turned toward the front of the plane, where the sun gilded the white carpet of clouds below them.

"Want to turn around and go back?" Skeeter asked, smiling. "The plane could have a sudden mechanical failure."

"No." Evaline replied. "But thanks for asking."

"Everyone can see you two were meant for each other," Skeeter added.

"Everyone but Gabe, apparently."

"He's an idiot." Skeeter banked the plane and headed southeast. "He's my best friend. And I think the world of the guy. But he's an idiot."

24

The day of Allison's evaluation arrived. Gabriel had promised that he'd stop in and see Evaline when they were in town. Throughout the workday, Evaline anxiously waited for the phone to ring so she could find out how the evaluation went and make arrangements for dinner.

Gabriel had called her each night from Obstruction Bay, and they'd talked of Allison, the weather, and what they'd been through with Stephen Durrell and Meredith, but they never discussed their future. Gabriel had admitted he missed her cooking and missed her in his bed, but never mentioned his feelings for her.

Evaline spent the day preoccupied with thoughts of Gabriel and Allison, and hoped that everything was going well for them. She finished up her paperwork, said goodbye to the staff, and took the bus home while she considered her choices for dinner and an evening spent alone after all. Having received no phone call from Gabriel, she could conclude that something serious must have come up to waylay him.

Chinese takeout and a quiet evening at home was a poor substitute for dinner with Gabriel and Allison. Feeling let down, Evaline unlocked the door of her apartment and put her purse in the closet. Then she poured herself a glass of iced tea and flipped through her mail, her thoughts far away from the bills in her hand.

As she was looking at the mail, she heard the doorbell ring, startling her out of her thoughts. Visitors were rare, and she wasn't accustomed to the sound of the bell. Evaline dropped the envelopes onto the table and walked across the living-room floor, her pulse racing. She leaned forward to look through the peephole. A dark-haired man oddly distorted by the lens loomed on the other side.

Gabriel? Her heart leapt into her throat. She pulled open the door.

"Gabriel!" she cried.

Before she could feign any self-restraint whatsoever, he swept her up and spun her around, grinning and hugging her. "City Girl!" he exclaimed. "God, how I've missed you!"

Then he pressed her against the wall by the door and kissed her as if he'd been starving for the taste of her, just as much as she'd been starving for him. Minutes passed, filled with nothing but the sound of their breathing and long, heartfelt sighs. They caressed each other, and reacquainted themselves with the touch of each other's bodies. Evaline felt herself blossoming for him in all ways, heart and soul.

Gabriel sagged against her, his forehead touching hers. "I'd almost forgotten what you felt like," he murmured. "It's been so damn long."

"Want to come in?" she asked.

"In more ways than one," he replied, kissing her under her jaw, which sent shimmers of delight down her neck and torso. He clutched her rump in his hands and pinned her against his loins, growling as he nuzzled the top of her shoulder.

"Gabriel!" she gasped, giggling. "What if the neighbors see?"

"What if they do?" he retorted. But he soon released her and followed her into her apartment, shutting the door behind them. Before she could take another step, however, he grabbed her and kissed her all over again, until she was breathless with wanting him.

She pushed at his chest and pulled away from his insistent mouth. "Where's Allison?"

"With her grandparents."

"No!"

He smiled and smoothed back her hair. "It's not like that, Evaline. She just wanted to stay overnight with them. And I thought that might work out just fine."

"Then she did well on the evaluation?"

"Outstanding."

"Oh, thank God!" Evaline grinned. "That's great, Gabe!"

"God might have had something to do with it, Evaline." His eyes darkened to charcoal gray as his expression turned grave. "But I think you had a greater part in her rehabilitation. And I will always be grateful."

"Oh?" She couldn't help but tease him. She swayed against him suggestively. "Just how grateful, Wild Man?"

"Wildly grateful." He smiled the slow smile of his that drove her crazy with desire, and then looped her arms around her hips, pinning her to him and gazing down at her, his eyes brimming with light and happiness.

"Want to hear what I found out today while I was stuck with Meredith's lawyers?" he asked.

"Shoot."

"I found out that you want to go to medical school."

Evaline flushed. "How did they know that?"

"They knew all about you. Durrell might have been as crooked as a dog's hind leg, but he was a thorough sonofabitch."

"It's true." Evaline sighed. "He promised that if I stayed the entire summer with you and Allison, that he and the Delaneys would fund my college education. But since I quit before the job was completed, all I got was my regular paycheck." She sighed again. "Looking back, I realize the college education bribe was just another of Durrell's dirty little deals, and probably wouldn't have materialized anyway."

"All that trouble for nothing, eh?" He winked.

"I wouldn't say that." She slipped her arms around him and lay her cheek on his broad chest. "I met you, didn't I?"

"Much to my good fortune." Gabriel held her in his arms and stroked her hair. "I also found out what you really think of me, City Girl."

Evaline flushed. "You did? How?"

"From a report you filed at the hospital. The lawyers had a copy."

"They let you read it?"

Gabriel chuckled. "No, but they gave me a summary. What you said about me was in direct opposition to the reports Durrell had filed. He and Meredith's parents were trying to make me look like a rat so I'd lose custody of Allison, and he'd get control of Meredith's money."

"That's why Durrell kept Allison drugged and hypnotized, to keep her from regaining her memory until he had the Delaney fortune in his pocket."

"Damn right." He shook his head. "After hearing Durrell's lies about me, you must have thought I was a real bastard at first."

"I did. Durrell told me that you had abused both Meredith and Allison. But soon after I met you, Gabe, I knew you weren't that kind of man."

He held her away from him. "That's why you pulled the gun on me that night!"

She nodded. "I should have pulled it on Stephen Durrell, had I only known."

He smiled at the wry tone of her voice. "Would have saved us a lot of trouble. But it turned out all right. In fact, Meredith's parents apologized to me for all the grief they'd caused. I never thought I'd see the day."

"That's wonderful, Gabe." She caressed his cheek. "It will be so much easier for you and Allison in the future, to have a decent relationship with them."

"Life is full of surprises, City Girl." Playfully, he pulled her hips closer to his. "And I've got one more."

"One more life, or one more surprise?"

"One more surprise, you little smartass!" He chuckled. "And this one's a real shocker." His eyes sparkled. "Meredith left half of her fortune to me."

Evaline went stiff with astonishment, and Gabriel laughed.

"Surprised, eh?"

"I'll say."

"When she found out about Stephen and Allison, she changed her will and then apparently confronted Durrell. But good old Stephen held up the legal system with his claims against me."

"I can't believe it!" Evaline exclaimed. "She must have had a considerable change of heart about you."

"I'll say. Too bad she didn't live long enough to enjoy her newfound maturity."

Evaline nodded silently, thinking how betrayed Meredith must have felt, because she knew firsthand the burning ache of betrayal.

"Know what I plan to do with the money?" Gabriel continued.

Evaline snapped out of her thoughts of Meredith. "Buy more plaid shirts?" She raised a brow. "Go to a chef's school in Paris?"

"Smartass!" He laughed again and squeezed her. "God, it's good to talk to you again!" He kissed her until she drew away.

"What *are* you going to do with the money, Gabe?"

"Build a lodge. Make Obstruction Bay the sportdiving destination of the Northwest."

"You mean a place with overnight accommodations and everything?"

"Yep. Fishing, boating, swimming, as well as good, down-home eating, using all local ingredients."

"Sounds like a job for Mandy Bayer."

"Mandy Bayer?" He snorted. "Maybe as an assistant."

"Yes, with a place like that, you'd probably want a trained chef, someone with experience."

"That's for sure." He paused and looked down at her, deep into her eyes, until Evaline thought her heart would burst with love for him.

"Ev," he began, trying to smile but losing the ability suddenly. "I don't want to scare you off, but—" He paused and rocked her against him as if he were suddenly unsure. His right eye started to squint.

He didn't know what to say.

"Scare me off? Come on." Evaline tilted her head and smiled. "You know I don't scare easy, Gabriel Townsend."

He swallowed. "You must know how I feel about you, Evaline."

"You've never told me," she put in gently.

"That's because I didn't think I had the right. I didn't know what to *do*," he retorted vehemently. "I hated to see you leave, but I couldn't figure out a way to ask you to stay. You have your career, your work—"

"I hate the city, Gabe."

"I couldn't ask you to give up your life to see if you and I could make a go of it, not when I was unwilling to give up mine. And we haven't known each other that long—"

"We know each other more thoroughly than most."

"But then I came up with the lodge idea. It could work, Evaline. You have that way about you people respond to, that way of making folks feel welcome and cared for."

"Gabe, are you offering me a job?"

He broke off and stared at her, his right eye squinting even more this time. She touched his cheek.

"What are you trying to say, Gabe?"

"I'm trying to say that I'm crazy about you, Ev, that I want you in my life, somehow, some way. I want us to build something together. A business, a life. We could do it, too. Just look at Allison. We work well together."

"Yes, we do." She brushed the hair at his temple. "Once we put our minds to it."

"Well, I've got a plan, Evaline. What do you think about this?" He pulled back and looked at her. "It will take me a couple of years to build the lodge and the marina. While I'm doing that, you can go to medical school here in Seattle. Skeeter can fly you back on the weekends for some peace and quiet with me at Obstruction Bay. And when you're done with school, you can be the doctor on call at the lodge, and maybe have a weekend clinic for the folks in the area. Most of them have to travel all the way to Port Angeles for any kind of medical treatment."

"Gabe, you've really been thinking about this, haven't you?"

"You bet I have."

"I can't go to medical school, though, and keep

working. I won't have enough time, not to mention enough money."

"Don't worry about it. You can quit your job and be a full-time student. The money's no problem."

"I can't ask you to pay for my medical education!"

"I'm not. Meredith is." He dropped a kiss on her lips. "And the way I see it, City Girl, she owes you."

"I'm not sure who owes whom—" she broke off. She knew the time had come to tell Gabriel about her past, before they got any further with making plans for the future. Her heart thumped wildly at the prospect, and she paused, unsure how to begin.

"What are you saying?" Gabe urged.

"There's something I've never told you, Gabe. Something you did for me four years ago."

"Four years ago?"

"Yes. You saved my life." She paused and looked back up at him.

"I did?" Puzzled, his brows lowered over his intense eyes. "How?"

"By making me realize that life was worth living, that I could reinvent myself."

"I did that? Four years ago?"

She nodded.

"It's not possible." He pulled back. "I would have remembered you, Evaline!"

"I was different then," she continued. "I hadn't become captain of my own soul yet."

Gabriel stared at her, speechless.

She tilted her head. "It's all coming back to you now, isn't it?"

His eyes poured over her and his expression was wide with incredulity. "How can this be?"

"You pulled me from the sea. I was half-frozen."

"You were that woman in the boat?"

"Yes, the one you took down to your cabin and crawled into bed with."

"It was the only way I could think of to get you warm."

"I would have died without your help. But the thing is, Gabe, I wanted to die."

"I sensed that, Ev, and I didn't know what to say to you. So I just recited all the poetry I knew."

"It was the best thing you could have done. Those words"—she swallowed, choking back a thick lump in her throat—"those words and your kindness meant everything to me. You couldn't have known."

"But you were—" He broke off and reached for her face, tracing the line of her sculpted cheekbone with the tip of his index finger. "You looked so different then—"

"I was scarred. I still am, Gabe, in many ways. But since I've met you, I barely think of my scars anymore."

"They're nothing." He bent down and kissed her, pulling her tightly into his embrace. "I thought there was something about you that looked familiar," he said, his cheek against hers. "I just couldn't put my finger on it."

"It's understandable. Plastic surgery changed my face quite a bit."

"Evaline, this is unbelievable!"

"I know. To be thrown together twice by fate—"

"—proves that it was meant to be." He looked down at her and his eyes melted as if they were made of quicksilver, and an endearing crooked smile crept over his mouth. Then he slowly slipped his hand up her neck and into her hair, and gazed at her until she thought her knees would buckle out of sheer joy. "We belong together, you and I."

"You think so?"

"I know so. And I know something else, too."

"What?"

"That I love you, Evaline. And I always will."

"Oh, Gabe, I've been waiting to hear that," she murmured as his mouth found hers again. "I love you, too."

He kissed her as he'd never kissed her before, claiming her for his own with his lips and hands, until he lifted her off the floor.

"Marry me," he said, sliding one hand under her knees until she was cradled in his arms. "Marry me, beautiful."

"I'd like that," she replied. "On one condition."

"Name it."

"That you always call me beautiful."

"Deal." He grinned and shifted her close against his chest. "Now where's your bedroom? We've got some serious catching up to do."

Evaline laughed and hugged his neck. "Does that mean you're staying for dinner?" She lifted a brow.

"Honey, I'll be here for breakfast, too, if you'll have me." He pushed open the door of her bedroom with his foot.

"Sometimes I think you love me just for my cooking."

"If you think that, beautiful, you've got a lot to learn."

"Hmmm." She nibbled his earlobe. "That sounds like an interesting proposition. I'm a fast learner, too. How about you?"

"Doesn't matter." He stood with her at the foot of the bed and gazed down at her. "We've got a lifetime to find out."

She stared into his eyes while her smile faded into a serious expression. "I know all I need to know for now."

"So do I, beautiful. So do I."

Let HarperMonogram Sweep You Away

※❦❧

FALL FROM GRACE by Megan Chance
RITA Award-winning Author

Lily longs to be free of the gang of outlaws who raised her—even if it means betraying her husband, Texas Sharpe. However, her plan for freedom backfires when Lily realizes her dreams of leading a respectable life will mean nothing without Texas by her side.

JUST BEFORE MIDNIGHT by Patricia Simpson
Award-winning Author

As a physical therapist for an injured teenager, Evaline Jaye lives in a rustic house with the girl's gruff but attractive father. Soon Evaline senses the presence of a spirit in the home...and an even stronger energy that awakens passions she has never known.

THE RAGING HEARTS by Patricia Hagan
New York Times Bestselling Author

The Civil War had taught Union army officer Travis Coltrane not to surrender his heart to anyone, but Southern belle Kitty Wright's wanton beauty proves a temptation too hard to resist.

WHISPER OF MIDNIGHT by Patricia Simpson
A HarperMonogram Classic

When the ghost of Scotsman Hazard McAllister is zapped to the present day, he sweeps Jamie Kent off her feet. Together they must solve a century-old mystery, falling passionately in love in the process.

And in case you missed last month's selections...
A KNIGHT TO REMEMBER by Christina Dodd
RITA Award-winning Author

A gifted healer, Lady Edlyn saves Hugh de Florisoun's life, only to have the knight claim her as his own. Torn by desire, it will take all Edlyn's will not to surrender to the man determined to win her heart.

HEAVEN IN WEST TEXAS by Susan Kay Law
Golden Heart Award-winning Author

Joshua West is sent back from heaven to protect Abigail Grier, the Texas beauty who once refused his love. As the passion between them ignites, Joshua and Abigail get a second chance to find their own piece of paradise.

THE PERFECT BODY by Amanda Matetsky

Annie March has no idea how a dead body ended up in the trunk of her car, no less a perfect body! When someone tries to pin the murder on her, sexy police detective Eddie Lincoln may be Annie's ticket to justice — and romance.

"Smart and sassy...a charming combination of mystery, romance, and fun." — Faye Kellerman

CANDLE IN THE WINDOW by Christina Dodd
A HarperMonogram Classic

Lady Saura of Roget is summoned to the castle of a magnificent knight whose world has exploded into agonizing darkness. Saura becomes the light of Sir William of Miraval's life, until a deadly enemy threatens their newfound love.

Winner of the Golden Heart and RITA awards